Knockout Raves For

OCT -.- 2010

TODD ROBINSON

Sex, Thugs, and Rock & Roll

"These stories will leave you wincing, smiling and wanting a shower and all the while you'll be begging for more."
—*Buzz Bin*

"Here's proof that the short story isn't just alive and well, but kicking . . . you right in the balls."
—**Rod Lott, Bookgasm.com**

"Be prepared to be shattered, shell-shocked and bruised, as Thuglit's emissaries write wrongs that are very, very right."
—**Sarah Weinman**

Hardcore Hardboiled

"So good, it's almost dangerous.
—*CrimeSpree*

"So hard-boiled, the shell is still on."
—**bn.com**

"Solid . . . will appeal to those with a taste for explicit violence."
—*Publishers Weekly*

"A showcase of new and exciting talent."
—**Charlie Stella,** author of *Shakedown*

"You have to look hard to find two consecutive pages that don't deal with sex or violence, but why would you want to?"
—**Otto Penzler**

Also by Todd Robinson

Hardcore Hardboiled
Sex, Thugs, and Rock & Roll

Published by Kensington Publishing Corporation

blood, guts, & whiskey

EDITED BY TODD ROBINSON

INTRODUCTION BY MAX ALLAN COLLINS

KENSINGTON BOOKS

http://www.kensingtonbooks.com

KENSINGTON BOOKS are published by

Kensington Publishing Corp.
119 West 40th Street
New York, NY 10018

All Kensington titles, imprints, and distributed lines are available at special
quantity discounts for bulk purchases for sales promotion, premiums, fund-
raising, educational, or institutional use.

Special book excerpts or customized printings can also be created to fit spe-
cific needs. For details, write or phone the office of the Kensington Special
Sales Manager: Kensington Publishing Corp., 119 West 40th Street, New
York, NY 10018. Attn. Special Sales Department. Phone: 1-800-221-2647.

Kensington and the K logo Reg. U.S. Pat. & TM Off.

ISBN-13: 978-0-7582-2268-8
ISBN-10: 0-7582-2268-8

First Kensington Trade Paperback Printing: June 2010
10 9 8 7 6 5 4 3 2 1

Printed in the United States of America

CONTENTS

Introduction

Max Allan Collins

What we tend to call noir fiction today—and used to label "tough guy" or "hardboiled" (a World War I term)—seemed to blossom into full bloodred with such novels as *Red Harvest* (1929) by Dashiell Hammett, *The Postman Always Rings Twice* (1934) by James M. Cain, and *The Big Sleep* (1939) by Raymond Chandler. But these landmark novels only represented the first *book-length* work from those three writers, who had developed their criminal craft in the short-fiction form.

More than that, the debut novels of both Hammett and Chandler represented recycling of short fiction originally published in pulp magazines. That a prestigious publisher like Knopf would endorse novels with such questionable pulpwood roots may seem unlikely, and one wonders if this new, natively American kind of crime story would have risen to critical praise, best-seller status, and Hollywood heights, had the editors at Knopf not been blessed with great taste and considerable foresight.

Both Hammett and his celebrated disciple Chandler were regular contributors to the famous pulp magazine *Black Mask*, and Cain honed his style at such "slicks" as *The American Mercury, Esquire,* and *Redbook.* Cain's prototype for his style of crime fiction, "Pastorale," appeared in influential journalist H. L. Mencken's *The American Mercury*—Mencken also instigated *Black Mask* as a vehicle to underwrite more overtly literary endeavors. With the notable exception of F. Scott Fitzgerald's first published short story ("Babes in the Woods"), it's doubtful Mencken's other short-story magazine, *The Smart Set,* ever spawned anything as lasting (in the literary sense or otherwise) as the work of Hammett and Chandler in *Black Mask* did.

The late 1920s—and the several decades that followed—were a time when the short story flourished. The short story was the TV of its day; half-hour programs dominated on radio and TV for many decades, indicating the degree to which short-form prose set the standard and form. Many films bragged in their credits of a screenplay's source being a *Collier's Weekly, Saturday Evening Post,* or *Liberty* short story (or serial).

These weekly magazines were mainstream entertainment, at least as popular as novels and probably rivaled movies. In the world of crime and mystery fiction, many of the most famous characters in the genre—Charlie Chan, Perry Mason, even Sam Spade—turned up in slick magazines, as a precursor to episodic television.

Cain, who currently suffers an undeserved diminished standing, was in the 1930s and '40s usually taken more seriously by literary critics than "mystery writers" Hammett and Chandler, though Cain, with his sexual content, was certainly the most controversial. Cain's preferred form was the short story, or the novella. *The Postman Always Rings Twice* was a notably slim volume, and Cain's second most-famous work, *Double Indemnity* (1935), was a long magazine story that did not appear in hardcover as a solo work (it first reached hardcover as one of the three novellas collected in *Three of a Kind* in 1943).

Cain was not alone among major names in crime fiction who preferred the short story. The hardboiled sensation of the 1950s, Mickey Spillane, during his approximately decade-long layoff between Mike Hammer novels (*Kiss Me, Deadly,* 1952, to *The Girl Hunters,* 1961), published one or two long short stories a year in such low-end men's publications as *Saga* and *Cavalier.* Why Spillane—then a writer as popular as Stephen King and with a character as famous as Harry Potter—chose to write short fiction is partly explained by his own preference for a shorter form. He explained that he felt the novella was the "perfect" length for a crime novel, and fans of '50s and '60s paperback publisher Gold Medal Books (and now Hard Case Crime) might agree.

That *Black Mask* and its imitators form the tide pool where the life of modern crime fiction began is surely beyond argument. Some key creators have not lasted, or have had their reputations fall—Carroll John Daly, the inventor of the private eye story (and a huge influence on Mickey Spillane), is a figure much mentioned but little read today. Daly's Hammer-esque Race Williams set the form and standard for the private eye, but the writer's rough pulp edges—and his inability to fashion a worthwhile book-length narrative—has left him important but passé. (Spillane himself told me, in a typically pungent fashion, that "Daly wrote great short stories—but he stunk as a novelist.")

Black Mask short story writer Erle Stanley Gardner became one of the most popular mystery novelists in the '40s through the '70s, and frequent *Black Mask* contributor Horace McCoy—probably the most criminally forgotten of the greats—fashioned several of the most effective crime novels of the twentieth century, including *They Shoot Horses, Don't They?* (1935) and *Kiss Tomorrow Goodbye* (1948). (McCoy's work is the template for Jim Thompson, whose paperback originals were essentially novellas.)

Not long after *Black Mask* faded away, *Manhunt* filled the hardboiled gap in the form of a digest-sized pulp with wonderful covers by the top paperback artists of the day—not surprisingly, the new magazine kicked off in 1953 with a four-issue Spillane serial. James M. Cain appeared in *Manhunt*, and Richard S. Prather, Evan Hunter, and just about every significant mid-century name in tough crime fiction.

During this period, *Mike Shayne Mystery Magazine* and *Alfred Hitchcock's Mystery Magazine* emerged as markets for the hardboiled tale, while *Ellery Queen Mystery Magazine* instituted a "Black Mask" department (recently revived in those pages); and any number of crime-oriented digest-sized pulps came along, often bearing brand-name authors or their characters—Rex Stout, Ed McBain, Charlie Chan, the Saint, and even *77 Sunset Strip* from TV (a series spawned in part by *Esquire* magazine short stories by Chandler imitator Roy Huggins, future father of Bret Maverick and Dr. Richard Kimble).

By the late '60s, however, the short story had become a marginalized form, and not just in mystery fiction. Now short fiction was the stuff of a few high-end publications, a handful of genre publications, and a smattering of small literary magazines. A writer could hit the lottery and get thousands from *Playboy*, or five cents a word from the handful of digests . . . or a complimentary copy of a literary magazine.

I started trying to write professionally in high school in the mid-'60s and it never occurred to me to try to market short stories—I went straight to novels. At the University of Iowa's Writers' Workshop, I kept writing novels, but soon learned the workshop format was kinder to short stories, and wrote a few. The literary crowd always understood that a writer goes to school in the shorter form. Still, my first sales were novels.

Frankly, I didn't even try to sell a short story until I was well-established—my first one was for an anthology around 1984, a good ten years into my career, and it was by request from an editor. In the '80s and '90s, the anthology market boomed and, thanks to Marty Greenberg, Ed Gorman, Bob Randisi, and a few others, guys like me got to write short stories by invitation. My wife Barb—the best native short story writer in my house—became a professional when those kind of invitations began rolling in regularly. Such anthologies are not gone, but they are an increasingly rare breed. Barb hasn't written a short story in a couple years (really a sad thing, good as she is) and has been doing novels in collaboration with her longer-form-oriented husband.

If the short story has never quite become a lost art or even an endangered species, it remains the place where crime fiction began, and has always been a breeding ground for new talent. Writers need on-the-job training, and short stories have always provided the major venue for that. With only *Ellery Queen* and *Alfred Hitchcock* left in the digest pulp field, and original-material anthologies becoming less and less frequent, that venue begins to look all but nonexistent. After all, it's not easy to sell to *Queen* and *Hitchcock's*, and the anthologies are usually by invitation only, so how does that aid the next generation of crime writers?

Understand I'm not incredibly anxious to encourage these talented SOB's. Somebody the other day talked about me as one of the best crime writers of the '80s, and I didn't mind hearing that, except I wanted to raise my hand and say, "Hey! Asshole! I'm still here!"

Anyway, a lot of these writers are breaking in on the Internet, and Thuglit.com has been, and continues to be, one of the best sites for contemporary tough fiction. Look back at the previous two volumes in this series and you'll see names that have already achieved esteemed status and even stardom. This volume has a few of those as well (Tom Piccirilli, for example) but mostly these are names not as of yet the household variety.

If history is any judge—whether we're talking Hammett's first story in *Black Mask* or pick-a-name-here in this *Thuglit* antho—that will change.

What hasn't changed is the desire of writers and readers to tell lean, mean stories that deal with the major conflicts of humankind—life and death, i.e., sex and violence—unflinchingly. In a form developed almost a century ago in the pulps and born again on the net, today's brightest writers provide some of the darkest tales you've ever read.

June 2009
Muscatine, Iowa

A Message from Big Daddy Thug

Welcome one and all to the third *Thuglit* anthology. To those of you who already know who we are, welcome back. To those of you who are wondering what the hell a "Thuglit" is, we're all about rainbows, puppy dogs, and whatever Celine Dion is up to. Would I lie? "Blood, Guts, and Whiskey" is the title of a Celine Dion song. Look it up. This book would make a great birthday present for your grandma, with stories to share for generations to come. Now stop reading this intro and just buy the thing. Trust me.

Pssst.

Are the newbies gone?

Good.

Suckers. I totally lied about the Celine Dion song. . . . Christ, I feel dirty just mentioning her name three times.

For the rest of you, once again, we've tossed the terrible salad of the dark and deadly, the gruesome and the glam, the vicious and the violent. Much like a . . . well, a terrible tossed salad (Editor's Note: choose definition of "terrible tossed salad" for yourself.). We've got some rising stars, some new masters, and a never-before-seen story from a legend taken too soon.

We've got badass bikers, 'roid-raging lunatics, double-dealing gangbangers, S&M psychos, and hellacious hitmen. We got *blood,* we got *guts,* we got *whiskey* (hence the title. Get it? We weren't being coy, ya dipshit). And it just wouldn't be a *Thuglit* anthology without at least one set of mutilated genitals, now would it?

We await our National Book Award. Or Nobel. Whichever one comes with the best gift basket.

Still waiting . . .

—TODD ROBINSON (BIG DADDY THUG)

Red Hair and Black Leather

Jordan Harper

She had an ass like a heart turned upside down and cut in half—and that's what we call foreshadowing, friend. But I didn't know that at the time, of course. All I knew was that it was a slow Wednesday afternoon at the bar and in walks this gal, red hair pouring over her shoulders, wearing a wifebeater and black leather pants. And all of the sudden the Cards game on the teevee didn't seem so interesting.

"Nice place." She pulled herself onto a stool in front of me, thumping a big leather purse onto the stool next to her. Strictly speaking, what she said was a lie. Jackie Blue's isn't much to look at—brick and linoleum, bars on the only window up front, old neon signs on the wall. But still it sounded like she meant it. She had a Southern lilt, not that twang that you get around here, and it made whatever she said sound like sunshine and kittens. Sexy kittens.

"Thanks."

"It yours?"

"Indeed it is."

"Well, I guess that makes you Jackie Blue, am I right?"

"Well, I'm Jackie, anyway," I said. I haven't answered to Jackie Blue in a long time.

"Jackie Blue . . . isn't that the name of a song?"

"By the Ozark Mountain Daredevils, as a matter of fact. You find yourself in the Queen City of the Ozarks just now, if you didn't know it."

She wrinkled her nose at that.

"Is that where I am? I had wondered. I hope you don't mind me saying, she doesn't look much like a queen."

"Well, take a look 'round the rest of the Ozarks and get back to me on that. Springfield don't look like much, but it beats the hell out of Rogersville or Monett."

She dropped a smile on me that peeled about twenty years off my old hide, which might have put me about even with her.

"Jolene," she said, and put out a freckled hand for me to take. It felt hot to the touch.

"Well now, that's the name of a song as well, right?"

She groaned a little at this. I guessed she wasn't a Dolly Parton fan.

"What can I do you for, Jolene?"

"I'll take a Wild Turkey neat with a Dr Pepper back, if you please."

That is a drink order that makes a man sit up and take notice. I poured the liquor in a highball glass and filled a twin for myself. Owning a bar, you want to watch things like drinking in the day. But there's exceptions for everything, and this was shaping into an exceptional day. She took a hard swallow of the Turkey. I could see it play havoc with the muscles in her throat but it never touched her face. I liked her even more.

"So now, Jolene—seeing as how you don't know where you are, maybe it's a pointless question—but what brings you to town?"

She smiled, but this time there was a little crack to it, like there was something that wasn't a smile underneath. She put her hand on her purse like it was fitting to fly off, then dug in it for some of those skinny toothpick cigarettes that ladies sometimes smoke.

"Jackie, I'll tell you what it is. I'm in town for exactly two reasons. One's to drink Wild Turkey. The other is to get laid."

I've had it every other way I can think of, but I've never had it served to me sizzling on a platter like that. There was something there in the back of the skull telling me that God made up his mind long ago that I'm not that lucky and the strings you can't see usually turn to chains. But sometimes you got to jump just 'cause the chasm is there.

Hell, what was I going to do, go back to watching the Cards?

I topped my glass to the rim, then hers. Then I held up that near full bottle of Wild Turkey up between us and poured the whole thing into the sink.

"Fresh out of Wild Turkey," I told her.

She laid that smile on me again and it peeled off another couple years so that now she was the older one, the one in charge.

"Maybe you want to close up shop early," she said, sliding off the stool.

"Maybe I do." I walked around the bar, hoping she couldn't see me tenting out my jeans. I threw the deadbolt on the front door and pulled the strings on the blinds on the window. Before I did, I peeked out into the parking lot, which was empty except my old truck. Maybe she parked down the street, I figured, and turned to ask her. The words got jammed in my mouth. She was in the corner of the bar, sitting on the glass top of the sit-down Ms. Pac-Man machine. I wondered if her ass was cold, seeing as how while my back was turned she'd stripped out of those black leather pants and didn't have a thing on except a pair of high-heeled cowboy boots.

"I thought this would be fine," she said, patting the video game table under her ass.

It was fine, all right. Fine, indeed.

* * *

And time passed slowly and, well, the way it did back when I was young and time seemed like it would last forever. Every now and then someone would rattle the door, as the regulars who couldn't believe I would shut the door came calling. A few times the phone rang, and I knew that had to be some right thirsty boys indeed who'd go home to look the number up to see if they could rouse me. But none of the noise bothered us at all, except once, later on, after the sun set and there wasn't any light but the orange glow of the Budweiser clock over the bar. A noise like a long loud rip of fabric went by. It was the sound of a motorcycle, something chopped and mufflerless. At that, Jolene stiffened under me like a deer who hears the step of a clumsy hunter. But then it passed and faded and after a few seconds she unlocked her joints and turned back into the slippery slick she-devil. Where there'd been fear in her eyes, I only saw thunder.

So we talked and then we'd wrestle some more, and then talk again. She told me about growing up in Georgia, about how her grandmother was an honest-to-God dirt eater who'd scoop soil off the ground and pop it in her mouth, embarrassing Jolene something proper. She told me about how football was king then and how she'd put her prom dress on layaway. She told me more than that and I noticed that none of her stories ever reached up into the past few years. What had happened to her since that prom stayed a mystery.

I talked too, and if she really listened, she might have noticed that I did just the opposite. Everything I told her was in the now, ever since I opened Jackie Blue's. Mostly stories about what the drunks did, like the time Mad Dog McClure opened up Mike Lewis's head with a claw hammer not a foot from where we now lay. Stories about bad men, but I didn't delve back into the dark days, back when I was bad myself.

So when we talked we kept our secrets. But when we wasn't

talking, there weren't no lies between us, and she saw me for who I used to be—a dangerous man. And I saw her in danger. So much danger. I got it in my head that maybe I was the man to get her out, and then I thought maybe that's just what she wanted me to think.

We slept on a bed of our clothes and woke around dawn, to the sound of songbirds outside. It was a sound that didn't fit in Jackie Blue's any more than if you heard Lynyrd Skynyrd coming out of the treetops. God, she still looked good in that morning light, and let me tell you: that was a thing I wasn't used to anymore. A man who owns himself a bar don't hardly ever need to go to bed alone, but what you wake up with is usually a poisoned head and possum bait smiling next to you, the kind you'd chew your arm off to get away from. But not her. I stared at her until my old eyes started to burn and then I took some time to look at me instead. The fur on my chest and belly had all faded from black to gray over the last few years, like I'd spent the time soaking in hot water and the ink had leeched on out. The gut had gotten bigger, but I hadn't gone soft. No, not yet. I still had some pretty good muscle, hauling kegs and tossing drunks. And under the faded India ink tattoos on my forearm, I still had some ropes of muscle. Maybe I wasn't just Jackie the bartender yet. Maybe there was still some Jackie Blue underneath, ready to bark at the moon.

She turned herself over, blinking in the sunlight, just as I was finishing pulling on my old leather boots.

"Good morning, cowboy," she said, not bothering to cover herself in the daylight. "Sorry to see you've already got yourself dressed. A lot of effort for nothing, if you ask me."

"Protein," I said. "This old goat needs protein if he's planning on walking, much less working, today. There's a diner down a block, should be opening about now. How do you like your eggs?"

She sat up and hugged herself, as if all the sudden she knew she was naked. Then she slipped that mask back on and leaned back to show herself, pale skin against the leather pants beneath her.

"I'll put you to work, Daddy," she said. "All you need is a little bit of that popcorn and a belt of brown stuff to get you back in the saddle. What do you say?"

Lord, even after the night she'd gave me there was something in me kicking its heels up for more. But I picked up my keys, partways because I truly needed some grub, and partways to force her hand. It was time to get some truth from the little lady.

"Over easy suit you?" I jingled my keys at her.

"Don't go." See, there was some of that honesty she showed me on the floor last night.

"Why not?"

She hugged herself tight again. "I need you. I need shelter, don't you see?"

"You hiding from a man?"

She laughed. "I suppose you could say it that way. I prefer calling him a low-down son of a bitch."

"And what's this son of a bitch want with a pretty little lady like yourself?"

"Can't you guess it?" She stood up in all her glory. "The dummy thinks we're still in love."

It's a story I can believe.

That don't mean I do, just yet.

"This dude got a name?"

"Cole."

"Cole? Just plain old Cole? Like Slash?"

"That's all I know to call him."

"That's all you know? And you're his woman?"

"Was. As of last night, I'm all my own again."

She'd met him in Tulsa, she said, and picked up with him and his boys. Bikers—called themselves the Sloppy Satans. That name meant something to me from stories I'd heard from some of my meaner customers. Oklahoma boys, I told her, who moved some Nazi dope up and down I-44.

"Cole weren't a Nazi," she said. "No more than anybody else, anyway."

I shook my head.

"I'm not saying the boys are Nazis. The dope is. You ain't never heard of Nazi meth?"

She shook her head.

"Some good old boy from around these parts, around twenty years ago, he went over to the library over at Missouri State—they called it SMSU back then—and found the recipe that the Nazis had for cooking up amphetamines back in World War II. It's the premier recipe for Ozarks meth. Our little contribution to that world."

She nodded, like something in her head just clicked. She pulled her purse close to her and then stood up to pull on her leather pants. It pained me to see her do it, even if it was fun to watch.

"I don't know from Nazi dope," she said. "What I do know is I'll take a whole lot of lip of a man if he's as much fun as Cole was, but I'll be damned if I'll let him put his hands on me. Last night, Cole had a little bike trouble—the ride had gotten real bumpy. We were all pulled over on the side of the exit, just where the highway is up the road?"

I nodded to let her know I knew where she meant. That was only a quarter mile from here.

"Well, I asked Cole when we'd be heading back to Oklahoma. Now, I'd ridden with him long enough to know that I came in a weak second place, if that, to that bike of his. But I guess I never saw it in him to smack me around like that."

She touched the side of her face, turning it towards me to examine. It looked flawless to me.

"And that was that, huh?"

She purred a laugh.

"I jumped the guardrail and marched through a couple of yards and then saw your place. I grabbed that there barstool and figured I'd start up a new life right then and there."

"Is that what you figured? You didn't walk into here like a woman on the run. You walked in like a goddamn cannonball."

She smiled. "Ain't you ever cut free of something and it made you feel wild?"

Not for a while, would be the truth of it. Not since I walked out of the life and into this bar. But the way she said it, and the way she looked, made me think that maybe I could do it again.

"Think that motorcycle man is looking for you? That why you don't want for me to leave?"

She stepped closer, put a hand on my arm. The whiteness of her made my skin look dirty.

"You ever dump a mean son of a bitch?"

I pushed her hand away and grabbed onto the bar.

"Is he coming? Is that why you're here?"

"I figured if he was coming, he'd come right away. It wasn't until I thought it was safe that I made my move with you. You see?"

I did. I saw that Jackie Blue's was on a back road, and while it might be the first place you'd find on foot, it'd be real easy to miss from the road, especially if Springfield weren't your town. And I saw that she knew that, and that she hadn't given that fellow near enough time to give up on her before the two of us got busy. But I also saw that it'd been near fifteen hours since she came through the door, and even as fine as she was, fifteen hours is longer than a man could look for a woman with his buddies in tow.

"If he were coming, he'd a been here by now," I said. "So there ain't no harm in me running to get us some breakfast. You can keep laying low here, and then the two of us can sit and figure out what the next part of your grand adventure is going to be once you leave here."

"That's what you want?"

I wanted to run across the room and mash myself to her. I wanted to sell the bar and buy a bike and see how far across the planet the money could get us. I wanted to shave the gray out of my hair and step back into my old boots and stomp and steal for enough money for us to last forever.

"Yeah," I told her. "That's what I want."

I drove over to Aunt Martha's Pancake House and ordered up a couple stacks to go. I picked up a *News-Leader* and took a seat, turning straight to the editorial page to read the letters from the loonies. There was one about how abortion stops a beating heart, one about how the school board was trying to teach kids evolution, or, as the letter put it, "from goo to you via the zoo." The last letter was about how the Ten Commandments needed to be posted up in every school. All three quoted the Bible in the first paragraph.

I love living in the Ozarks.

"Jackie?"

I looked up and there was Pinkle. Don Pinkle, that is, looking every bit the methed-out redneck that he was. He stood there Nazi-dope skinny with a sad, scraggly goatee and bags under his eyes that looked like full-grown slugs. If he'd slept in forty-eight hours, it had been forty-eight hours ago. He flashed me a smile, but that isn't the right word, because there wasn't nothing flashing in that brown meth mouth of his, just teeth, yellow and orange and brown like dry dog food. He came by the bar some nights with some of the boys, every once in a while getting on a rebar crew to earn an honest dollar—which must have felt lonely and out of place in his vinyl and Velcro wallet. He never tipped on a drink, not once.

"Pinkle," I said like it was the whole conversation, and tried to get back to my newspaper. But he wasn't having it.

"Went by the bar last night."

"Did you now?"

"Wasn't open."

I dropped the paper, seeing as it was clear he wasn't going away.

"Now, Pinkle, don't you think I know that?"

"Knocked on the door and everything."

"Well, trust in your senses, boy. We were closed."

"Thought I heard something," he said, scratching a scratched-up face. His nostrils stood out bloodred and ragged against the trout belly of his skin. "That's why I knocked, see? But nobody answered."

"Hear voices? You? You can't tell me that hearin' voices is some sort of strange occurrence in your life, the shit you've got floating in that lump of gristle you probably call a head. I bet it sounds like happy hour in there most times."

"I thought maybe you were in there with someone, is all," he said, trying to give me a saucy look. "Ain't nothing to it but to do it, right?"

I stood up fast and took pleasure in how he scurried back a few steps. Sometimes folks forget just how big I am, or what I used to be able to do. Sometimes I forget myself.

"And I thought," I said, "that what I do in there or don't do is exactly one hundred percent none of your goddamn business. Care to tell me how I got so misled about that?"

Just then a waitress called out, saying Pinkle's food was ready and that mine was getting bagged up.

"That's a whole lot of food for a body," he said, looking at my order. "Got yourself a tapeworm?"

"Got something to plug that hole I'm getting ready to stomp into your head?" I asked back.

"Not meaning to aggravate you," he said, holding up his palms.

So I took a few deep breaths and just told myself that the dumb twiddlepatted motherfucker is too stupid to barely breathe, much less know when to leave well enough alone. I was wrong, it turns out. Pinkle really is stupid, just not as stupid as I gave him credit for. Not that I figured it out by his next move, which was to try to pay for his breakfast with a hundred dollar bill. It was early yet and of course the joint couldn't handle that, so I groaned and paid for his while mine was still being put together. I didn't even ask where he'd gotten the hundred. I didn't want to know.

"Could you throw in a dollar extra?" he asked me with a sheepish grin. "I need me some quarters."

"You need to be laying off that dope," I told him, but pushed the quarters across anyway. "And you need to not think about setting foot in Jackie Blue's until you're ready to pay me back, hear?"

He grabbed his food and hotfooted out the door. I went back to the waitress, who was kind of cute, and gave her a wink. Well, the goat had really woke up, hadn't he?

"Some dude, huh?"

"Yeah, people suck," she said. "Bank on it."

"Rosy disposition." God, I wish I knew what it was about girls with too much eyeliner and a bad attitude that got to me. Then I thought of Jolene grabbing the brass pole that ran under the bar and I knew that I was good to go again.

"Mister," she said, pushing my bag of food over to me. "Work the night shift at a diner some time, and then you can tell me about how great people are. Especially people like that one."

I was about to tell her about how I worked a bar and knew how people could be, when it struck me that there was something strange in the way she'd said "like that one." She stressed the *that* like she could still see him, so I turned around, and there he was at the gas station across the street, jabbering into a pay phone. I didn't like that. And then I remembered that hundred dollar bill, and I liked it all even less. There was plenty of ways that a man like Pinkle could get some cash money, none of them nice. But to have a fresh hundred to spend on breakfast at the end of a binge, that didn't set right. *It was probably nothing*, I thought, but decided I'd walk over there and see what he had to say. And then he looked up and saw me crossing the street and dropped the phone. A piece of paper fluttered to the ground in his wake.

A big semi rolled past the road and by the time it passed, Pinkle had a good head start. Besides, I wasn't going to win no footrace with a meth head. I stopped at the phone and picked up the paper scrap. Then I dropped the breakfast. There was an out-of-town phone number scrawled on it, with one word under it, and that word was *Cole*.

The chopper was a beauty, all silver fire and wheels. It slouched in front of the front door of Jackie Blue's, which hung open. The wood around the doorknob was splintered like someone had kicked it open. He couldn't have been there long—less than ten minutes had passed since Pinkle made his call. In fact, when I climbed out of the truck I could still hear the bike's engine ticking. Then that sound was ripped out of my ears by a scream coming out the door. I ran inside, my fists balled at my sides, hoping he didn't have a gun.

He probably had a gun.

The insides of the bar looked like someone had picked the whole place up, turned it upside down, and given it a shake. The register was popped open and the cash drawer hung crookedly out, the shelf lifted to search out the underneath. Bottles had been shoved off the shelf, some of them breaking on the floor. A cloud of booze stung my eyes and plugged my nose. All this came to me out of the sides of my mind. Right there in the foreground was a big old boy with an arm inked with jailhouse tats he had wrapped around Jolene's throat. His other hand muffled the screams with his palm. Jolene's eyes bulged out over his hand, and her own hands didn't fight his but instead clutched her black leather purse.

"Just stand back there, Pops," he said with an Oklahoma twang. "Just keep a cool head and we can all walk out of this."

"Funny words coming from a man just trashed my bar."

He barked a little laugh at that.

"Brother," he said, "I just got here. This little bitch"—he gave her a shake for emphasis—"is the fucking source of all our troubles, yours and mine. I don't know how she's been playing you, but if I had to guess, I think I could. I know how she suckered me."

He took his arm away from her throat and cupped the crotch of her leather pants. She tried to say something through his other hand, but it kept her muffled.

"Played me but good, brother, and now she's playing you. When I came through that door she'd done cleaned your register out."

I took a step forwards. The place was cleaned out, all right.

"You really Jackie Blue?"

For the first time in a long time, I said yes.

He shook his head sort of sad like. "Well, that's what I get for opening my big fat mouth. I done told this cooze enough stories about Jackie Blue back in the day to fill her head with 'em. See, my pops used to ride through here, and he always told me that back then the hardest man in the hills were Jackie Blue. And so when we'd ride by, I'd always have to tell this bitch here about it. I guess I might have oversold you and made Jolene here get some mighty bad ideas."

She tried to shake her head, but I could see it was true— she'd known just who I was the moment she'd walked through the door. Makes sense. Lucky is just what you call someone when you don't know how smart they are.

"That may be, son, but still all the same, if a gal wants to take her leave of you, it's best to let 'em go without a fuss. What do you say?"

He laughed and yanked Jolene's purse out of her hands. He shook it and dumped it out on the floor. First came all my money that she stole and then came pinkish white bricks, one, two, three.

"Brother," he said as I watched the Nazi dope pile on the floor, "it ain't the leaving so much as the stealing that bothers me."

Well, damn.

"All right," I said. "I see it now. She done played you and then she played me. Figures. So you take what's yours and get on out and we'll call it a day. How's that sound?"

"Sounds fine," he said, then turned to the woman. "Scoop that shit up—leave Jackie Blue's money—and let's get going. Let you have one last ride before you get yours."

"No," I said. "You misunderstand me. The lady stays."

He looked at me like I gone plumb crazy. "Jackie, I know she's got a snatch like hot butter, but come on—this bitch is pure poison. You can't want her to stick around after she tried to rob the both of us."

"That's so. But as much as I might like to see it, I can't let you hurt her. See, even if it was partway, or even in total a lie, that girl made me wake up last night—she made me see who I am. And no woman under the protection of Jackie Blue is going to get dragged off and dealt with by no biker piece of shit like you."

The fear hit his eyes and I thought it was going to be easy, but then it went away. At first I wasn't sure why, but it's that his young ears heard them before mine did—the sound of a group of motorcycles rolling down the road.

"Now, Jackie, I got all sorts of respect for you, but I got to think of my own image too. Can't let my boys think I got taken by a slut and a geezer."

He reached behind him and pulled a little flat pistol. He moved the girl in front of him, as a shield like. His boys were rolling into the lot—I had about fifteen seconds to make this right.

I walked in, stepping to the right, putting Jolene totally between us. That suited him fine, he thought, as I'm not going to hurt the woman. But also it meant he couldn't see me to shoot me. I took Jolene's head in my hands—our eyes met and I laughed—then I slammed her skull straight back into Cole's nose. He dropped and just for a second I stood holding Jolene by the head like I was getting ready to lay a Hollywood kiss on her.

But instead I tossed her to the side so I could stomp Cole while he's down. Three times did nicely. Then I picked up the pistol with my right and his shaggy greasy hair with my left and I dragged him to the door, just in time for his three buddies to come to full stops on their bikes. The dust swirled up and their engines roared and I stepped into the storm of it all dragging Cole behind me.

By God, I felt good.

"Welcome to Jackie Blue's," I said.

The Return of Inspiration

Tom Piccirilli

I was back in Frisco and I still had no idea why I was there.

It had something to do with the fact that my wife had tossed me out and New York had turned sour for me. Her attorney had chased me from our apartment and her girlfriends had iced me from our social circle. My buddies had to meet me in secret so their wives wouldn't know they were consorting with the enemy. They were getting more and more worried all the time until we could only hang for a few minutes at the kiddie park while their children played. My pals were always late and fled quickly. I sat on that fucking bench watching screaming kids so often that the cops finally rousted me for being a potential pedo.

For a year my publisher had been hinting at dropping me unless my novel sales improved greatly. They didn't improve, greatly or otherwise. My last royalty statement had been for $12.35. I had resigned myself to the possibility that I wasn't destined to retire to St. Croix anytime soon.

Another buddy had started hitting it big in Frisco as an underground performance artist. He played to audiences of a few hundred every night, which didn't seem very underground to me. He tried to explain exactly what he did, but I got too confused trying to picture how the bale of wire, the unicycle, the fifteen-pound weights, and the penis puppets all went together. It proved the limitations of my imagination, but he invited me out West anyway.

The word got around the circuit that I was coming to town. I didn't even know there was a circuit, or that such circuit would care about me in the slightest, but there it was. My mysteries never got reviewed. My horror novels had a sixty-five percent return rate. But my whitebread erotica stories had started getting some weird buzz. Even before I got off the plane I had three readings set up. One was at a sex bookstore, one at a sex shop, and one at a sex club. I began to sense a predominant theme attempting to impress itself upon my life.

By the time I got to my buddy's apartment he was already gone. The Europeans had gotten wind of his act and he was off to east London for a two-week show. Things moved fast in Frisco. He left a note saying the place was mine for the duration. Food was stocked and he'd conveniently left a map out on the kitchen counter with the bookstore, sex shop, and club marked in red pen. He told me that people who lived in San Francisco didn't call it Frisco and I was doomed to look like a dumbass tourist. He wished me luck and was kind enough to leave me some cash in case I was strapped. It was fifty bucks. Clearly the concept of strapped didn't go hand in hand with the penis puppets.

The lady running the readings was named Miss Tress. She called and told me she was a big fan of my fiction. She thought it was wonderfully humorous, how I was always writing about my goofy alter ego getting into such ridiculous situations. I didn't have the heart to tell her that I didn't have an alter ego. I told it like it was, but nobody wanted to believe me. I didn't blame them; I didn't want to believe it either.

Miss Tress asked if I wanted to put on any kind of a presentation. She said many of the speakers brought up onstage their spouses, lovers, slaves, doms, troupes, entourages. They chose music, lighting, and a couple had smoke machines. They carried paddles, masks, costumes, plushies, pony-wear, ball-gags. I asked how they read with ball-gags in. She ignored me and said speakers liked to be playful before the audience. They often embraced their sexuality onstage. I had embraced my sexuality many, many times before but never on a stage. She said the best speakers knew how to use props to their advantage. I looked around my pal's apartment and noted handcuffs, rope, duct tape, and excessive amounts of razor wire. The unicycle was propped in the corner. Christ, he even had a smoke machine.

I told her I'd just need a copy of the anthology with my story in it. It was a book called *Naturally Naughty 3*, edited by Alison Wonderland. She said that was excellent—Alison was the main attraction of the show. She hung up and I stared at the phone like I wanted to call someone, but I didn't know who.

I hadn't seen Alison since my last visit to Frisco six months ago, where she was the headliner and I'd read sixth out of six. She'd been expecting someone else. They were always expecting someone else. It was all right, I'd learned to live with it. I was sort of expecting myself to be someone else too.

But after the reading at Betty's Puss and Whips shop, Alison and I had thrown back a few drinks and done a curious dance around each other. She wanted to know where a vanilla fudge pudge like me had gotten enough imagination to write the stories I did. She was a dark, lovely woman with burning eyes, glossy black hair, and a molten fascinating core. The surface drew me in, but it was what smoldered beneath that really hooked me.

We had taken a run over to her apartment, where she threw down a sexual gauntlet that had left me horny, shaken, and with a little too clear an insight into my own contradictions. I was a perverted prude. I was hardwired to be weak. I liked to be stomped but not too much. I liked being on my knees but only if someone appreciated it. She was so powerfully submissive that she'd scared the crap out of me. I didn't cower but I came damn close. I was angry for a lot of reasons I understood and many I didn't.

I hadn't been able to become the dom she needed. I couldn't raise my hand to her. When I thought of a dom I thought of two guys named Dom that I'd known in high school. They'd both been bullies. I already had bad associations. When I thought of a sub I thought of Captain Nemo on the *Nautilus* or roast beef hoagies with lots of mayo. I figured I wasn't going to be in the proper frame of mind to perform at a club called Beat Yer Ass.

I was eager and nervous to see her again. We hadn't spoken or e-mailed since our encounter. I read her blog for any hint of me that might turn up. She talked of many lovers and situations, but never of me. It left me remotely jealous and a little bitter.

Two days later, the fifty bucks was long blown. I was in a cab heading towards the BYA. It was the kind of town where you could mention the name of a club and all the cab drivers would already have the best route mapped out. I was impressed.

The BYA proved to be a decent-sized space that reminded me of some East Village bars. Dark, somber, but with a constant blur of activity in the back corners. A stage had been set up with tables covered in paraphernalia. Some objects I recognized. Many I didn't. My curiosity was piqued. Dozens of books were stacked far to one side. There was no microphone or stool where a reader might sit. A large sign boasted a dozen names. Mine was number eleven out of twelve. I was moving up. At the top with a bullet was Alison Wonderland. The insecurities and self-consciousness began to hit hard.

The joint was crammed. Women in see-through nighties and leather halters with their tits exposed wandered past me. Men in chaps and crushed velvet suits glided past. There were riding crops, canes, cricket paddles, strops, leashes, and zippered leather masks on view. The masks had holes for the eyes and mouth and nostrils but not for the ears. I knew I was going to have to enunciate clearly and really project.

A young woman approached almost warily, slinking up to me hesitantly as if she might slip up on me unnoticed. Since I was staring right at her I didn't quite know how that could work, but I was new to the scene. She wore a black silk halter and a latex skirt and not much else. She looked underage, had a heart-shaped face and cornflower eyes that would normally make me think of girl-next-door wholesomeness if not for the venue being packed with folks waving their naughty bits around.

She looked into my eyes, going deep and not stopping. I didn't know whether to blink or not. I stared back at her and she flinched.

"You're full of rage," she said.

"Me?"

"You've killed many."

"Me?"

"You've destroyed many men and women. The ones you hated and the ones you loved."

"Lady, you've got me mixed up with somebody else."

"If not yet, then soon."

"Say what?"

"Your anger, it cuts into me. I want it. Don't give it to any-one else. I want it. You can punish me. You can murder me if you want. I don't care. Flay me, dump me in the bay. I'll sign a suicide note. They'll never find you."

It was a nutty enough dialogue to normally make me roll my eyes and grin, but I wasn't smiling. Icy threads of sweat prickled my scalp and ran down the back of my neck. She spoke with more conviction than I'd probably ever spoken about anything in my life. I backed away from her and her hand shot out and clenched my wrist.

"I'm yours."

"I don't want you," I said.

"She's not worth bleeding."

"Who?"

"Alison. I know what you want."

"And how the fuck do you know that?"

"She'll never fulfill you. She can't inspire you."

"Look, seriously, I think you—"

"Please."

The girl had some muscle to her. I snapped my arm back twice and still had a hard time breaking her hold on me. The third time she released me.

I wanted to ask her what the hell she was talking about. I wanted to ask exactly why she thought she recognized in me some overwhelming urge towards pain and frenzy. I opened my mouth and she stood on her toes, leaned in, and kissed me.

She said, "You can kill me whenever you want," and faded back, step-by-step, as if consumed by darkness in a well-lit room, until I couldn't see her anymore.

I recognized Miss Tress from my last reading. She spotted me and crossed the place with her hand held out like a duchess. She was decked in full head to toe pink rubber wear. I had images of her tripping, falling, and bouncing around the room like a handball.

She drew me into the wings of the stage. "Are you all right? You look a bit . . . put out."

"I think I just had a run-in with a fan."

"Trouble?"

"Not really. I've just never had a fan before."

She snorted. "Have you ever been to a reading at a club like this?"

"No," I admitted.

"Well, let me just fill you in . . . you see, reading is, ah, optional."

"Say what? Reading is optional?"

"Yes, as I mentioned, most of our speakers like to . . . perform and put on something of a display for the audience. A cabaret."

"A cabaret."

"Yes, their . . . well, their bodies become their art, you see. Their bodies, their acts of worship, become their fiction. Very few of them actually read."

I blinked at her. "Most of the readers don't read?"

"That's correct."

No wonder the penis puppetry brought in the big bucks. I was in the wrong game and getting deeper all the time, and I still didn't know what it was. She smiled at me like she thought my stupidity was pitiful and kind of cute. I blinked at her some more. "What about those of us who do read?"

"Well, tonight, you're the only one who does, if you choose to."

I sighed. I turned on my heel and started to walk out of the place when the stage lit up.

Alison Wonderland, wearing a pink teddy and garters and fishnet stockings, wafted out. Noise and activity heightened in the shadows, but there was no applause. The rest of the lights dimmed. The darkness crept across me. My breathing slowed and grew shallow. My back itched like I was covered in leeches.

"The show's beginning," Miss Tress said.

Alison pressed her hands against the stage wall and assumed the position. I'd seen a lot of street dealers hit that position in

THE RETURN OF INSPIRATION / 23

alleys flooded with flashing lights, but I'd never seen a beautiful woman do it of her own initiative. Her head hung low. Her disheveled, black shining hair covered much of her face. It got me going. It filled me full of lust and dread and a little fear. I wanted to see her eyes.

A prettyboy with muscles like cannonballs, wearing a little Tarzan loincloth, stepped past me. He held a thick belt in his hand. He lingered beside me in the dark, allowing the moment to stretch and progress. Alison waited, as immobile as stone.

"Who's he?" I asked.

Miss Tress said, "Her dom."

Six months ago she'd been living with two guys. I'd met one of them. This guy wasn't him. Maybe it was the other one. Maybe she'd pulled in a third guy to pick up the slack in bed or help make the rent. It set the prude in me on edge. I didn't know where I'd gotten such puritanical angst. The perv in me really wanted to check out the tableau, sit back and watch it all play out. I wanted to push. I wanted to be pushed. I began to tremble.

I knew Alison best through her confessional prose. She'd offered herself honestly to the world. The angle of her jaw energized me. The curve of her ass plucked at my guts. I was turned on by her and starting to really burn. I wanted to feel her nails digging in hard. Her flesh clapping mine. I had been shamed by her. I was furious with her. I should've at least rated a half-inch column in her blog.

The dom's oiled muscles and good looks offended me. That subtle hint of envy ratcheted up in my belly. It lifted me onto my toes. I didn't understand it. A rage and a sudden insane need swept over me. The dom looked cool and almost bored. He was slack-jawed. He didn't even have his lips set for what he was about to do.

My heart hammered and my pulse tripped along at an increasing rate. I became light-headed. I felt like I'd been doing wind sprints all evening. Sweat slithered down my face. I stepped over to him.

"You!" I said. "You her boyfriend?"

He wheeled to face me and went, "Wha'?"

"Alison's boyfriend. Her lover. You him? You one of the two or three?"

"What? No."

"Well, who the hell are you then?"

"Chad."

"Chad?" Even his name offended me. "Chad! You a reader who doesn't read? Fuck you, Chad!"

"What?"

"Take a walk! We don't need you here tonight. You've been demoted. My lips are set, buddy!"

"Wha'?"

The look in my eyes scared him. The sound of my own voice scared me. He backed away and his jaw grew even slacker. Any other day he could probably twist me in half, but right now we both knew I wasn't in control of myself. That put me in control of the situation, maybe.

Before I knew what the hell I was doing I walked out on-stage. There was a spattering of noise, a mixture of murmurs and disappointed yawps. Fuck them too. I stared into the shadows for a moment and saw bodies turning in motion, rolling over on couches, in the carpeting, doing their own thing. I looked for the wholesome girl and didn't see her.

I didn't have cannonball muscles. I didn't stink of vegetable oil. I wasn't a dom. I didn't know what I was and this might not have been the place for learning. This was where you went to embrace an understanding of yourself, not discover it. I was unmasked. I had my clothes on but I was naked, exposed before leather men and rubber women and pony people and six-foot-tall plushie toys. For people devoted to the flesh, they sure wore a lot of shit.

I moved up behind Alison. The veins in my throat stood out. I didn't know what to say so I went with an old favorite. "Hi."

She remained frozen in place but her muscles tightened even more. She'd assumed the position and wasn't going to move an inch. These people had rules and laws and habits I couldn't even guess at.

"What are you doing here?" she whispered.

"I'm sort of curious about that myself."

"Go away, someone else is—"

"No," I told her, "nobody else is. Chad had to fly back to the jungle."

"What?"

"Evil white bwana was knocking down the trees. The chimps needed protection."

"What the hell are you talking about? Everyone's watching."

I looked around and said, "Some of them, maybe. But most of them are already kind of busy. It doesn't matter. They're not real. They're made of latex and stuffed with cotton."

"You're crazy!"

I got up close and breathed on her neck. I sniffed at her hair and swallowed hard. Six months ago I had tried to make love to her but didn't play her game. I'd been consumed by fear of her sexual intensity and conviction. It had turned me on and torn me down. I'd left her tied to a bed and in complete control. I'd felt gypped and pissed with myself for the last half a year. The air between us began to heat with possibility.

I pressed my hand to her back and gently stroked her skin. I drew my knuckles across her shoulder blades. I brought my lips to her ear and for an instant took her earlobe between my teeth. It made her frown. It made me frown too.

"We have unfinished business, you and me," I said.

"Take off your belt and whip me."

"I don't have a belt."

"You don't have a belt?"

"No."

It broke her from her station. Her heels came off the floor and she started hopping in place on her toes. I wondered about the willpower it took to hold her hands to that wall like they were nailed there. Jesus, she was strong. I wanted that strength.

"Why don't you have a belt?" she asked.

"I just don't."

"But why not?"

"Not everybody wears belts, you know! Goddamn!"

"Take off my panties."

"You're pretty pushy for a submissive, lady."

"Do it."

I did it. I was off to a bad start. I slid them down her legs. She had a cherry tattoo on one cheek. She'd written about it more than once. One of her lovers had taken her to the tattoo parlor and given it to her. A sign of ownership. I instantly hated it. I wondered what it was like, waiting beneath the needle, taking the pain merely because someone else wanted you to. I knew what she could take, but what could she give? Could I find my inspiration?

Her ass was crimson, bruised, and striped from the hands and implements of her lovers. My breath hitched in my throat. I couldn't believe someone would want even more punishment. The muscles in my back went rigid.

I hissed, "Jesus fuckin' Christ—"

"Don't. This is what I want. It's what I need. Do you understand?"

I said nothing.

"Do you understand?"

"No," I told her. "Jesus Christ."

"It's my need. I need you now."

"Well, that's nice to hear."

"Spank me."

All the sparking black vibes that had been going on between us began to tighten inside my chest. She was angry too. On some small level she must've felt gypped the last half year as well.

"Take charge," she urged. "Do it."

"Listen—"

"Do what I say," she ordered.

My skin was on too tight. "You want me."

"Yes."

"Say it then."

"I want you."

"No, damn you, say my name."

She said my name, and her control wavered. A little thing like that, it took us off the stage and into the moment, into each other. I felt the reins of power shifting back and forth between us. My hate grew and waned. I didn't know which was better. I was still on my feet and not my knees. What did it mean?

"Spank me," she said.

"Stop telling me what to do!"

"Spank me. Do as I say. Beat me. Punish me. I want scars."

"You're already covered with them."

"I want more."

Her unruly hair covered her face again and I swept it back, grasping handfuls. I pulled gently at first, and then harder, until her face was pulled aside to my own. She didn't seem to want to kiss me. Good. I kissed her anyway. Her mouth arced into a small grin beneath my lips. "Bend me over," she ordered.

I forced her down and said, "Grab your ankles."

"Oh yes. Spank me. Now!"

"Seriously, it would be really nice if you quit yelling at me."

I'd never hit a woman in my life. I didn't want to hit her now. I thought of the razor wire and what my buddy might do with it, to himself and to others. I clapped her ass. She grunted but I grunted louder. It hurt to do it. I wondered why any of us signed up for this. I wondered if I could ever learn to ride the unicycle. I grimaced while she champed her teeth. I struck her again. She drew a breath so deeply that her whole body quivered. I had soft hands but they were strong. Typing a quarter million words a year had its benefits. They were already stinging. I spanked her faster and harder. It felt like she was doing it to me. My face reddened, the pain grew. I couldn't look at the crimson of her flesh anymore. I nearly wavered. New York no longer seemed so bad. I'd never been to the top of the Empire State Building. I suddenly wanted to hit Lincoln Center and take in the opera. There they only sounded like they were being whipped. I slapped her ass and clamped my hands on her cheeks, squeezing them tightly, plying them. Flesh on flesh was one thing. I could almost wrap my mind around it. But canes and riding crops and belts were beyond me. I wanted contact. I wanted muscle.

She said, "Do your hands hurt?"

"Not as bad as my heart."

"Good. Do it harder."

I glanced over at the books on the table, the ones that wouldn't sell, my stories unread. I felt worthless. I usually did. Maybe if I'd had a better agent I wouldn't have had to be here at all. Chad hovered in the wings. I snapped to attention and gave him the finger. Chad shrank back and cowered in the shadows. This was her dom? These people were all insane. I started backhanding her. I mixed the game up. Her thighs were smeared with our mixed sweat. I hit her again and she called me sir.

I said, "Don't ever say that."

"What, 'sir'?"

"Quit it."

"Yes, master."

"Forget that noise too, damn it."

"What?"

"Speak my name," I said. "My name has meaning. You can call anybody sir."

"I call you sir."

"Save that shit. My name is mine. Do you understand?"

"Yes." She said my name the way my high school principal had when he'd handed me my diploma. With a touch of pride, a little surprise, a dash of disappointment, and beneath it all a thrum of coy derision. That bastard! I hit her again and her whole body rocked. If she hadn't been so used to the position I would've knocked her across the room. My hands were burning. My blood was burning.

The floor was wet with her tears. Maybe some of mine too. I was dripping. Salt lined my lips. I laid my palms against her cheeks and felt the heat rising from them. I got in closer and pressed myself against her. She said, "Tell me to release my ankles."

"Why do I have to tell you? Just do it."

"Tell me."

"You act like this means something. It doesn't. It's another stupid game. Aren't you tired of them?"

"Tell me."

"Christ almighty. Release your ankles. Get up."

She got up and nearly fell over. I had to grab her. I reached around and tightened her across my chest. She slumped and could barely stand. She looked me in the eyes and her gaze was dominant and consuming. This one, oh yeah, she was dangerous. I held her up and kissed the side of her throat. Her pulse throbbed against my tongue. I was rewarded with a brief, knowing smile. It was at once beautiful and erotic and gleeful. I wanted to lash out at her some more just for that. She was deep in my head.

I thought, *Look what's become of me already. Look at what*

I'm becoming. What books will I write now? Will my sales improve greatly? I might fall off a unicycle and break my fucking neck but no way was I touching that wire or turning my johnson into a Muppet.

"Tell me what you need, Alison. Tell me what you deserve."

"You've made it hurt. I withstood the pain. I've earned your hate and your love."

"Maybe. But what have I earned?"

"Only what I choose to give you."

"That sounds like a rip-off."

"It's not. You'll love it. You love it already."

"What?"

"Me."

I sighed loudly and the stage echoed it and my sigh worked its way through the room into the dim recesses where it caused a few of the ponies and plushies, the rubbers and the plastics, the latexes and the leathers to look up and glance my way. It was the sound of the damned outsider wondering why he'd ever barged his way in. One fucker neighed at me.

"Don't say it if you aren't sure. If you don't mean it."

"I'm sure. I mean it. Don't question my intent again."

"All right."

"Tell me that you understand."

"I understand."

"Now take me. Right here. Now. If you want."

"No," I said.

"Stop fighting me."

"Funny you should say that."

"Now," she told me.

There are times you need to play around, and then there are times you just need to get the job done. I was reserved. I was shy. I had more issues than *Time* magazine and *National Geographic.* But I dropped my pants and pressed myself into her from behind and did it without another thought to the circumstances or the place or the people. She'd earned my love and my hate.

Alison shuddered and actually let out a sweet laugh as I made my whitebread love. It fueled a facet of me I'd never met before. But as I continued I knew I was in an act of transition, that I would never again be the person I'd been thirty minutes ago.

Maybe we were done with the pain portion of the evening, maybe it was only really beginning. I couldn't tell. I had to defer to her. I yanked her hard against me, my teeth gritted, vicious words escaping me, aware of her smile.

It inspired me to try harder. If only my high school principal had known what I needed maybe I wouldn't have gotten suspended so often. Her eyes were full of hard fought knowledge, a glimmer of shock that she was with me and we were right for each other, at least for the moment.

I was starting to realize that the symbols of our lives follow us through every inch of the day and night. She urged me on and said, "Yes, that's right, you know what to do for me." I supposed she was right. I reached down and clawed at her skin, making her bleed, watching it flow over the cherry tattoo that had been given to her by another man. It was mine now. She was mine.

Afterwards, Miss Tress and Chad the belt boy started for us. I shot them a look that stopped them in their tracks. Alison could barely walk. I'd been too rough and yet not rough enough. I had to refine my touch. It would take time. She would teach me. She held on to me tightly and rested her face against my chest. I found her clothes and got her dressed.

The night was just getting started for the rest of them. Chains clanked, saddles creaked. The audience was alive with choking and warbling and hee-hawing.

I moved her towards the door.

"You still living with other men?" I asked.

"Yes."

"You're gonna kick 'em free."

"I can't do that."

"We'll see. I'm moving to Frisco and I'm going to be your guy."

"Nobody calls it Frisco. It's San Francisco. You sound like an idiot."

I got a cab and we climbed in. I gave the driver my buddy's address and when his eyes met mine in the rearview he shifted his gaze away. Good.

"I gave you what you needed, Alison," I told her. "Now it's my turn."

"And what do you want?"

"We're going to order a pizza, have some wine, and watch a goddamn movie. *Vertigo* or *Bullitt*. They take place in Frisco."

"Nobody calls it—"

"We're going to make out on the couch."

"And then what?"

"And then we're going to screw again, and I'm going to croon in your ear. And you're going to love it. And then you're going to write me into your goddamn blog. You understand me?"

"I understand you've got a lot more to learn."

"Well, there's the fucking revelation of the century."

"Shh," she said, "you're in my hands now."

"You're in mine. But you teach me what you can, if you can."

"I can," she said. "You're going to bleed me."

"Maybe not."

The cab slid through the streets and I stared at the unfamiliar city, waiting for the fog I'd always read about to rise. There was none. The night became clearer as we went along. I thought of those I hated and those I loved. I welcomed my rage. The wholesome-looking insane girl had been wrong. Probably. Alison could fulfill me. Probably. I wasn't actually going to kill anyone. Probably. She was worth bleeding. And if, in the end, I found out differently, that other girl would be waiting for my touch, my heart, my teeth, my unwritten books, my vicious and endless need.

Cut

John Kenyon

James used to love his job, but Hollywood had fucked up everything.

What's not to like? Somebody with the crew calls you in, gives you a name and a location, maybe hands you a photo. They slip you a wedge of cash with the promise of more later. You find the guy, clip him, and report back for another wad of bills.

Then came that cocksucker Quentin Tarantino. Now, *Pulp Fiction* was a great movie, but it set loose a pack of guys with twice the budget and half the talent. Unable to compete story-wise, they compensated with blood. Pretty soon there was no such thing as a classy hit; the red stuff had to spill. It wasn't long before there were buckets of it being flung at the camera, and every hit had to be a performance.

If you think whitebread America eats up that escapist shit, you should see the way criminals react. It's like their deluded self-image projected twenty feet high on the screen. Soon, instead of the movies reflecting society, society was working hard to keep up with the movies. Now it's not enough to simply end a guy. The bosses want *proof,* they want you to *make a statement.*

That's why James was sitting on the El with a human heart on ice in a Playmate cooler on his lap.

"Did your ambulance break down?"

James looked up to see a young guy in a shirt and tie holding on to the rail. The guy gestured to the cooler.

"I did see a heart or something in there, didn't I?" he asked. "I know it's none of my business, but I couldn't help but notice."

Jesus. James was usually pretty cool about things, but he freaked a bit, thinking he was going to have to follow this guy and whack him, or else explain to the cops about why he was carrying a heart around in a cooler. He wanted to kick himself for continually opening the lid to check the contents.

Then he remembered the guy's original question about his ambulance. The guy thinks he's what, a doctor? Then James realized the guy assumed he was one of those transplant dudes who rush organs to the hospital.

"Budget cutbacks," he said. The guy nodded.

"That sucks. So what happened? Car wreck or something?"

James still had eight or nine stops to go, and didn't really want to get into a long thing with this guy.

"I can't talk about it. Patient confidentiality, you know?"

The guy nodded again. "Oh, sure. Right. Well, keep up the good work."

The train pulled into the station a moment later and the guy moved towards the door and exited. James set the cooler on the floor between his feet and hoped everyone else either minded their own business or assumed it was his lunch.

An hour later he sat outside the boss's door, the cooler back in his lap. The office was in the back of a dry cleaner, and the fumes always nauseated him. It didn't help that he kept thinking about what was in the cooler, or how he'd gotten it.

This one had been a typical job, a guy who owed the boss a ton of money and gave no indication that he intended to pay it back. James was never sure what the cutoff was, but six figures seemed to be enough to put out a hit. The boss started asking for a souvenir from each job a few years back, content at first with the odd finger or ear. But the more of those fuckin' movies he watched, the more depraved he got. It escalated to eyeballs, then nuts, and now finally the topper: a heart.

This was the first one. Everything else James just stuck in a plastic bag and carried with him, but this little sucker was like carrying a decent-sized cut of meat. He didn't want it to start stinking on him, so he iced it.

Jacko stuck his head out of the door of the boss's office and waved him in. The boss, a short guy with a completely bald head, an ill-fitting suit, and short, stubby fingers, reached out for the cooler.

"Whattaya got for me Jimmy, my boy?" James hated the artifice in the boss's talk, but the money was good enough to help him ignore it. If the little butterball wanted to play mobster, let him.

James handed over the cooler and watched as the boss slid back the lid.

"Jacko, get over here and pull this thing outta the ice. What are you, one of those transplant guys?" the boss said to James, laughing, as Jacko pulled the plastic bag from the cooler. Water from the melted ice dripped from the outside of the bag and onto the boss's desk.

"What the fuck, Jacko! Get something to clean that up! I don't want heart shit all over my desk, you idiot!"

Heart shit, James thought. Never heard blood described quite so colorfully. He jumped in to rescue Jacko.

"It's just water from the ice, chief," he said, knowing the boss liked it when James called him that. "So, are we good?"

The boss held the bag up to eye level and gazed at the heart, seemingly wary, as if worried it would suddenly start beating.

"Yeah," he said, smiling. "Did that son of a bitch suffer?"

James knew the drill, and laid it on thick.

"Pulled it out of him while he was still breathing," he said. "The guy saw his own fuckin' heart beating in my hand for a second before he died."

In truth, James had strangled the guy in a motel room, put him in the tub, suited up in plastic coveralls, and then carefully opened the guy's chest and taken the heart out. He stuck it in a Ziploc, dropped that in the cooler he'd pulled from the back of his closet, and then filled the cooler with ice from the machine at the end of the hall. His car was broken down again so he had to take the El. It was a hot day, so he stopped at a convenience store on the way to top off the ice. He felt strange standing behind the place, gently emptying the ice from the bag around and over the heart, but figured people would think he was icing down a sixer.

"Excellent. Once word of this one gets out, people will think twice about stiffing me," the boss said. "Okay. Get this thing out of here."

"You don't want to keep it?" James asked.

"What, like a souvenir? This ain't Navy Pier. It's evidence in a murder, you dumbfuck. Get rid of it."

Great, James thought. How do you get rid of a heart? He'd been tempted to just kill the guy, dispose of the body, and go buy a cow heart or something at the butcher. How would they know? But he didn't want to fuck it up the first time, so he'd gone through with it to a T. Now he had a cooler with an iced heart in it and no idea where to go from there.

He got back on the Red Line and took it all the way north to Howard, then exited and went down to the street level. It was late by that time and there were few people around, so he walked behind a store down the block, pulled the bag out of the cooler, wiped it down, and tossed it into a Dumpster. He thought about pitching it, cooler and all, but then he wouldn't have his cooler anymore—and besides, the thing had to be covered with his fingerprints. He dumped the ice behind the Dumpster and headed back to the train and home.

The next day, while reading through the paper and waiting for someone from his crew to call with more work, he skimmed the want ads. He liked imagining another life, one in which he didn't kill people for a living. One ad caught his eye: "Transport worker for a transplant program." They wanted someone who could drive organs from one hospital to another within the city for transplants. How perfect was that? He certainly knew the drill, he figured.

That afternoon he was back on the El with a cooler in his lap, but this time there was no heart inside. He'd gotten the job, surprised at the lax background check and cursory interview. There must not be many people eager to cart organs around in a cooler, he guessed.

They gave him a polo shirt with a logo on it, a special cooler that didn't look a lot different from his Playmate, and a pager. When he got a page, he was to call in, go wherever they told him to go, and then take the organ to the right hospital. It wasn't much different from his other job save for the fact that the person in question was already dead when he got there.

A couple of days later he was back at his kitchen table with the paper open in front of him when his cell buzzed. He pulled it out and found Jacko on the line.

"We've got a job for you," he said. "Come in."

James shut the phone and headed to the door. He then remembered that he was on call for the transplant office, so he grabbed the cooler, stuffed his polo shirt inside, and then went out.

The boss was impressed with the cooler.

"You're really getting into this, huh?" he said. "Nice cover. You'll be using it today, kid. This is an important one, and I want it taken care of immediately."

He gave James a name, told him where to find the guy, and then waved him out. Jacko handed him some cash as he exited. James stuffed it into his pocket and went out to do the job.

Hits didn't usually bother James, but he worried about this one as he climbed the stairs to the El platform and waited for the train. In his line of work, he occasionally came up against people he knew—it's a small world on the wrong side of the law—but this one was close to home . . . literally. Davey had lived in the apartment below his when they were growing up, and had dinner a lot of nights with James's family while his single mom held down two jobs. It wouldn't be like capping his brother, but jobs like this really made James rethink his career choices.

Then again, he knew Davey would help, because he could just ring the bell and walk right in, no sneaking or strong-arming needed. He did just that when he got there, and Davey let him inside.

"What's up?" Davey said, heading across the room to sit down in a chair in front of a TV showing some reality show, leaving James to shut the door behind him.

"The boss sent me," James said, catching his attention. "You owe him money or something?"

"You kidding me?" Davey got up and moved towards the apartment's kitchen.

"Stop," James said. He pulled a pistol from his waistband. "I asked you a question."

"Jesus. You're serious," Davey said, visibly shaking now.

"Come on, James. How long we known each other? You wouldn't really kill me, would you?"

James raised his eyebrows as if thinking about the question. "Why shouldn't I? Job's a job, right?"

"But I'm not just some guy, James. I'm me. That's gotta mean something."

"'I'm me'? Real profound. I'm gonna need more than that, Davey," James said. "You into him for a big gambling debt or something? I mean, this has gotta be big. We're skipping right over ass-kicking and leg-breaking to the big lights out here. Why does he want you dead?"

Davey leaned back against the wall and slid down it until he was sitting on the floor.

"It's Tracey," he said. "That's gotta be it."

"His daughter?" James said. "Little Tracey?"

"*Little* Tracey is nineteen now, man, and she's smokin' hot. She came on to me at a party a few weeks ago, and I've been bangin' her ever since. I didn't think he'd find out. I guess he did. Guy's so protective of her. If he only knew."

"Makes sense. He did seem unusually worked up about this one," James said. "He told me he wanted this done today."

Just then the pager on James's belt started beeping. He unclipped it so he could see the number, then pulled out his cell phone and made the call. He was told to go to Evanston Memorial to pick up a kidney and take it to a hospital on the south side.

"You still got that Cutlass?" he asked. Davey nodded. "Pack a couple of things, nothing too obvious, then get the hell out of here. I get the wheels, you get your life."

"How am I gonna get out of here?"

"If you don't shut the fuck up and do as I say, it'll be in a body bag, okay? Now look, the boss wants me to cap you, cut out your fuckin' heart, and bring it to him. I got an idea about how to appease him, but if you show up somewhere with your ticker still thumping away in your chest, we're both gonna get topped, you got it?"

Davey nodded again, silently, then went to his closet and started pulling things out to throw in a suitcase.

Jacko was waiting for James when he pulled up at the back door of the dry cleaners. It was after five, so Jacko was there to let him in.

"Nice ride. When'd you get that?"

"Today. Consider it a fringe benefit of a job well done. Don't worry, I don't think anyone's gonna report it stolen."

Jacko laughed knowingly and followed James into the back of the store. Even though the machines weren't running, the place still reeked.

The boss was sitting behind his desk. James waited to be waved in, then set the transport cooler down.

"How'd it go?" the boss asked.

"He wasn't happy, but as you can see, there wasn't much he could do about it," James said, gesturing to the cooler.

The boss opened the lid and looked in. This time he didn't wait for Jacko, but instead pulled the bag out himself. He held it up for inspection.

"This one I'm gonna keep," he said, his eyes narrowing to slits as his mouth clasped into a tight grin.

James was startled. "What about it being evidence?" he said. "Don't you want me to get rid of it?"

"No, not this one," the boss said. "This one I'm tempted to cook up and eat. I want to devour this shitheel, you understand?"

As he continued looking at the bag, his eyes widened. He turned it from side to side and poked at the organ inside with a finger.

"What the fuck's going on, Jimmy?" he said.

"What, chief?"

"Don't you 'chief' me. This doesn't look like a heart," he said. He set the bag on the desk and pulled it open.

"Do you believe this guy, Jacko? He brought me a fuckin' liver or something. Thinks I'm an idiot." The boss reached inside his jacket and Jacko did the same. James was quicker. He pulled his pistol out of the back of his waistband and put two bullets in each man before either could unholster their gun. As the boss fell, he grabbed at the edge of the desk. He pulled the bag down with him and the kidney slid out and skittered across the dusty floor.

James had just lost one job and knew he couldn't afford to lose the other. Remembering what the transplant people had said about keeping things clean and cold, he figured the kidney was no longer any good.

He went to the desk, pulled open drawers until he found what he needed, then went over to the boss. James flipped him onto his stomach, cut away his jacket and shirt, and prepared to do a little surgery. For once he was glad for the dry cleaning fumes, hoping they'd cover the smell of what he was about to do.

"Bet that fuck Tarantino never thought of this," he said, making the first cut.

Pick's Place

Colin O'Sullivan

A gecko sticks to the outside of the window, attracted to all the lights inside, the flashing faux-retro disco-bar bulbs the owner Pick got from some junk off-load. The gecko could be dead for all we know, plastered there, like a rubber toy some kid licked and flung, foot suction pads sticking to the surface—or is it just some damn creature, plain giving up in the summer heat? We're all a bit like that in here this evening, flung, stuck, and giving up— Pick setting the beers in front of the three of us, Gert, Mixxy, and me; Pick taking our money and keeping the change. He doesn't even thank us anymore, and we never offer, we've been here so long—years I mean, and communication is such a labor we don't care how out of pocket we get. Our lives are all torpor anyway, only early thirties, but still, bad luck, bad decisions, the usual. We're in a bar after all, what kind of story were you expecting? That's what has us here staring at a gecko, and at Pick, his Takamine electric guitars hanging over his head. We don't even mind that he picks his nose the way he does—only one of the reasons for his moniker—rummaging like that, same hands he pours our beer with, same fingers he uses to flip nuts into our bowls, same dirty bowls we stick our heads over and sniff like the dogs we are.

Mixxy is really Mick, a straight London guy with a gay nickname. He doesn't like it but that's the way with nicknames, they glue to you and you can't do anything about it.

Gert's another regular guy and he must be from Germany or someplace. We forgot to ask, and it's too late now. We've known him for years and it would be rude.

I'm Milly, and that's not a nickname. My parents called me that and thought it was a nice name for a pretty girl like me. Maybe they meant Molly. Who knows? My parents were Irish, and people easily get confused.

Three of us here, we're not really from anywhere, that's the way the world is now, full of wanderers. Pick seems to be the only stationary thing in our life. He's always standing there, doing his job. That's admirable. A couple of Japanese girls enter and smile and wave at him, and Pick smiles and waves back, though he senses trouble. We don't see many natives in here anymore—maybe they're all scared of us. I overheard someone call us vampires once, thought that was a bit of a stretch.

When Pick locks up and the other two have staggered off somewhere, I go upstairs to a room over the bar, Pick's place, and soon he has me on my back, legs in the air. When we're done, I keep my legs up, hoping the sperm will stay in and at least one swimmer makes it so I can become pregnant. There seems to be little more that I'd want from a life. I'd even stop drinking. Plus, I'd have more of a right to be here. Pick has his stance going on, that kind of look, eyebrows and forehead lines, as if all he's ever wanted was to be in a shadowy '30s film—or better, a novel. He chooses this moment (me: legs akimbo, him: scotch and ice cubes swirling) to say that if it's gonna be a guy, he wants him to be called Marlowe, and if it's a girl, maybe Marlowe. I ask him, does he mean the playwright or the private investigator? He says: what playwright? It's then I wish the sperm to flow back down and the swimmers not to bother. Pick's English is pretty good. It's not that we don't understand the words we send out; it's that we don't understand each other.

Gert's on about the things he remembers from childhood. No gecko tonight, unfortunately, no such distraction. He's saying: orange bedclothes, a bucket he used to get sick into when he had some virus or chicken pox or whatever used to cause that yellow bile to up and spew-burn. And Debbie Harry. On a big poster looking down at him. Not all sexy and sultry as you'd expect, but in a peach scarf, strangely conservative, incomparably beautiful. No one has ever surpassed Debbie for Gert; he set his standards very high from the onset. No wonder he failed and is here. He still has *Autoamerican* on cassette. We all sigh at this, remembering cassettes, how they were once our future. In Japanese they have a word for this feeling of nostalgia, *natsukashi*. Shame we don't have an accurate word in English, nostalgia too wistfully sepia, not quite cutting it. I like listening to him talk about Debbie Harry, except when she's within the same sentences as virus, pox, and spew: she doesn't deserve that. I say this to him and he starts to weep a little, as if he's betrayed her. Well, he has. Pick's good at moments like this and brings us more drink and keeps the change for himself.

It's all your fault, Pick.

Pick smiles.

Every night one of us says that to Pick, and he always just smiles, a crooked, leering grin that he's been working on.

It was Mixxy who said it this time. And when we say it, it's like we mean every word of it.

Mixxy says he hides out in the bar because he is afraid they will come looking for him. He says if they find the people he's killed that it'll be the end of him, and of us, as if we are all complicit by listening to him and drinking with him. We like these stories he tells; he sounds so sincere. And Pick never smiles when Mixxy's in the throes of the telling. I wonder sometimes, sometimes get a shiver—like what if even one of the stories was actually true? He says hiding in a bar in this part of town is so obvious that the police would never look. They're probably looking for murderers in the decent part of town, some guy trying to blend in with the norms, not here in the docks. Mixxy says he doesn't know what it would be like to be in a Japanese prison. Says he's heard horror stories, abuse, things being stuck up asses. One of us at least is tempted to say, what's new and original about that? But no one says anything, we just look up at the guitars hanging, wonder who ever plays them. I never seen Pick use his fingers on a guitar, just sticks them in his nose, or up me.

A cockroach this time scurries past my bare feet as I go towards the bed in Pick's place. Pick is ready already, and I've yet to take all my clothes off. Sometimes I don't even take the shirt or bra off anymore. It's not about that now, just getting a job done. I don't know why there is so much wildlife in Pick's bar and natty apartment; something is always crawling around when we're there. Pick says there are lizards about too, and I think of Mixxy and Gert and say: yeah, I know. Pick is on me then, delivering, and as I lie back after—it doesn't take long, nothing about life really does—I feel it squiggling up me, some tiny reptile thing making its way home perhaps, making its way to where it should really belong, a nice place where Debbie Harry isn't befouled, but handsome in her peach scarf, and cassettes were in people's hands and loved, and people had names that weren't dirty but were their own real names in their own real places. Pick holds me tight and I can forgive him his dirty bar and the way he picks his nose, and I can forgive him the pretence and everything else. He's the only worthwhile thing in our life, me and them boys. Why do I say life and not lives? And I can forgive Mixxy too for the things he does, and why those two Japanese girls never came back, and the screaming behind the building with Gert and Mixxy laughing, and I heard shouts in Japanese, words I can understand now, words of hateful protestation, and I try to block them out and think of Pick instead. How he'd get them pregnant too, if they wanted maybe, those girls, but it was too late for them, too late. He's good like that, many of the natives are just like that around here, decent, taking care of us, putting up: Pick especially, pouring out the beer when he knows it's what we need. Some nuts in our bowls. He's always standing there, doing his job. That's admirable. The police have yet to come and ask a single question, and so we wait, stuck, given up, and Pick never says a word to anyone, just serves us.

These Two Guys . . .

Craig McDonald

"So what about Saturday night?" Angelo checked his speed as they rolled through the small village—a notorious speed trap—and raised an eyebrow.

Davey James was rooting through a sack lunch. "Don't know, A," Davey said. "Let me run that by Alex."

"What's to run by?" Angelo Grapelli shook his head, picking up speed now that they were out of the little village. Saturday nights had always been a given until the past two months. Saturday nights were drinks, dinner, and more drinks with their ladies du jour at La Vecchia.

At least that was so before Davey had begun sparking the recently widowed Alexis DeCastro.

Jesus.

Far as Angelo Grapelli could tell, that skinny Dutch bitch Alexis was drawing his partner Davey's teeth.

Angelo frowned, palming left onto a county two lane. He gestured at Davey's lunch bag with his right hand. Angelo's fat fingers were spangled pinkie to pointer with big, sharp, and shiny rings. "What's today's?"

Davey said, "Fat-free pretzels, tuna fish salad in this funny little plastic bowl . . . sliced tomatoes, and some fresh vegetables. Bottled water."

"Sounds healthy," Angelo said. "How much you down now?"

"Was three hundred and thirty . . . three hundred and twenty-five on a good day," Davey said. "Down to two hundred and eighty."

Angelo nodded, sour-faced. "Jesus, Davey, you look like you've lost a whole guy—hope this doesn't affect your work. Gotta say, you're less imposing from the gates, my man."

Davey shrugged, chomping on some baby carrots, talking around the orange debris. "Nah, A, I'm getting *stronger*. Benching three hundred and twenty now. Sounds more impressive to bench more than your own weight."

"Sure," Angelo said, stepping carefully. "Sure, if some stranger could tell what you can lift just by lookin' at ya. I'm just saying, before, you were like a damned tank comin' at some guy. Now, you're just another big guy."

"Don't sweat it, Ang." Davey spooned down some tuna salad, smacked his lips. "You got specific complaints? I let you down so far? 'Cause if you've got specific complaints, we can talk about those. Otherwise, we're just jawin' and if we're just jawin', it's a dumb fucking topic and one we want to get off of, right now."

They locked eyes; Angelo blinked first. And hell, he was driving—had to watch the road.

"Nah, I got no complaints about any of that," Angelo said. "Hell, no." He shrugged. "I'm just sayin', Davey, you know?"

"Well, just don't."

Angelo tossed his cigarette stub out the window. Lit another. He frowned when he saw Davey roll down his window. Angelo suddenly realized he couldn't remember the last time he saw Davey light one up himself. "So, you'll tell Alexis about Saturday night?"

Davey didn't answer for a while, then said, "Yeah, well, Alexis, she's not much of a drinker, see."

Yeah.

Alexis wasn't much of anything, near as Angelo Grapelli could tell. She was the beaten-on wife of some deadbeat Mexican grifter. Alexis DeCastro had lost her son about six months before her old man got clipped. The woman had been the De-Castro family's only legitimate wage earner, working a parimutuel window at a thoroughbred track. When that racing season ended, the trotters started running at the other end of town, and Alexis shifted to that track.

Angelo's current steady lady was Molly, a busty, leggy red-head he'd met at the Red Fox Gentleman's Club. Molly was the joint's prettiest pole dancer. Molly was always the one selected to appear in all the newspaper ads for the Fox. That made her a minor celebrity in certain circles.

Angelo tightened his grip on the wheel. "So that's just a way of saying 'no fucking way,' huh, Davey?"

"We could do dinner," Davey said, chewing his tuna and staring down the hood. "But we could branch out a little, you know? I'm frankly up to here with La Vecchia and that sad-ass crowd—all the wannabes and never-weres and almosts jawin' and lyin'. And all the civilians who come and stare and try to eavesdrop 'cause they've heard it's where The Boys like to hang out. Jesus, it's just tired, A, a tired fuckin' scene."

Angelo bit his lip. He reached down to the ashtray, sucked hard on his unfiltered Marlboro, and then ground it out and tossed the butt out the window. "They still let a man smoke at La Vecchia," Angelo said. Angelo and Davey had personally seen to that. The joint sat on the wrong side of the city corporation limits, rested in township jurisdiction. There were only three township trustees, all old men, so they weren't hard to manipulate—not hard to cajole into passing a smoking exemption for La Vecchia.

"That's the other thing," Davey said. "You go into that place and *everyone* is fuckin' smokin'. It's like eating inside a damned car muffler. Who needs it? You walk out of that joint stinkin' like some whorehouse ashtray on dollar night."

Angelo couldn't *believe* this shit. Did someone kidnap Davey and replace him with this scrawny prissy replica? Angelo shifted gears: "Alexis have any notion as to how you contributed to her, *ah* . . . widowhood? Any pillow talk yet about how you did her old man?"

Angelo could feel the weight of Davey's death stare—those dark dead eyes on him. He kept looking straight ahead. At bottom, it was all really Angelo's own fault. Luis DeCastro had been asking around for someone who would clip his wife . . . open the door for Luis to get some insurance money when his wife Alexis fell. Someone talked to someone who talked to Angelo who recommended Davey.

But plans went sideways. Lonely Davey had taken out Luis DeCastro for reasons that still bewildered Angelo. Then, more stunning, Davey had moved in on the woman he had widowed.

"No, she don't fuckin' know," Davey said. "She will never fuckin' know, and if anyone thought about seeing Alex know, that someone would fuckin' rue the day he fuckin' made that big ass fuckin' mistake."

Davey slapped one big hand to the dashboard to brace himself as the car went into a skid to the berm. With his other hand, Davey wrapped his fingers around the butt of his gun—didn't even bother drawing it clear—just pointed it in the direction of Angelo's head. If he pulled the trigger, Davey would just be out a sports jacket. Hell, the damned thing hung on him like a tent now, anyway.

Angelo had his hands off the wheel now. He started to reach, then saw Davey's hand under the too big sports jacket and raised his hands. "I fuckin' resent the implication of that last statement of yours," Angelo said. He slowly reached down, shifted into park, and put his hands back up. "Jesus, Davey! Look at us! I was just askin' a question." Angelo swallowed hard and lowered his hands. "That was no fuckin' threat, Davey," he said. "I know you construed it as such, but it was not a damned threat."

Davey looked at him with those dead black eyes. "Yeah? You swear?"

"On the soul of my dead daughter, I swear, Davey."

Angelo reached down, shifted back into drive and then rolled off the shoulder and started picking up speed again. "What's happened to you, Davey? What's happenin' to us?"

Davey put away his gun and dipped his hand into his bag of pretzels. He held it out and Angelo took a handful.

"I don't want this thing with Alexis messed up," Davey said. "You start raggin' on my gettin' small, then you ask a question like that about what Alex knows about what happened to her ex . . . you bein' you and all. Me knowing you like I do, Ang . . . well, wheels start turning in my head, you start bustin' my balls that way. Pieces starting fitting together into a picture I don't fuckin' like and won't abide. I get this notion you've got a notion to try and fuck up what I've got going with Alexis."

Angelo shook his head. "Jesus, Davey, what kind of traitorous fuck do you make me for? You're happy, maybe first time in your life, and I'm gonna go monkey with that? You believe that? We've known each other since we was, what, eight? Nine? I'm frankly disappointed, David. Let's not go this long and suddenly let some woman get between us."

"Let's forget it," Davey said.

"Sure, sure." Angelo checked the mirror, said, "You two starting to talk some long-term thing?"

"It gets talked about," Davey said. "We'll see." He ate some more carrots. He offered the bag and Angelo declined: "Nah, eat too many of those, you'll friggin' turn orange."

"That's a myth," Davey said.

"Nah, I seen it happen," Angelo said. "Remember that one that danced over at the Lair? The blonde with the nipple rings?"

"Yeah. What was her name?"

"Hell if I know ... some cartoon name ... maybe Bambi. We only went out about half a dozen times. But she started eating all these little carrots just like those ones ... went on a juice diet ... she turned orange."

"No shit?"

"Nah, it looked like one of those fake tans," Angelo said. "Kinda tan you get out of tubes or from sunlamps ... just this kind of off-orange. Right down to the whites of her friggin' eyes. It was like lookin' at a TV with bad color balance. Disturbing ... like a jelly bean with tits."

Davey half smiled and sipped his bottled water. He resealed it and said, "What's the drill?"

"New tavern, just opened. It's on the county line, but our side. Guy who owns it is an ex-vet."

"Iraq?"

"Yeah, but from the first time around. You know ... Bush One."

"A Desert Storm vet, huh? This will not go smooth," Davey said.

"Expect not," Angelo said. "I was in there the other night. Guy's an ex-Ranger. Goes six-three, maybe six-four, and probably two hundred and sixty—all muscle. Why I said, you know, three hundred and twenty, you'd dwarf the cocksucker."

"Don't sweat it," Davey said. "We'll get her done."

The place looked more like a VFW hall than the sticks tavern it was conceived to be. Davey looked at his watch. The wristband was loose now and Davey had to reach across with his right hand and twist the face around to where he could see the time. Eleven A.M. Davey reminded himself again to have his watchband tightened. Angelo saw Davey adjusting the watch and smiled crookedly. Davey flipped Angelo the bird.

A man rose from behind the bar, wiping his hands on a dishrag. He said, "Hey, fellas." Neutral, not even mock cordial. Davey narrowed his eyes, getting this feeling like they were maybe already made.

The tavern owner was big enough—probably six-three bare-footed. Broad shoulders and a short sleeve shirt to show off mature muscle. *Imposing* was the word for the tavern owner. Even if Angelo hadn't told him, Davey would have made the big vet for an ex-Ranger.

The keep said, "Township laws are a little hinky out this way. Can't serve you anything hard until after one P.M."

"That's the shits," Angelo said, taking a stool near the TV. "Well, make mine . . ." He paused, looking at tap pull knobs, then said, "A Sam Adams."

Davey didn't really want a beer—all those empty carbs—but he didn't need Angelo bitching at him either, particularly in front of this Goliath that Davey was supposed to maybe muscle. Davey said, "Amstel Light for me." That wasn't much better than ordering nothing. Davey thought he could hear Angelo's eyes rolling sideways to appraise him. That damned mock smile was on Angelo's face again.

The keep tossed down a couple of cardboard drink mats and placed frosted mugs atop them.

"Nice touch, frosting the glasses," Angelo said. "Real classy."

"Glad you fucking approve," the keep said.

" 'Spect we'll run a tab," Angelo said.

The keep said, "No, these two are on the house. Enjoy 'em. Then I'd ask you to leave. I know who you are. I was warned by others who you've shaken down. I ain't playing that game. Closed discussion."

The keep was standing close by the bar now, his arms at his sides. He was standing closest to Angelo, who blinked several times, then said, "Come again?"

Davey scowled and sipped his beer. He figured the tavern owner had something close at hand on a shelf under the bar. A club—maybe a ball bat or a tire iron. Or maybe a handgun . . . perhaps something bigger, like a sawed-off. The keep was looking at Davey, sizing him up. Davey shot the sleeves of his loose fitting jacket, covering up his watch that sat sideways on his thinner wrist. There was enough space between the band and the bones that Davey could have slipped his own big thumb in the gap and still have had wiggle room.

The stranger said to Davey, "What? You sick or something? Cancer, or the like? Looks like you've lost a shitload of weight."

Davey heard Angelo cluck his tongue. Davey sipped more beer and said, "Nah. I ain't sick. Just cut back on my bad diet habits. Got tired of eatin' gym jockeys like you for breakfast. Tired of havin' chunks of guys like you in my stool."

The man behind the bar shook his head. "That line wasn't funny when Phil Hartman coined it fifteen years ago."

"I think we need to educate you a little on the way things work out this way," Angelo said. "This thing we offer, it's what you call, *compulsory*. It's not an opt out kind of thing." Angelo frowned and said, "Your name, it's Tom, ain't it?"

"Tom, yeah," Tom said. "But you ain't staying long enough to need my handle again."

Angelo slapped Davey's smaller arm. "This dude's got himself a temper, eh, Davey? I can see it building. What do you think? Guy's a Desert Storm vet. Think he's maybe got that, what you call it? Gulf War syndrome? Some headcase shit like that, maybe? Read me an article about all these guys, they get back from Iraq, they got temper issues. First thing they do, they flip and beat on or kill their old ladies. All these Gulf War guys, they're all damaged goods. Head cases, you know? How's your old lady, Tom?"

"I'm single," Tom said evenly.

"Me too," Angelo said. "Mostly. Though old Davey, here, he's got himself a woman. Getting himself skinny to spark her more. High school shit, ain't it?"

Davey said, "A . . ."

Angelo switched directions, said, "Think we got us a 'roid monkey in Tom here. What do you think, Davey? Apart from the fact that 'roid junkies are nearly all homos, they've got anger control issues too. All those hormones go to work on 'em. Maybe they lose it too, 'cause the pills shrink their balls."

Davey toyed with his beer mug, pointedly keeping both hands wrapped around the cold mug where Tom could see them. Despite the beer, Davey's mouth was dry. He felt sweat stains spreading under his arms. Davey looked Tom over again. Davey decided that on his best day, he still couldn't take the retired Ranger hand to hand. And Christ only knew what the professionally trained soldier could do with a firearm. It was a revelation to Davey—that he'd met a man he considered more than his match. Tom shot him a glance, then turned his full attention back to Angelo. In that instant, Davey knew that Tom had also decided he could take Davey. But Davey sensed Tom had reached that conclusion a good while before Davey arrived at it.

Angelo said, "Think we're gonna have to take this asshole apart. What do you think, Davey?"

"I think Tom has opted out on the program, A. I think we walk."

Now Angelo and Tom were both looking at Davey. Davey hefted his mug to drink more, then changed his mind and sat it down.

"Looks like the one opting out on the fucking program here is you, Davey," Angelo said.

Now Davey took a drink. He put down the mug, keeping

both hands on the bar so Tom could see them. Looking at Tom, Davey nodded, said, "Could be, A. It could fucking well be."

Angelo was seething. Red-faced, he said, "This cocksucker's got you cowed! That's it! You're fucking afraid!"

"That could be half of it," Davey said.

Tom was scowling now, confused. Like he was trying to grasp the dynamic, to decide if this was some arcane ploy they were running on him.

Angelo turned to face Davey. "What's the other fucking half?"

"I'm sick of the life, A," Davey said. He drained his beer. "Time for a new line of work. Maybe time to be self-employed, like Old Tom, here. So I'm walking, Angelo. You got any brains left, you'll follow me."

"You fucking believe this?" Angelo said to Tom. "Davey here goes sweet on some cooze he widowed and he turns pussy on me. Fucking unbelievable. Drops a ton of weight, goes soft, quits smoking and drinking. You fucking imagine that, Tom? Big bastard like you—you imagine letting a fucking woman draw your teeth like that? We wrap this up, first thing I'm doing is I'm gonna go visit that pathetic bitch and let her know how you did her husband, Davey. Save you from your fucking self."

Dave swiveled on his stool. "You are a fucking dead man, A."

Tom bit his lip, said, "Take it outside, you two."

Angelo said, "You shut the fuck up, Tom. Sorry, but I gotta teach this smaller-but-still-fat fuck Davey here a fucking lesson. And I'm afraid you're the lesson, Tom." Angelo's hand dipped into his jacket for his piece. Tom reached under the bar, got clear first.

Angelo shuddered and then looked down at his nearly severed right arm and the spreading red stain in the center of his shirt. His lips and chin were sprayed with blood. Angelo said, "Well, fuck me." Then he fell backwards off the barstool, arms spread and eyes to the ceiling.

Davey's hands were still flat on the bar. He'd never even tried to draw his own gun. Tom's sawed-off was now leveled at Davey's heart. Tom said, "One barrel left, asshole."

"You don't need it," Davey said, calm now. "I'll help you get him out of here, bury him out back, I guess, and then clear out."

Tom considered that. He lowered the gun, but kept it at hand. Davey said, "We go back, me and Angelo, like you guessed. But it's been strained for a long time. And this latest, over my lady, that was the breaking point. Fuck, I nearly shot him myself on the drive over here."

Davey stood up carefully, looked at the tables, and walked to the closest one. He moved the ashtray and condiment tray to an adjacent table and pulled off the table's vinyl red-and-white-checkered tablecloth and spread it out on the floor next to Angelo's body. He looked up and said, "Tom, you want to help me wrap this fucker up in this thing, or what?"

The vet stowed his gun under the bar and came around to Davey's side. Tom locked the bar's front door and then Davey took Angelo by the ankles and Tom got him by the shoulders and they rolled Angelo over onto the plastic sheet. Tom took another tablecloth off another table, and they bundled up Angelo, then wound several turns of duct tape around the body to hold the plastic in place. Davey rose and waved a hand at the spotless floor. He said, "Neat fucking job. Not a single blood-stain."

Tom said, "I can take it from here. You bein' his friend and all. Just get your ass out of here."

Davey said, "Nah. I owe you for your trouble. I tried to talk him out of this. And like I said, he and me go back. Least I can do is see A in the ground. I'll take his legs." Before he stooped down, Davey took a look around at the tavern and said, "You've really got a real nice place here, Tom. I *like* this joint."

Tom shrugged. "That's great," he said.

They hefted Angelo's body up between them and lugged him out back and through a stand of shoulder-high weeds down to the bank of a small stream. "I own the acreage back here—all flood plain," Tom said, "so there's no danger of anyone developing this later and digging up your friend here."

They dropped the body there, then went back to the bar together to fetch a pickax and two shovels. The creek bank was relatively moist and the digging went quickly. Tom said, "Think that's big enough?"

Davey turned his head to one side, narrowing his eyes and measuring angles and depth. He said, "I'm worried about erosion. Hate for you to have to do this again. I think we should go deeper. Maybe a little longer too."

They dug for another twenty minutes. Davey looked at the mounting dirt pile and decided he didn't want to have to deal with more than was already there. He said, "I think we're good." They muscled Angelo's body into the hole. Davey groaned and pressed his hands to the small of his back and said, "Jesus, I'm too old for this. Think I pulled something."

Tom nodded and dragged Angelo's body farther towards the top of the hole so his feet would fit in. Davey said, "You know, I'm looking at all that plastic and thinking it's a mistake—gonna slow down decomposition." He reached into his sports jacket's pocket and pulled out a switchblade. He sprung the blade and handed it down to Tom. "For the tape," he said. "I think we ought to unwrap Angelo before we bury him."

Tom nodded and set to work on the duct tape, his back to Davey. "Makes sense," he said. "Back doing any better?"

"Yeah, better," Davey said. "That place of yours really is a nice one."

"Thanks."

"So nice, I've decided to take it over."

Davey shot Tom twice in the back of the head, pressing the gun up tight behind Tom's ear to muffle the sound.

Tom fell across Angelo's body, most of his head gone.

Davey tucked Tom's arms into the hole and bent the big man's legs at the knees, forcing those in too. When he was done, it looked like Tom was humping a checkered mummy.

Davey set to work filling the hole.

Community Property

Pearce Hansen

"Three months, Gordon. Maybe four if you don't stress yourself out, if you give up burning the candle at both ends, and if you're lucky."

Gordon heard Doctor Benson's words on an intellectual level, but forced their meaning to wash over and past him. All his attention was on the MRI scan printout of his abdominal region, trying to see if he could spot the tumor for himself. But it was no use: to his untrained eye the MRI was only a jumble of color representing his internal organs. Gordon was irritated to have no idea what was supposed to be there inside his body, and what was the cancerous parasite betraying him.

Doctor Benson's hand touched his arm. Startled, Gordon turned away from that hypnotic MRI to look down at his plump, pretty primary-care physician. There was nothing wrong with plump, he considered as he eye-fucked her up and down. He was on the husky side himself, after all.

"You can get another opinion if you like, in fact, I recommend it," Doctor Benson said. "But I've run the tests more than once and there's absolutely no doubt. The MRI is only confirmation. Would you like me to point out the malignancy on the display?"

"No," Gordon said, refusing to look at the MRI again, wondering why he wouldn't make this last acknowledgment of a truth he'd suspected since the first night he'd spent hugging the toilet bowl and vomiting up blood. Instead, he focused his attention on Doctor Benson.

"Linda," Gordon said, using her first name for the first time in their acquaintance. That old seductive croon had entered his bass voice. "Linda," he repeated, letting his unspoken offer color his words. He had nothing to lose anymore, after all.

Linda looked at the floor from under lowered lashes, avoiding his eyes. "Good luck, Gordon." Her voice was soft and almost regretful, but the shutdown was firm.

"Don't waste any time," Doctor Benson said to his back as he left the examination room.

Out in the parking lot, Gordon lit up a Marlboro and started hotboxing it, toking hard. He noted five missed messages on his cell phone when he turned it back on. He grimaced as he saw that four of them were from his wife, Yang. The fifth was from his attorney Chris Kellum, and Gordon hit REPLY as he walked towards Yang's Mercedes, touching his thick head of hair to make sure his coif was still immaculate.

"Gordon," Chris said on his end as he caller IDed Gordon's cell. "We have to talk, my friend."

"I know, I know," Gordon said as he hit the alarm button on his key ring. Yang's Mercedes chirped a greeting as he reached it and gave the hood an affectionate pat, admiring the perfect lines of his soon-to-be-ex-wife's car. The Benz was top drawer, a 2008 S65 AMG, and Gordon enjoyed its luxury as much as he enjoyed the taunt he was sending Yang by keeping it from her.

"Don't you blow me off again, Gordon," Chris shouted, loud enough that Gordon had to pull the cell away from his ear a bit as he threw down his smoke and got into the Benz. Gordon hit the SPEAKER PHONE button and tossed the cell onto the passenger seat as he buckled up, chuckling to himself even as he did it. He'd always been a careful man (except in his love life of course) and a lifetime of habit was hard to break even now when it didn't matter anymore.

"How long have we known each other, Gordon?" Chris asked, voice a little lower, a little calmer. "She says she wants her Benz back as part of her share of the community property. I'd say she really just wants the closure. You sign the papers, you show up tomorrow in court and hand her the keys, and I'll bet I can keep her from fucking you too hard."

Gordon laughed out loud as he started the engine and lit another smoke. "You don't know Yang as well as you think you do, Chris. The divorce is just her opening salvo, and the Benz is just the first trophy she's going to scalp off me. She's going to burn me down to the waterline. She's taking this all the way no matter what I do. Besides, I don't really have to give a rat's ass anymore." Gordon realized he'd said too much even as the words came out of his mouth, but it was too late to backpedal.

"And what exactly do you mean by that statement, my friend?" Chris asked slowly, his attorney brain chewing hard on Gordon's words.

Gordon pulled out of the Kaiser Hospital parking lot and took Broadway west towards Oakland Civic Center, thinking hard himself. He powered down his window and flung out his latest butt, then fumbled another from his pack and lit up while he drove one-handed.

"I'm dying, Chris," Gordon said, wondering even as he uttered the words why he was burdening his friend with the information. Maybe he was trying the fact of his imminent death on for size. Maybe he wanted Chris's legal brain to show him some kind of loophole from his upcoming death.

"Jesus," Chris breathed, and was silent for several seconds himself. "Get your ass over here, Gordon. Screw the divorce, you shouldn't be alone right now."

"You always were a good buddy, Chris," Gordon said. "I'll be in touch." He reached over and picked up the cell phone, ended the call. But it started ringing again immediately. Gordon powered down his window again and tossed the cell out of the car without bothering to see if it was Chris or Yang vying for his attention.

Gordon reached Jack London Square and turned south along the Estuary to the industrial park his office was located in. He entered the lobby, took the elevator, and entered his office. His secretary Sarah looked as relieved at his arrival as if he was the Second Coming.

"She's been burning up the phone lines," Sarah said in that husky Midwest drawl that had turned Gordon on since the first time she opened her mouth at her job interview two months before. "I just about ran out of note paper keeping track of her calls. Oh, yeah: a process server came by, but I refused to accept whatever paper he was trying to hang."

"Good work, babe," Gordon said, reaching up to make sure his hair was unmussed. He angled to get a look down the front of her low-cut dress at her cleavage, but realized he was just doing it from habit, going through the motions. His heart wasn't really in it today, so he just took the paper listing Yang's calls from Sarah and walked past her towards his office.

"Gordon," Sarah called out from behind him, and he turned. "Is everything all right?" Was that honest concern he saw on her face? Or did she only smell the possible end of her meal ticket?

Gordon made himself try to smile, not realizing that the facial rictus made him look anything but pleasant. "Everything's fine."

Sarah nodded as though she wanted him to think she was relieved, but he sensed she had more to say and waited in unaccustomed patience. "Do you think your wife knows about us?" she blurted after a moment, her face gone a little red.

Gordon almost laughed at the irrelevancy of the question, but restrained himself. "You have nothing to worry about, Sarah. Why don't you take the rest of the day off?" As he saw the pleasure fill Sarah's face, Gordon was moved to add: "Hell, take the rest of the week off. I've got some things to attend to and I'll be away from the office for a few days. Here's an advance paycheck to tide you over."

Gordon ignored her murmured appreciative words as he made out a company check for a month's wages to the girl. "Cash this right away," he said, figuring Yang would be attaching his assets soon enough.

He watched Sarah's perky ass as she left, remembering how that tush had felt when he'd clutched it with both hands as they did it on his desk yesterday, and she'd called out his name over and over. But now she was gone, and he was alone.

Gordon lit up a smoke as he walked back into his office. He hit the wet bar behind his mahogany slab desk, poured some Walker Red neat, and tossed it down his gullet without the scotch even touching the sides of his throat on the way down. He poured another tumbler and sucked hard on his smoke as he moved to stare out his window, which took up the whole outer office wall.

His office was on the fifth floor, and he could see Yang's S65 below in his reserved parking space, he could look across Embarcadero to the Estuary, the deep water shipping channel separating Oakland and Alameda. High-end apartment buildings and condos paraded out of sight to his left and his right on the Oakland waterfront. Across the water he saw the low skyline of Alameda's upscale homes, sprawled under their omnipresent canopy of trees like a high-end version of *Leave It to Beaver*. Yachts and cigarette boats crowded slips and marinas on both sides of the Estuary.

It had taken Gordon four decades of hardscrabble labor to earn this view, to belong in high-priced commercial real estate like this. He'd come straight out of the trailer, nobody had handed him a thing, and he'd never asked for any favors. He'd built this consultancy from scratch, all by himself. But right now, with the knowledge of his upcoming demise forcing him to take a step back and examine his life objectively, Gordon realized that the good life had always been just out of arm's reach for him no matter how much cash he threw around. What had he been chasing, giving up his irreplaceable time to scamper after?

Doing his best to keep it equally impersonal, he also thought about his soon-to-be-ex-wife Yang, and wistfully recalled their first meeting over in Shanghai. She was a part-time model, she'd even done some bit parts on Chinese TV, but she and Gordon had met when she was moonlighting as a taxi driver and she'd picked him up at the airport. Yang was northern Chinese, almost as tall as Gordon at six feet even, thin but shapely with ivory skin paler than Gordon's own. He'd had to have her, and the trophy of merely bedding her hadn't cut it at the time. He'd slapped a wedding ring on her finger as soon as humanly possible.

He admitted to himself now that he'd been an abject failure as a husband. He knew he was a proficient enough lover. Women had always wanted more of him than he was willing to give. But with Yang underfoot twenty-four/seven as his wife, Gordon realized that he hadn't the foggiest idea of what to do with a woman outside the bedroom.

His infidelities had been nonstop, his emotional unavailability had hung over their home life like a pall, and Yang finally got fed up. Lo and behold, Gordon discovered that she had powerful relatives, both in China and the United States. Her seemingly placid beauty concealed a ruthless dragon nature as aggressive as Gordon's own. And now that she was royally pissed, she was going to gut him in the settlement.

Gordon was surprised to find he actually liked this side of Yang as much as he feared it. Seeing her flex her claws made him wonder what their marriage would have been like if he'd tried even a little bit. Now he'd never know, with a tumor time bomb in his belly, and Yang's scorched earth version of a divorce looming over everything Gordon had managed to accomplish in his life.

Gordon sat at his desk and opened the drawer. He pulled out his Desert Eagle XIX, and unholstered it from its shoulder rig. It was only the six-inch barrel, but he'd found that the ten-incher hung up too much on the shoulder holster when he was competing in quick draw competitions, or at the combat hand-gunning range he trained at every weekend religiously.

Gordon spun in his leather office chair and faced his reflection in the office window. He put on a gunslinger's snake-eyed scowl as he held the Desert Eagle up, as if for his reflection's inspection. "Draw pardner," he said, pointing his pistol at his mirror image. "*Bang,*" he said softly.

As the gun was in his hand, it was only natural that Gordon would hold it up in front of his face for a better look. Twisting and turning the 50-caliber Magnum as he examined it from multiple angles, Gordon reflected on how easy it would be to just stick the gun in his mouth and pull the trigger.

He holstered the Desert Eagle, stood, and took off his Brioni suit coat to strap on the shoulder holster. Gordon buttoned his coat back up, ground out his latest smoke, and lit another. He looked at his reflection again, twisting from side to side to see if the holstered Desert Eagle bulged too conspicuously as it hung down the length of his ribcage. He decided it looked okay.

He started to reach up a hand to reflexively smooth the thick mop of hair on the top of his head, but stopped with a grimace. He dug his fingers into the hair, ripped off the toupee it actually was, and tossed the hairpiece to the carpeted floor where it lay like a dead poodle. He examined the revealed, reflected, bald Bozo-like dome of his head, scalp pale from years out of the sun. He left his office for the last time, pistol still holstered under his coat.

Gordon drove Yang's S65 around aimlessly for a while, even through his distraction able to enjoy all the bells and whistles in this automotive piece of community property. The heated leather seats, the harman/kardon surround sound currently featuring Rush Limbaugh on the station preset, the agile handling and the feeling of overwhelming power barely constrained within the six-hundred-horsepower V12 engine. There was no way Gordon would let Yang have this car back, even though he knew it was stubborn spite as much as possessiveness on his part.

Gordon drove and drove, towards where he didn't know, all around the East Bay. What was he looking for, now that all meaning had turned to ash? Where was he going to, besides the upcoming grave? He couldn't say, but he knew that as long as he kept driving he didn't have to think, he could just react. As long as he kept sharking forwards, he could pretend he was safe, and that Yang wasn't hot on his tail eager to prove just what a failure his entire life had been.

He was in Berkeley when he finally decided on a semi-ultimate destination: Grizzly Peak Boulevard up in the Hills: a winding, scenic stretch of highway where he could let the S65 off its leash, really let it howl on those curvy inclines and slopes. It would be an easy enough thing to twitch the steering wheel to the side on one curve or another, send the Benz rocketing through space on a fatal, final ride down to impact. If he wanted to, of course. He'd decide when he got up there.

Gordon reached for another smoke as he headed up Ashby, planning on taking Claremont up to Grizzly Peak. But the pack was empty, and Gordon tossed it out his open window as a black guy stumbled backwards out of a storefront about half a block ahead of Gordon's approaching Benz. Two white boys with guns followed the man out the door. As Gordon continued getting ever closer, he saw one of the kids raise his pistol and shoot the black guy. The man fell backwards on his ass with one hand clutching the side of his gut, the other hand palm out and fingers splayed at the end of his outstretched arm, palm facing the gunmen as if in supplication or defense. The second gunman shot the man in the face, and the man's arm lowered to the ground as he subsided the rest of the way onto his back.

Gordon floored the gas pedal, the S65's powerful engine making him feel like he was riding a Valkyrie charger; he should have had Wagner blasting from the harman/kardon instead of the DJ's current neocon monologue driveling pointlessly from the speakers.

The two gunmen froze and whirled to face Gordon as he bounced the roaring Mercedes half up onto the sidewalk, accelerating like a rocket even as he aimed to make sure he missed the black guy's body on the sidewalk. For some reason Gordon didn't want to feel the guy's corpse under his tires.

Time slowed down, nothing existed but Gordon, his Mercedes war wagon, and the two men in front of him. Everything to either side was a blur pouring past, irrelevant bystanders pointing in slow motion. All Gordon's attention was focused on the two gunmen as their staring openmouthed faces got rapidly closer, limned in a crimson glow in his eyes. Gordon realized he was literally seeing red as a keening sound leaked from his mouth, and spittle flecked his lips in a dense foam.

In the last few instants, one of the gunmen started to jump out of the way while the other one raised his pistol and started shooting at the Benz, at Gordon actually. Gordon ignored the bullet holes starring the windshield as the supersonic rounds cracked through the interior of the car past his ear and out the rear windshield like angry hornets. The Mercedes was doing at least eighty as it clipped the fleeing gunman in the hip and sent him spinning through the air to the side like Jackie Chan on crack.

Gordon could see the unbelieving look on the other gunman's face in the final molasses-slow instant as the Mercedes folded him over at the waist and pinched him in half against the lamppost behind him. Gordon saw guts spewing out the guy's mouth even as the Mercedes's hood folded in half around the lamppost, the airbag deployed, and the Benz came to an instant apocalyptic halt.

The expanding airbag slammed Gordon in the ribs like a jack hammer, and there was a red blossom of pain in his face as the airbag surrounded his head and upper body and blocked his vision completely. Gordon clawed in panic at the bag, which pressed him like a prisoner against his seat. Finally he calmed down enough to grope the keys out of the ignition and rip at the fabric of the bag until it deflated.

Gordon scrabbled the belt off, wrestled the warped door open, and half crawled out. Broken glass crunched underfoot as he reeled drunkenly to the front of the car, which was hissing like a tea kettle as steam escaped the ruptured radiator. The black guy's corpse was lying in the gutter, what was left of his face pointing at the sky. Gordon ensured the gunman he'd crushed against the lamppost was dead too, shooting him in the head with his Desert Eagle, which had found its way into his hand somehow. The 50-caliber round almost made the kid's head evaporate as it hit. The other gunman was nowhere in sight, and it occurred to Gordon to wonder just where he was.

He strolled into the dry cleaners that the three men had vomited forth from, the Desert Eagle dangling nonchalantly at his side. The second white boy was in there leaning against the counter, hopping on one foot with his ruined leg dangling, holding a middle-aged black woman from behind by the throat, his pistol muzzle pressed against her temple as he lurched around on his only working leg.

Gordon looked down at the guy's hip and leg as the woman writhed and contorted her face at him; the kid was panting hard enough that his breathing was a series of yelping snarls. His hip actually looked dislocated from when the Benz had sent him spinning through the air, and his foot was twisted at an impossible angle. His leg was swelling so fast, it looked like a balloon filling to press tight against the inside of his pants leg.

"You're not getting far like that," Gordon observed. The kid's eyes glittered, but that was his only response.

"Homicide in the commission of a robbery," Gordon mused. "You're looking at lethal injection, or at least life without parole.

"You're trapped," Gordon continued. "There's no escape for you, you're doomed." Gordon studied the kid closely as he spoke, but his words seemed to have no impact. Instead, the kid was listening to the distant, approaching sirens.

Going for a psychological whipsaw, Gordon focused on the black woman, who trembled in her captor's grasp, eyes pointed as far away as possible from the pistol pressed to her head. "What's your name?" Gordon asked, seriously interested despite the distraction she represented.

"What?" she asked, looking at him in disbelief.

"What's your name?" Gordon repeated.

"Larella, I'm Larella."

Gordon returned to looking the kid deep in the eyes, trying to reach him for some reason. "You're scaring Larella, son. Is that how you want to go out, how you want to be remembered? The kind of scumbag that does a woman wrong?"

Gordon waggled the Desert Eagle but kept it down at his side. "Let Larella go, boy," Gordon said. "Let's keep this between us, go out together like men."

The kid's face slowly sagged into stillness, and his gaze seemed to turn inwards for an endless moment or three. Then he grinned, flung Larella off to the side, leaned back against the counter on his one good leg, and whipped up his pistol to fire at Gordon.

Gordon grinned right back at his current best friend as the kid's shot missed and the bullet whizzed past Gordon's head to his right. Gordon's Desert Eagle spoke three times in reply, every round on target: triple tap, two to the body and one to the dome. The kid's bloody rag of a corpse slid down the counter to lie on the floor, disjointed from the three 50-caliber black talons.

The black woman was pressed back against the wall as if trying to get as far away from Gordon as she could. Gordon looked at her with interest, the grin still on his face as he objectively noted the woman's revulsion towards him. "You liked it," she hissed in accusation.

Gordon's grin widened even farther as he realized she was right.

She escaped out the door away from Gordon, knelt next to her husband's body, and commenced to wail and grieve. Gordon holstered the Desert Eagle and followed her out at a stroll, ignoring the approaching sirens and the shocked babble of all the surrounding bystander drones on this busy Berkeley street.

Yang's S65 was still wrapped around the lamppost; the almost-headless dead kid was still folded in half, face-down on the hood with arms outstretched. All the Benz's windows were shattered. Safety glass lay strewn all around it on the sidewalk, and fluids drained away into the gutter as though the car was bleeding to death. This fine piece of German machinery was totaled.

Gordon felt a momentary pang at the waste of a $200,000 car, but then he chuckled at the irony: this was one piece of community property Yang wouldn't be able to hold over his head anymore. He even considered showing up at the divorce proceedings tomorrow. If he signed, Yang would get half his shit. If only she knew, all she had to do was wait a bit and she'd get it all, one hundred percent.

Gordon buttoned his Brioni jacket as he ducked around the corner, snickering to himself at the comedy of it all. The first emergency vehicles were arriving on the scene, and he needed to be rapidly elsewhere. He also needed some fresh smokes and a drink or three as soon as possible.

It was good to be alive again, even for however short this little upcoming bit might be.

News about Yourself

Scott Wolven

For EJS

The fall brought some cold nights and the pond had the thinnest sheet of ice I'd ever seen. I pointed it out to Richard as we walked around the old farm, eighty acres, talking about how he wanted me to tear the buildings down and how fast I could get the job done. We looked inside the first two barns, then just walked around. We spooked some deer that were bedded down in a field near some old apple trees. The barns all looked the same inside, I was pretty sure of that. We passed by the pond again.

"Ice melts from the bottom," he said. "I never knew that till a couple years ago."

We stood on the point, where you could see across the Hudson River. Richard worked a farm on the other side, up in Greene County. This farm, outside of Red Hook, had been a project his younger brother was going to start, before he passed away in late summer. No illness, no warning. Richard was going to have the barns and outbuildings torn down, to make it a neater parcel for developers. He didn't have a choice. He couldn't very well run two farms. The fall had been very slow for my logging business and I was more than happy to help Richard complete the demo and keep my machines working. I hadn't talked to Richard or his brother since high school. His brother and I had been in the same class, with Richard a couple years ahead of us. The three of us had been great friends when we were kids. I knew his brother had gone on to college, been a fraternity man, and come home to work. He was an officer in the fire department. The past ten years or so, I just waved to them while they were working out in the fields if I happened to be in Greene County visiting my folks. I'd been out of prison about five years at that point.

"I can do it," I said. "It will take me a week. I'll leave the stub-ups in place for the utilities, so if you decide to bulldoze below grade you won't hit anything." Only four of the seven barns were electrified and only two of those had water.

"The electric is dead back to the pole," Richard said. "How much?"

"Twenty-five hundred," I said.

"That's not enough," Richard said. "You have to make money too."

"I'll make money at twenty-five hundred," I said. "My trucks are sitting right now, I've got to get them on a job. Might as well be this one."

Richard nodded. "My family will appreciate that."

"How's everybody doing?" I said.

"It was a real shock," Richard said. "We're watching out for each other." He looked around at the old farm. "I almost never came over here, unless he asked me to. I don't know what he planned on doing with it." He swallowed his sadness. "But I know he had plans for it."

I nodded. "Please give my best to your mom and dad."

"I will," he said. We started to walk back across the property, towards our trucks. "Remember we used to play so much basketball?" he said.

"Sure," I said. "You guys had the only court that was dry in the rain, inside your barn."

"Once he got into the fire department, that was a big part of his life," he said. "He was a good judge of men and fires."

"I bet he was," I said.

"Time goes so fast," Richard said. "Time is not watches and clocks and calendars." He opened the door to his pickup truck. There was a shot in the distance. "Muzzle-loading season opens today," he said. "I'll see you, Ray."

"See you, Richard," I said. I stood there as he pulled away. He had work to do on his own farm.

I started right away the next day. Brought my two big trucks up, along with a skid steer. Two of my regular guys were working with me. We ran the work in an orderly fashion. One of the guys would climb into the rafters of the barn with a logging chain and hook onto the main beam. We'd hook the other end to the skid steer and pull, which usually made the barn collapse. Then we'd load the wood and debris into the trucks with the skid steer and haul it back to my woodlot, about ten miles away. We drove with the flashers on and I followed in my pickup truck to grab anything that fell onto the road. Three barns fell that first day and we were able to haul most of the stuff off.

The next morning at the farm site, there was a man in an SUV parked by the big house. He got out of his truck as I pulled up. He started talking before I opened my door.

"What are you doing?" he asked.

"I'm handling a job here for the Brodersons," I said. My two guys were there already, and I waved at them to go ahead.

"This isn't going to developers," the man said. "You can't do that. The town won't allow it."

"I think you're trespassing on private property," I said. "Hit the road."

He shook his head. "I've got people coming from the town with a Dutchess County sheriff," he said. "We're going to put a stop work order on you."

I looked down the dirt road towards the barns. My guys were hustling, already had the big chain hooked up and were ready to tear down another barn. I gave them the thumbs-up and the skid steer lurched forwards. I turned back to the man as the barn collapsed.

"Wait on the road for your people," I said. "Get off this property." The man looked at me like I was kidding. "I can hook a chain on your truck and drag it to the edge of the property," I said. "Or you can drive it there."

"Do you know who I am?" he said. "I'm Cal Sheely."

"Like I give a fuck," I said.

"Who are you? Some tough guy?" he said.

"Find out," I said. "If you want to get in a fight, I'll help all I can."

Cal sized me up and must have decided I was tipping the scales too much to mess with. He got back in his SUV and pulled to the edge of the road, off the farm. I kept my eye on him. He sat there for almost an hour before he pulled away. We had loaded up the truck at that point and were ready to make a haul back to my woodlot. I called the guys over.

"Let's make a change today," I said. "Let's put all the structures on the ground right now, as quick as we can. Then we'll load and haul them. It will make for a messy work site, but that's how I want it done."

They agreed and we ripped down all but the last barn when I saw some trucks pulling into the farm entrance. I stopped working and slowly walked up to see who it was. Two men from the town, a sheriff, and the man, Cal Sheely, I had seen earlier. I recognized one of the men from the town. It was Ernie Pickens.

"Hey, Ray," Ernie said to me. He pulled me to one side.

"This guy's got everybody in an uproar, says the farm is covered in asbestos shingles. Says you've been hauling it near town. It that true?"

I pointed at the remaining building. "It's tar paper, Ernie, with regular shingles. There's no asbestos here."

"Okay, okay," Ernie said. "Will you let us inspect it?"

"It's not my property," I said. "Call Richard. If you get the okay from him, it's okay with me."

Ernie walked up to the other men and got on his cell phone. He walked back to me next to the last barn after a minute.

"Richard says okay," he said.

"Do what you want then," I said.

He motioned at the last structure. It was the largest barn, the only one still standing. We opened the big swinging doors. It smelled like wet hay.

Inside was an old fire truck.

"Maybe he was restoring it," Ernie said.

The truck must have been brought in on a flatbed. All the tires were flat. It was a dull red and most of the gold lettering had been scraped away. The axes on the sides showed rust. I climbed up into the cab. There was a yellow legal pad sitting on the front seat. There was a list of things that needed to be fixed on the truck. Along with a list of names. Richard's name was on it and his dad's name. It was a list of guys that he would have wanted to be on the truck with him. Some of the guys were already long dead, like his grandfather. My name was there. It said "Ray Cooper, my good friend."

I stepped outside, into the sunlight. The sheriff was there, smoking a cigarette. I walked over and stood next to the big farmhouse. My two workers were there and we waited until the town was done. Ernie walked over to me.

"There's no asbestos here," he said. He said it loud enough so Cal Sheely could hear him. Sheely walked away and sat in his truck while we worked. Finally, he took off.

After they all left, we chained up the fire truck and dragged it out of the barn. We chained up the main timbers and the beams snapped like matchsticks as the structure collapsed. The guys got busy putting the debris into the big dump truck and hauling it. They cleaned up the site pretty well and we were done a day early, as it turned out.

I called Richard to tell him I was done and about the truck. The next day there was a check in the mailbox from him with a note that just said: "Thanks." A couple cutting jobs turned up over the next couple weeks, and I ended up being busy into October and beyond.

It must have been a year later, in the late fall. I was having a bad time of it, for several months. I had a dream and woke up suddenly in my own bed, my heart pounding. The dream had been that the old fire truck was running, with lights and sirens going. I got into my truck and drove over to the farm property. The truck sat in the field where I'd left it. It was too old a model even to have lights on it. Rifle shots came across the morning air and I thought about how much the hunters would hate it if I somehow got the siren to work. I got back into my truck. Something kept me from walking into the woods and fields in my tan jacket and taking my chances. Among the trees and the evergreens and the deer.

It was a couple summers after that when something came my way. It was late August. I was sitting at the garage to escape the heat, downing beers with Jimmy Work, and he started to talk about this guy that owed him money.

"Who is it?" I said. Jimmy had tattoo sleeves. He'd done about eighteen years overall and I met him inside after knowing him outside, which is pretty rare. He was a big guy, walked like a biker, and had a lot of biker friends. Sometimes he hooked people up with drugs—if the buy was big enough and he was sure it was safe. He made sure the rent was paid. Cash.

"This guy, used to be on the town board around here, till he moved," Jimmy said. "Now he owns a store and used car lot over by Saugerties. Cal Sheely and his oldest son."

I drank a beer like it was water. "You don't say," I said. "How much is he into you for?"

"He's owed me eight grand for over six months," Jimmy said. "I just thought about it today and started to get angry."

"Do you know where he lives?" I said.

"Yeah," Jimmy said. "I know where he lives."

I emptied another beer and so did Jimmy. "Let's go talk to him," I said.

"Yeah," Jimmy said. "Let's go talk to him."

We got in Jimmy's work truck and Jimmy drove over the bridge, into Kingston and headed north. He cut off the main road, until we were riding north right along the Hudson River, with big houses and huge lawns on either side of us. It was almost dusk on the river. Isolated by at least two miles from the other houses was a white, Italianate fake mansion with an attached garage.

As soon as we pulled into the driveway, a black German shepherd mix came out and started barking at us. Jimmy pulled a silver whistle from his pocket and I knew it was a dog whistle, but I couldn't hear it. The dog put its tail between its legs and lay on the driveway. Jimmy and I got out of the truck and walked through the open garage. I was carrying a claw hammer that I'd picked up off the floor of the truck.

We walked through the garage, through the house and ended up out back by the pool. There was a young girl and boy there, probably neither of them more than fifteen. The girl was in the water and the boy was sitting under a big umbrella, talking on a phone. He stopped talking when we came out of the house, through the back screen door.

"Hi," the boy said. "My dad isn't here."

"Is he at the car lot?" Jimmy said. "He's selling us a car."

"Oh," the boy said. He looked at the hammer I was carrying. "He should be home any minute." The girl kept swimming in the pool, glancing at us.

"Where's your brother?" Jimmy said. He pointed at the phone next to the boy and the boy tossed it to him. Jimmy tossed the phone in the pool.

"Cape Cod," the boy answered. He picked his head up and listened. "I think that's my dad," he said. A car door slammed from the front of the house and we heard the dog give some friendly barks. The boy was smarter than he looked. "Don't hurt my dad," he said very softly. The girl stopped swimming.

After I smashed his arm and shoulder with the hammer, Cal opened the floor safe in his bedroom and paid Jimmy what he owed him, plus the rest of the contents of the safe. We brought him back downstairs, out to the pool. The boy still sat under the umbrella and the girl was wrapped in a towel next to him. The dog lay on a chain run in the back of the yard.

Cal got up off the grass and started to run for the trees at the edge of the property. He was trying to carry his right arm, the one I'd smashed, with his left. He was limping. He was overweight.

Jimmy pulled a pistol with a silencer out of his coveralls and drilled Cal once in the back and then again in the side of the head. The blood flew, like a red shadow coming out of Cal's head in the last of the fast fading sunlight. Then Jimmy shot both of the kids, the girl and boy, twice each, through her towel and through the baseball shirt the boy was wearing. We got back into Jimmy's truck and left. We didn't speak, all the way down the road and across the bridge. When we stopped at the garage, I got out and got into my truck. I might have waved as I left. I forget.

The outrage in the community, not for Cal Sheely, but for his children, was tremendous. The BCI questioned Jimmy twice, at his garage. Nothing ever came of it.

I didn't see Jimmy for a while after that, but I was out in the woods working in the spring and I turned around and there was his blue beat-up work truck.

"Hey, Jimmy," I said.

He waved. "You were never there," he said. "So sleep easy."

I nodded. He got back into his truck and pulled out, down the logging road I had cut.

I thought about the list of men in the old fire engine. I didn't belong on that list. Maybe I had never belonged on that list.

Trauma Dyke

Derek Nikitas

This whole fucking country's got a motto. It's *pura vida,* and it means pure life, it means chill, it means when life gets you down, put up your feet, sister. But I'm fired up with purpose and I lift my legs for no man.

Costa Rica can kiss my ass, but I'm here anyhow with a bunch of off-season tourists. Americans like me, Canadians, Germans, Swiss. We lean over this bridge abutment and gawk down some fifty feet at the crocs lazing in the muddy Río Tárcoles. Just their backs eased up from the muck, studded with traction like truck tires. The bus driver said locals fling live chickens sometimes, just to see the frenzy.

So it's like I figured: fuck *pura vida* when there's something to kill.

Our tour bus waits outside the dusty lot of an open-air market where you can buy big green coconuts with straws stabbed in them, or little lottery tabs that the natives snap open and toss on the floor when they're losers.

On the road from San José to Quepos we stop at every rickety village to grab a handful of native Ticos from the dusty roadside, bus crammed past capacity, so they stand in the aisles with wet armpits in your face, lunging at you as the bus rounds mountain curves. It's what you get for a three-buck fare, five sweaty hours each way.

I paid a couple thousand for a last-minute flight from Buffalo, transfer in Atlanta. Closed up the consignment shop, packed my duffel bag, dusted off my passport, and scrammed. So fast, my girl Jess had no clue I was gone till I called her from the airport in San José last night. Told her I was in Cleveland sorting shit out with my dad. Lied to protect her from my . . . my whatever. Absconding, you could say, but you'd be wrong.

At customs they asked my intentions. I said kayaking, ziplining, and surfing—all the same shit Cameron Diaz did on her travel show. They eyed my dreads and the studs in my face and my bulldog forearm tat and my scratch marks, but they let me pass. They're used to granola lesbos flooding down for Endless Summer, I guess. Nothing memorable about me, which is just what I want.

What I didn't tell Jess and I didn't tell customs was this: I'm here to kill a man named Moose Walther. I'm here to saw off his cock and cram it through his left eye socket. Or better yet, store it on ice, cart it back to this here bridge, drop it down for the crocs to chew. Tell me how you break that news to your girlfriend while she sobs long-distance on the phone?

We bus along the coastline and hit Quepos, a concrete patch with beach-themed shops, then onwards past forests where the belladonna and the birds-of-paradise burst color among leaves big enough to swaddle a dog. The bus hemorrhages its passengers at a surfboard rental shop, the Miguel Antonio National Park just across an inlet from the beach, and the coconut oases. Taxi drivers sitting in their windows, leaning over their roofs, barking the obvious.

I got nothing but a rucksack to my name, and here nobody knows that name. I pass the clay artisan booths, hit the nearest palm-roofed cabana, and order a chilled Imperial, the national beer. The bartender tries to stuff a lime in it but I snatch his wrist to stop him. Three fresh scratches run down my forearm, sliced through the middle of my bulldog tat, and the bartender grins banana-wide. You're something else, lady.

I studied the maps. I'm a couple kilos away from Moose Walther and I can feel his old venom stinging in my blood. I need his scalp right now—no delay, no recon, no plan. I'm past the dream of scot-free, ever-after vindication. Instead I'm just praying my info is legit and current. Praying to God, praying to Satan, I don't give a fuck. I'd be a better bitch, but I'm just the one that Moose Walther made me, twenty years ago.

It's kicking a hundred degrees, even at dusk after a flash monsoon, and I walk the upwards slope away from the beach, past little b&b haciendas and rental bungalows. A long brownish snake ripples up the roadside opposite, keeping pace. I wonder if it plans to tempt me.

I'm all wet dog and panting by the time I reach the hilltop, beer boiling in my gut. My tank top is drenched. Squat brown howler monkeys sway through the tree canopy overhead, and their call is like a bar full of men hooting at a pole dancer. My starvation points me to an open-air restaurant just seating for dinner. The tiki bar and live calypso band tell me this is no bargain joint, but if it's to be my last dish, I want the coconut crusted mahimahi.

I sit along the panorama overlook and vie for a view for Moose Walther's joint. No numerical addresses in Costa Rica, just landmark directions. His I have engraved on my brainpan, a kilometer east of the Parque Pacifica Resort. But I can't see it from here because everything's buried in foliage, and I don't have my bearings. Soon enough, the end of this.

Craggy islands rear up from the silvery Pacific—valleys so lush with green, the purple stormcloud horizon. The overlook is level with the treetops, so cue the gangly squirrel monkeys.

They swing in from the branches, cat-sized with wrinkled pygmy faces. They pose on chairbacks and tables for food scraps and the shutterbug tourists are suckers for the con. Calypso shimmers metallic on the night.

I stuff my contempt a few minutes straight and think of Keira, our daughter. Jess's daughter if you want to get biological. Keira's four and trades on and off month by month between us and her dad. This is our month, and I'm gone, and I may never make it back. Costa Rica is everybody's heaven, but away from Keira I can only appreciate the longing it delves out of my soul. I got a crayon sketch of hers folded up in my pocket—three stick figures all in dresses, holding hands with their heads together like they're the spokes of some wheel that almost seems in motion.

My fish, asparagus, and white wine arrive, and on the far side of the tiki bar three people take a candlelit table. Two of them are Ticos, or at least Hispanics—a woman in a floral print dress and a girl about ten with rainbow-beaded hair and a one-piece swimsuit. The third is Moose Walther.

The gouges on my arm slow burn and I can feel his violations all over again. I'm twelve, on display in my half shirt by the light of Toledo truckstop vending machines, holding Zelda's hand while a fat faceless trucker sticks his pinkie in my navel. I'm swooning with the mainlined dope Moose used to twist my mind for six months straight. Moose is not there, is everywhere, omnipresent.

Moose is here, firing through time and flaring up like a chronic blight. He's got two new females within his reach, a dour-faced pair gussied up to look like sunshine. One of them's just a little girl, the same—

I was still prepubescent the night of my rescue, the big Toledo police truckstop sting of '88. Zelda and a posse of truckers arrested, three underage abductees saved, but pedophile pimp Moose Walther was a phantom in the night, an FBI profile, a televised most wanted exposé, a Costa Rica refugee, after all this time.

To see him now, he's gone mostly bald, gained thirty pounds of flab—but he's still the seven-foot slouching beast I remember. He's still a lecher, his arm around that ruined Tico girl, smearing her against him. Twenty years of healing gutted with a pitchfork, but I brought this on myself by coming here. From across the restaurant he sniffs his nose at me. Not a flicker of recognition, and I'm almost insulted.

The dinner knife in my fist is sharp enough to stab between ribs, but I'm starry from beer and caught off guard. My adrenaline drains like a menstrual flood. Who the fuck am I all of a sudden? I'm a wannabe riot grrl who runs a consignment shop in Buffalo. I don't put blades in people's hearts, especially not ghosts like Walther, flashbacks who aren't even there.

My wicker chair scrapes the floor behind me. The purple clouds are pulling back from the sea, and the squirrel monkeys scatter, chirp warnings at each other. I weigh nothing and everything at once and the axis tilts and the mosaic floor is moist on my cheek. I try to sleep. The attic windows are boarded but the winter seeps in. I lie on the floor because the bed is tainted. I can't escape because Moose and Zelda know my home and they promise to slit the throat of everyone in my family if I try. My address, the life I lived before.

A damp napkin on my face brings me around. My medics are a waiter, a bartender, a few leering tourists. They lift me back onto my seat and offer orange juice, a blanket, a taxi, but I hold my head and wave them off. Moose is twenty feet away and watches with the smirk of an eel, his smoldering power.

He used to tell me there was an invisible thread connecting each of us to God, twining out of the crown of all our skulls. He told me if I scorned him, he'd cut that thread, and I wouldn't be lifted to heaven when I died. His worst threat of many, and to exorcise it, I've cut the thread myself, every day. I fold it into a little loop pinched between my fingers, and snip it with scissor fingers. Easy.

I pick at the fish, pay my bill, muster the guts to walk the gauntlet past his table. The sunset spreads red through the restaurant and Moose has donned his sunglasses. The little girl hangs her face and eyes me askance. I flex my hands. The tendons in my neck are taut enough to snap twigs against. The trees are alive with the twitter of birds.

When I'm out of sight I sprint, cut through the resort complex past the suites and the pristine pools shaped like water droplets. The banana trees curve their fruit upright in virgin green bunches. Don't let the beauty distract from your hate.

Just one private residence at the end of the road. The mission clay-tiled roof emerges from the canopy, then the stucco walls and the garden fountain, the marble-tiled courtyard, everything wrapped in a black iron fence with ten-foot rails. The gate doors are clasped with a wrapped length of chain and a padlock.

I hunch in the dusty road with my hands on my knees and gasp for air. Two iguanas peer at me from a shaded brush. Inside the gate, a Tico guard in a white tank top and cargo shorts stands to attention from his lawn chair. He's got a machete in his grip and his brow folds low over his eyes. He wraps his free hand on a fence rail and watches me like he's the one who's an inmate.

"Do you speak English?" I say, still heaving from my jog. I take gulps from a water bottle stowed in my rucksack. The road behind me is empty save the darting mosquitoes.

"English, *sí*," he says, and there's the grin I expected.

"Who lives here?" I ask.

The guard taps his machete against his shin. He says, "I don't tell."

"You're not allowed to say? I'm looking for my uncle's house, but there aren't any address numbers around here, so I'm trying to figure it out, you know?"

"Is no yours uncle house here, lady."

"How do you know?"

"Is private name," he says.

"You don't even know who he is, do you?" The iguanas have retreated, like they know, like they smell the fear I give off in my sweat. The guard shrugs in answer to my question, so I say, "How long have you been working here?"

"Eh, maybe, fie weeks."

"How much do you get paid a week? Slave wages, right?"

He shrugs again and stops tapping his blade. He looks back at the house.

"I know he's out to dinner right now," I say. "I'll give you seven hundred American dollars if you let me inside. Before he gets back." I crouch and reach back into my rucksack. The gesture spooks the guard, but his skeptical brow lifts when he sees the money stack. "Here it is," I say. "All of it, right now. In your hands."

The guard raises his chin, nostrils flaring, like he's offended. He says, "Two thousand American dollars."

I push the money through at him, flap it around like a dead trout, but he doesn't grab. I say, "Listen, *señor,* I don't have time for negotiations. This is all the money I have. There's no two thousand dollars. There's seven hundred. I didn't want to mess around with you, so I just went ahead and offered all I had."

"One thousand eight hundred dollars," he says.

I reach through the fence with my left hand, index and middle fingers in the shape of scissors. I mimic a cut just over the top of his head. His eyes pivot upwards almost white. "Snip," I say to him, then I kiss the v-shaped crook of my own two fingers.

"You should leave now," he says. He lays the flat end of the machete over his shoulder and hoists his chin even higher. I see his jugular pulse, and I think back to—Jesus, just yesterday, think back to Zelda slinking into my shop around closing time, fresh off parole and seeking teary talk show forgiveness. The thick veins running under the crude black prison tats scraped into her neck.

She said, "I'm sorry to come here like this, and I don't mean to cause trouble."

Right now I push that bitch from my brain and tell the guard, "All right, Pedro. If you don't take this money now, I'll have to come back later, and you might get hurt."

He chuckles with his tongue shoved in his cheek.

I continue, "The man who lives here is named Kyle Walther. People used to call him Moose, but I doubt they still do. He's an international criminal, wanted by the FBI for running prostitution rings in the United States. His prostitutes were mainly underage girls, most of whom were kidnapped and drugged and held against their will and raped, repeatedly."

The guard sits back down in his lawn chair, lays the blade over his lap.

I say, "Maybe you know this, maybe you know zilch. I'm one of his victims. I was twelve years old when he drugged me and stole me from a party and kept me prisoner for six months before I was rescued. It took me twenty years to find him, but here I am. I intend to make him dead, even though I know it won't prove anything. But that's my business. I'm going to do this, or I'm going to get myself killed trying, but either way, here's your money. If you don't take it now, I'll be back later. I don't think you want to get hurt, and I don't really think you want to hurt me, now that you know my story. So the best thing to do is take the money and let me inside this gate, isn't that right?"

The guard spits on the courtyard tile and refuses to look at me. From around the bend in the road behind me hails the slow crush of rocks under tires, the squeal of suspension springs. I only have time to lift my rucksack before a dark SUV pulls up with its headlights burning my pupils. Dusk has moved on to night while I've talked with the guard, and now the streetlights kick on with an electric rush.

The guard begins to work the chain wrapped around the gate. The tinted driver's side window melts with an automatic whir. The wheelman's a portly Tico with a penciled-in mustache and a dinner jacket. He's the driver, but Walther and his two victims are in there, in the backseat, just out of reach. I know without seeing them.

"What are you doing here?" the driver says.

The stars on the skyline twirl. I have to shove my hands in my jeans pockets to keep them from shaking. My eyelids go slack for the improv skit where I tell the driver, "I'm just looking for something to eat, dude. I been on the road all day and—"

"No beggars," he says, and shoos me off with a limp wave.

Back down on the beach the cabana's in full swing. One by one I peel fives off my money stack and convert them into canned beers. The swash tumbles in white flashes out on the dark shoreline. The sea chides me.

I rent a hammock and beachfront camp space, but I'm swimming in beer and forget where it was I meant to sleep. There's a bonfire draw and I'm the moth. A mariachi plays for loose change. I sit in the sand and hug my knees and swoon and think how this might be if I were someone else.

I greet people with names and mix them up too soon, but everybody smells like spice and the sea. A girl with blond cornrows and a bikini top dances against me. Where I touch her skin it's dusted with dry sand. She's from Germany and her arms are greened like gauntlets with overlaid tattoos, scenes from the Garden of Earthly Delights.

I have never loved any other but Jess. I have never loved. Someone spots a sloth lousing in the crook of a tree. The German girl's named Astrid, or ought to be.

"I'm here to study the turtles on the Atlantic coast, an internship," Astrid says.

"A woman named Zelda told me this was the best place to hide," I reply.

"From what do you hide?"

Men sing in unison and the bonfire embers linger like insects on fire. I say, "Men who chew girls like tobacco," and Astrid has draped herself across my shoulders. Her mouth, my neck, her hands, my flesh. Shirtless men hoot like howler monkeys, a camera flashes. I shove Astrid off her driftwood perch. She pitches backwards in the sand. My beer can glances off her forehead. She curses German and hunts for her lost sandals. She screams at me like a nursery rhyme: "Trauma dyke, you're just a poseur trauma dyke! Would've been straight if not for the rape!" Simian hoots of approval accompany her song.

But I'm already stalking beyond the light. I cannot be loved except by hurt. I cannot be at rest, unless death. I'm laced with his ugliness all the way down to the marrow. *Pura fucking vida.*

The road is black as I climb it again, sweating even at night. I pass rental bungalows tucked in the trees every hundred feet along the roadside, built into the thickest trunks like elvish enclaves. Behind the slatted shades, families and honeymooners dream under spinning ceiling fan blades in the shape of ficus leaves.

Tico guards are posted at each hobbit gate, and one sits in his lawn chair with his head hung forwards, snoring like a call to the jungle. Even my footsteps don't wake him. I slip his machete off his lap. The hilt is padded with electrical tape but the blade is sharp.

My rucksack and money are lost, and I don't know where, and I am beyond the need. This demon in me took wing the moment I recognized Zelda. She stood in my store beside my checkout counter and said, "I'm on parole now. I know I'm the last person in the world you wanted to see, and I was so afraid to come here, so ashamed, but I wanted you most of all to know how much I repent, how much I owe to God."

Over the years I learned not to think her name anymore. I learned to pantomime a self that even I believed—an entrepreneur trading in vintage and ragtag clothes, a woman's lover, a substitute mother. I didn't drink or go to nightclubs. Foreign film rentals came in the mail on weekends, and I suppressed a growing urge to scrapbook. That was before yesterday, before Zelda came.

"Do you know where he is?" I asked her while I folded capri pants into a pile.

"I don't concern myself with people like him anymore," Zelda said. Nobody else was in the store except the faceless mannequins. The sign was flipped to CLOSED, but Zelda had tested the door and found it unlocked.

"If you honestly repented, you'd let them know where to find him."

"I just want to forget about the past." She spoke with a sedative drawl.

"You can't repent and forget," I said.

"I don't expect you to forgive me, I really don't."

"He abandoned you, and you protect him?" I said.

"My only concern is God. Have you been saved?"

The width of a counter was between us. I said, "You goddamn know where he is."

She spread her hands on the countertop and weighted herself against them with a long sigh, like I was just too much to bear, too unforgiving, too unredeemable. She wore sweatpants and a sweatshirt and a small gold cross around her neck. Twenty years ago she sat on my chest with her knees crushing my arms while Moose Walther broke through my body. She'd stood guard outside the trucks.

Now at the Walther property the streetlights again paint my shadow. The chain that earlier twined the gate doors now sits coiled like a rattler on the marble tile. The guard's lawn chair is empty. This is my grace because I would've been helpless otherwise, even with my weapon. I'm only sorry that I can pay the guard nothing but karma. He's not here to thank.

The gate creaks like a question. The tiles are slick under my sneakers. The small fountain spills its contents endlessly and my fingers slip through its reservoir as I pass. I taste the water from my fingertips. The night humidity pulls me out of my own pores, and I'm adrift on the drunk I have nurtured. All along the forest the monkeys watch from their thousand perches and recognize this ceremony as their own.

The door latch clicks and pulls me into a room decked with Tico folk art, clay monkeys, and pinwheels. Bright birds chirp inside of three suspended cages, and the floors are more marble tile. The light cones upwards from two lamps on either side of a leather couch where Moose Walther sits hunched forwards with his elbows on his knees, sweat on his scalp.

He says, "I thought I recognized you."

"You're the one who left the gate unlocked," I say as I shut the door behind my back. Through the archway the house spreads out in compartments that blend ever more deeply with the lush forest beyond it. I can see the ocean from here, I think. I can hear its rush.

"It was an invitation, not a trap. Whatever happens, I want you to know I'm through with all that. I live here without drugs or alcohol, or anything of the sort."

"You're surrounded by whores. I saw them, a woman like Zelda and a child like I was."

Walther flinched, sucked air through his nostrils. "They're my family. My daughter."

"Your family," I say, and I don't want to believe. He has lived utter lies before.

In the Buffalo ArtPark is a ten-foot sculpture of a monkey

cobbled together with rusted junkyard parts and found art—
Keira's favorite piece. Last summer when we were admiring the
monkey, Keira spotted a friend of hers from preschool. She introduced me to the girl's parents as "my mommy's wife." Right
now I'm too drunk to think deep about why that occurs to
me—people and monkeys cobbled together out of junk.

"How did you find me?" Moose Walther asks.

I shiver even in the stinging heat. His voice is the echo of the
drugs that stole months from my life and anesthetized the pain,
until the daylight delivered it all back to me in one blinding
burst. I tell him, "Your old whore Zelda gave it to me."

He kneads his swollen face. "I figured as much," he says.

I step to the nearest birdcage and clumsily unlatch the mesh
doorway. Walther doesn't stop me. He watches the machete I
hold against my thigh. The parakeet inside the cage flitters from
perch to perch, unsure of itself, until it warbles in a tuft of color
through the archway, towards the sea.

Yesterday evening I took flight. In my consignment shop, I
burst over the counter, and I haven't stopped lunging since. I
tackled Zelda into a clothing carousel and we were a jumble of
other people's abandoned attire. She was trapped beneath me.
My hands clutched her neck. Cartilage snapped and shifted deep
inside her throat. Her eyes went wide and wet and her face
tinted violet. Her frantic fingernails gouged three parallel lines
across my arm. She had already told me where to find him, but
she wasn't absolved. I tore away her gold cross necklace and
fed it into her wide, silent mouth. I left her, the door unlocked,
for the world to witness, for Jess.

"We spoke on the phone a few days ago, Zelda and me, after
she was released," Moose says. "She told me she found you and
Jessica—"

"Don't you dare use her name," I say.

Moose raises both hands and nods demurely, mockingly.

"I'm sorry—I'm just saying she was glad to find out that you two had made your lives together and put what we did to you—put it behind you. I know how difficult it must've been. I think about who I was every day." He reaches for the table beside him, but it is only a glass of red wine he grasps. He swishes the liquid in the glass and sips, a gesture I remember, the emperor who turns down his thumb.

"We cope," I say. I scratch the denim on my knee with the blade.

"You don't know how glad I am to hear that. I want you to be happy. If there's anything that I can do to make you happy, I want it. I have money for you, and for Jess. I'm glad to think that in spite of all this ugliness that I put you through, when I was young and foolish, at least something good came of it."

"Sometimes I wonder if her and I are tainted, because you brought us together."

"No, don't think that. Just be happy in your life."

"Don't you fucking tell me what to do, and fuck your playing cupid bullshit."

His surrender pose again, wineglass dangling by its stem from his crooked thumb. He says, "I understand your anger. I've felt it against myself a million times, every day."

"I came here to kill you," I say.

"I was hoping we could talk through this instead."

"Tell me something. Why didn't she roll over on you? Zelda. If she knew your whereabouts all this time for twenty years. She could've had a plea bargain. Don't tell me you're all that mesmerizing."

He downs the rest of his wine, wipes away what dribbles on his chin. Maybe down here in Eden he found God walking among the mango groves. Maybe what he thinks he's drinking is the blood of Christ. He says, "She didn't know until she was released. I reached out to her then. I got in touch with her because I knew we could have a chance to forgive each other. I even invited her down here."

"Funny," I say. "She wanted the same from me. Did you send her to find me?"

"She wanted to. All I did was encourage her."

"But you didn't expect her to cough up your address."

"I knew it was a possibility. Look, forgiveness is for your own mental health."

"I know the routine. I've seen *Oprah.*"

"Zelda and me—"

"Zelda's dead. Within five minutes of asking my forgiveness. I strangled her." The shudder in my voice, the stage fright. This moment, rehearsed in my nightmares for two decades, but I couldn't prep for the swarm of old pains and fears that frenzy around my head. He's faking meek, the *puta.* Any second this man on the couch will leap forth and devour me. He has that power. His talk is poisoned honey. Doesn't matter that I have a machete. It dissolves in my hand.

We both hear it at once: the stick of bare feet padding across tile. Moose lifts himself off the couch with his face contorted. I almost lose my balance, still dizzy from drink, thinking I'm cornered for some ambush. But into the archway comes his supposed daughter, the little half Tico girl with her hair all beaded, white nightgown. She squints in the light and holds between her cupped hands the bird I released. It bobs its tiny pink head.

"Papa," she says to Moose, but continues in crystalline Spanish I can't understand.

Moose halts her with his hands and with a command. He is suddenly afraid of me.

"Do you speak English?" I ask the little girl, and she nods at me suspiciously.

"I taught her, from when she was a baby," Moose says. He's

trying to feign that I'm just another American friend dropping by for a drink, one of daddy's old associates. I can see he wants it to be true, wants me to harmonize, for the little girl's sake.

"What's your name?" I ask her.

"Miriam. My bird flies into my room."

"But you caught him," I say. "Good job. How old are you?"

"Miriam . . . ," Moose says.

"Nine years," Miriam says. The thread is invisible, but still I can see it winding upwards from her crown, up through the ceiling, up into the heavens. She raises the bird towards me.

"I was a little girl once," I say.

"Miriam—"

The black tape wound around the machete hilt is slick with my sweat, but I won't let it go. The blade sings like a distant wave on the shoreline. Somewhere on the beach, a vendor cracks a coconut in half and the meat inside is flawless white. Here in Moose Walther's home, the pastel green walls are showered with a hundred tiny plastic beads. They dribble on the floor like candies, and soon the grout between the tiles channels liquid red. I have a daughter I will never see again. The bird flitters against the ceiling, frantic for exit.

Moose drops in supplication, beats his palms on the marble. Out in the night stray monkeys squawk answers to his howls. I crouch beside him and whisper, though I'm sure he's beyond hearing.

"Forgive me," I say.

Before I leave, I wash my wet hands in his fountain. I listen to the music of the tropics.

'Demption Road

Justin Porter

Cass always woke slowly. He moves his feet, feels the dense, worn-down heels of his boots rasp on the wooden edges. He moves his hands, runs them over his body. Scratches where he finds an itch and rubs sore, scarred knuckles.

He draws up his heels, bridges a little, lifting his lower back off of the assortment of blankets padding the pile of wooden planks he slept on. Rolling onto his side, he puts his hands together like a prayer between his knees. The joints would ache if he allowed them to pillow each other. He would never be able to sleep like that, his hands so occupied, so confined. Eventually he sits up, opens his dun-colored eyes, and looks out at the place he'd built.

His place.

Sunlight streams in through the windows, dust motes playing within the rays like ecstatic children. Between each aperture, an accentuated dark. The corners seem to swallow light and pass shadows.

When Cass had claimed the warehouse as his own, his bed

had lain in the heat of one of those windows. He had woken, angry and abrupt, his eyes opening first, to those hellish rays of sun. That night he slid the pile of boards to a darker corner, his hands soon studded with splinters. They still sported dark spots where bits of desiccated wood lay driven beneath the first layers of skin.

Head aching, throat dry, he casts about his bed for the bottle from last night and, like most mornings, it's empty. He shouldn't have bothered. If he woke to find a bottle at all, it would always be empty.

Cass stands up, shirking his clothes around him, his pant legs out of the tops of his boots. His belt buckle sits dead center. He reaches overhead, stretching, passing his hands through the sunlight from a higher window, feeling warmth. Turning, he drops to a crouch and slides a hand under his rolled-up jacket. The jacket that held his head as he slept. He notices with distaste a sizable wet spot from when he must have drooled the night before.

Under the jacket, his hand bumps something and grasps it. Cass slides the object behind his belt buckle and makes sure to pull the hem of his ripped and spotted shirt over it.

What Christina awakes to is an unyielding hardness in his back, shoulder, and under his ass. His knees ache at their awkward position. He could see the alley around him and feel that the parts of his body that weren't protesting were against garbage bags.

Rubbing at his face, he smells the perfume that he had put on the night before. "My flypaper," he had joked to his roommate as he got ready to go out, indicating a small bottle. His roommate had shaken his head, mystified, but secretly happy with himself for being cool with so counterculture a roommate.

Christina smells the rancid garbage on two sides. He smells his skin and clothes, which hold traces of the things he had done the night before. The things he had done willingly and with enthusiasm.

And the things he had not done willingly.

The enthusiasm of others.

Both had been part of his plan when he left the house the night before.

Christina was thin, delicate even. Narrow of shoulder and hip, willowy and beautiful. His face's bones, his large eyes, and his harshly pouting lips made some of the baddest faggots gasp. Forget themselves, forget not to fight over these bitches. Christina knew that. And loved it. Loved to make these men put the boots to each other.

Thugged out, heavy knuckled, and big dicked.

Christina loved them all and they loved him.

He feels that maybe they had loved him a little too much too far this time, as he braces himself against the alley wall and stands up. Feeling the sore places on and inside his body, like the echoes of a canyon scream.

He pushes off the soiled brick and puts his weight on his left ankle. Crying out shrilly as the joint buckles, Christina topples into a pile of garbage. Cries of outrage replace cries of pain.

He drags the pieces of himself together and wraps his arms around his knees, hugging. And from somewhere back, back before the hateful words, the clenched fists, and the fast push out of a door that held safety on one side and hell on the other— before all of those things—he remembers that there used to be arms that held him. Protected him from everything, including himself. A ghost of that whispers in his own clutching arms.

Tears reach his mouth and are tasted before he knows that he is crying. Once he notices, it comes hard and fast, pushing and shoving to get out, as though it knows it has just this one chance.

He wracks and shakes.

He turned nineteen yesterday.

* * *

Cass pats his pockets as he walks to the front entrance. A tiny key lies in the folds of a pocket. It had rolled out once while he slept, and he had lost sleep and patience finding the damn thing. But he wasn't that bad off, some had lost blood.

He later found it between the slats of his makeshift bed.

The only new thing on the building is the padlock that Cass had bought for the warehouse's only entrance. The tiny key opened it. Cass had robbed three people to get the money together to buy what was originally a bike lock. He saw messengers, and all of them had the same one. He figured that it must be good.

Cass removes the metal pipe that he slid through the door's mechanism to keep it shut at night. From one end of the pipe, he unloops the chain and lock and takes the key out of his pocket.

Outside in the fading sunlight, he chains it shut and slams home the lock's struts. Cass glares up at the setting sun and walks towards a group of other men like himself who had already started a fire in an old oil drum. That's when he hears the crying. He hasn't heard anything that broken since four years ago when he caught one of the older bums fucking a young runaway that had been stupid enough to think fellow victims don't prey on each other. Cass remembers the look of fear in the kid's eyes after Cass had beaten the rapist to death. Like his life had just gone from bad to worse. Cass had walked away disgusted.

But this crying sounds older and it lacks the grunting hiccups that accompanied the other. It is coming from around the side of the warehouse.

Christina gave up trying to stand. The torrent quality that his crying had taken makes it difficult to see. Any attempt to choke it back just made it worse.

While the tears fall vertically, the memories spanned panorama.

The shouting, the hitting, the words. Learning the lesson that you were an idiot and a faggot at school and then learning the same lessons at home. You were an idiot for not being able to handle geometry and you were a faggot for painting your fingernails. *You wanna be a little girl? Fine. We'll start calling you Christina at home, not Christian. You wanna be a chick, you can be a chick, fucking little faggot.*

So absorbed is Christina, that he feels, rather than sees, that somebody is standing over him. Somebody large and somebody silent. Still struggling to draw an uninterrupted breath, Christina looks up into Cass's face. He would have collapsed farther inwards if it had been possible. This isn't like at the club or last night. He's sober, for one. For another, at the club, he was prepared to be used. Prepared to like it.

But this is the next morning, when he's hungover and hurting. No safe words out here. Not that he set them up for last night, but you know, it was a possibility. Not here, with this huge scary man standing up, staring down with the most beautiful and emptiest eyes Christina has ever seen on another human.

Cass isn't sure what he's looking at. It's small, like a kid, but the face has some age. Slightly built like a girl and there's makeup, but it is also clearly male. What the fuck is it doing out here? Not a safe place for anything that looked like that. Cass could remember some people who would find a way to use it.

Christina tries to stand up again, tries to at least be on his feet when whatever was going to happen next, happens. But the ankle buckles again, and his whole leg from toes to hip rattle with a painful vibrato. As Christina falls, an arm shoots out and grabs him above an elbow. Not painfully, but not gently either, and it makes pain easy to imagine. Christina looks and Cass is holding him up with one hand. He turns and guides Christina to uncluttered ground.

Having been taken out of the scattered trash and worse, Christina finds it easier to stand without help. He looks around at the blasted buildings and warehouses that surround them like broken teeth in a beaten man's mouth. He looks down at himself, brushes the clothes that cover him. He tries to ignore the whitish stains and the rips that are new, settles the shirt more comfortably, more for a way to figure out what to do next. The silent one next to him still hasn't fully let go of his arm, but relaxes the grip a little.

Christina cuts his eyes at Cass, unable to keep a slight flirt from his mouth corners and eyelashes. "Where is this?" His voice forced falsetto, Christina gathers the protections that life had forced upon him little by little. Now standing and confident again.

Cass just looks at him. No expression yet.

Christina casts him a withering look, frustrated. *Great,* he thinks. *It's Lennie from* Of Mice and Men.

Christina lowers his register and answers in the voice he inherited from his parents. "Where are we?"

"Squa—squats." Cass's unused voice chokes on the first syllable before allowing him the pleasure of a full word.

Oh shit, thinks Christina. This is bad—first they spend the whole night rough with me, then they fucking dump me out here. Fucking assholes going for the whole experience I guess: snatch, gang rape, and dump. Then it occurs to him that maybe he was the only one enjoying a fantasy last night. He shivers and grabs around himself, shrugging all the way out of Cass's grip, who just lets his hands fall to his sides.

"I need to go here," Christina says, his slim hand holding what looks like a postcard.

Cass stares at the words on the card. A few of the smaller ones jump out at him, some of the ones he knows, but mostly it might be any language for all he's concerned.

"I can't read," he says, with just a hint of something in there with the gravel.

"What do you mean?"

"Forgot how."

"Ooookay." Christina throws up his hands, placing one on a hip, wincing when a broken nail catches on the fabric. The other hand on his cheek, Christina stands, hip shot, and says: "It's the Old Souls Halfway House." The card is still facing the same direction toward Cass.

"I've never heard of it," Cass says.

"Fuck. Well, can you tell me where I can catch a bus?"

Cass shakes his head. "We're too far out here for that. You're gonna have to walk."

Christina sighs and straightens up, looks around like some species of very dramatic waterfowl, and demands: "Which way?"

Cass points vaguely.

"What are you, some kinda fuckin' retard?"

Cass turns slowly and looks at Christina from the direction he was pointing. Nothing changes about him, but something buried deep in Christina—something that's maybe buried deep in all of us—tucks its tail between its legs.

"No," Cass says, and then after a moment adds: "I'm not."

"Right. Well, I guess I'll just start fucking walking . . ." Christina says, taking exactly one step before his ankle buckles, causing him to shrill out and drop to one hand.

"What's the matter?" Cass asks.

"What the fuck, are you blind?"

"No."

Christina flourishes an impatient gesture at his ankle.

"My stupid ankle is totally fucked! Help me," he demands imperiously, extending one shattered-manicure hand. Wrist cocked at exactly 45 degrees, fingers reaching. He shrieks again when Cass pulls him to his feet as though he wants to get launched into orbit, rather than simply stand up.

"Jesus Christ! What the fuck's the matter with you?" Christina says, shaking his arm out from his shoulder.

"Nothing," Cass says, speaking his truth.

"Can you help me find the shelter? I need to get checked out. After last night."

"What happened last night?"

"Some guys I know kept me in a van for three hours taking turns."

"Oh." Cass's features wrinkle and his tone darkens.

"Don't knock it till you've tried it, sweetheart."

Cass shakes his head. "I'm too big for that now."

He moves closer to Christina and ducks under the injured arm that matches the ankle. Then he straightens up a bit, allowing Christina to stand and walk.

"I'm Christina."

"Cass." Then thinks for a minute. "But that's a girl's name."

"You have antiquated gender biases."

"What?"

"Never mind, let's just walk."

Cass looks around after walking for what feels like hours, but judging from the sky and light patterns, it can only have been one.

"I'm not sure if we're going the right way," he says.

Christina sighs and sucks his teeth in irritation. "God. I thought this was, like, your neighborhood or something?"

"It's not anybody's anything."

"Yeah, well, whatever, but I think the buildings I see up ahead are familiar."

"Then I guess you don't need a guide."

Christina stops and looks at him. Cass can see his fear's fingertips in his eyes, edging up and peeking out. The boy he had saved from the rapist had the same look in his eyes. This time though, Cass is sure he's seen as the savior and not the big-ger of two wolves fighting over a scrap.

"Let's go," Cass says, and walks ahead, past the shaking Christina.

"What the fuck do you mean, you're lost?" Christina shrieks.

"Just what I said." Cass rolls his eyes, but other than that, nothing is obvious.

"I thought this was your hood or whatever!" Christina is still shouting.

"You said that already, and what did I tell you last time?"

"I don't fucking remember! Fuck!"

"I said it wasn't anybody's anything. Now stop shouting. You're gonna draw out the wolves." Cass looks around obvi-ously at the buildings surrounding them that appear to be empty, or at least abandoned.

Christina does a quick head twitch look around, seeing nothing but figments of imagination in the windows. But imag-ination shape-shifts mice to werewolves and back again.

"Hang on," says Cass as he walks towards a pile of slag near the stairs and doorway to one of the buildings. Nervously, Christina follows, picking his way through the trash and bot-tles on the balls of his feet, the heels scrabbling for purchase amid the chunks of the pavement.

Cass addresses the gray, shadow-clad heap.

"Yo, you know where there's a shelter around here?"

Christina goggles at him. "What the fuck are you doing? There's nobody there."

Cass ignores him and stares at the heap.

Christina turns and decides to go it alone when a voice that seems to be using barbed wire and poisonous snakes for vocal cords speaks up.

"Da journey man would ask a queschun of him dat see all,

da gospel wh'a him speak, and the scripcha wh'a him lun as a buay and now remba."

"Uhhh, yeah," Cass answers. "What can you tell us about the place?"

The shape shifts and twists, a head rising from the amorphous rags. Its hair (that which there is) sticks straight up or hangs in grease-shellacked hunks. Both eyes are milky, but they focus on Cass. The skin is brown, wrinkled, and desiccated like a crack-addicted walnut.

"You can'na even 'magine wh'a da cost a dis here eran' gone need dee spendin' of." The face pauses and the rags shift, evoking an image of a large bird caught in an oil spill that is trying to ruffle its feathers.

Christina turns and tugs on Cass's sleeve.

"What the fuck's he saying? Is he Jamaican or something?"

"No. And shut up," says Cass, eyes never leaving the living heap wedged into the corner of the stoop. As if prompted, it kicks into life again like a carnival's automated fortune teller.

"You'a al'reddy on dee pat', keep you'a feet tru'a and you'a purpows strang. Keep you'a 'art on you'a task an' you'a han' on you'a blade and you be allri'. Remba wh'a I sed. Go'an whichoo. Keep tru'a."

"What the fuck . . . ?" Christina whispers as he turns to follow Cass, who is already down the street.

"He says we're going the right way," Cass says over one large shoulder.

The sun sinks as the terrain of empty buildings continues strange around them. The only sounds are their heartbeats in their ears, their breath passing their lips, and their footsteps. Christina has given up trying to talk to Cass. Each question was met politely, but tersely.

Ahead of them in the street, a darkness deeper than a project hallway with a blown lightbulb detaches itself from the buildings and spaces between, or seems to rise from the paving stones. As the distance closes, Christina shrinks to Cass, who seems to swell and spread the light that is lacking. As that distance is halved and then quartered, the darkness ahead gives way to individual shapes.

Men.

And in Cass and Christina's road.

One shape takes the angle point of what becomes a wedge-shaped blockade. That shape pushes back the hood of a Raiders sweatshirt that has seen better millennia, never mind days. The exposed face is dark like ebony and smooth like something more. Its voice is loud.

"The fuck you want here?"

Cass shifts weight to both feet and makes his normally impassive face even blanker.

"Just to pass through, we're not here for anything."

"Cass . . ." Christina whimpers.

"Man says, pass through 'n shit, like that's just something you do. Please. Why the fuck we shouldn't just tax your ass?"

"We don't have anything you want."

"What do you got?"

"I just said, nothing."

Christina is starting to mold to Cass tighter or perhaps to hide inside him. Cass shakes a shoulder irritably, trying to dislodge him. Christina stops sticking to him, but a hand remains, holding on to Cass's shirt sleeve.

"Nobody has nothing . . . plus, I think my man back here wants a taste of that thing you got with you . . . Miss Thing over there." He gestures first over his shoulder to a huge man in a very old bubble jacket, and then over Cass's shoulder at Christina. Christina whimpers, but slides a hand into a pocket.

"No," Cass says.

The leader moves forwards to Cass and gets in his face. Cass holds his ground, unmoving. The leader slowly moves a hand towards Cass's pants pocket; a ripple goes through the mass of men behind him. Cass feels a hand searching his pocket, and when it feels like the leader has his hand good and deep, he clamps his own hand down over the wrist and holds it there. The leader tries to pull away stupidly, giving Cass the delay he needs to clamp his other hand on the back of the man's neck and hold him while he whips his head forwards. There is a crack and a soft yielding as the man staggers back, screaming and clutching his face. Cass's hand flies under his shirt and behind his belt buckle. He lifts out something old, and steps forwards while the leader has his eyes behind his hands. Cass slams the object into his chest. The body folds, caves, and becomes slightly less so, doing a full-on marionette slump all the way down to stillness.

Cass looks at the group, and gestures at the body.

"There's your tax."

The mass falls upon the body, now gone from alpha to beta, ripping and twisting, clothing stripped and pockets gone through. In the resulting chaos, Cass and Christina move on while the moon rises higher and decorates the dome of the sky.

"Cass . . ." Christina trembles, voice shaking.

Cass grunts by way of answer and acknowledgment.

"Is that guy . . . ?"

"If not just then"—Cass lifts his right hand in a fist and opens it abruptly, fingers spread—"by now for certain."

"Oh."

They walk.

The buildings grow less whole. If the pair could run fast enough, the city might decay around them like flip-book animation. The streetlights would fade and burst one after another. And so it seems, because light flees to hide in the shadows. Finally, each walk to the next streetlight becomes like several lights at the end of several tunnels.

In the distance something shakes and moves, passing through a pool of light like a shark moving too close to the surface. A block before it reaches the pair, it reveals itself to be a long white Cadillac.

Christina starts to slink towards the side of the road, near the buildings, when Cass shoots out a hand and wraps it around his upper arm, holding him in place.

"Don't run, they'll only chase."

Christina shakes, but stands. Then when Cass prompts, they both begin walking again. Little by little the car and the pair get closer, until finally it stops moving. When their feet carries them parallel with the car, the back window rolls down with a whirring noise, morphed in the silence from a whisper to a shout. Sly and the Family Stone's "Everyday People" sprays from the stereo.

Cass stops and holds Christina close to his side, his grip the same.

"What you got there, soldier?" a voice from inside the car asks. A voice that sounds like nothing at all.

"I don't have anything," Cass answers, the hand holding Christina tenses as he tries halfheartedly to bolt.

"That's not true. I think you better put it in my car."

"What? This?" Cass asks, shaking the arm holding Christina.

"It'd make a nice addition to my stable."

"Since when does a pimp in this place," Cass says, his free hand making an all-encompassing gesture, "run boys?"

Christina squawks and tries to pull free.

"I run it all, soldier, now put that pretty little piece in my car."

"What are you offering?"

"It gets in the car, and you don't go in the trunk."

Cass pauses and looks at Christina, who meets his eyes unflinchingly. Exactly what Cass needs to see.

"No," Cass says, turning to go. He feels, less than hears, Christina sigh.

"Yes," the voice answers, as a barrel pushes itself out of the darkness behind the window.

Cass looks at the gun, and then cranes his head down a little to look into the darkness, only to have his eyes met with nothing. He lifts back up and turns his eyes to the road ahead and lifts the hem of his shirt.

"I'll fight."

"So will I," Christina pipes up.

"You'll die," the voice answers.

"So you'll have nothing but bodies. And I promise, I won't make it easy," Cass says.

Silence answers from the window. The barrel goes back inside. A hand reaches out, manicured, adorned with rings. The smallest finger sports an elongated nail. Between the rest of the fingers is pinched a folded wad of cash.

"My second offer. Put the slip in the car."

Cass looks at the money for a moment and then turns away. He drops the hem of his shirt and the pair moves on, leaving the car behind them. Cass waits for the shout, or the shot, or the movement of the car. But none comes. What he does not do is look over his shoulder to check. He just walks, and after a few feet he says to Christina, "So, you'll fight, huh?"

Christina lifts his head defiantly.

Cass snorts and releases his arm, letting him walk on his own.

The road stretches.

Slowly, whether it's dawn, or functioning streetlights, the world gets brighter. Cass looks around him and sees that some of the buildings sport lights, some of them are even whole. Towards the center of the block is one brownstone far larger than the others. It looks the way city houses must have looked before enterprising landlords chopped them up into apartments. A crowd sits around the entrance to this one. The gathering has the look of a thug's red carpet. Skinny junkies sit alongside iron freaks studded with jail ink, fresh from Gen-Pop. Impassive men in monochrome seem to twitch constantly, hands reaching for the deadly lumps that used to be underneath their clothes. Ladies stand among them, black, white, chicana, and boriqua, each looking like razors dipped in silk and gold.

As Cass and Christina come close, eyes swivel to take them in, but they are still a block away. Cass slows up, and Christina looks at him sideways as he mutters under his breath.

"Fuck." Cass's hand twitches to be filled and it rests just on the outside of his clothes near his belt.

"It's okay," Christina says, placing a hand on his arm and shaking it a little.

"The fuck you mean, 'It's okay'?" Cass asks.

"This is the place."

Cass looks again, sees the building is in good shape, that this isn't just another pimp/hitman/crack house sitting in the middle of the squats like a hornet's nest in the swamp, spewing out fast-moving danger. As they draw closer, Cass sees that there is nothing aimed at them. No guns, no knives, and not even a look. They are watched, but the eyes seem to look at them, and then beyond them, like there is another image to see.

Cass hangs back, unsure. Christina, for once, is ahead and is already heading up the stairs when he looks back at Cass's hesitant form.

"It's okay," says Christina. "This place is safe. I know people here."

"I did what you asked. I got you here. What else is there?"

Cass is looking at Christina, noticing that there is nothing of the boy-victim in Christina's eyes now. Christina watches him a little before answering.

"You might as well come in and rest, get a cup of coffee."

Then Christina sniffs—very meaningfully and very fey. "A shower?"

Cass looks around at the crowd and then realizes what is so odd about the whole scene. The crowd is totally silent. Nobody is talking shit, nobody is posturing, hitting on the women. Nothing.

Cass looks up at Christina again, who throws up his hands and flounces back down the stairs. He grabs Cass by one arm and walks him up the stairs to the entrance.

"C'mon, it's not a big deal. Besides, you helped me out, maybe these people can give you some clean clothes or something to eat."

"A drink?" Cass asks, remembering the empty bottles by his bedside.

"We'll see," Christina says noncommittally as they enter through the open archway. As they pass, a collective sigh goes up from the group behind them.

The front room holds nothing beyond a large, graffiti-scarred wooden desk. Cass eyes the room, right hand straying close to his belt buckle, the other held a little ways from his body in an absent warding gesture. Christina, moving with a confidence that Cass sees for the first time, walks straight up to the desk. Cass leans with his back against the desk so that he can see the whole room. He looks over his right shoulder and down to see the book set on the desk. Christina is busily writing his name into it with a cheap ballpoint pen that's attached to some dog-eared packing twine with a piece of lint-crusted duct tape.

"Christian?" asks Cass.

"Parents," Christina answers.

"So . . ." Cass trails off, the question audible in his tone.

"They gave me the other one when they saw what I was," he says again, his tone dull. He steps away from the book and gestures for Cass.

"I ain't signing shit," Cass says, looking around the room again.

"You have to or we can't go in," Christina says.

Cass sees that there are two doors leading out of the room. They're currently shut. Cass looks at Christina and defiantly walks to one of the doors and gives the handle a no-bullshit jerk. The door doesn't even flex on its hinges. He looks at the door again, then walks to the other across the room and pulls. Same.

"Told you," Christina says, mouth twisting into a smirk.

Cass shrugs as if he was never really concerned, walks over to the desk, and signs the registry.

"Cass?" Christina says.

"Yeah?"

"That's it? Just 'Cass'?"

"Yeah."

"No last name?"

"Forgot it."

Christina looks like he's going to push the issue when the right-side door swings open and in walks a stone-faced woman, gray hair done up in dreads. They're bound at the back of her head with a blue bandanna. One lock has escaped and is hanging down the side of her face. Her face looks as open as the two doors had been. It's decorated with a nose and eyebrow piercing; one side sporting a faded tribal tattoo. It looks like the years must have been rough. Looks like she'd been rougher.

"What," she says. She doesn't ask. She doesn't exclaim.

"I was told to come here if I needed to get tested. I need to get checked out. I was raped last night." Christina says it the way you'd explain something that happened to you years ago.

"Who's that?" the woman says, indicating Cass without actually looking at him, using a hand missing two fingers.

"He helped me get here in one piece."

"Okay. Follow me," she says.

Christina starts to walk, and then turns to check on Cass, who hasn't moved.

Christina widens his eyes, and impatiently gestures at Cass to follow. Cass starts forwards, getting almost to the door before the woman turns and acknowledges Cass for the first time.

"You can't bring weapons in here."

Cass does his best puzzled look.

"I'm not."

The woman just looks at him, then she extends her right hand, palm up, her left arm crossed, the left hand resting in the crook of the right.

"You look like the kind of guy who hasn't been unarmed since he was in utero, and even then I'm sure you were trying to figure out a way to strangle something with your cord."

Cass looks at her a minute, then lifts the hem of his shirt and places the object in her hand, holding on to his end for a moment.

"Nobody is born like that," Cass says, holding her eyes, "and I want that back."

They both look down at the sharpened screwdriver that Cass always carries. When he looks up, she is watching him, and smiling.

"Point," she says, and turns around to lead them through the door.

The three walk into the next room, with its humans standing in clumps that probably should have been lines. The nature of the place gave organization the finger.

A woman with two children rests against one wall, their burns conspicuous against otherwise beautiful, coffee with cream skin. The wounds look fresh. Cass guesses that this place was probably closer than the hospital. The woman would push herself from the wall and yell for somebody to come help them. Cass thinks to himself *good luck*—but to his shock, somebody comes right over with rolls of gauze, disinfectant, and tubes of something. Cass isn't sure if it's going to be enough, but at least they are being helped. He looks away, and the person that ran to the family's aid was getting one of the kids to uncertainly smile and then giggle.

Just as Cass is looking away, Christina grabs his sleeve and tugs him along.

"Take a seat here," the woman with dreads tells the pair and walks away.

"Thanks, Izabel," answers Christina.

"Izabel?" Cass turns to Christina. "You know these people already?"

"She introduced herself while you were staring off into space," Christina answers.

"This place is strange."

"Why?"

"People here are getting help, that's unusual for a shelter."

"It's not exactly a shelter," Christina says.

"What do you—?" Cass starts just as Izabel returns and beckons to them. Christina jumps up and tugs Cass along by the arm.

They are taken into a different room, where Izabel moves to sit behind a weather and God-knows-what-else beaten school desk. She takes some forms from a drawer. When she sees the pair still standing, she waves impatiently to two chairs on the supplicant side of the desk. The pair sit. Izabel tries unsuccessfully to get her pen to work before fishing inside the desk for another.

Izabel turns to Christina.

"Name?"

Christina answers.

"Reason for being here?"

Cass listens to Christina answer in a monotone, and watches Izabel being impassive. Because he's heard enough nightmares, and seen plenty of people who didn't react to them, he wanders off to look at the rest of the shelter.

He ducks through the doorway, briefly looks over one large shoulder to check if his leaving is noticed or if it even matters, and sees Christina and Izabel talking to each other, absorbed. So he turns left and collides chest to chest with a dead man.

Cass jumps back from the unexpected contact and his hands raise up a little, his right twitches towards the now vacant spot behind his belt.

While his hands and body do the automatic, his jaw drops when he recognizes the face.

"Scabs?"

The man just looks at Cass and smiles.

"But, I saw . . ." Cass remembers the night years ago when the kids had come through the squats. Kids, yes, but in adult bodies, and looking for fun without consequence. Harsh young men with mean habits. Scabs had tried to get them to share. Scabs, being the kind that was looking to get whatever he could into his body, hadn't been thinking. He was probably still not thinking when the last boot had fallen on his twitching corpse. But here he is in front of Cass. Whole.

Scabs just smiles at Cass again, his eyes unfocused, vague.

Cass stares at him and says: "So you made it after all? What did you do? Come all the way here? Somebody help you?"

Scabs just smiles, and pats Cass on the shoulder as he moves past him and around another corner leaving Cass to stand in the hallway.

Cass shakes his head, says to himself, "Brain damage is a bitch."

Cass keeps going into the central room, crowded with faces and stories all fighting for validation. Harried workers, distinguished by their focused looks, dart among them, passing one so they can be free to help another. Cass walks towards a staircase near one corner, expecting to be turned back at any second, but he isn't. Even when his feet touch the bottom step, and then eventually the top landing, he is ignored.

On the second floor quiet spreads out, rising like heat from the noise below. On this floor, rooms flow off the main hall, each lacking a door, each empty until he comes upon the last room on the right. He looks in and sees a young boy sitting on the edge of a bed, at the boy's feet is a man hunched over. As Cass leans further into the room, he can see that the man is lacing the boy's shoes. Cass sees the boy's face, and recognizes him from years ago, when he had beaten a man to death to save the boy from violation; the kid hadn't changed a bit. He looks up at Cass, this time with none of the animal fear in his eyes that was there the last time. Cass raises a hand, palm out, and the boy smiles shyly in answer. Cass turns his head and looks at the man.

And looks into the face of a man he had beaten to death those years ago.

The face of a man bent on raping a child.

The man's eyes are as empty as Scabs's. His hand pauses around the boy's feet, still gripping the weathered sneakers. The same hands that had held the boy's head down as he fumbled at his belt, now tie the boy's shoelaces. Cass roars and bowls the man over, slamming him into the corner, upsetting a table with a crash. Cass levers his shin and knee across the man's hips, his weight pinning him in the corner. His left hand twists in the neckline of his shirt, his right crashes into his face, once, twice, three times.

With no visible effect.

Cass keeps hitting; he switches hands, he stands and stomps, down heels leading, and while he can feel his hands and feet hitting something solid, the man just stares at him and does nothing. There is no blood, the man's face is whole, his body does not rock with the impact.

Cass stands and stops hitting. His breath comes in heaves and chokes. His victim still hasn't moved, and when Cass feels a light pressure on his arm, he whirls and sees the boy there, watching him and smiling. Cass turns fully to regard the boy when the man, from his place in the corner, scurries around Cass and hides behind the child, cowering.

Cass reaches to move the boy aside and have a fresh crack at the rapist but the boy won't move.

"What the fuck is going on here?" Cass says in a loud voice to nobody in particular.

"If you're finished flexing, I can explain it," Izabel says from the doorway. Behind her Christina looks on.

Cass points at the man behind the child. "He's a rapist. Of children."

"We know," says Izabel.

"I beat him to death three years ago."

"Oh? Was that you?" Izabel says.

"He was trying to rape him," Cass says, pointing first at the man and then the boy. "He's supposed to be dead."

"He is," Izabel says.

"What?" Cass hears his voice rising as he moves further from his normal self-control.

"Come downstairs," Izabel says.

"Not leaving him alone with the boy. What the fuck's wrong with you people?"

"Charles is fine. Perfectly safe."

"If you motherfuckers are pimping kids out of this fucking place, I swear to God!" Cass yells.

"Downstairs. Now." Izabel's voice is its normal, even tone as she turns and walks away.

Cass, at a loss of what else to do, follows.

Downstairs, somebody has placed a cup of coffee between Cass's fingers, which he clutches like a prayer.

Izabel watches him. The way in which she does is not one that Cass could remember seeing for some time. Appraisal without fear. A look that had not been turned on Cass in the fifteen odd years since he got his growth.

Christina sits off to one side, watching Cass, but with every inch of the fear that is absent from Izabel.

Cass looks up from the steam hovering over his cup. "What the fuck is going on here?"

"You're dead."

Cass shifts, the balls of his feet touching down, grinding into the floor, ready. "You're going to press charges for a piece of shit like that? Besides he's not even hurt."

"No, I mean that you are currently dead."

"Right . . ." He looks up at Christina.

"These people of yours are fuckin' nuts. You want to stay? Cool, hang out with the cult. I hear the Kool-Aid"—Cass looks down at his hands, still gripping the cooling coffee, and adds—"or in this case the coffee, is great."

"Cass . . ." Christina starts.

"I'm fucking out of here."

"How else do you explain what you've seen here?"

"That I spend most of my free time drinking, and that it's bound to have some effect on my mental state. I just didn't expect it so soon."

"You've seen two dead men here. And you know it to be true," Izabel says.

"Maybe I wasn't as enthusiastic as I thought with the child-fucker."

"What about your friend in the hallway?"

"That junkie retard was never a friend of mine. How the fuck do you know that anyway?"

Cass stands up and walks towards the doorway.

"There's nothing out there."

"I'm going back home."

"You're past that point, all that waits out there are circles and jackals."

"That's different for me how?" Cass asks, looking behind him at the blue eyes between the dreadlocks, now unbound and framing the severe face.

"You died last night. Alcohol poisoning. In two days your body will start to stink with enough rot for some of your neighbors to move and lean against another warehouse."

"I didn't drink enough last night for that." But as Cass tries to bring up a memory he finds himself reaching for things with less substance than the steam rising from his coffee.

"Yes. You did," Izabel says.

"And him?" Cass asks, pointing at Christina.

"A guide."

"Seems to me, I did most of the guiding. I killed to get him here."

"A guide still, and a toll."

"A toll?" Cass looks at Christina who still looks as fey and as slender as earlier, but has lost the defenselessness. Has lost the softness—and his eyes weren't tough—more like ageless now.

"Your task. Your burden. Your price of entry. The man upstairs? The one you killed? He is doing the same. The boy that was once his prey is now his master in a sense. He serves as you have served."

"And the men I fought to get here? The people I spoke with?"

"Demons, supplicants, and lost souls."

"And this is 'heaven'?" Cass's voice is heavy with sarcasm.

"It's a way station, and one that has to make sense to the people passing through it. This is what your life held. This is what your transition of life resembles."

"Fuck this," Cass says and turns to walk out. He gets as far as the front room. The doorway that leads outside opens in his hand. Outside, the occupiers of the stoop stare in hungrily. But not at Cass. They look into the shelter as if eyes could salivate and not have it mistaken for tears. Cass stops. He hears Christina's voice behind him.

"Out there is nothing. You'll be fighting and running every day. There won't be any change for you."

Cass looks at him. Christina standing hip shot, body saying *fuck you*, eyes saying *please don't go*.

"I did what I told you I'd do. I'll take my chances out there."

He turns his gaze to regard Izabel, who has come to stand sedately beside Christina.

"She gets it," Cass says, nodding his head to Izabel.

"He's new," Izabel says, regarding Christina.

He looks at Christina again and feels compelled to speak. Thinking as he did that he spent more words this day than in a lot of days before. "I lived in the squats because it was a choice. I'm not about to go back to letting other people choose now."

"But there's nothing out there, this is all for you to step through."

"When I believe that, I'll have another choice."

He sees Izabel nod to herself.

Cass holds out a hand to Christina. Christina places his hand lightly in it. Cass squeezes and then holds his palm out to Izabel. Instead of shaking it, she places Cass's screwdriver in it, handle first.

Cass nods, tucks it behind his belt buckle, and walks back outside.

Mr. Universe

Glenn Gray

I know it. If it weren't for the humongous juice dosages I woulda been Mr. Universe. I mean, if not Mr. U then something pretty close, like maybe Mr. A. I had it all, the genetics, the proportion—and I could pose like a professional dancer. Not like some faggot, but I mean I could flow through the moves like honey in slow motion pouring from a bottle. I was on my way.

Then friggin 'roid rage.

And just because I killed my best friend with my bare hands don't make me all that bad a guy either. It was the shit. Christ, I loved the guy like a brother.

We're in the locker room at Iron Plate Gym, me and my best friend Stevie, all revved up 'cause we just got our first juice delivery from Big Bobby. Fuckin' Bobby and his white '79 Corvette. Never knew how that guy with twenty-two-inch guns fit in that thing anyway.

Big Bobby handed me a crumpled paper bag with a few boxes of Deca and a bottle of D-bol tabs and said, "You're on your own," and went to work out. He threw in a few darts so we'd be ready to start right away. Big sport.

We're staring at all this gear in the bag and I'm thinking that this was it, that I'm gonna be in the big time now. That's right. I was primed to get huge like the other freaky gym monsters. Only bigger.

Stevie fishes out a syringe and I pull out a box of Deca. I howl and say, "Look," as I chomp off the top of the cardboard box and dump the vial into my hand, spitting the wet flap onto the floor. We're carrying on like two friggin' kids.

I pinch the glass up to the light and say, "Breakfast of champions," and we both bust out and do a high five. Joey Napoli walks in and looks at us, so we cool out. We go into the small bathroom, barely big enough for two guys on their way to the kingdom of huge.

I grab the dart from Stevie, peel open the wrapper, and pop off the needle cap. I snatch a bottle of rubbing alcohol from my gym bag and splash some on toilet paper and wipe the rubber top of the vial. I stick the needle in, turn it upside down, and suck out the full 2 cc's of oily stuff.

I say, "Me first."

Stevie says, "Fine," and then he says, "Dude, I ain't shootin' your ass."

I call him a pussy and say, "I'll do it myself." I face the sink and undo my sweatpants. I let them drop to expose my glutes.

I wipe my skin with alcohol, lean on the porcelain with one hand, and say, "Bombs away," then plunge the spike, push down hard, forcing the Deca into my ass muscle. It stings a little and I could swear the juice started to work right then and there—but I know it ain't so.

I felt like my life had changed somehow, like I was in some new exclusive club. I guess I was. At the time I thought the change was for the better, but little did I know it was the beginning of the friggin' end.

* * *

One time me and Stevie meet this older guy at the gym; his name is Richard and he tells us if we want to really be cool we should get into Manhattan and forget about all this Long Island suburban crap. They're all losers out there, he says.

I think, *Whatever,* but I have a feeling this guy is weird and one night we go into the city, a place downtown in the West Village. I forget the name. It don't matter and all I remember is people screwing around all over in these dark concrete chambers. I was like, friggin', yeah.

It was some sex club and you had to be a member and this guy Rich just showed a card at the door and the bouncer said, "Go 'head, boys." Guess he'd been there before.

There was this amazon chick in shiny leather pulling a guy around on a leash and he's licking her black spiked boots and she's kicking him and he just keeps apologizing. Man, what a pussy the guy was.

Me and Stevie look at each other and almost at the same time we say, "What the fuck?" And then we just start cracking up. Richard glares at us like we should chill out or something. Like we're breakin' the rules or some shit.

Another naked lady has her hands tied to a wood beam above her head and this guy in a mask is whipping her. He's got the littlest dick around, like a turtle head poking out from his fat sack. Not that I was lookin' or anything. This lady moans in the dark and then he rams her with the handle of the whip. She lifts her legs off the ground like she's riding a Jet Ski and screams so loud it hurts my ears.

After a couple beers I gotta go to the can, so I weave my way through the stone chambers and smoky haze, like I'm exploring some ancient tomb or something. In slashes of light, I see this skinny guy wearing only cowboy boots lounging inside one of those long urinals like he's at the beach, one leg draped over the side. And he's loving it.

I stood in the shadows, eyes burning with the smell of urine and smoke, thinking, *What the fuck?* I watched two guys finish spraying the cowboy with piss like they're putting out a fire. He rubbed it in like lotion and groaned and said, "Next."

He's lookin' at me and smiling—and I really had to go, so I ended up taking a whiz on his boots.

After a few months of juicing like an animal, I'm getting huge and Stevie slows down on his shit and tells me, "Maybe you should cool it for a while."

I tell him, "No way," 'cause I'm getting jacked and I want to enter a show. Probably the Mr. Long Island to start things off.

Stevie says, "What about college?"

I say, "Screw that." I keep training and training and getting bigger and bigger.

Stevie is getting ready to go to college. Mr. Frat Boy. I got my eye on the Mr. Teen USA contest the August after graduation in Venice Beach, California.

Somebody tells me that Venice is the mecca of all bodybuilding and that fires me up even more.

California, here I come.

Another time, a group of us cut school on a freaky warm April day. We hop in Stevie's Chevelle and cruise over to Jones Beach.

We packed a cooler full of Bud quickies we picked up at 7-Eleven. Sherrie and Michele were in the car with us—Michele with her blond hair falling over her shoulders, smelling like goddamn spring flowers or something. I knew that Stevie liked Michele 'cause she was much hotter than Sherrie, but Michele liked me and it was obvious. She kept saying things to me like, "Wow, you're getting so big," and, "I love your muscles," as she scraped her spike-like fingernails across my forearm hair.

I could see Stevie out the corner of my eye with that stupid look on his face.

I don't like to say it, but Stevie just didn't have what I had, you know? Even though he was my best friend and all, he just didn't have good genetics, I guess. You need the genetics to win shows. That's what I read in *Iron Man* mag.

And even though he juiced for a while it didn't seem to do anything. Me, I just got bigger and people told me I could probably win a big show some day. I already knew that though.

When we get to the beach, we spread out a towel and blast some Van Halen and kick back. That was when I told Stevie I was gonna go to California after graduation.

He says, "That's stupid, dude."

I say, "Really?" Right then I wanted to punch him, hard. He was leaning back on the towel, hands behind his head, like he had everything under control, like some wise old man.

He started telling me about all the college crap and says, "What're you gonna do? Be a muscle man?" And how was I gonna make money and all that.

Like all of a sudden he's got some attitude like he's better or something, like he's gonna be some doctor or lawyer. Guy's clueless.

So it was great 'cause right then Michele comes jogging up to the towel with her tits bouncing in her tube top, nipples hard, and says to me, all flirty like, she says, "Come down to the water, hot stuff." In my head I was laughing like crazy.

She has her hand out, so I take it and she pulls me up.

As we saunter away hand in hand, I turn back to Stevie and he's got that stupid smirk on his face again.

I'm smiling, feeling like a pig in shit.

Things were going pretty much as planned with the California trip and all, except me and Michele were getting kinda tight and she was getting a bit latchy. I could never understand these chicks.

The whole thing was starting to get on my nerves 'cause I had big plans, you know? To be Mr. Universe. I didn't need some whiny chick getting in my face.

She says things like, "You know you're taking this muscle stuff a little too serious," and, "You're still taking that shit, 'cause I think your balls are getting like little grapes."

When she said that last thing I let the back of my hand sort of slide across her face, not really like a hard slap, but she took it that way, her face getting all red and splotchy. And all the crying. Man, it was crazy. I'm lookin' around, rolling my eyes.

I said I didn't mean it. It just happened, like a little switch in my skull clicked or something. I knew the juice was fucking with my head.

She just cried.

And then she really pissed me off 'cause she said, "Why can't you be more like Stevie?"

I lost it.

Lucky I didn't hit her because my fist smashed right through the Sheetrock wall in my basement.

The next time I go to the city with Richard, it's just me and him. Stevie says he has to study. We end up back in Greenwich Village. I was like, whatever.

We're in this smoky bar and two guys are making out and I say to Richard, "The heck is that?" These guys were like hairy and shit and had some muscle and it just didn't look right.

He says, "The city, just the way it is."

We leave that place 'cause he says I got all quiet, and I was. I was trying to make sense of the shit I was seeing.

So he takes me to another place that's more of a disco club and there are some chicks, but they're making out too. Hot chicks no less.

Rich just smiles, shrugs.

I say, "I'm outta here."

After a while, Stevie stops training altogether 'cause he says he's got some other stuff to focus on and why don't I chill too. Take a break. And I'm thinking, yeah, right.

I'm bigger than ever and my neck feels like it's gonna explode out of every shirt I wear. My thighs rub together on the inside 'cause they're like two tree trunks, and I got cuts and veins running all over my body like lightning bolts.

I up the juice dosages 'cause I figure it's three months to the show in California and I wanna peak out right on time.

I start cutting some classes at school, but it doesn't matter 'cause it's the end of the year and I got better things planned anyway. Like I'm ever gonna need the crap I'm learning.

I'm gonna be Mr. Universe someday.

I'm right on target for huge success as I see it, but nobody sees it like I do. I feel like I'm living in my own little world. Everyone else is just putzing along.

It's going great until Michele calls me and she tells me she's pregnant.

One time near the end of all this I'm at Richard's house and we smoke a joint, suck down some beers, and were cranking Led Zeppelin.

He takes out a sandwich baggie and it's got a lot of different colored pills in it. He pulls out a red one and says, "Take this, it'll really relax you."

I ask what it is and he says, "A downer."

I shrug and take it. Not long after, I'm feeling really groggy and weird but it's kinda cool.

Richard falls back on his bed, looking at the ceiling, and says, "Man, I know a way a stud like you can make a lot of money."

I say, "Really?"

He starts telling me about how muscle dudes can go into the city and pose for guys and get paid tons of cash.

I say that sounds kinda fucked and he says, "No, it's cool."

I'm really starting to feel funny and he says, "Try it, take off your clothes. I'll show you."

I stand up, thinking I gotta get out of there, and he says, "Where you going?"

I step back. He hops up and walks towards me, smiling. I see this big happy mug headed my way, a weird look on his face, just like I thought all along.

The last thing I remember is his hand cupping my nuts before the switch clicked.

When I can see straight again, he's crumpled on the floor with a bloody face staring up at me and he's breathing funny and trying to talk.

I just say, "What the fuck?"

I don't remember driving home.

Michele actually says, "What if we had it?"

I say, "You gotta be kidding."

She says, "We'd be a family."

I start telling her about how there's no way a guy like me can have a baby now, at this age, especially with all the plans I had. I'm thinking to myself, *Can she really be serious?*

I ask her what is she gonna do when I go to California in a couple months and she says, "Yeah, right."

I tell her we gotta get this situation taken care of pronto and she cries and says, "No way," and jumps right out of my car at a stoplight.

I have to roll alongside her in the car for about a mile before she gets back in. With a face like a rock-hard boulder, staring straight ahead, she says, "Fine."

*　　*　　*

Not long after that, Mrs. Cartwright from the main office pokes her stupid head into my English class and says there's a phone call for me. I figure it must be serious, 'cause no one ever gets a phone call like that at school.

When I pick it up it's my mom. She says, "Come right home after school."

I ask her why and she says to just do it and her voice sounds funny. I'm thinking, *okay, this is weird.*

When I get home she leads me to her bedroom where she's got all my 'roids scattered out on her bed. She's got the pills and the vials and all the syringes spread out. She's got tears in her eyes and she says, "What's this stuff?"

I smile 'cause I know what she's thinking. She found my stash. Before I can answer, she says, "Well, what is it, uppers or downers or what?"

I chime right in, grinning, "Yeah, and sidewaysers too."

She doesn't like that and bursts out crying. I tell her to calm down and then I tell her about the juice and how it's really a good thing. That she should be lucky that I'm not doing hard-core shit. And how come she's going through my stuff anyway?

She tells me to just wait until my father gets home.

When he walks through the door, my mom tells him the story. He comes to me, and as he throws his hardhat onto the chair, says, "Wipe the grin off your mug."

I say, "What grin?" and I can see he's had a crappy day.

He says, "You're a fuckup." He starts to swing at me and I duck.

The switch clicks.

My head spins and things just happen. I clock him on the side of the head, and he falls back into my mom. They both crash onto a desk and end up on the floor. Shit.

I scoop up the 'roids and bolt.

* * *

I jump into my '76 Monte Carlo and tear down the street, tires screeching.

I don't even know where I'm going.

I slide a Black Sabbath cassette into the player and Ozzy is yelling and I crank up the volume and the speakers are thumping and I can't believe I just smacked my old man.

I swerve onto the main strip near my house and some guy cuts me off. In a fuckin' Pacer no less. He doesn't even wave or anything, and this pisses me off. I speed up, getting alongside this guy. He knows I'm right there and he doesn't look at me, just stares straight ahead and we're going faster and faster.

I lean over and crank down the window, almost losing control and the wind is blowing in my face. I yell, "Hey, douchebag," and he just ignores me.

I pull closer to him and start running him to the curb—now he starts honking and he slows down 'cause he has no choice. Then I see him take a sideways glance at me.

He's starting to shit in his pants.

We finally come to a halt and I jump out of the car, running around the front towards him. Now he looks like a chickenshit. He's got a pencil neck. He throws it in reverse and slams a parked car before he speeds away, smashing a couple garbage cans in the process.

I do a loud, *"Yee-haa,"* and yell full-out, *"That's right a-wipe."*

I slide back in my car, feeling pumped, and decide to go over Stevie's.

When I get to Stevie's, I see that Michele's car is parked out front and I wonder what the fuck is going on.

I make my way around to the side door that leads to the basement where Stevie's room is and I let myself in. My head is really hot now and I feel like I got a wicked headache. My heart is racing like never before and my body feels like it's tingling.

When I get to the bottom of the stairs, I see the two of them sitting on the bed and Stevie's hugging Michele. What are they, like long-time lovers? They both see me and turn and jump and Michele starts right in saying, really fast, "We were just talking," and, "I needed somebody to talk to."

Stevie is saying, "Hey, man, what's up?" And, "It's not how it looks." And he's got that stupid smirk on his face.

It was the smirk that really did it for me.

And the switch goes off.

The switch has a loud bang and I swear, this time, I can actually hear the sound like a sonic boom. *Boom Sheeeesh.*

The rest is a blur.

Later, Michele tells people how she never saw a person pick someone up by the neck with one hand, only in cartoons. And she never, ever, saw a look like the one I had in my eyes.

She flew out of the room screaming and got help. Nobody saw what happened next, not even me, 'cause I don't remember anything, just the click and then the white flash.

All they know is that when the police came in, I was sobbing and had Stevie's dead body draped across my lap.

They say I was mumbling something to him and rocking him like a baby.

Green Gables

Dana King

Harvey Hastert's story is about a woman. Call her what you want: a dame, a broad, a skirt, a tomato, a babe. Just not a frail. This one was definitely not a frail.

Harvey made a mint selling equipment that fell off the backs of Patton's trucks driving across France and Germany, earning ten times his military pay on the black market by January of '46. Any normal crook would have sold his sister to a Tijuana impresario to stay in Germany. Harvey only saw homesick soldiers tired of occupation duty, agitating for a ticket on the next boat stateside. And if someone else wanted it, Harvey had to have it.

That's how he got his extra Luger. The first one was mint: Harvey took it off a dead SS officer when he stole the guy's Iron Cross. He was showing it off to Luther Brumm when he noticed little Shep Hickey nosing around a couple of dead Krauts. Shep was from Kentucky—such a 'billy, he showed up at the induction station in his bare feet. His daddy told him the Army will give you boots, boy, leave your'n here. Kid so shy he even stammered on words that started with S. Harvey went to check out what interested Shep and saw the other Luger still in one Kraut's hand. The gun was in Harvey's pocket ten seconds later, Shep sniffing around like a kid with his candy stolen.

So Harvey's nature called him home, just because everyone else wanted to go. Got him involved in one of those demobilization riots the Army doesn't talk about, American soldiers in the streets all over the world, wanting to go home. California wasn't even home enough for some of them; they rioted there too.

Harvey lucked out at his court-martial. He'd been so busy stealing stuff he didn't realize he had enough points to go home if he'd kept his mouth shut. The Army had plenty to do without providing three hots and a cot for a malcontent they were going to ship out anyway. They traded his stripes for a general discharge and called it even.

Harvey started going to the Green Gables Ballroom in West Mifflin a month after he got back. No pressure to look for a job, he could live a couple years off what he brought back if he didn't spread it around too much. Kept wearing the uniform, general discharge be damned. Made him look like he was fresh off the boat. The girls liked that and Harvey was tired of paying for it. Every fräulein he knew was on the make for something: cigarettes, food, even chocolate. Harvey screwed a girl in Stuttgart once for a can of Heinz ketchup and a Hershey's bar he'd stolen out of a POW's Red Cross package.

The skirts loved medals. The court-martial killed his chance for a Good Conduct, but Harvey still had a unit decoration and an ARCOM he got for moving more diesel farther and faster than any other supply sergeant. The medal was a bonus; Harvey made five hundred bucks profit on the champagne and scotch he had stashed in the trucks. The Bronze Star he filched when its rightful owner stepped on a mine was gravy.

Harvey went to the Green Gables two or three nights a

week. He didn't mind spending money on the girls and he had a lot more of it than most GIs coming home. Harvey was cooling, considering his options. The end of the war freed up a lot of money. Schmucks were climbing over each other to work for it. Harvey only had to find a way to pick up what fell through their fingers.

The first time he saw her was a Thursday night, May 9th. Good-looking, not a knockout. Nice figure, brunette hair cut in a bob. Every time her dance partner twirled her, the polka-dot dress showed more thigh than the Hayes Office would let you see in a movie.

She didn't lack for partners. A dance or two with one guy, then one with another. She doled out slow dances like water in Death Valley, never ignoring anyone so much he'd lose interest.

There were ten girls as pretty in the Green Gables every night. This one had more. Call it charisma, an indefinable something that attracted men even if they knew it was a bad idea. Her sugar drew them like bees. Harvey had to have her.

He moved like smoke through her admirers, not waiting his turn, not quite cutting the line. When he got his dance, he saw she wasn't as tall as he'd thought, and her nose was bigger. She still wore that aura like perfume.

Her name was Stella Postelwaithe. "Like Stella Dallas," she told Harvey.

"Who?"

"You know. Like in the movie. Barbara Stanwyck?"

Harvey heard of Barbara Stanwyck. He didn't know Stella Dallas from Stella D'oro. Stella Postelwaithe sounded like some stuck-up society dame, which this one definitely was not. Hers wasn't the kind of class money bought. Stella wore it like the polka-dot dress: a nice introduction, but the real attraction was the possibility of seeing her without it.

Just two dances that first night. Stella made a pout when the second ended. "I have to go," she said. "I come here every Thursday night." She leaned in and pecked Harvey's cheek like he was her brother. Not quite like a brother. Second cousin, maybe.

She left with an older guy, a heavyset stiff in an expensive suit who looked like he might be a gimp. Hard to say for all Harvey saw of him. Her leaving with him made Harvey want Stella even more.

He made appearances Saturday night and the next Tuesday. He took a girl home on Tuesday and thought of Stella. Spent all day Wednesday and Thursday thinking about Thursday night.

He got to the Green Gables earlier than usual with no desire to be part of her entourage. Once Harvey knew what he wanted, knew what the others wanted, he knew how to get it. Too fast and she'd see it coming and string him along. He'd play Stella Postelwaithe like the prize fish in the pond. Which she was.

They met at the Green Gables six weeks running. Each time they danced more, and each time she left with the fat guy. He seemed fatter every time Harvey watched Stella leave with him. Definitely a gimp. Must be loaded too. Just walked in and Stella would finish that dance and beg off for the night.

Harvey asked about him on the fourth Thursday. Stella put him off. He pressed a little the next time and a little more the week after that. Each time she put him off with less enthusiasm.

The seventh Thursday was June 20th. Harvey remembered because it was his old man's birthday. When Harvey asked her to dance she took him by the arm and said, "Let's get out of here."

He took her to a joint a few blocks away, a nice place where the booze wouldn't break him. Harvey drank highballs; Stella favored gimlets. After the usual banter, Harvey pushed ahead with the sixty-four-dollar question.

"Do we have to talk about him?" Stella said. "This is so nice."

"We have to sooner or later," Harvey said. "It took me six weeks to get you all alone and you still have to be back to meet him at ten thirty. You married, or what?"

"What if I was?"

Harvey gestured to include the whole lounge. "We're here, aren't we? This can go either way. It's up to you."

Stella looked around the dark bar. "Not here. Is there someplace we could go? Close by?"

"Sure. The Green Gables?" Harvey paused for effect. "Or someplace else?"

Stella didn't pause at all. "Someplace else."

So there it was. Harvey knew a flop a few blocks away that didn't advertise the hourly rates in neon. He paid the check and they took a cab. So Stella wouldn't be seen.

No one asked any questions of the single man with no luggage taking a room. Harvey let Stella in a side door. They didn't talk much upstairs, not after the polka-dot dress came off, which was before the light reached every corner of the room. Harvey barely got Stella back to Green Gables in time to meet the gimp. She hadn't even told him the guy's name.

They didn't waste time going to the bar the next week. Harvey brought a hip flask with him and Stella packed a few cosmetics in her purse so she'd look more like a woman flushed from dancing than a cat in heat.

The third week Harvey and Stella were out the side door before the band got all the way through "Come Rain or Come Shine." They knocked off the flask almost as fast as Stella lost her dress.

When the time came to leave, she sat on the edge of the bed with her stockings half up. Harvey stopped knotting his tie when he saw her just sitting there.

"You know I don't want to rush you," he said, "but we have to get a move on."

"I know." Stella pulled a stocking over her knee, hooked it to her garter. Then she started to cry. "I hate this."

"Hate what? We don't have to come here. It's just that it's so close and we don't have much time."

"No, the place is all right." Stella wiped an eye with her wrist. "It's this part I hate. Going back."

"Then don't go. You never said one way or the other, but if this guy's your husband, you're not a fanatic about it. Leave him."

Stella breathed deeply and looked away from Harvey, then back, then away again. "It's my father."

"What about your father?"

"My husband." Stella spit it out like a bad cherry. "He's a big shot in the little town I'm from. Brookville. Ten years ago my father made some bad crop investments and had to mortgage the farm. Things didn't turn around and Dad couldn't pay the note."

Harvey looped the tie around his neck for a second attempt at the knot. "So? This guy run the bank or something?"

"Or something." Stella finished fastening the first stocking. "It was a personal loan. If Dad defaults, title goes to . . . to . . . I don't even want to say his name. God, I hate him!"

Harvey checked the knot in a mirror over the dresser and slid into his jacket. "He'd do that to his father-in-law?"

"Not so long as Dad *is* his father-in-law. That's why I can't leave him." Stella stood and gripped Harvey's arms, rested her head on his chest. "I hate the thought of that slob on top of me, especially after I've been with you. It makes me sick to think what he did while you were winning those medals you wore the first time I saw you."

Harvey grunted something Stella took to mean she should go on.

"His father—he's dead now, thank God, he was as bad as my husband—got him classified 4-F. We'd see them driving their big cars. Always had plenty of gas. Sugar, butter, whatever everyone else had rationed."

"There's nothing you can do?"

"Not while Dad's still alive. He'd have nowhere to go if

David—that's his name, David Postelwaithe—threw him out. I'd lose everything if I left too, but I wouldn't need much. A good man. I could be good for the right man."

Harvey took a second to add things up. He knew there was more here, just not how much. "This sounds pretty dramatic," he said while Stella finished with her stockings and slid that polka-dot dress over her head. "I mean, Mack Sennett would have you tied to the railroad tracks by now."

Stella slapped his face. "You don't believe me? You think it's funny. I made this up as a joke for you? Go to hell." She picked up her purse. "I'm going to be late. Let me out, please."

"Whoa! Slow down." Harvey almost rubbed his face, redirected the hand to take Stella's wrist. "I didn't mean anything by it. You have to admit it's kind of a screwy story to feed someone all at once. Is there something I can do to help?"

Stella smiled, her eyes wet. "You are helping. These little two-hour vacations you give me every Thursday help. You give me something to look forward to for the rest of the week. There's nothing more you can do. It's up to me, since Dad had the stroke. I just have to find some way to get Dad out from under."

They avoided the subject the next Thursday and it hung over them like snow clouds, cold and dismal. Harvey waited until they were almost dressed again before he brought it up.

"How're things with your old man and the farm?"

"The same." Stella kept getting dressed while she answered. "They won't change. The doctor says Dad won't ever get better. He can take care of himself pretty well, but he can't work, and he can't afford to take on any more help. When he dies, the whole farm reverts to . . . him."

"And you." Stella shot Harvey a look. "As the wife, I mean."

"I suppose, though I'll never see the farm again. He'll sell it before Dad's cold. Then I'll have nothing. Not Dad. Not the farm. Just . . . him."

"That's a bum deal." Harvey tried to slide it in so smoothly Stella would answer without thinking. "What kind of money are we talking about here?"

"A hundred and forty thousand dollars," she said, buttoning her dress.

A hundred and forty grand! And that was not the full value of the farm, just what the old man had to borrow. The economy was heating up with so many coming back from the service. So was inflation. Harvey's German nest egg got smaller every month. A chance to move in on that kind of dough wouldn't come along again, not for a guy in Harvey's league.

This was one of those times when you found out who had their boots on. Harvey knew opportunity only knocked once; this was the first time it ever danced with him. He checked her story. There was a Griffin farm in Brookville. Big one. He drove his Packard up there, two-and-a-half hours each way. Read the plats and tax rolls. The place worth at least two hundred and the old man already had the down payment on his final, permanent address. Harvey didn't push for too much on the mortgage angle. People in small towns don't share secrets with strangers.

The way Harvey saw it, Stella's father was the fly in his ointment. Harvey didn't know if the old man would die in two weeks or two years. When he went, Stella would be as free as she'd ever be. Postelwaithe could do what he wanted. Stella would get over losing the farm when she had no more family there.

Of course, she'd have nothing. Someone like Postelwaithe would have no trouble rigging the divorce. He could even trump up some evidence to show Stella had been sleeping around, how he was the injured party. The fact that Postelwaithe wouldn't have to trump anything up never entered Harvey's mind.

If Harvey wanted Stella *and* the money—which he did—it was Postelwaithe who had to go. Harvey could hire it done.

Frank Amato was thinking of giving him something better to do than making money in fews and twos loan sharking. That meant someone else would know. Frank could move in on him, maybe even rat him out . . . Harvey had to do it alone.

He smiled thinking of it. Through North Africa, Sicily, France, and Germany he'd never fired his weapon except on a qualifying range. Didn't know where it was half the time. Now he was home, safe and sound, planning to kill a man.

He'd do it too.

He almost killed that Jew adjutant in Metz, the one who threatened to write him up for not getting ice cleats forwards quick enough to support Patton's push to Bastogne. Threatened to send Harvey forwards himself—Harvey busy trying to get a thousand cartons of Luckies into Germany while things were still in flux. Funny, he would've used the Luger for that one, had it all planned out, but Captain Greene found something more important and left Harvey to fight the war his own way. Postelwaithe wouldn't be so easy.

Harvey saw only one downside: he might get caught. Everything else was aces. Stella would be free, with all of Postelwaithe's money, the farm waiting in the wings for the old man to cash in so Harvey and Stella could cash out. Harvey could play golf all day if he wanted, shoot pool all night, finish up with some Stella. Frank Amato would find a place for someone with Harvey's initiative if things got boring.

Casing the job was easy. People were used to seeing him around Green Gables, so he came and went as he pleased. Harvey'd excuse himself to use the men's or catch a smoke, sneak outside to explore the alley beyond the side door where Postelwaithe always came for Stella.

One Thursday in August he brought Stella back early, said he had someplace to be. She looked at him funny, like maybe her feelings were hurt. Didn't say anything. Harvey didn't worry about it. He'd make it up to her in spades.

He needed to know what time Postelwaithe arrived, and if he came alone. Harvey's reconnaissance had found a good place to see the door without being seen himself, next to a trash bin near the service entrance.

Postelwaithe pulled up in a Caddy at ten twenty, sat in the car and smoked until exactly ten thirty. Alone. Harvey kicked himself. He could have taken Postelwaithe right there and been done with it, but he hadn't brought the extra Luger and didn't have his escape route planned yet. Harvey made himself calm down; he'd be back. Three more times Harvey checked Postelwaithe's habits. Sometimes he came five minutes earlier, sometime five minutes later. Always alone.

By mid-September Harvey was ready. Canceled his date with Stella. Said he had to work. Met a couple of friends, right gees who'd know on their own to say he left them later than he did, if it came to that. Picked up a car from a curb in Lawrenceville where the owner really should have known better. Mapped a route back to his car that gave him a chance to dump the Luger in the river. Even if the cops came around to him, his hadn't been fired, and the slugs wouldn't match. Worst could happen was it would look like a frame.

He crouched by his trash bin at ten o'clock, listening to the occasional rustlings of rats on the inside. Overcast night, no light except what the streetlights showed, which wasn't much after Harvey broke two of them.

Postelwaithe parked at ten seventeen and sat in the car smoking. Snatches of Frankie Carle's "Rumors Are Flying" floated through the alley. Harvey saw the glow of Postelwaithe's cigarette when he turned his head, smoke wafting out the driver's window.

At ten twenty-eight by Harvey's watch the car's dome light came on as the door opened. Postelwaithe walked around the front of the car, his right shoe making a rasping sound on the gritty pavement as his bad leg turned in the toe. Harvey walked quickly, didn't run. He made it as far as the car's trunk when Postelwaithe reached for the door to enter the Green Gables.

Harvey called out, "Postelwaithe! Mr. David Postelwaithe!"

Postelwaithe stopped and turned. Harvey walked towards him from behind the car. Postelwaithe built half a smile, like he might know Harvey. *He'll know me in a minute,* Harvey thought, holding the Luger out of sight down against his right leg.

Close now, no more than five feet apart. Postelwaithe looked younger from here, no more than thirty. Unblemished face, clear blue eyes. Hatless, a thick head of blond hair combed straight back off his forehead. He said, "Yes? I'm sorry, I don't recognize you."

Funny thing, Harvey thought he might have recognized Postelwaithe just as he pulled the gun level and shot him in the belly. The Luger made more noise than Harvey expected in the alley, reverberating between the close brick walls like thunder in a canyon. The noise fazed him for a second, long enough for Postelwaithe to recover from the initial impact of the shot and move towards him.

Postelwaithe came after Harvey with the assurance of someone who knew how to handle himself in a tough spot. The leg made his move jerky, slowed him down. Harvey pushed the gun into Postelwaithe's fleshy midsection and shot him again. This time he went down.

Harvey risked a quick look up the alley. Trouble could only come from one side. Escape lay the other direction, over a fence to the hot car parked a block away. No footfalls sounded. Only Postelwaithe's moans as he struggled to catch his breath.

Harvey placed the muzzle of the Luger to Postelwaithe's head an inch above the right ear. Their eyes met, Postelwaithe's searching for some explanation. Harvey said, "You should treat women better." His shot made a Rorschach pattern of brains against the Green Gables's wall.

Harvey ran back past the trash bin thirty yards to the fence, scaled it in one jump. No one on the street, the car right where he left it. He threw the gun into the Mon from the Rankin Bridge. Harvey was home, in bed, by midnight. He never even heard a siren.

He dozed off and on all night, waiting for the morning news. Never occurred to him to turn on the radio, like it wouldn't be real until he saw it in writing. None of the three major papers had anything until the *Post-Gazette* came out with a special around ten o'clock. Harvey bought a copy from a newsie outside a drug store on Braddock Avenue. He snapped the paper under his arm like his interest was no more pressing than what the Pirates did last night and made himself take his time walking home.

He made the headlines.

ATTORNEY GENERAL'S NEPHEW
SHOT TO DEATH IN WEST MIFFLIN

Harvey's guts coiled as he read down the page.

David Postelwaithe, 28, nephew of Pennsylvania Attorney General Byron W. Dworkin, was shot to death outside the Green Gables Ballroom in West Mifflin last night.

Harvey's mind ran on two tracks, part reading, part thinking of what he'd got himself into. He kept reminding himself he was clean. No one had seen him, the gun was in the river. He had an alibi as long as Lou and Brownie didn't play the wrong riff. The attorney general's nephew. Harvey wondered how much heat Lou and Brownie could handle if it came to that.

The *Post-Gazette* article had more.

Postelwaithe, a marine who earned a Navy Cross on Guadalcanal, had returned to the area to rehabilitate his right leg, almost severed by a mortar round on Okinawa.

Things Stella told him crowded the newsprint from Harvey's mind. About how Postelwaithe knew someone on the draft board. Hoarding ration coupons. He pushed the thoughts aside. All politicos had pull with the papers. A good flack could make Bruno Hauptmann sound like Pope Pius XII.

Police are looking for a man seen in the company of Mrs. Stella Griffin Postelwaithe several times over the past few months. Details are unavailable, but Mrs. Postelwaithe is rumored to have described a man who had accosted her on multiple occasions at the Green Gables.

Harvey turned to the continuation on an inner page thinking she might have described anyone. Everyone there danced with her.

Page thirteen had more facts of the crime, comments from the police and not-quite witnesses from the Green Gables. Nothing more about the investigation or whether they had any good leads.

A sidebar story covered four inches of three columns near the inner fold. People who knew Postelwaithe, led by a comment from Stella.

"Dave and I met dancing, he knew how much I loved it," Mrs. Postelwaithe said. "He couldn't even walk when he got back from the war. He told me he would rather have died over there

than see me shut up in the house all the time, so
he encouraged me to go dancing at least once a
week while he got his therapy. He gained a lot
of weight when he couldn't get around and was
finally starting to get back into shape. He said
he was looking forward to going with me in another month or so."

What else would she say? Name one woman who says her
dead husband was a malicious SOB who manipulated her. Harvey still knew—*knew*—he only had to let some time pass and
Stella and the whole setup would be his.

Another quote caught his eye, three inches down the sidebar.

"A wonderful man," said Homer Griffin,
Mr. Postelwaithe's father-in-law. "I would have
lost the farm when I got sick. Davey took care
of everything, even gave me the mortgage to
burn at their wedding rehearsal dinner."

Harvey was still trying to reconcile that with what Stella
told him when the police kicked in the door to his apartment.

Stella made a great witness. Sobs were heard on several occasions in the gallery when she bravely and without tears told
how much she loved her husband. How Harvey accosted her and
didn't want to take no for an answer. Under cross-examination
she admitted to leaving the Green Gables a time or two for a drink,
to avoid causing a scene. No one could identify her at the flop
they'd used for their trysts; Harvey had been too careful getting her in and out.

The jury took less than three hours. The judge's grim smile
as he read the verdict form and passed sentence showed his satisfaction at a rare opportunity for real justice.

Harvey barely had time to get the routine of Death Row down before he read a three-day-old article in the *Press* about Stella. Story below the fold in the regional section, how her beloved father fell down the cellar stairs in Brookville reaching for a mason jar. Broke his neck, dead when the ambulance got there, despite Stella's frantic attempts to revive him.

A sidebar had an interview with Stella, recapping her tragic year. "I can't stay in Brookville anymore," she said to the reporter. "Losing David and my father within a year. There's nothing here I can bear to look at." The article went on to say she was selling the farm and moving to New York. Already looking for an apartment in Manhattan to take advantage of the year's single saving grace: rising property values.

Harvey kept looking for an angle. Saw guys get weaker as their day approached, like they were disappearing before his eyes. The electric chair just gave someone an excuse to pronounce them. Not Harvey. He asked for the paper every day, stayed current on world events. Acted as though it mattered, like it would be important to him when he got out. The guards gave him a grudging respect. Always on the grift, never giving up. He told them war stories they didn't believe, even though the most outrageous ones were true.

The warden at Western Pen thought of himself as enlightened, wanted the inmates to feel connected to life around them as much as possible, even the walking dead. Let them join the general population for movies twice a month, if they wanted to. Most didn't. Harvey went every time. Wrists and ankles shackled, he sat in the back of the mess hall, no other prisoner within twenty feet, his chair chained to a table so he could see. Caught a lot of good movies that way. *Casablanca, All the King's Men, Going My Way.*

The last one he saw—a week before they ran the current through him—starred Barbara Stanwyck. Not *Stella Dallas*, the one his Stella recommended to him. This one he'd missed, it came out while he was in Europe. Harvey's minute sense of irony was pretty well shot by then—four days and counting—so he didn't recognize his kinship with the Fred MacMurray character in *Double Indemnity*. Walter Neff. A man who killed a husband for money, and for a woman. He didn't get the money, and he didn't get the woman.

Pretty, isn't it?

Death of a Rat

Eddie Bunker

A witness to the murder of the Soledad guard had been sent to San Quentin awaiting the trial. He was kept on the hospital's third floor. To reach him, you had to get through the hospital entrance by showing an identification card, with mug photo, name, and number. That got you into the hospital infirmary room, normally used for treating cuts and dispensing cold pills. At the other side of this first room was a gate of steel bars painted white. A guard stood behind it, checking passes and identification. He had a board affixed to the wall with a hundred and fifty-two name tags, inmates who worked somewhere in the hospital, from laundry room to surgical nurse, clerk to the prison psychiatrist and the chief medical officer's clerk. Inmates who worked in the hospital wore green jumpers, which differentiated them from non-workers in blue chambray shirts.

A couple weeks later the chief prison psychologist gave his clerk a list of men he wanted to see. The clerk dutifully typed up the list as a "request for interview." He put it on the psychologist's desk. It was signed and given back to the inmate clerk to be forwarded to the custody office where the actual passes were

made up and distributed throughout the cell houses by the graveyard shift. This time, however, when the clerk got the signed list
from his boss, he put it back in the Underwood and added two
names and numbers, "Clemens, B13566," and "Buford, B14003."
Both were young "fish," age nineteen and twenty-two, and neither had been a year in the House of Dracula, the nickname for
San Quentin. Folsom was the Pit, and Soledad, the Gladiator
School. Neither would admit it, but both wanted to be the stuff
of legend in the prison underworld. During the night a guard
walked the cell house tiers, putting passes (called ducats) on the
cell bars of convicts who were wanted somewhere by someone.
Clemens was wide awake and waiting when the guard passed
his cell. Buford got his when he woke up.

They met on the Big Yard after breakfast. Neither had any
appetite. Instead of hunger, both felt the hollowness of fear
deep in their stomachs. Normally they would have joined some
partners hanging out in the morning sunlight near the north
cell house until the mess halls cleared and the whistle blew for
work. This morning they wanted to hang out quietly until it
was time to take care of business.

"Is that fuckin' whistle late this morning?" asked Buford.

Clemens shrugged. "I ain' got no fuckin' idea. I don' even
know what fuckin' year it is."

The work whistle blasted through the morning, causing an
explosion of pigeons and seagulls. The latter flew over the yard
and shit on the cons, as if getting vengeance for the whistle's
blast. They were cursed in return. "Flying fuckin' rats." (In an
attempt at retaliation, a few convicts would put Alka-Seltzer
tablets inside pieces of crushed up bread. The birds swooped,
ate, and soon went crazy as the Alka-Seltzer fizzed inside of
them.)

The Big Yard gate was rolled open and convicts streamed
out to their jobs in the lower yard industries. In minutes the
yard was empty save for the cleanup crew and those who had

night jobs. Lined up near the south cell house rotunda were those going to sick call. A guard was picking up ID cards. When he reached Clemens and Buford, they showed the ducats and ID cards. He beckoned them. "Follow me." The guard led them along the line to the infirmary door. Because they had passes, they had priority over those who were in the sick call line on their own. He took their ID cards and put them with the others, to be returned when they left the hospital.

At the grille gate across the infirmary, they handed their passes through the bars. The guard keyed the gate. "You know where you're goin'?"

They nodded and he waved them through. The corridor ahead was long. A few inmates and free personnel were coming and going. The psychiatric department was halfway down the hallway. Instead of turning through the door, they kept going to the rear. On the left was an elevator. Inmates used it if they were patients or assigned to. Others went up the stairwell, which was the route taken by Buford and Clemens, two and three stairs at a time. On the second floor they turned in and went to the X-ray department. They swiftly removed their shirts and tossed them under a bench. Now they wore the green jumpers. Anyone who didn't know better would assume that they were assigned to the hospital work crew. Clemens slapped Buford on the back. "Let's do it, homes." He opened the hallway door and out they went.

As they reached the third-floor landing and started to turn in, an elderly correctional officer came out and nearly collided with them. "Slow down. Where's the fire?"

"Sorry, boss," said Buford. "We're late." If the guard had asked for what, there would have been no reply, although Clemens's sweaty hand held the taped handle of the shiv in his pocket. It was fifteen inches long overall, and the tip of the blade had been stabbed through the bottom of his pocket and the steel pressed against his thigh.

"Okay, go on . . . just take it easy." The guard went down the stairs and they went through the door. To the left were the rooms. It was cleanup time and the doors were ajar. A chicano janitor was squeezing a wet mop in a wheeled bucket and wringer. The first door went into the nurse's station. It was open; the nurse was inside.

"Where's the rat?" Clemens asked Buford.

"At the back . . . around the corner."

"How we gonna get by the nurse?"

"That's what these green shirts are for."

"Let's go do him up."

They walked past the nurse's office without a challenge, and nodded at the chicano mopping the floors. Men in the rooms, mostly wearing nightgowns and jeans, glanced up as they went by, but suspected nothing and said nothing. With every step Clemens's tension increased. When they turned the corner and saw the correctional officer reading a newspaper, Clemens got momentarily dizzy. He expelled a lungful of air.

The officer sensed, or heard them, as soon as they turned the corner. The way they moved made him stand up and put the paper down. He saw the green blouses, but the hallway was a dead end ten feet away.

"Hold it. Where're you going?"

Clemens literally lost his mind. The tension was too heavy and he snapped. "Gimme them motherfuckin' keys, pig!" He didn't wait for the response, but pulled his shiv and stuck it straight into the officer's stomach, an inch below the ribcage.

"*Ahhhhhahhhhh! God!*"

Buford stepped forwards and put a hand over Clemens's chest. "Cool it." And to the officer: "Better be givin' up them keys."

"I don't have them," he said, blood spraying out of his mouth.

In the cell, the witness, a black queen, heard the officer bang his back on the door when Clemens stabbed him. The queen got up to look through the observation window. She saw what was going on and ran to the window overlooking the air well at the center of the building—and began screaming: *"Help! Help! Help! Murder! Oh, God, help!"*

From nearby windows came responding voices, but not of help. "Shaddup you dingbat motherfucker!" "Shut the fuck up, dick sucker, snitchin' nigger."

In the hallway, Clemens and Buford had the guard seated in the chair, unable to resist, blood coming from his mouth and down his shirt. He held his belly and hunkered forwards. "Don't have keys," he said.

"Yeah . . . yeah." Buford was turning the guard's pockets inside out. Nothing.

Unexpectedly, the female nurse in the white uniform came around the corner. She took a couple steps before she realized what was going on. She turned and ran, with Buford in hot pursuit. Patients were sticking out their heads, but on seeing the nurse running and yelling they stepped back and closed their doors. When they were questioned, and they would be, they would give the standard convict answer: "I didn't see nuthin', I didn't hear nuthin'—and I don't know nuthin'."

The nurse's office had a panic button, but Buford and his shiv were too close behind for her to turn in there. Instead she hit the stairway door and went through on the fly, screaming, *"Help! Help! Help!"* as she leapt and fell and rolled down the stairs, miraculously not breaking any bones and still screaming at the top of her lungs.

As Buford started down the stairway, his will ran out and fear filled him, sapping his strength. The nurse hit the first floor and ran into the main corridor.

Clemens came up behind Buford. "Did she get away?"

"Yeah, yeah. What're we gonna do?"

"C'mon!"

Clemens led the way to the second floor and turned in. "Best pray right here."

"Pray. What the fuck!"

"Yeah, pray they pass on by to the third floor."

They heard the pounding feet and excited voices. "Go ... go ... on three." Four officers bounded past to the third floor.

Wordlessly, Clemens pulled Buford's sleeve and led him out of the second floor and down to the first. The main corridor had a dozen or more convicts looking towards the door into the stairwell and buzzing.

The corridor was long. The exit door was beyond the barred gate and infirmary.

"Suck it up, dawg, an' let's go." He started walking with Buford on his heels.

The elderly guard on the barred gate was arguing with convicts on the other side. "Gonna want us," the convict said. "We're the surgery crew. They've been calling us on the loudspeaker. Here—" He brought out a yellow assignment card. It said "Hospital - Surgery."

"Wait," said the guard as he picked up the phone and checked with control, holding down his voice. "Stand aside. When they need you, they'll call." At the same moment, he looked back over his shoulder to Clemens and Buford in their green hospital worker blouses. The guard nodded and turned the key in the barred gate. Buford and Clemens slipped out into the Big Yard.

"*Lockup! Lockup!*" blasted the public address system. Convicts looked at one another, shrugged, and began to slowly file into the vast cell houses.

In the dark hours before dawn, the sound of boots crunching and the tall shadows made by prison floodlights gave notice that guards were on the tiers. They took Buford first and went

DEATH OF A RAT / 157

back for Clemens. On the way down the rear steel stairs, the nightsticks rose and descended. One blow gave off the hollow sound similar to that of a breaking egg. It was actually Clemens's breaking skull. He was in a coma for a week, and would be a mumbling idiot for the rest of his life. That saved Buford, for the guards were afraid of what they had done. Their reports said he had fallen down the steel stairs to the concrete floor.

The sun was rising and the baby pigeons and other birds were making an inordinate ruckus that most convicts slept through, when Buford was walked across the prison to the adjustment center. There was the bang and slam of gates opening and being shut until they got him into a cell on the bottom floor of the north side of the a.c., among half a dozen men the officials thought were the most dangerous in the entire prison system of sixty-eight thousand.

The Last Dance

Stuart Neville

Treanor's Bar never tried too hard to be an Irish pub. Maybe that's why on a busy night you could find more Irish people there than any bar in the city. I don't mean white guys trying to adopt some kind of ethnicity to ease their Caucasian guilt, but real honest-to-God children of Eire.

Plenty of bars gave you the shamrock treatment, Guinness on tap and fiddles on the walls, but Treanor's was the real thing. It seethed with that self-righteous jingoism and sense of injustice that only comes from Ireland.

Do I sound bitter? Well, I have good reason to be. That's why I got out, got away, across the ocean from Belfast to Boston. I couldn't stand the hate anymore. But still, at least once a week, I felt drawn to this sorry excuse for a bar.

This one night, the place was empty save for an old duffer counting change on a tabletop, Mickey the barman, and one stranger who occupied a stool two seats down from my favorite spot. The stale smell of old beer filled my head. Mickey raised an eyebrow and grunted as I limped towards the bar. The weather had turned cold and damp, and my left knee didn't like it one bit.

I loosened the collar of my work shirt. The ID laminate clipped to the pocket proudly told the world I had achieved the office of warehouse manager. I wasn't quite a regular at Treanor's, not a part of the furniture, but Mickey didn't have to ask what I wanted. A pint of Smithwick's was ready for hoisting to my lips before my ass was even settled on the stool. I grimaced at the creaking in my knee.

"Quiet tonight," I said.

"Yep," said Mickey.

And that was the sum total of our conversation most nights. Tonight was different, though. Mickey leaned forwards as he pretended to wipe down the bar. Mickey never wiped down the bar. The beer stains on there were older than my car, and it's been a long time since that piece of shit was new.

Mickey inclined his head towards the stranger. "See that guy?" he whispered.

I tried hard not to look to my right where the stranger sat staring at a shot of whiskey and a pint of Guinness.

Mickey rested his chin on his hand, obscuring his mouth as if the stranger might be a deaf lip reader. I should point out that Mickey isn't the brightest. Between you and me, he knows just enough not to eat himself.

"That guy's been here a half hour," he said.

I shrugged. "And?"

"And he hasn't had a sip. He just sits staring at those glasses like they're gonna start doing tricks or something."

By now, the old duffer had finished tallying his wealth and he approached the bar. "I'm a little short, Mickey. Can you stand me the twenty cents?"

His accent, or what was left of it, sounded like Cork to me. I'd seen him here before, always alone. He probably came to

America expecting to make his fortune. The sight of him terrified me. Not because he was a scary guy, you understand, but because he looked like my future. I shuddered and put my glass down.

Mickey sighed, pulled a glass from under the bar, and brought it to the tap.

"You're always a little short, Frankie. Drink this one up and go home."

Frankie smiled and reached for the glass full of froth. "Thanks, Mickey. You're a good lad."

He gave the stranger a sideways glance and shuffled back to his table. If the stranger noticed, he didn't let on. He just sat there, staring at his drinks, his shoulders rising and falling with his breathing.

The patchy overhead lighting cast this man in glints and shadows, picking out the ridges and valleys of his face, making it look like a skeleton mask. His hands were spread flat on the bar, as if supplicating themselves to the drink, and their lines gave away his age. Mid-forties, I'd say, about my age, maybe a year or two older.

Mickey leaned back into me. "What'll I do?" he asked.

"He's paid for them, hasn't he?"

"Uh-huh."

"Then what the fuck do you care? He can piss in them if he wants."

Mickey's face creased. "But he's giving me the creeps. He's not right. Look at him. Does he look right to you?"

"No," I said, "but neither do most of your regulars."

"I'm gonna ask him what's wrong." Mickey didn't go anywhere. "Will I ask him? I'll ask him. Should I ask him?"

"Jesus, Mickey, if it'll calm you down, go and ask him."

Mickey looked to the stranger, then back to me, then back to the stranger again. He straightened and moved along the bar.

"You all right, there?"

The stranger didn't respond.

"Mister? Are you all right?"

"Mmm?" The stranger looked up.

"Is something wrong with the drinks?"

"No," said the stranger.

"You haven't touched them."

"I don't drink anymore." The stranger's eyes moved back to the glasses in front of him. His accent, hard and angular, made me study him a little closer. He was West Belfast, like me. My own accent had been buried beneath almost two decades of Boston living, but his was fresh.

A furrow appeared in Mickey's brow and his tongue peeked out from between his teeth like he was figuring out his taxes in his head. "Then why'd you buy 'em?"

"Because I could. Because I can drink them if I want," said the stranger. "But I don't want to. I don't need to."

"I'll have them when you're done, then," I said. I am not a proud man.

The stranger turned towards my voice, the light shifting on his face. The skeleton mask slipped away and I saw him fully for the first time. He said something. I don't know what, offering the drinks to me maybe, but I didn't hear. My heart was thundering so loud it drowned everything else out. I had to fight to control my bladder. My left leg, my bad leg, throbbed with memory.

Sweet Jesus, I knew his face. Some nights, when sleep shunned me, there was nothing in the world but his face. Other nights, when sleep was more forgiving, it was his face that dragged me back to waking.

The stranger's lips moved some more, and now Mickey stared at me. Mickey said something too, but it sounded like blood rushing in my ears.

"I know you," I said.

Mickey looked back to the stranger, whose face had slackened.

"You're Gerry Fegan," I said.

"No," he said. He turned back to his drinks. "You've got me mixed up."

His fingertip traced a line through the beaded condensation on the glass of stout.

"You're Gerry Fegan from Belfast." I lowered myself from the stool and limped the few steps to where he sat. I pointed to my left kneecap. "You're Gerry Fegan and you did this to me."

He kept his eyes forward. "You've got me wrong."

Mickey's mouth hung open as he watched.

I grabbed Fegan's shoulder and he winced. "Look at me, you piece of shit. You smashed my kneecap. You and Eddie Coyle. You would've done the other one, only the cops came."

Fegan turned his face to me. It was cut from flint. "I don't know what you're talking about. You're thinking of someone else."

I moved tight to him, his shoulder pressing on my chest. "Do you remember me?"

"No. I don't know you."

"I'm Sean Duffy. You and Eddie Coyle dragged me into an alley behind McKenna's Bar on the Springfield Road because I bought the wrong girl a drink. Remember?"

"You've got the wrong fella."

"She was Martin McKenna's fiancée, but I didn't know that. We had a dance, that's all." I looked down at my leg as the pain flared in my knee, a keepsake from the bad times. "The last dance I ever had. McKenna found out about it and he had you and Coyle do me over. Do you remember, Gerry?"

Fegan reached up and took my hand from his shoulder. "It's not me."

He got off the stool and turned to the exit. I went after him, hopping and limping to catch up.

"What was it, a crowbar?"

He kept walking. I reached into my pocket and found the plastic box cutter handle, the one I used at the warehouse. My thumb settled on the button.

"Whatever it was, it did the trick. I couldn't walk for a year. My father had to carry me to the toilet. You better stop, Gerry."

The box cutter came out of my pocket, the blade sliding out from the orange plastic handle with a stutter of tiny clicks. Fegan reached the door.

"Stop, you bastard."

He looked back over his shoulder and saw the blade in my hand.

"Easy, Sean," Mickey called from somewhere behind me.

Fegan turned his body to face me.

"So, what are you doing here?" I asked. "It was on the news last month. All the old crew, McKenna and McGinty, all that lot. There was a feud. Someone did them in. Is that it, Gerry? Did you run away in case whoever did them came after you? Did it all catch up to you?"

My hand trembled with adrenaline, my voice shook with hate and fear. I had dreamed of this, of taking from Gerry Fegan what he took from me.

"You didn't run far enough," I said.

Fegan took one step forwards so the blade quivered beneath his chin. "No," he said. "I can never run far enough."

I felt Mickey's lumbering presence over my shoulder. "Jesus, Sean, take it easy. Put the knife away."

Fegan's eyes locked on mine, cold and shiny and black as oil. No fear leaked from him. One movement of my wrist would open his throat, but the terror was all mine.

"He won't do it," he said. "He's not like me."

I brought the blade closer so it reflected light onto his skin. "I will. I'll do it."

"No, you won't. You can't."

What started in my belly as a laugh came out of my mouth as a whimper. "Why not?"

"Because you're better than me," he said.

From the corner of my eye I saw Mickey sidle up to us, a baseball bat gripped in both hands. "Sean, put the knife away. Mister, whoever you are, just turn around and get the fuck out of here."

I felt the tears then, bubbling up from inside me. Stupid, helpless child's tears. Hot, scalding tears. "But look what he did to me. Just for a dance. I danced with the wrong girl and look what he did to me."

A memory moved behind Fegan's eyes. "McKenna told me to do it. He never said why."

"So?" The words hitched in my throat. My legs threatened to crumble beneath me. "If he'd told you why, would it have made any difference?"

Fegan didn't think about it for long. "No," he said.

My legs had trembled all they could, and now they betrayed me. Fegan caught the hand that held the box cutter and let my body fall into his. The knife left my fingers and Fegan's arms snaked around me. His breath warmed my ear.

"Martin McKenna's dead now," he said. "Him and the others, they're all gone. But it wasn't a feud. They've all paid for what they did. I made sure of it. Everybody pays, sooner or later."

"Not you," I hissed. "You haven't paid."

"I will." His arms tightened on me. "But not tonight."

I had a second or two to wonder where the knife was as Fegan and I danced in the doorway of Treanor's Bar.

He slipped it into my pocket and his lips brushed my ear as he said, "I'm sorry for what I did."

Then he was gone.

Mickey's thick arms took my weight as the door swung closed and the cool night air washed around me. He guided me back to the bar, towards my stool, but I veered to the right, to where the shot of whiskey and pint of Guinness remained untouched. The black beer was still cold as my shaking hands brought it to my mouth.

Like I said, I am not a proud man.

The Cost of Doing Business

Michael Penncavage

The wall clock with the round, wide, inlaid smile and gloved arms is pointing west and east, symbolizing the start of a new business day when Charlie Whitman, just like clockwork, hears the familiar *tinkle, tinkle* of the door charm. Charlie is facing the wall, restocking the cigarette sleeves after being plundered by the morning rush. But he knows who it is.

Just like going to the dentist, but on a daily basis.

"Morning, Charlie."

He slams the last of the packs into the pocket and turns around. "Morning."

Wade Brown gives his belt an affirming tug, but his belly and sidearm have different plans and his pants sag back down pathetically. He walks over to the stack of donuts alongside the coffeepot. He picks up a chocolate-frosted, reconsiders, picks up a cruller, reconsiders, picks up a jelly, reconsiders, picks up a powdered, smirks and proceeds to eat it in three quick bites, just like each morning. The coffee comes next. He pours it into a large Styrofoam cup, leaving plenty of room for milk and sugar. Wade takes a sip and frowns. "This pot fresh?"

"Fresh enough."

"Tastes like mule piss." He chuckles like he always does, as if amused with his own jokes. "Though, that's not to say I ever drank any."

Charlie ignores the comment as he wipes off the counter. It's spotless, as always, but his hands need something to do.

He wonders how much today will cost him.

Wade, coffee cup in hand, begins thumbing with fat, chubby digits through the magazine rack. "You get that new titty magazine in yet?"

"Not since yesterday."

Wade casts Charlie a disapproving glance that a mother would give to a misbehaving child. "You'd best get on that distributor of yours. Tell them that there are eager fans waiting for Miss Fourth of July." Wade grabs a *Field & Stream* and *Hunting* magazine from the rack.

Charlie watches as Wade begins to make his way towards the door and thinks, *Only ten dollars, I'm getting off easy,* when he sees the fat man bend down and pick up one of the boxed window fans that had just arrived earlier in the week.

"Weatherman says it gonna be a hot one today. Summer's almost on us." Tucking his magazines under his armpit, he picks up the cooler and shimmies through the door with the same *tinkle, tinkle.*

Charlie slams his hand onto the counter, causing the brass dish of Take One, Leave One pennies to careen up and crash onto the floor. He closes his eyes and tries to calm his temper before the next customer walks in.

It's been six months since Charlie moved out of the city, leaving the pollution, congestion, and memories at the border as he passed into the country. In the city he owned a convenience store also, but it was a twenty-four-hour joint there, not a six-to-six. He ran it a little over twenty years, with the naive belief that once you had handled your first crazy drunk you could handle any type of customer.

That is, except for the ones that came in coked-out and toting a ten-gauge.

His wife, Betty, had been working the register. Charlie had been in the dry goods aisle and could not hear what was going down, not until the robber screamed at Betty for not emptying out the cash drawer quickly enough. Charlie reached the front of the aisle to see Betty take a blast to the chest, point-blank. He lunged at the kid, who was not a day over sixteen, and received part of the second blast to his leg, sending him careening into a rack of cleaning products.

It went dark after that.

He was discharged from the hospital two weeks later. Three more months passed and the store was sold, the apartment as well, and Charlie was transplanted four hours to the west and a world away. He found a nice town named Westbend, a bit off Interstate 79. It seemed like the ideal place to start over.

Or so he had thought.

It's during the grand opening week that Wade makes his first visit. It's an odd time of day. Charlie is in between wrapping the unused rolls from the morning crowd and prepping the meats for the early lunchers. Twenty years of dealing with people from the homeless to movie stars and everyone in between gives Charlie the knack of being able to instantly tell if a customer is going to be trouble.

And he doesn't like what he sees one bit.

Wade is in uniform but he's a mess. His boots are scuffed, shirt unbuttoned, pants wrinkled, and face unshaven. From the doorway, he's surveying the store like a building inspector trying to determine if it's up to code.

"Looks a hell of a lot better than the old place." He finishes his overview and tips his hat to Charlie. "Wade Brown. Town sheriff."

Charlie smiles politely and introduces himself.

"I see you got that smell out of here."

"Excuse me?"

"The smell," repeats Wade. "I don't think the fellow who ran this place before you was a big fan of showers. Immigrant, I think. Skipped back to Japan with their relatives when they couldn't foot the rent."

"China. They were Chinese. And he moved back to Los Angeles to be with his parents," Charlie corrects. He can't believe what he's hearing.

"Whatever." Wade's eyes are bloodshot, as if he's been up all night. Still, they have an unnerving sharpness to them. "I heard you're from the city."

"That's right."

"Well, I think you'll find the people here a little more pleasant to deal with than the ones you're used to."

"That's . . . good to know." Charlie places the last of the wrapped breakfast rolls into the same wicker basket he used in the old store. He walks behind the meat counter and begins preparing some premade sandwiches.

"Yep, you'll find a whole lot of things different here than in the big city." A *tinkle, tinkle* sounds and Charlie looks up just in time to see him passing through the front door.

Impulsively, Charlie glances over at the wicker basket. It's a whole lot more empty now.

It doesn't get any better. The following day, again during the lull, the door tinkles and in steps Wade. Charlie had been up half the night pondering what to say to the man.

"Morning, Charlie," he says, the same silly grin plastered across his face. "You got a pot of regular on?"

Charlie is auditing the morning receipts and nods his head. "Over there."

"Fresh?"

"As always."

"You gonna pour me a cup?"

Charlie looks up from the till and Wade begins to chuckle. "Just kidding. Wow—I wish I had a camera. The look on your face!"

Wade's smile grows even wider as he grabs a Styrofoam cup and the coffeepot with his ham-hands. "Yes. That's good. Nice and hot." He prepares his coffee and begins the donut ritual again, manhandling them all until he invariably chooses the powdered. Charlie watches the big man inhale it.

"You know what today is?" asks Wade as he ducks down one of the aisles and out of view behind the soda and juice refrigerators.

"No. What?" asks Charlie as he makes his way around the counter to see what Wade is up to. He'll be damned if he is going to get lifted again—sheriff or not. As Charlie reaches the aisle he almost collides with Wade. "Looking for anything in particular?"

"Just browsing," replies the sheriff as he takes a sip of coffee. "Like I was saying, today marks the anniversary."

"Anniversary? Of what?"

Wade motions with his index finger down the street. "It was four months ago today that Pete Mingers's hardware store went up in flames. Burned right to the ground."

"They ever learn the cause?" Deep down, Charlie isn't sure that he wants to know.

"Fire marshal, that's my cousin Larry by the way, wasn't a hundred percent certain. Being a hardware store, Pete kept a good deal of wood on hand. Hell, if you can burn down an entire forest with nothing more than a cigarette butt, I guess it wouldn't take much to raze a store, now would it?" Wade shrugs his shoulders and removes a pack of cigarettes from his pocket. He pats his shirt and then his trousers. "You wouldn't happen to have a light, would you?"

Charlie stares at him for a moment.

"Wait. I found one." Wade lights up and promptly pockets the matches.

"So, no official cause for the fire?" Charlie finds that hard to believe.

"Nope. I suggested it was an accident. Larry agreed," answers Wade. "Ol' Pete just sucked up his losses and moved back to the city—that's where he was from originally. Don't know what happened to him after that. But then, he was never the friendly type to start with." He tips his hat and heads for the door. "Well, got to go. See you real soon."

Charlie spends the afternoon pondering. Along with the store, the lease also includes the apartment above with roof access. On afternoons, prior to the pre-dinner-errand rush, Charlie finds he can relax on the roof and get some sun while still being able to watch the storefront below. He can tell if a passerby will head into his store or not. Customers during that time of day have a concentrated, constipated look. No time for chitchat or lollygagging down the street. It's simply get in—make the purchase—and get out.

Charlie hears the faint rattling of a doorbell, followed by two voices. He glances down and sees Wade stepping out of the bakery a few doors away, licking his fingers. He begins walking towards his squad car before stopping and turning around. He's sporting that mischievous grin again.

Charlie hustles down the turret staircase that leads into the store's backroom. With his lame leg, it's not nearly as fast as he would like. He steps out on the store floor just in time to view

Wade pocketing a pack of batteries. Suddenly, Charlie has reached his limit.

"Three seventy-five, Wade."

"What would that be?"

"The AAA batteries that you just dropped into your jacket— they're three seventy-five per pack."

The sheriff looks at him narrowly. "Well, it's a good thing you told me the price then! Three seventy-five's a bit steep for batteries don't you think, Charlie? Especially when I can go over to Multi-Mart and get them for a buck cheaper." He places the item back onto the display, giving it a little pat as if to keep it in place. "What do you think about losing a customer though?"

"I think I'll live," Charlie replies.

Wade glances over at the grill that is used to cook breakfast sandwiches. "Can I get a pork roll?"

"Sorry. Grill's closed." The last thing Charlie feels like doing right now is handing out free food.

"Damn. That's a real shame."

A *tinkle, tinkle* sounds as a customer walks in.

Wade tips his hat and begins walking over to the exit. "Well, off to catch me some criminals. Be seeing you, Charlie." And with that he is gone, leaving Charlie with clenched fists and a face full of frustration.

A shotgun blast goes off and the box of canned corn Charlie is holding strikes the linoleum floor, sending cans off in all directions. He races to the front of the store to find Betty slumped down behind the register. A growing pool of blood surrounds her. Blood covers the products displayed on the shelves behind her, and still more drips from the ceiling tiles in large globs. Somehow she is still alive. She points an accusatory finger at him. "Your fault," she mutters, coughing up blood. "All your fault."

* * *

Charlie wakes up with a start, heart pounding, clothes covered in perspiration. With his thumb and forefinger he rubs the sweat from his eyes and tries to erase any lingering images from the nightmare. It's been a week since the last one. Possibly a new record. For the longest time it had been a nightly occurrence.

Charlie stops gulping the air and inhales through his nose and tries to relax, just like the yoga class he took with Betty. Instead of helping him settle down, it makes him immediately realize that he has a very big problem. There's a heavy smell in the air—one that he immediately recognizes and almost causes him to soil his shorts.

The bedroom window is open, but the night air is still and it's not doing much to ventilate the apartment. Charlie moves slowly through the pitch-black room. His bare foot smacks against the corner of the dresser and he winces in pain but doesn't dare turn on the ceiling light.

He gropes for his keys and cell phone on the dresser and slides them into his pocket. Slowly, he makes his way out the back door of the building. He uses the fire escape to reach the alley below. It is only then that he dials 911.

Five minutes later the firemen show up. A minute after that, a police cruiser arrives. He half expects it to be Wade, but it's not. Instead it's some deputy he's never seen before. Probably someone who had gotten on Wade's bad side and was banished to the graveyard shift. A guy from the gas company shows up next. He chats with the firemen for a moment and then drives off.

One of the firemen walks up to him. "We'll have the gas line shut off in a minute. Once we get the call from Fred Stevens, that's the gas man, we'll wait it out, just to make sure nothing happens."

"Thank you," replies Charlie as he stares at the building. One of the firemen is propping the door open with a brick.

"Consider yourself lucky, sir. From the amount of gas in there, one spark would have not only taken the building out, but probably the whole block. Going forwards, you should make a checklist of things to do before you close up each night, such as checking that griddle."

"Good advice," says Charlie, not caring to point out that he has such a list tacked to the back room wall, next to the phone. "Inspect Grill" is item five, right after "Turn Off Coffeemaker."

It happens at the end of the day this time.

"Afternoon, Charlie."

"Afternoon, Wade." Charlie doesn't bother looking up from his ordering form, but instead watches him from the corner of his eye.

The sheriff makes his way to the candy, manhandling a dozen different bars before shelling and shoving a Snickers into his mouth. "Heard you had a bit of a pickle here last night."

"Nothing too serious."

"Problem with the stove?"

"It's been taken care of."

"Can I get a pork roll?"

"Grill's closed for the day."

Wade lets out a grunt. "You run a crazy establishment here, Charlie. The stove's off during the day and on at night. You keep that up and it's only a matter of time before you either lose all of your customers or end up burning this place to the ground. I, for one, would just hate to see that happen."

It's the sarcasm in his voice with the last sentence that makes Charlie stop what he is doing and look up at the man. But Wade has said his piece and before Charlie can reply, the sheriff is out the door.

*   *   *

Charlie doesn't sleep much that night. He lies in bed, staring up at the ceiling, thinking about his old store. His thoughts go to Betty for a while, thinking about their honeymoon, their anniversaries, their years living in the city. Happy times.

But mostly he thinks about Wade.

He's right on time the next morning.

And the next.

And the next.

In at nine fifteen. Out by nine twenty-five. It's rare anyone else is in the store and Charlie realizes Wade likes it that way. Makes it much easier to wreak havoc.

"Glad to see the building still standing," remarks Wade as he looks around.

"Must be the checklist," replies Charlie as he stands behind the counter, trying to keep focused on the crossword puzzle that he never seems to start.

"Funny thing about checklists," says Wade as he fondles the donuts again before devouring, like always, the powdered. "They're never as complete as you would like them to be. There's always that one extra thing you forget to write on the list, and that's the one that always bites you in the ass," he says, laughing. He grabs a cup and pours himself some coffee. "Goddamn, Charlie," he gasps after taking a sip. "This is some nasty shit you brewed this morning!"

"I'm using a different blend," Charlie answers, using his pencil to point to a canister on the shelf. "Thought I'd give it a try."

"Tastes like you pissed in it!"

"That's because I did," Charlie answers, not bothering to look up from the crossword.

Wade looks at him for a moment before breaking out into laughter. "That's a good one. Good to see you're finally getting a sense of humor." He frowns after taking another sip and drops the cup into the wastebasket. "But switch back to the old stuff."

"Once I use it up, you'll be the first to know."

"Better do it quick," says Wade. "You might lose a customer."

Charlie doesn't reply.

"Say, where's your antacids?" Wade asks, clearing his throat of some phlegm. He spits into the garbage can.

"Same aisle as the toilet paper."

The sheriff disappears for a moment. Charlie can hear him cracking open one of the plastic bottles. "My wife's cooking," he says, walking back around the bend. "I keep telling her to lay off the spices. She says she is, but I don't believe her." Wade makes a fist and taps his chest as if trying to burp. "Ugh. Damn heartburn. Been popping these suckers for the better part of a month now. Doesn't seem to be doing much good."

"Maybe you should go see a doctor?"

"Hell, no," replies Wade. "Bastards charge me a hundred bucks and give me a prescription that's no different than this crap," he says, placing the antacids in his pocket.

Wade adjusts his hat and pulls the door open. "See you to-morrow, Charlie."

Charlie doesn't reply as he continues staring at the cross-word. As soon as he hears the door tinkle closed, he walks over to the plate of donuts, and, like every morning for the past three months, tosses them into the garbage. He glances at the clock. Nine seventeen. A shelf life of fifteen minutes. Three dollars a day for a dozen donuts that he buys from a round-robin of donut shops from surrounding towns. If there's ever an investigation, they'll never be able to uncover a pattern. Plus, like all of Charlie's regulars know, he hasn't sold donuts in months. He looks down at the pile of sweets in the bin. *A waste,* he thinks, *but it's the cost of doing business.*

At least he buys the rat poison that he sprinkles onto the powdered donuts at wholesale.

A month later there's a cover story about a beloved small town sheriff who suddenly, tragically, succumbed to kidney failure. On page ten, at the bottom, is a small blurb about the local convenience store and its expansion plans.

Son of So Many Tears

Hilary Davidson

"Go in the peace of Christ," intoned the elderly priest as Maire Kennelly made her escape. Her heels clattered on the stone steps as she distanced herself from the few penitents whose addiction to early morning mass was as keen as her own. She was glad to be out of the church, a fact that surely meant another dark mark on her soul. It had been seven years since Maire's last confession, and when she thought of her soul now, she pictured a Victorian silhouette with edges sharp and refined but coal-black to the core. As she turned onto the sidewalk, she wondered what effect words of absolution could have on it now. "Saint Rita, hear my prayer," she began to recite silently, when a flame-haired woman in a black trench coat stepped in front of her.

"Pardon me," Maire said, stepping to one side. The woman moved to block her path.

"Maire Kennelly? Janey Saxon. We've met before." She smiled and put her hand on Maire's arm. "Last week was the seventh anniversary of your son's trial and I wanted to ask how you felt about—"

"You're a *reporter.*" Maire hissed the last word and jerked her arm back. "I have nothing to say to you."

"Well, plenty of people are interested in what Brendan's doing now. So many viewers called us about the show we ran last week. If you would—"

"Let me alone." Maire took a step back.

"We've been trying to locate Brendan but we can't find him," said Janey, flashing a toothy smile. "Nobody knows where he's gone. I was hoping you could help . . ."

Maire stepped onto the damp grass and when Janey Saxon blocked her path again, she hit the reporter's shoulder with her big black purse. The dyed redhead swiveled and Maire followed her glance. There was a black van on the street with a man standing behind it, holding a camera.

"How dare you," said Maire, her voice rising. "You're nothing but a—a *vulture.*" She rushed down the sidewalk as quickly as her heels would allow her.

"Did he leave the country?" Janey called after her. "Is he hiding out from his victims?"

Maire kept on, her heart racing. *Saint Rita, don't let me fall,* she prayed. A year before, when she turned sixty-five, a reporter had so flustered her that she'd tripped in front of her own house and fractured her forearm. Maire slowed her pace now to look over her shoulder for the reporter and the van but saw neither. As she approached her house she scanned the street. When Brendan was first arrested, there were local news reporters and then national ones camped out in front of her house. Maire had installed an iron fence along the property line and planted a privacy hedge behind it. Even though she only occasionally heard from reporters now—the anniversary of the trial always brought them out—she liked the privacy it afforded her, the way it shielded her little house from prying eyes. The downside, which she hadn't realized until everything was in place, was that the fence and hedge made her house immediately identifiable in a modest Queens neighborhood of green lawns and painted gnomes and year-round icicle lights.

She snapped open her handbag and extracted her keys, wondering if she needed to bring out that big lock she used to keep on the iron gate. *It's a lot of bother for arthritic hands,* she thought as she walked up the flagstone path to the house. She unlocked the front door and stepped inside. As she shut it behind her, something struck the back of her head. Her keys clattered to the floor as everything went dark.

Maire heard the sound of something smashing as she came to. Her vision was blurry and her head throbbed, but she realized it was her own kitchen spinning around her. She closed her eyes and took a shaky breath. She wanted to touch her face—the left side felt like it was burning—but she couldn't move her arms. Her raincoat had been pulled off and tossed in the corner. She was sitting in a wooden kitchen chair, her hands tied behind her back.

"You're awake," said a man's voice. She opened her eyes and glared at him, fury trumping fear.

"What are you doing?" she said, her voice hoarse. She heard another crash.

"Knock it off," the man called out. He was in his early twenties, with blond hair and a goatee. His face was turned away from her while one hand tapped an impatient beat on the Formica countertop. There was another crash and a second man bounded into the room.

"This place is like a museum!" he said, grinning. He was also young, but muscular and dark-haired. "Doilies and shit everywhere. Hey, Grandma," he said, turning to look at her. Face on, his face was haggard and his eyes blank and glazed.

"What are you doing in my house?" said Maire, staring at him as his face came into focus.

"Whoa, she's an old hag, like you said, bro," said the dark-haired man.

Maire wanted to snap back at him, but her insides were quivering. She gritted her teeth to keep herself from sobbing.

"Where's your cash, Grandma?" said the dark-haired man.

"There's money in my purse," said Maire. "That's all you'll find in the house."

Her good black handbag was lying sideways on the table, its mouth wide open and its guts spilled over the table. Her lipstick and compact and tissues were lying in the midst of coins and stamps and lined bits of notepaper. A prayer card to Saint Rita lay on top of her checkbook. There were no bills on the table. They must have pocketed those already.

"All this nice shit," the dark-haired man said, bouncing on his heels and cracking his knuckles. "I know you got something stashed away for a rainy day."

"Enough, Ray," said the blond man, sounding exasperated. The words were met by an affronted look. "Fine, look for her money. Just don't make so much noise. We don't want anyone coming over."

"Whatever, man," said Ray, disappearing through the doorway.

The blond man's eyes swept past Maire and drifted to the kitchen window. He was watching something in her backyard with a concentrated expression on his face. Maire twisted her wrists apart slightly, but the bonds were tight. *Trussed up like a turkey in my own kitchen,* she thought. Indignation gave strength to her voice. "You should be ashamed of yourself, beating an old woman and tying her up."

The man's head snapped around. "Ashamed? That's funny, coming from you." There was cold fury in his voice, and his eyes narrowed as he stared at Maire. "Where is he?" he finally said.

"Who?" Maire asked, thin lips quivering slightly.

"You lie to me and I'll cut your eyes out of your head." His gaze went to the window again, but his eyes seemed barely focused.

"You're at the wrong house," said Maire, her heart pounding out of her chest.

"You're Maire Kennelly." The man looked down at her and stepped closer. In his right hand she saw a flash of a knife blade opening up. "You don't remember me, do you?"

She looked into his eyes. They were blue with flecks of green and gold mixed in. Handsome eyes, but fatigued-looking, like someone who hadn't slept in days. They were memorable and yet not at all familiar to Maire. "I don't."

"Your son used to bring me over."

"Patrick?"

"No. The other one."

Maire stared into his eyes, but she barely saw the man in front of her. One of Brendan's little friends. All grown up now, and with a knife in his hand.

"I didn't come here to steal, though I can't say the same for my buddy." He moved a little closer to her. "I want to know where Brendan is. You're going to tell me."

"Seven years," said Maire. Her eyes were tearing up a little, and her voice was quavering.

"What?" The man put the blade of the knife against the edge of her jaw. She felt the sting of the tip of the knife. It was like the sting of a hornet, hot and sharp.

"It's seven years since . . ." She was staring into the man's eyes and speaking with careful deliberation.

"Where is he?"

"I don't know." Her gaze dropped to the hem of her black skirt.

The words were barely past her lips when she felt a searing pain on her jawbone. The blond man had slid the knife down an inch. She looked at him and saw his eyes, almost as shocked as she was. She saw blood on the knife in his hand and a wet patch on her skirt, darker than the black fabric.

"I told you not to lie to me," he hissed. "You were there with him in court every day, every single fucking day. Always by his side. You knew what he did and you didn't care." The scent of his breath was vile, like something had died in him but hadn't had a burial. *His soul,* Maire thought. Brendan had done away with that, and this was the husk that remained. She closed her eyes in anguish and guilt and began to pray to Saint Rita before she passed out again.

When she came to, Maire could hear the young man's labored breaths. He had moved a few feet away from her. When she opened her eyes, she kept her head bowed.

"I remember you praying in court," he said softly.

Maire nodded slightly and glanced up at him. He was flipping the knife closed and swinging it open, a movement that was jittery but hypnotic. Maire's eyes followed the blade, now wiped clean. The phone rang shrilly behind her. The man blinked in surprise.

"Who's calling you? It's not even nine."

"It could be my daughter."

"She live around here?"

"No. Philadelphia." Maire swallowed, the dryness of her mouth making her throat ache. The phone continued to ring.

"You don't have an answering machine?"

Maire shook her head. The blond man picked up the receiver and slammed it down. Less than a minute later the phone started ringing again. The man looked at it and cocked his head.

"Maybe it's your son calling." He grabbed the receiver and held it against his stomach. "Say hello and nothing else." He held the receiver against Maire's ear and bent down to listen.

She mumbled a soft "hello" and tried not to gag at the smell of his breath.

"Maire Kennelly? Janey Saxon again. Don't hang up! I just want to ask you a couple questions about Brendan. I won't quote you if you don't want—"

"Who the hell is that?" hissed the blond man, moving his head back slightly.

"Reporter," whispered Maire.

"Oh." He looked at the receiver—Janey Saxon's high-pitched voice was still chirping out of it—and pulled the cord out of the wall.

"Reporters always come around this time of year," said Maire.

"Guess I'm not the only one looking for Brendan." He was interrupted by the dark-haired man, Ray, who stalked into the kitchen holding a china figurine in one hand, its head obscured in his fist. "Man, this shit is all over the house. You think it's worth something?"

The blond man shrugged. Ray smashed the figurine against the wall and watched the pieces fall to the ground. "I thought maybe there's, like, diamonds hidden in them. They're all over the house. But nothing." He looked annoyed. Then, staring at Maire, he brightened. "Fucking A, Paul, you cut her face good. You look even more like a gargoyle now, Grandma."

"Cut it out, Ray."

"What's the matter with you? You were all excited about doing this, now you look like you came to a funeral. You're depressing me, man."

"I need more time."

"Grandma holding out on you?" Ray turned his full attention to Maire. His black eyes held hers, making her think of a nocturnal animal whose eyes were all pupil and no iris. "Where's your boy hiding, bitch?" He slapped her across the face once and then again. Then Maire turned her face forwards and glared at him. She tasted blood, and fury extinguished her fear.

"You are nothing," she spat out, blood trickling onto her lips.

Ray kicked her hard, hitting her leg and sending the chair toppling to one side. Her head narrowly missed the floor, but something snapped in her wrist and she cried out in agony.

"Stop it!" the blond man yelled, shoving Ray to one side and hitting him into the countertop. The knife flashed open again but she felt her bonds go slack and realized he was cutting her free.

"What did you do that for, man? I was going to get it out of her."

"Get out, Ray."

"That's what you say to me, the only one who ever tried to help you?"

Maire curled her knees to her chest and pulled her right arm close to her with her left. The bone had to have fractured; the pain was so intense. The blond man, Paul, was on his knees in front of her, looking at her arm.

"You wouldn't be nothing without me, you little fuck, you hear me?" Ray slammed his fist onto the Formica countertop. Paul stood up and grabbed Ray's arm. For a second, Maire thought Ray was going to hit him, but the big man seemed to deflate before her eyes. "You don't want my help, fine," he muttered. He turned his dark eyes on Maire. "You didn't get nothing you didn't deserve, bitch." He headed out of the kitchen and a moment later the front door slammed emphatically shut.

Paul crouched next to her. "Can you stand up?"

"I think so," whispered Maire. "But my wrist . . ."

He put his arm around her back. His head was so close to hers that she breathed in his awful breath and her head swam again. But he helped her to her feet. "You want to lie down?"

She nodded and he helped her through the doorway and down the dark hall and into the front room. It was a disaster, she realized as he eased her onto the sofa. The room looked like it had been hit by a cyclone. There was broken glass and crystal all over the bare wood floor, and pictures had been torn down from the wall and smashed. Even the framed family photographs had been swept off the end tables and crushed underfoot. Maire automatically reached down with her left arm, picked up a silver frame, and set it on the table.

"Who's that?" Paul asked.

"Vincent. My grandson," Maire said, fussing with the frame.

Paul stared at it for a moment. He knelt down and picked up the photos, propping them up on the table again. "That's your daughter Caitlin. And Patrick. I remember him. He died just after Brendan was acquitted."

Maire nodded sharply, her eyes filling with tears. Paul moved to the other side of the sofa, where Maire couldn't reach, and picked up more pictures. "You don't have one of Brendan." He said it flatly, but a question lurked within.

"How could I?" said Maire softly. "After what he did."

"So you admit it now."

Maire shrugged with her left shoulder and shook her head.

"I thought you'd defend him till your dying day." Paul sat on a chair and looked at her appraisingly. "You and your rosaries, always beside him. I wanted to strangle you back then. Dreamed about doing it with a rosary. I never understood how you could stand by him."

"If you had a child, you'd know."

"He raped kids. How could you overlook that?"

"I believed he was innocent."

"All those boys testifying against him? You thought we were all liars?"

"I thought . . . I hoped that it was a mistake."

"A mistake?"

Maire looked at him and wondered how she could ever explain. She had spent years praying to Saint Monica, because she felt that there was a bond between them that bypassed time and geography. Like Monica, Maire had had three children and a violent-tempered husband and a mother-in-law who made her life a hell on earth. And like Monica, she had recognized that one of her children was a bad seed. But that was the very thing that gave Maire hope. "A priest once told Saint Monica that it was not possible that the son of so many tears should perish," Maire said softly. "He was right. The son she despaired of, the one who made her life agony, he became one of the fathers of the church." Paul looked at her blankly. "Saint Augustine, Monica's son. It gave me hope."

"You thought Brendan was a saint?" There was acid in his voice.

A saint. What a laugh. Maire had named him for an Irish saint, Brendan the Navigator, and where had that led? "Of course not," she said. "But I hoped he'd get . . . better."

"So he was sick?"

"I'm not excusing him . . ." Her voice got louder when she saw Paul's pale cheeks flush bright red. "But anyone would have to have been ill, very ill, to do what he did."

"You thought he was innocent. What changed?"

It wasn't a question anyone had ever put to Maire before, because she never talked about Brendan, not to anyone. But she had thought about this very thing, long and hard. When had she lost her faith? She could trace it to a day, to an hour, to a half-choked confession over the phone. "I don't know," she said sharply.

"You're lying again. You've got the worst tell I've ever seen."

"Tell?"

"Like in poker, a tic that gives you away. When you lie, you look at your lap, like there's a rosary waiting there."

Maire looked at the front window and almost jumped out of her skin. "Water," she said.

"What?"

"A glass of water. I'm sitting here with my arm broken. You could at least get me a glass of water." Her voice quavered.

Paul gave her a long look. "Don't move," he said, getting up and retreating to the kitchen. Maire looked back at the window, the face of the red-haired reporter she'd seen at the church swimming in front of her eyes. *Are you all right?* The woman mouthed with her bright pink lips. Maire shook her head and thought she'd lose consciousness again, it throbbed so painfully. Janey nodded and skittered away from the window. Paul came back, a glass of tepid tap water in a glass ringed with a shamrock pattern. He handed it to her with a shaky hand and watched her drink. "You had these glasses years ago," he said.

She closed her eyes for a moment. "You said Brendan brought you here." *Help is on the way now,* she thought. All she had to do was keep him occupied a little longer. Talking about Brendan made her insides frigid and her heart stone, but she could manage it for a few moments, if she had to.

"He said if I came over I'd get a treat. Said his mother was the best cook in the world. Stupid kid I was, I fell for that." Maire's eyes followed him as he paced. "Treat for him first, of course. Then, after he was done, he gave me pie and ice cream." Paul stood still for a moment. "Rhubarb. Cherry. Blueberry. Made me wish I had a mother who cooked for me."

"You came here more than once?"

Paul sat down again, but he was jittery, kicking one heel against the chair. "He brought me over here a few times. One of the reasons he got away with it, you know. His prick lawyer kept hammering that home. 'If Mr. Kennelly was hurting these boys, why on earth would they go back to his house to have it happen again and again?' " He kicked the chair really hard, then looked at his leg as if it were an entity separate from his body.

"Are you all right?" she asked.

"When I'm up for days my muscles get jumpy."

"Up for days?"

He gave her a look that was halfway between pity and frustration. "I'm tweaking." Her blank look made him snort. "Meth. I've been up five days. Ray's pushing three weeks."

"That's a terrible sin, desecrating your body."

Her words made him smile and look away. "My body was *desecrated* a long time ago." He stood up again and paced in a circle around the chair. "You can't know how happy I was to find something that kept me from sleeping."

Maire watched him, so filled with sadness that she couldn't catch her breath.

"I'm sorry," she said softly.

He gave her a bewildered look. "That's the first time you've apologized . . ." He stared at her, realization dawning on his face. "It's true that your other son died of an overdose, isn't it? Right after the trial."

Maire nodded and dropped her head to her chest. When she tried to speak, a huge sob shook her body. She held her breath for a moment and watched fat tears drop onto her black skirt, close to where the blood from her jaw had dripped down. She felt Paul's hand on her chin, lifting up her face. "Brendan molested him too, didn't he?"

She cried softly for a little while, finally wiping her eyes and nose on her sleeve. "I didn't know," said Maire. "I never even suspected. Brendan was fourteen when his father died, Patrick was ten. Caitlin was already eighteen and out of the house. I had to go back to work to support us. Couldn't afford a babysitter, so I left Brendan in charge of his brother."

"And he abused him."

"I didn't know until the end of the trial," she said. "I called Patrick to tell him the good news, that Brendan was free, and he cried as if someone had died. He was living out in California then, as far from the rest of us as he could get. I told him he should be on his hands and knees praying. It was only then that he told me . . . what Brendan had done." She shook her head. "He hung up on me and I tried to call him back. I tried and tried and finally that night I got his landlord on the phone. He went up to Patrick's apartment and found his body. An overdose, like you said."

"He killed himself?"

"Accident or not, who could say?" Maire stared down at her skirt.

"That's why you changed your mind about Brendan. But by then, it didn't matter." His hands were drumming against his thighs. "So where is he now?"

Maire shook her head.

"I can't believe you're still protecting him. He's responsible for the death of your other son, you know that?" His voice was getting louder. "You know how many other deaths he's caused? How many drunks? How many addicts?" He towered over her. "You're going to tell me if it's the last thing you do."

Maire laughed suddenly, a short, mirthless sound that was almost a bark. "That would be a threat if my life meant anything to me." Paul's blue-green eyes stared at her. "Do you think I want to go on living like this, knowing I gave life to a monster? This is hell on earth. I wish I were dead."

Paul shook his head disbelievingly. "When the trial was on, somebody asked you how you were getting through it. You said it was faith. What happened to that?"

"I put my faith in the wrong things," she answered quietly. "I have committed a mortal sin and I . . ." Her voice trailed off. "I can't even take communion now. I'd have to go to confession first. I'd have to tell a priest my sins, and there are too many to tell."

"Hiding your son from me is a sin." Paul sat down on the couch next to her. "You know he's guilty."

"And you want revenge," Maire said, staring straight ahead.
"It's not just that." He put two fingertips on her bloody jaw
and gently turned her face to his. "I think about what he's doing
now. I think about him hurting other kids."

Maire stared into his eyes for several heartbeats and took a
deep breath. "He can't hurt anyone."

"I need more than just you telling me that," said Paul.

"If I tell you where he is, you have to promise me something."

"Anything."

"You'll put an end to my suffering. I don't mind how you
do it, so long as you do."

"Put an end . . ." Paul stared at her in disbelief.

"I can't kill myself. A Catholic can't do that," Maire explained. "But it would be a mercy if—"

At that moment there was a crashing sound and shouting,
and men with guns yelling, "Don't move!" and a camera crew
behind them getting everything on tape. Paul was shoved onto
the ground, a patrolman's knee shoved into the small of his
back as he was cuffed. "No!" shouted Maire. "You can't take
him away! Let him alone!" No one listened to her. Another cop
frisked Paul and pulled out a small baggie from the pocket of
his jeans.

"This is Janey Saxon, reporting live from the home of Maire
Kennelly, mother of accused sex offender Brendan Kennelly.
Mrs. Kennelly's quiet home was brutally invaded this morning
by a pair of drug addicts . . ."

Maire closed her eyes and sank back against the couch, offering no resistance to the medics who swarmed around her.
There would be no release and no absolution for her.

Maire refused to press charges, but Paul was arrested for
drug possession, denied bail, and shipped to Rikers Island
awaiting trial. Janey Saxon had spotted his partner leaving Maire's

house, but the police hadn't found Ray. For all Paul knew, he was headed back to San Diego. One morning Paul was told he had a visitor, and he was stunned at the sight of Maire on the other side of the glass. Her silvery hair was freshly permed and she was wearing a black suit and red lipstick. One side of her face was healing from dark bruising, but the cut on her jaw looked as if it had healed without a stitch.

"You look better. Healthier," she said when she picked up the telephone to speak to him.

"Maybe orange is my color," he said, and gave her a slight smile.

"I've thought a great deal about what we talked about, the last time I saw you," she said carefully. "I told you about Saint Monica. Now I want to tell you about Saint Rita."

Paul stared at her, wondering if it was the blow in her front hall or the fall in the kitchen that had jumbled her brain.

"I started praying to Rita after the trial, when I finally knew what my son really was. Do you know anything about Saint Rita? Her life was a hell on earth. Her husband abused her and her sons were terrible creatures. She prayed for them, for all of them, but the only relief she got was when they died."

Paul took a sharp breath.

"The last thing my son Patrick said to me was: *Take care of Vincent. Don't let Brendan get him too.*" Maire blinked back tears. "It hit me then, my grandson was in danger. Brendan wasn't going to stop. *I* had to stop him." She took a deep breath. "Brendan could read me like a book, just like you did, and I thought he would realize that something in my heart had changed. But with Patrick's death, it was easy to explain why I was . . . different. After Patrick's funeral, when Caitlin had left with her husband and boy, I made dinner for Brendan. It was never hard to get him to come over for that. He always said I was the best cook in the world."

Paul swallowed hard.

"Do you think anyone's listening to this?" Maire said idly. "Be an interesting test, won't it? So when Brendan came over, I served him dinner. And that was the end of that."

"You mean you . . ." Paul's hand shook and he gripped the receiver.

"It had to stop. It was the only thing I could do."

"But how did you . . . get . . . rid . . . of . . . ?"

"There's a rather large freezer in my basement," said Maire. "The next time you come over, I'll show you." She sat straight in her seat. "You've a fine way of listening to an old woman prattle on. Almost as good as a priest." She started to get up. "Keep in mind you made me a promise," she said, leaning close to the glass. "I intend to hold you to it."

Faith-Based Initiative

Kieran Shea

Every Monday at a quarter past five, Father Mike Hogan takes a corner stool at The Raised Jar.

Mondays are Father Mike's days off from the bleak, celibate trade of the doomed at Sacred Heart down in Asbury Park. Shepherding the indigent, the guilty, the infirm, and more and more these days, the totally fucked.

Typically, Father Mike settles in at the end of the mahogany, tucks into a recycled stack of Sunday papers I save for him, maybe orders a thrifty special off of the menu. Curried stuffed potato skins and Manhattan clam chowder are keen with Father Mike. Never more than two pints at a sitting lest it get back to the fretful diocese brass.

The Raised Jar's owners, Ed and Eleanor Campbell, love the old man to pieces. Hell, everybody does. What with his coaching the summer hoops league and the shore homeless shelter, the man is a local saint. The Campbells comp Father Mike too, because he hooked them up with Ethan and Luke, their two adopted Korean sons.

There's no TV in the bar, so Mondays are a dead shift behind the sticks, and because of this I've gotten to know Father Mike pretty well.

He reads thick, political biographies and both of us think James Gandolfini is totally overrated. I'm lapsed, but what the hell. Father Mike keeps trying.

"A seltzer, Gabe."

I arch an eyebrow. "No Guinness tonight, Father?"

Father pats his pockets like he's forgotten something.

"No," he says. "My stomach's been acting funny. Just the soda, please, Gabe. No straw."

"Fruit in it?"

Father Mike shakes his head no and rakes his scalp-cut with his fingernails. I smile and gun him a large soda, tapping it down on a coaster in front of him. His skin is scarlet from the cold walk up to Long Branch. February low off the New Jersey coastline makes the sea air slash like a razor. From where I stand I can smell the stale smoke drifting off his faded blue Knights of Columbus windbreaker like an old attic sheet.

What can I say? The priest likes his Winstons.

I stick a black plastic swizzle stick in my mouth and switch it back and forth with my tongue as Father Mike slugs back some of his seltzer. Setting his drink down, his eyes bore into the space on the bar between his scabbed hands. And then Father makes a noise that sounds almost like a child stifling a hiccup.

Father can't hold it. He starts crying.

I reach for his forearm.

"Hey, Father. Hey, now. Hey."

"I know, I know. I'm sorry."

"Hey, nothing to be sorry about."

He backhands some tears. "It's been . . . it's been hard."

"I know, Father."

"Hard for me, Gabe. Hard for the other priests, but they're younger. Ethiopia. Sierra Leone. They've seen worse where they come from."

"I know, Father. It breaks my heart."

"Horrible things."

"It'll get better soon, you'll see."

With fractured grief, Father Mike stares into my eyes and starts to cough, a heavy smoker's jag.

Two other patrons at a lone two-top across the room look up from their burgers and I shoot them a look. They go back to their specials while Wendy, our sole waitress on Mondays, refills their water glasses.

I let go of Father's forearm and go old school.

I pour Father a double of Tullamore Dew.

After closing, our grill cook, Miguel Morales, sits near the back door of the kitchen. He's peeled out of his checks, apron, and chef's jacket, and changed into his street clothes—some ratty sweats with a black zipped hoodie, swollen dirty sneakers, and a red Fila trucker's cap. Miguel kind of leans and sits on a short stack of four green milk crates, arms resting on his thighs like a whipped prize fighter.

After I called Father Mike a cab, we had about a dozen other bar and dinner customers. Ed came by to cash out the register with a security escort about a half hour ago, and he gave Wendy a lift home. It's part of my job to turn out the lights and set the alarms. Because it's a light night, I gave Miguel a hand breaking down the kitchen and running the dry mop over the mud-colored tiles. Eight dinner tickets all night long. Clean up was a breeze.

Miguel and I are drinking our second shift beers before heading home. The scent of bleach and lemon cleanser from the floor is stifling. I pull on my brown Carhartt jacket and shake my keys.

"Light night, huh?"

Miguel looks up.

"Mondays at The Jar . . ." I go on, taking a slurp from my beer. "Macking."

Miguel mutters something I can't hear.

"What's that?"

"S'not right, yo."

"What's not right?"

"Father Mike."

I chew my lip. "Yeah, well. Hey, what're you going to do? Scumbag kids."

"Still. S'not right."

I zipper up my jacket and adjust my watch cap in the shine of the glassed doors of the standup convection oven behind the line. I rent a garage apartment a stiff ten-minute walk from the bar, and if I get a move on I can probably catch a shower and maybe ESPN *SportsCenter* before midnight and dreams. In ten hours I've got class over at a Rutgers satellite. Economics.

"Somebody should do somethin', yo."

I turn and tilt my head. Miguel is looking at me now, his brown eyes dead on and hard. I wait a beat.

"Do something?"

Miguel's head bobs.

"Yeah."

I eye him up and down.

"What? You?"

"No. Me and you."

I bark a short laugh, but Miguel's face stays stony.

"You're serious?"

"*Sí.* I totally serious."

"Get the fuck out of here, Miguel."

Miguel throws up his hands. "But Father Mike, he does so much, man. My cousin? Enrique? Fuck. His little girl got sick and Father Mike was, like, paying for her meds an' shit. Does it all the time. Father, he give when no one care. Old Italian ladies yell: Latinos ruining their *parroquia* and I's like, fuck them. But Father Mike sticks up for us. You don't know what that's like, G."

Miguel is right. I have no idea what it's like.

I grew up middle class with broken family roots one county over. I attend college on my own dime because I can't pour beer forever, and I'm dating a cherry-haired, Irish bombshell with great tits who adores anything I do. I have prospects. Young guys like Miguel, from the battered, carved-up houses in the trashed, flagged parts of all these Jersey beach towns, the cheap apartments and forgotten residential tracts—it's got to suck. All feared and shunned. Clawed their ways out of the brutal guts of one country into another's just to be squashed in the slack and scapegoated. It was Father Mike who talked to the Campbells into hiring Miguel on the line at The Jar in the first place.

I try to talk sense into him.

"Miguel, come on, man. Think about it. What're you going to do? Like in a perfect world I'm sure there'd be some justice out there and those sickos who trashed Father Mike's church would get theirs."

"Yeah."

"But I'm sure the cops are doing everything they can. Just forget about it, dude. It's their problem."

"Ellos saben la mierda."

I finish my beer.

"Yeah, well, they may know shit, amigo, but sooner or later they'll figure it out."

Miguel sulks. "Been, like, three weeks, man."

"So?"

"So? *So?* Someone like me, I do somethin' like that? Like . . . *bang*, jail. Throw away the key."

And I think, maybe Miguel just needs another beer. Fuck, I know I do. I saunter into the dining room and reach over the bar to pour us a couple more Harp Lagers from the tap. I walk back gingerly and hand him his. We drink our third beers pretty much in silence until Miguel leaps up and punches a hole in the drywall.

"*Hey!*" I shout.

Miguel is up now, pacing. "Like I know, man! Like I know who did it, G!"

"You? You know who trashed Sacred Heart?"

"*Sí.*"

"No shit?"

"Yeah. No shit. Enrique knows too."

"Enrique?"

"My cousin. Says last month Father sees this homeboy hitting some girl bad, so he stop to help. Fucked Father all up. Bryant. That's the guy. Bryant guy say he gonna get even, fuck Father Mike for good. And, yo, people, man . . . they saw it. Everybody saw it! Him say all this shit, but nobody say nothin' to police. Nothin'. Word is, homeboy brags about what he did. Proud."

"What's this Bryant dude's first name?"

"*No se. Pinche puta.*"

"Where does he live? Up here? Does this piece of shit live down in Asbury proper or what?"

"Nah. Down Neptune."

"Neptune?"

"Yeah."

I remember Father Mike weeping at the bar and slowly I begin to feel my shoulders tighten.

I cannot imagine the humiliation, the suppressed rage Father Mike feels. A real boot in the face. Paint and garbage and broken stained glass everywhere. Graffiti describing acts of pedophilia. Dog shit stuffed in the chalice. Sacred Heart's statue of the Virgin Mary had her eyes blacked out and her hands chopped off.

"We need a lookout, yo."

"What? Wait. Who? Me?"

"Yeah. Jus' a lookout."

"I don't know, man."

Miguel paces. "Enrique an' me we teach this *maricón* respect, yo. You don' have to do nothin'."

"Fuck. What the fuck, Miguel?"

Miguel rolls his shoulders. "Back in an hour, G."

Three more beers and Miguel makes a call from the kitchen's phone. Ten minutes later a dented, tan Toyota minivan picks us up half a block down from the bar. We climb in and I slide the side door closed.

"Enrique, este es Gabriel."

Enrique is slightly taller than Miguel and bigger across the shoulders. He has a closely shaved head, full goatee, and wears a heavy lined black and tan flannel shirt over a gray sweatshirt. From where I sit in the back, I can see a dark green shadow of an ornate tattoo creeping up from below his collar to the base of his skull.

Enrique pulls into traffic and doesn't acknowledge me at all. The radio plays some Latin talk show, real low, the DJ's rapid-fire prattle sounding like he's trapped in an oil drum. A minty air freshener with a Salvadoran flag on it swings from the rearview mirror and there are kids' toys all over the backseat. I adjust my legs. There's easily a half a dozen empty McDonald's and White Castle sacks on the floor.

Enrique points below the glove compartment and turns the wheel.

"Compruebe el bolso . . ."

Miguel unzips a duffel at his feet, rummages, and zips it back up.

"Galán."

Via the side streets we pick our way over to Route 71 and head south towards Neptune. I'm more than half drunk but

I'm thinking how bad this all is, about how I'm about to royally fuck up my life and maybe after a few beers this isn't the best idea to go vigilante, but fuck it.

Miguel gestures to me without looking back and the two of them in the front seat speak so much rapid-fire Salvadoran *caliche* slang that I can't keep up with my restaurant Spanglish. They laugh and Enrique catches my eyes in the rearview mirror.

"*¿Tu es un amigo de Padre?*"

I steel myself. I look back and nod.

And I am. I am Father Mike's friend. Beery drums pound the courage and I think: *fuck this guy Bryant, this lowlife motherfucker.* Father Mike is a stand-up guy doing real things to help real people and this Bryant piece of shit deserves some kind of payback for destroying the church. The fucking coward. A good ass-kicking sounds dead fine with me. But then I think, *Ah . . . fucking hell.*

I should have just gone home.

We troll by Bryant's butt-ugly, aqua-colored ranch house and pull around the block and park just off an access alley. Enrique and Miguel tell me to follow their lead and we move fast across the backyards. Apparently Bryant sleeps in the basement of his mom's split-level. It's a rec room arrangement with a sliding glass door exiting onto a cheap red flagstone patio all chemoed with weeds of neglect. I guess Enrique and Miguel just figured the back door would be unlocked because Bryant is a lazy ass kid or maybe if it was locked they'd just smash it in. Regardless, somewhere several houses away, a chained up dog catches our scent and goes positively apeshit. We wear latex gloves from the restaurant and black ski masks.

From the sliding glass door, I see Bryant passed out on a plaid couch in the blue glow of a DVD player's cue. Skinny guy, maybe twenty, with a whisper of a beard and short dreadlocked hair. There's a low, cruddy coffee table in front of the couch with a veritable skyline of spent Steel Reserve 211 malt liquor cans on it, the towering jewel of this city being a huge, red, translucent bong. A short stack of porno DVD cases are also on the coffee table. One case is flipped open and the cover is propped up in our direction like a greeting card. Even in the ghostly blue glow from the television, I can read the title from outside on the patio: *Big Wet Hiney-Hos #7*. Bryant's right hand is shoved down the front of his boxers. Guess he passed out mid-stroke.

I feel like I'm having a heart attack as I watch Miguel unzip the duffel and take out a youth-sized Rawlings aluminum baseball bat. He tracks the door open, crosses the room quickly, and chops fast before Bryant can focus out of his ganja coma as to what is happening. The bat catches Bryant at the top of his forehead with a hollow *thwok* and he flops back down on the couch. Miguel pops him again just to be sure he's out cold and Enrique slips farther into the basement, taking up a position on the stairs leading to the top half of the house, in case Bryant's mother comes padding down mid-assault.

Miguel steps back across the room and slides the door almost closed. Behind his ski mask, his eyes lock with mine and he quickly makes hand signals with a latexed forefinger. He taps his ear. *Listen.* He points in several directions from behind the glass and touches just below his eye. *Keep an eye out.*

I nod sharply at Miguel, and he turns and takes a fat roll of silver duct tape from the duffel and proceeds to wrap Bryant's mouth shut, wrapping the tape around his head several times like a mummy. Miguel binds Bryant's hands and feet as well.

Finished, Miguel steps back and gestures to Enrique. As instructed, I do a quick survey of the backyard, right then left, and then look back at the scene within. Through the cracked sliding glass door, I see that Enrique now has the bat and I hear two quick whooving sounds as he sails it through the air. Each swing ends with a grotesque, wet crunch as Bryant's kneecaps explode. Bryant rockets awake like a bucking animal. The screams against the duct tape are awful.

Lights pop on. I blink away the blur.

A voice upstairs cries out.

"Jeremy?"

Holy shit. Bryant's mom. Holy shit. Oh shit. Ohholyfuckingshit.

I can see Bryant's mom up in the foyer. In a pink bathrobe, she is enormous . . . and she is fumbling with what looks like a shotgun. She shrieks something indecipherable and Miguel charges up the short stairs to the foyer to take her out. He snatches the shotgun from her hands, flips it, and jabs the stock square in the woman's wide forehead. Bryant's mom crumples to the floor with a thud, hammy arms and legs out akimbo.

Enrique doesn't appear rattled by the interruption. Leisurely he takes a can of red spray paint from the duffel bag and gang tags the basement paneling above Bryant's heaving body. When he finishes, Enrique kicks Bryant in the shoulder and points at the wall.

Behind the tape, Bryant screams again, bug-eyed. The paint drips down the wall like a diagram drawn in blood.

Bryant's face shines with tears and snot. The veins in his neck are wires.

"¿Padre Mike?"

Bryant whines as Miguel turns out the lights in the foyer upstairs. Enrique whispers.

"¿La próxima vez?"

My mind tumbles the translation: Next time?

Bryant freaks.

Enrique hisses, *"Machete."*

A month and a half goes by and I keep waiting for the police to come a tap-tapping on my apartment door, or strolling into The Raised Jar's kitchen, or finding me in class, wrenching the handcuffs on me in front of a room full of slack-jawed peers. But no. Nothing. Not a peep. No aggravated assault charges or attempted murder charges or anything. The cops eventually link Bryant to the desecration of Sacred Heart but there's nothing in the papers about him or his mom or the attack.

Miguel doesn't speak of that night, until one Friday we're both in the walk-in refrigerator together.

I'm shouldering a case of Amstel and I have the necks of a couple bottles of the house white in my right hand. Crossing his arms, Miguel blocks the heavy, pebbled metal door.

"Hey, Miguel."

"Sup?"

"Can I get by?"

Miguel squints. "Father Mike . . . right thing, G."

I shrug. "You hear anything?"

Miguel shakes his head.

"Me either," I say.

Miguel laughs. *"Somos fantasmas."*

"Huh?"

"Boo!" He points at his chest then at me.

"Ghosts?"

"Sí. Ghosts. We ghosts. And Enrique and me, we owe you, G."

I look away. "No, you don't."

"No. We do."

I catch his eyes. "Okay."

Miguel's face goes flat, hard.

"But Enrique, yo, he has doubts."

"Doubts?"

"Sí."

"What do you mean fucking doubts?"

"Doubts, yo. You . . . *no familia . . . entiendes?* We cool and all, but I tell him and I tell him, but he's like . . ." Miguel shrugs. *"¿Quién sabe?"*

I puff out an incredulous snort.

"D'fuck, dude?"

"Hey, amigo. I jus' tellin' like it is."

I shove past him.

I step out of the walk-in into the heat and clattering chaos of the kitchen and I look back at Miguel standing in the walk-in's doorway. He flashes me a crooked upside *M* with his fingers and winks and starts laughing. Howling actually.

Mara Salvatrucha. MS-13.

And I remember the sound of Bryant's breaking knees and I head to the bar.

The bar, the bar, the motherfucking bar.

Mahogany and Monogamy

Jedidiah Ayres

The first time I saw Janis I knew she was a ballbuster. That was part of the appeal, honestly. Mom had been one and my kid sister, Denise? That's all I got to say. But Janis had something special and I'm not just talking about her industrial-strength rack and bear-trap thighs. She also had that elusive thing that I just can't resist, and if I knew what it was I probably wouldn't have a story to tell.

We had our own song, "Sweet Child O' Mine." It was our first dance. She danced, that's what she did, and when it got to the "where do we go?" part, she slowed way down and tried to grind it outta me with her hips. Then she did something strange. She stopped and looked me right in the eye. It made me pop. She rocked my world with just a look, then kept on dancing. Sure, she helped lotsa guys do the same, but me? After the first time I saw her, there wasn't anybody else, you know?

You're never gonna find anything, my old man said, written down in a book. He was a loser till the day he died, fucked over and left by my mom, but he did manage one memorable line near the end when the lucid spells were brief and unpredictable.

He was talking about when he first met my mother. He said he knew she was the one for him because she made him wanna grow up and produced the previously impossible in his life— mahogany and monogamy. I thought it was just a nice rhymey thing to say till that night.

Janis didn't notice anything special about me at first, and that was okay. Working at the Beaver Cleaver, she didn't meet many prizes, and to look at me, you'd not stop and think, "Guy's a sex machine" or "What's his secret?" But people change. They do grow up. They can surprise you sometimes. Gimme a chance and who knows? Could might be I make an impression.

Could be I'd made a life change. Could be I'd got my shit together. Could be I had fifty-thousand dollars in a gym bag in my trunk. Could be.

The thing about a guy like me having that kind of money on him? Yeah, it means somebody else is short that much. I never invested in stocks or had a business. I never went to high school or had anything fancy education-wise and I never paid taxes unless you count cigarettes. Which, come to think of it, maybe you should. Because, damn if they don't go up all the time, for real. So, yeah has to be somebody missing it.

The question then, is who?

Relax, might not be an Einstein or any other brainy hebe you care to name, but I'm not as dumb as you might initially think. It's not like I robbed a bank and got my picture took, or ripped off some solid citizen who'd wanna bring lawyers into a fair fight. And I ain't about to take on no badass, because I know a thing or two about when I'm outta my depth.

No, it was just Benji, that skinny tweaker with the fuzzy upper lip you wanna scrape for him. Seriously, I'm no square, but damn, some motherfuckers just ain't intended to wear mustaches. I took it from a hole in the wall behind his medicine cabinet. Just stumbled onto it and took it.

Pee-Wee, the guy who runs Carl's Bad Tavern down off Cherokee? He sees me getting up to leave the other night and slips me twenty bucks to take Benji's ass home. Benji's passed out in the bathroom, puke everywhere except the fucking toilet and a cloud of that rat poison he smokes stinking up the place.

Not one to look a gift horse up the ass, I take the twenty and put him in my Chevette. Thought about just dumping him around the corner, because he stank like he'd been practicing, but I shut that shit down because it was time to get a little forward-thinking in my game. In the future, could be Pee-Wee knows I'm solid for this kinda thing. Could be he thinks of me first, next time. Could be some regular gigs coming, or at least a free drink now and then. Never know. Could be.

I wasn't about to fuck with that possibility by taking the man's money then not doing what it is he says he wants, like some short-sighted asshole who thinks he just played a man. So I took Benji back to his place, wasn't far, and let myself in with the keys I found in his pocket. Not a part I relished, reaching into a man's pants like that—especially a stank-ass motherfuck like Benji—but, like I said, I wanted to do this right. I was already thinking about future jobs.

Maybe I'd get some of those disposable rubber gloves, if this was gonna be regular. You know the kind they make them wear at Subway to make sandwiches? Or maybe, and this is even better, talk to my cousin Rob, the plumber. Find out what he does when he's gotta reach into some shit water and find a wedding ring, because you know plumbers don't fuck around when it comes to that. Hell, I could just get some Ziploc bags and put them on. Would be cheaper. If I paid taxes, I bet I could write that off.

I was getting a little carried away, but it felt good, being trusted with a job like that. Pee-Wee was a serious guy. . . . Shit . . . That was something else. Stop calling him Pee-Wee. He was connected to real people, and I didn't wanna blow any chance I had with him now by offending him. Herman hated that nickname.

The way I saw it, it was time to take a little responsibility. Time to think about a career. Not that shoveling shit outta bars was a career I'd like to have, but you know, it was a start. I'm sure Janis didn't wanna climb a brass pole for amateur gynecologists the rest of her life.

I brought Benji inside the door and no further. Fuck him if he thought I was gonna tuck him in or give him a bath. Not for twenty bucks. No way. But, I'd have a look around, thanks. It was how I made most of my money anyhow. A little B&E here and there, I wasn't above it. The beauty of this was, it was E without B, and Benji wasn't conscious the whole time, wouldn't have any idea how he got home when he woke up.

Benji was poor white trash, up and down. His basement apartment had plain white walls decorated with black light posters of like Pantera and hemp plants and shit. His clothes weren't in the dresser except for some underwear and socks, and those that were on the furniture and the floor were one pair of jeans—black and ripped, like the ones he was already wearing—and heavy metal T-shirts. There was no jewelry (surprise, surprise) and no electronics worth taking.

There were cassettes all over the floor, not in the cases, which is something that personally really irritates me. It was the same story with the VCR stuff. Couple tapes just marked with pen: *Missing in Action, The Running Man, Bloodsport.* Say what you want about his lifestyle, his taste in movies was righteous.

Pisser was, I didn't find any drugs. Turned over his mattress, checked the freezer, behind the toilet, went through all his food, a jar of mayonnaise, some Sanka and Kool-Aid. I was so frustrated, I went back to his grungy-ass bathroom and grabbed his razor. Didn't bother with any water or foam. Shaved that shit dry. Bled a little, but still looked better. Shit, that was two favors I did for him in one night.

When I put the razor back in the medicine cabinet, I noticed it was a little loose, like it was on a hinge or something. I gave it a little tug and it swung open, revealing a little hiding spot in the wall.

Fuck, there was a lot of money.

It was arranged in those neat little stacks you see rubber banded together in movies. I didn't even count it, just threw it in a gym bag and drove straight to the Beaver. I peeled off a couple hundred and went in looking for Janis.

Could've been my walk or the intensity in my eyes. Could've been the super-heavy testosterone vibes pouring off of me. Or could be she just saw me changing a couple C-notes for singles. Whatever it was, she knew right away that I was different. She put on "Sweet Child O' Mine" before I could even request it. She got every penny too.

I started hanging out at Carl's every night. I'd keep my eyes peeled for losers ready to pass out or puke in the john. Fifty-thousand dollars was a nice start, but not exactly enough to re-tire on and I was serious about making a good impression on Herman. Besides, I couldn't tell anybody about my good for-tune, because when a little shit like Benji had that kind of scratch? Right again, somebody else was missing it.

That was one thought causing me mild discomfort when it came up. How had Benji come upon that much money? When? And what the hell was he spending it on? I decided it wasn't my problem and I didn't want to know, so I shut down that nega-tive shit quick. The way I saw it, if I kept up my regular sched-ule and didn't get flashy, I had it made.

The only change in my routine was stepped-up visits to Janis. Most nights, I'd come in with a single hundred-dollar bill and leave when it was gone. Though I realized I'd made a tacti-cal mistake that first night bringing two hundred in and spending it so quickly. Janis had come to expect a little more from me, but so had I, and I was trying to show a little discipline. So it was one hundred every night . . . let's not go crazy, you know. I was trying to pace myself a bit and make her work a little harder for it.

Janis wasn't the only one working a little harder for her money either. Herman had noticed me and given me a couple more disposal jobs. Nobody I knew, though. I had to dig out their IDs and find an address, and then I had to figure that shit out. Got to be, I was calling cabs and going with them to make sure they got inside. Oh well, it's like they say: you gotta spend money to make money. Yeah, I was, most of the time, blowing what Herman gave me on cab fare. But I was counting on that back end score once I got them home, and most of the time that worked out. A couple times there was a pissed-off wife or mean-ass dog waiting for me, but it was a safe bet anybody passing out at Carl's doesn't have much waiting for them at home.

I heard a preacher on the radio once say, "Love is patient. Love is kind." All I could think was: he didn't love Janis. It was getting a touch restless between us. She was less patient, I was less kind, and we were becoming something of an item. One night during my dance I guess she felt I was being a little stingy because she stood up suddenly and said, "What the fuck, Ethan? I am not doing one more number for a lousy hunnerd bucks. We're halfway through the first guitar solo and I barely got thirty-five outta your tight ass!"

Well, that pissed me off a bit. The way I saw it, I'd been spending my money on her exclusively for some time now and hadn't got so much as a friendly hummer to show for fidelity.

"At least one of us still has one," I said, and left with money in my pocket for the first time. I decided she'd got her last score off of me.

Did I stop going? Hell, no. I still went every night after leaving Carl's, but I wasn't a one woman man anymore. No, I spread the wealth. New girl every night. I'd watch Janis out the corner of my eye and I could tell my being there pissed her off. The tension between us could tune a piano. Could be our thing had gone to the next level. Could be I was in my first serious relationship. Could be, I was finally growing up. Could be.

The night they broke Benji's arm, everybody assumed it was over sports action. It happened from time to time. That or drugs. Everybody knew that happened when you fucked around with the drugs. I had to keep it to myself that I suspected it had more to do with some missing cash.

He came into Carl's, his right arm hanging off him like a purse. He clutched it with his left, but was stumbling and running into shit every few steps. When he used his left to steady himself, the right would swing free and he'd scream loud enough to stop traffic in other neighborhoods. Before he passed out, he pleaded for somebody to get him a fix and get him fixed, just don't take him to no hospital, he had warrants.

He should've been a little more cautious about the company he made an announcement like that in, because there's a couple sick puppies in there just curious enough to try setting his arm without any idea of what they're doing. And nobody was gonna give him any drugs without cash up front.

When those dudes got tired of playing with his arm, I nodded at Herman, who took out a fifty this time. When I came to collect it, he grabbed me and whispered, "Take it easy tonight, huh?"

I looked into Herman's eyes and my asshole puckered. That guy looked scary. Maybe I'd just met the edge of where my hard ass turned to pussy, but he was like E. F. Hutton or some shit—I was listening.

"No hospital. Get him a fix."

So, what do you think I did?

I knew the arm needed to be set and secured, but shit, I

mean, I didn't know any better than those biker fucks what I was doing. At least I scored him some good shit. Some shit anyhow. I never trucked with that stuff, so I don't really know from quality, but he slept through it all and I wandered alone in his apartment again. I think the place had been tossed, but it was hard to tell.

I felt a bit responsible looking at the kid, laying there with his busted wing, bound with a fuckload of scotch tape. I stopped for just a moment and let the feelings match up to the thoughts about what exactly my role in this had been. It was a rare quiet moment of reflection for me.

"Look. You fucked up. That's who you are; the guy who fucks up. I'm just the guy who benefited this time. The way things go, man. No hard feelings."

He groaned through his opiate stupor and I continued.

"If it makes you feel better, I ain't blowing it on pussy anymore. I mean, yeah, a little bit, but I got bigger plans then that." In truth, I felt a little guilty. In fact, I didn't even get a dance that night.

I was back the next night, though. Lil' Debi was starting to get the bulk of my business. I'm not sure if it was her looks or style or what. She had big bangs that were stiff if you touched them and favored a very strong strawberry-scented perfume. It kinda smelled like she'd used a whole pack of ChapStick on her crotch, and maybe she had, but I suspect the real appeal was her name. There was something kinda kinky-sexy about thinking I was getting dry humped outta my money by a snack cake.

Since Janis was there, I was playing my usual Mötley Crüe pick, "Don't Go Away Mad (Just Go Away)." I liked to think it bugged the shit outta her. I closed my eyes at the moment and sought out Janis's gaze with my mind. It pleased me to find it white-hot at the base of my skull, and I savored it a moment, knowing that the jealousy of a woman tasted sweet.

So, it shocked me when I opened my eyes and saw Janis on

the other side of the room, not paying me no nevermind. So surprised I was that I pushed Debi off my lap unceremoniously and spun around to see who was looking at me.

Couple mopes dressed in nylon tracksuits and wearing jewelry, just bringing down the property value over in the corner, talking with Don the bartender. Following his pointing finger over in my direction. Didn't stick around to find any shit out, didn't help Debi up. Just left quick, before they could talk to me.

Five in the morning, my phone woke me up.

"Mmmm . . ."

Whispered: "Ethan?"

"Mmmm."

"Hey, I just got off. I need to see you."

"Janis?"

"We need to talk. Meet me at Uncle Bill's."

I found Janis at a booth, three Kools in the ashtray and one in her lips. She shoved the coffee she'd ordered for me into my hands. "Hope you like cream and sugar."

She let me finish the coffee in silence, watching me intently while the whites of her eyes swelled with deep drags of menthol. She held my empty hand and sent electric tickles up and down my arm with her touch. The look in her eyes was intense and expectant—if our song was playing, I'd probably have wet my pants. It should have scared me, but I was only flattered. When I set the empty cup down, she said, "So?"

"Yeah?"

"What did you do, Ethan?"

"What are you talking about?"

"Why are those scary guys looking for you?"

Immediately I half stood and looked around. "What guys?"

"You know, the ones at the club? What do they want from you?"

I shook my head. "I don't know. I've never seen them before."

She smiled and grabbed both my hands in hers. "You can tell me, baby."

Apparently it was some kind of turn-on. Danger hung off me like ten inches. We got a room at the Motor Inn and danger threw a party. Afterwards, she slept and I watched TV till she got up about noon. Her makeup was a mess and her Tawny Kitaen hair bunched at odd angles from all the product and sweat and sleep. Her eyes worked hard at a twinkle when they met mine, but—and maybe it was the daylight and not insincerity—the effect was sexy as . . . well not very. But when she dropped the sheet and walked to the bathroom, there was a pleasant tingle south of my navel.

I'm not sure what she'd heard from loose talk at the club or what she'd managed to get out of me during our little romp. Could be she's smart. Could be she's wired with a sixth sense for money matters. Could be I'm transparent. Could be . . . Because when she comes out of the shower a few minutes later, wrapped in a towel and looking sweet and fuck hungry simultaneously, she lets that little motel-issue napkin fall and in the same instant nails me with, "So, how much we got?"

Nobody at the Beaver knew my last name. Janis had my phone number and that was it. She was the only one who could tell those scary guys in the sweatpants who I was. That made us partners, she figured. Partners in what?

Dude. Spending, of course.

Now, I'm not hypnotized over snatch so bad I can't see what's going on here. But come on . . . I am just exactly what you think I am: horny, lonely, and a bit low on the old self-esteem. And if not this, then what the fuck is it money is supposed to buy for you?

So?

"Fifty."

"Fifty!" she says like I just won her a teddy bear popping balloons at the fair.

"Fifty-thousand bucks, baby. All for us."

Being the meat in a fuck sandwich with Lynda Carter and Erin Gray? Flying copilot with Jan-Michael Vincent? The Hair Club for Men? These were things I had given serious thought to over the years. Life expectancy was not. Had I devoted some time in consideration of it, could be some things I'd have done different.

Could be I'd not have started smoking at eight years old. Could be I'd never have told that loudmouth Brian Belisle about fingering Tanya Hopeck behind the Dumpsters in junior high. Could be I'd not've stuck around St. Louis after stealing fifty-thousand dollars.

Might've turned out I'd not been such a sickly kid, gotten my ass kicked every day by Jeremy Hopeck or into some serious shit with an opportunistic stripper. But I'll tell you what, nothing would've stopped me from smoking, fingering, or stealing in the first place.

It was going to take a couple days for Janis to wrap up her affairs. Minor things like getting some money she was owed and finding somebody to take her cat. But the plan was to leave town together, go to Vegas or New Orleans, live fast and loose for a while. Forget my future working for Pee-Wee. Guess I could call him that again . . . not to his face mind you, but he scared me too much to wanna be around. I was gonna see how much happiness, or at least pleasure, I could make the money good for.

In the meantime, we agreed it would be best for us to continue our regular routines, so as not to call attention to ourselves. At least she should. I'd already got some attention. So, I gave her a thousand in walking around money. Enough, I figured, for her not to nag me for a bit, and too little for her to split on me with. She left me at the Motor Inn for work around six.

I was too antsy to stay at the motel, so I jumped in my car for a drive. Flipped the radio to 94.7 and scored an omen. "Sweet Child O' Mine" blasted from my shitty speakers and I rolled down the window, wishing my hair were still thick enough to wear long. It'd feel good to let it whip around in the breeze while driving. Crossed the Martin Luther King into Illinois and started cruising the east side, thinking long as she was playing this whole relationship mercenary style, might as well get some strange while the getting was good.

The song ended and another GNR tune immediately kicked in—must be twofer Tuesday or some shit. Deciding to check out the Ten Foot Pole, I headed south. That's when the omen took a darker turn.

Normally, you can't catch shit on the radio. Seems I always have to twist the dial immediately after one good song, so back-to-back ass-kicking tunes usually make my day—let alone Guns followed by AC/DC. But the thoughts I was beginning to have? Shit was dark. "Got You by the Balls" followed by "Dirty Deeds Done Dirt Cheap" sunk my mood. For real.

Would you be surprised to find out she'd told the six-million-dollar man and his butt-buddy exactly who I was and where I lived? Okay, she didn't know herself, but she knew my name and I'm in the book. So, no, I wasn't too surprised either, to come home to wash Ginger and Mary Ann off of me and find my apartment torn up.

I smiled a little smile, knowing that they hadn't found shit. I thought of zero sum nights, rooting around somebody's home, going through drawers and closets and under rugs, behind paintings and coming up empty-handed. I thought of how frustrating that can be and the smile grew a little broader.

"Fuck you, greasy fucks," rolled off my tongue as cool and understated as Bruce Willis might ever accomplish. I grabbed some clean clothes and skipped the shower. Who knew if they were watching the place? I went out the back door and down the fire escape. Even if they saw that much, I knew I could lose them down the alley and I'd parked the car three blocks away in caution.

I crossed the river again and ditched the car. I staked out the Beaver, waiting for Janis to get off. It was a long wait, but I didn't mind. I was savoring the thrill of playing the game a step ahead of these yo-yo's. Janis came out half past four, with three other girls and a big ape. The girls got to their cars, the bouncer went back inside, and I did a half crouched run up to Janis's passenger side.

"Judas Priest, Ethan! You scared me," she exclaimed as I let myself in.

"Hey, baby, I just couldn't wait to see you." I kissed her and felt the hesitation on her end. Could be she thought she'd never see me again. Could be she was afraid I knew about her betrayal. Could be she was scared of what I might do. Could be.

She recovered quick, though. She smiled and grabbed my junk while she stuck her tongue down my throat. "You're supposed to lay low, but I'm glad you're here."

"Baby Doll, I hope you got paid, because I've decided. Fuck your cat, we're leaving tonight." See how she likes that.

She didn't. She looked concerned. Chewed on her bottom lip for a second, but just like the calculating cunt I knew she was, she improvised just swell. Switched gears and went with plan B. "You're right. I don't wanna come back to this shithole ever again. Let's go now!" She kissed me quick and started the car, all smiles. The sincerity of the twinkle in her eye chilled me. Felt like a block of ice in my intestine.

I sat back, a little unnerved, and said, "Airport."

* * *

At least, I'd taken the liberty of changing our plans. Miami never came up in our talks, so I figured I'd be safe enough there to do what I had to before disappearing for good. Now I needed to take the driver's seat, be the man here.

She played it through convincingly enough, if I hadn't known better. She even liked my new assertive style. It was different for her, following the leader. At the Beaver, or any other place like that, the women control everything and tell you how it is.

She slept against me in our first-class seats and I pretended it was sweet. I pretended we had a future and were a team. I pretended all the way to the hotel, all the way through room service and the lazy sleepy sex before the nap.

I woke up an hour later and looked at her lying on her side, turned away from me. I let some light in through the window and took in the view. Really was something. I thought I should find another girl soon and come back here again. I turned around and looked at Janis. Looked clean and sweet and had that something—that definite something I still couldn't put my finger on. I slipped back into pretend mode, and while I was there, thought about our future.

Took a long hot shower. Scalding, really. Stood under the stream, walking through what I had to do. When I realized the hot water wasn't going to run out, I turned it off and scrubbed myself completely pink with those big white towels. When I stepped out of the bathroom, Janis was sitting, the sheet pulled up to her armpits, talking on the phone. She was whispering into it while I looked at her from the doorway.

Snapped me back. She never missed an opportunity. In truth, it made me love her just a little bit more. I thought: *That's my girl. You're so smart. And capable. I want to be just like you someday.*

She quickly hung up when she saw me watching.

"Who'd you call?"

Beat. "Oh, just Trish at the club."

"Yeah?"

"Yeah, I told her I wasn't coming back to work and where the spare key for my place was. She's gonna take care of Angus for me."

"You tell her where we were?"

She looked at me, confused. "'Course not. I didn't say anything about a 'we.' Just said I wasn't coming back to work, would be gone a while." She was pretty smooth, I gave her that.

I still had time for pretending, so I sauntered, yeah, sauntered over to the bed and dropped the towel dramatically. She responded by rising to her knees and dropping the sheet. She smashed her world-class knockers against me and put her head on my shoulder. A regular Chrissie Hynde. I tilted her chin up to look at me and said, "Let's get married."

When I came back to St. Louis, six months later, I was tan. I was dressed smart, I even talked differently. I had come into my own. I had gone into business for myself, used the money to buy in bulk. That's what they say: you gotta spend money to make money. And what do you know? They were right, this time. What ten thousand will buy wholesale will go for thirty, thirty-five retail.

And I wasn't out of my depth, like maybe you're thinking. Certain things you experience really prepare you for down the road events so that you know when the shit comes down, you're going to be ready. For me, it was killing Janis—when I drowned her that afternoon while she was talking about weddings and shit, like she was really into it. When we'd gone off to a private spot along the beach and she looked at me and said, "I want to spend the rest of my life with you," it was just the opening I was looking for.

I said, "Honey, you're going to," and did it right then and

there. Knocked the wind out of her with a stomach punch, then onto her back in two feet of water while I sat on her shoulders. She died looking into my face, knowing I knew all about her plans for me, and I was reborn looking into hers knowing I was all grown-up now and could take care of myself.

We'd taken a trip out to Key West to celebrate our engagement and I left her without ID. She'd had a few drinks by that time and had drowned, not been strangled, so I wasn't sure if they'd think she was a murder or an accident, but I didn't care much. I didn't think anybody'd try too hard to connect her to me, let alone find me across the country. I figured by the time anybody who gave a shit enough to put it together got around to my last known address, I'd have changed my identity and moved on.

And I did all that. I became John Connor, which was respectable enough. I figured the only thing looking for me was a cybernetic assassin from the future, and if he looked anything like Arnold, I could see that coming a mile away.

I came back to St. Louis for shits really. An odd feeling of destiny pulled me back just to look at the old stomping ground with my new eyes. I went to an afternoon ball game and drove through Soulard and Dutchtown just to see it again. I rolled up on Carl's Bad Tavern and thought, *What the hell?* and went in for a taste.

Nobody recognized me, which confirmed to me that I was one hundred percent changed. I casually sat at the bar and ordered a scotch, which I'd taken to recently. The bartender was new and I asked him where Pee-Wee was, used the name and everything.

He looked around nervously, hoping nobody'd heard me and it tickled me to see the discomfort in his eyes. "Herman's out right now. You wanna leave a message?"

"Nah, just thought I'd say 'hey' if he were around." I finished my drink and got up to leave when one of the regulars—I couldn't remember his name—stopped me and said: "Hey, I know you, right?"

I looked him right in the eye and gently clapped his shoulder. "Not even close," I said, then took out a bill and put it on the bar in front of him. "Bartender, a drink for my new friend." And I was gone.

I spent the rest of the day sightseeing and stopped in for just a sec at the Beaver. *What a shithole,* I thought. Guess I'd come up in the world. Didn't even stay for a whole minute. Went to PT's, which was more my speed now. Had a couple drinks and was getting a private dance when "Sweet Child O' Mine" came on the sound system.

Shit.

Wasn't prepared for it. Hadn't heard that song in months. Not ashamed to say, I got a little misty-eyed and sang along under my breath. Nah, fuck that, I got up and left in a hurry. The girl called me an asshole and I didn't argue. I walked out and bumped into a couple unhappy patrons on the way to the door.

Was pacing, trying to wash the song out of my system, walking along the riverfront, on the way to the car. I always liked looking at downtown from the east side at night. The river rolling under the bridge was soothing with the lights from the casinos reflected on its surface.

"I used to love her," I whispered, to change the tune in my head.

Could be I was so intent on calming the fuck down, that I didn't see him follow me. Could be my thoughts were elsewhere all the way to the hotel. Could be he took me completely by surprise at the door, me thinking it was room service. Could be, but I'm not sure.

I'm not sure because I never saw his face, just the knife. Even when he stood over me after ransacking my room (rather poorly I'd say), I didn't have to look at his face to know who it was; just the way he stood there and the way his right arm hung funny.

So, I don't know. Maybe I was inviting it. Maybe I'd put it together some time ago. I mean, all the guy had to do was remember where he'd passed out. And maybe Herman told him who'd taken him home that night. Why not, right?

Fucking Benji, man.

Could be I wasn't so smart. Could be he wasn't so dumb. Could even be she wasn't so guilty. Fuck. Could be.

Who Do I Have to Kill to Get a Little Respect Up in Here?

Brian Murphy

Alajuela, Costa Rica.

Oh man, just to get some respect around here.

After too long and too many encounters out of the ordinary, you start to wonder just what it's going to take anyways. It's not like you're a tourist. You start to wonder if maybe it's just too much to hope for—respect. Sometimes you wonder, "Who do I have to kill?"

Still, you stay loose, you roll away from punches, then you beat a few heads. Bar Sin Problemas. Your idea. The bar and the name.

A rock 'n roll bar without problems, in a dangerous barrio somewhere in Costa Rica? Bar of no problems? You must have been out of your mind. It's a crash and burn bar for the locals unless you get a little respect around here.

Weeks ago, when the beer distributor for the two national brands—Pilsen and Imperial—still hadn't taken away the old neon beer sign outside with the old name, some kids drove their panel truck underneath the sign and you got up there with a can of oil-based black spray paint.

As quick as you sprayed "Bar Sin Problemas" up onto the plastic, it ran—the words melting in black angst, running down the front of the sign. Barely legible. Spooky though. At night, the sign on, it cast a pale yellow silhouette down onto the parking lot in front of your place.

The black lettering, spiked and wicked-looking, sometimes make you lose your bearings. Take you back in time. When you drive up on your Harley, it looks like a punk bar on Wells Street in Chicago—1979. Maybe that's why you did the sign up in the first place.

Your kid at the bar took potshots at you that night—the day you did the sign. Yeah, it was Sunday. Yeah, the joint was closed. Yeah, maybe he didn't hear that it was you outside, screaming, "Mario, it's me Sal. I locked myself out!" Maybe he didn't hear you pounding on that front door.

But you figured he would have had to hear you once you climbed onto the roof and kept screaming that it was you. You thought he'd wake up and walk out, see it was you, wave, and go through the bar to open the front door.

After that didn't happen, you figured he might hear you on the roof, banging and crashing like a storm without rain. And if he didn't hear any of that, then for sure he'd hear the dog, Iggy, barking right in front of the door to the bunker he slept in.

Maybe it was the dog's barking that finally caught his attention. You were practically at the end of the building. When he did come out, waving the pistol like a drunk Pancho Villa, he then ripped off four shots right at you.

All you'd wanted was for him to let you in with his keys, not show you what a maniac you'd hired to manage your bar. You dove for a drainpipe, and a portion of the roof came off and somehow wrapped itself around you like armor as you fell.

You wondered if he didn't know it was you all along. Costa Rican humor. Some such shit. Or maybe he was showing you how tough he'd be on intruders.

You fired his ass, chased him the fuck out, hitting him with his mattress all the way through the bar—a long one, like, as long as a bowling alley.

Now, your language deficiency—poor Spanish—is probably digging you a big enough hole that maybe you and the bar, will fall through it any minute. Hell, maybe you'll end up in China if you fall far enough.

You may as well have been in China. Your customers? They may as well be speaking Chinese. For all you know, they are. No one talks behind your back after you fired Mario. With as much Spanish as you know, they just say it to your face. Then smile so you buy them a drink.

Rock 'n roll suicide.

So you need another guy—a manager. Bilingual. The city you're in, this is a need that sorely screams to the locals, *"Gringo. Ready to be fucked."*

That's what you're thinking tonight, while you drive down to The Infernero, Alajuela's "Little Hell," to buy some coke. You're thinking that you have definitely got a problem at the bar of no problems. So what else is new?

When you hit the road into the barrio San José, you give your bike a little gas, then glide past the sleeping neighborhood.

Past that, just down the road, silhouettes dance by an old wooden bus stop, under the lone streetlight. That's where you're going.

Like always, whenever you see a dope supermarket on the street, you automatically feel a breeze charged with electricity blowing onto your forehead. Winter or summer, no matter where you are, you feel the heat of commerce.

New York, Rio, or Chicago, it's all the same. Dangerous

business—the twenty-four-hour variety. Everyone is welcome. It's how you grew up. You just always believed there had to be places like this. You're in second gear. Puttering.

The houses have disappeared. There's just decaying brick shacks—crash pads. For laughter. For tears. For quick sex. Anything where harm of some sort can be done in private.

At the bottom of the first hill, barrio San José, the Zamora street crews are out in force. Laughing and dancing to Limp Bizkit throbbing out of a boom box someone has set on the hood of a car, parked in front of the first shack at the bottom of the hill.

There's a soccer ball in play. Taxies and cars stop briefly. Tattooed boys run up to the open windows with large plastic bags filled with grams of coke. Transactions are quick, but rarely mirthless. This is Central America. Everyone knows how to laugh. Even when they're dying.

These guys, the boys you call the "Down, Down Boys"— Zamora's crew—they all come to your bar. These guys are for the most part, your best customers.

They have the first post that you drive by, down at the bottom of the hill.

"Down, down. Boys." They liked that. They know you've been down, down before—maybe will again, someday. One night at your bar, you played the Zamora boss and some of the kids Iggy Pop's "Dum Dum Boys."

When you translated the lyrics while Iggy mourned the passing of all his boys, they all went nuts. They all wanted to be "Dum Dum Boys"—fearless and peerless. Their own revolution against all the ills and poverty that did its level best to keep them on the street. They loved that too.

Mi Cumpa. Mi Cumpa. Screams go up when you rev down into first gear, then drop your feet. Sometimes you stay and try a conversation. There's ten or eleven guys out tonight. They run to shake your hand. You're a humble celebrity. You've been tough enough down here. It's one of those places in the world where guts and a proven nutcase streak get you even further than money. Money ain't shit down here. Anyone can have it. It's just paper.

You'd flogged some kilos of reefer to Beto Zamora—the boss—before the tax people arrested him, his mother, his lawyer, and half his family. This is a place where you've always been treated well.

The Zamora without tattoos—the eldest brother, the straight businessman—was out on the street the very next morning after the bust, peddling coke. Zamora balls, tattoos or not.

He was there to let the city know that the show was going on without Beto. *Sin Problemas.* You drove down that morning also. With a bottle of tequila and a rose for the mother. He understood.

Finally workers drifted back—the tattoo boys. But the main tattoo, Beto Zamora, he was locked up tight. You miss him. He at least had advice.

Another night at the bar, he'd made a very small space between two fingers, then howled, "You're only this far from fucked, Gringo." Slamming down his shot, he came over and gave you a bear hug. Pointing to his chest, he said, *"Igual,* Gringo, *igual."* Same as me.

You dropped by the prison at San Sebastian and hung out with Beto for a while after his arrest. He had everything in there. Still, you'd already been in one five years. No matter how much you have inside, you still can't come and go. Not even Beto Zamora. Any freedom you got—it's got to have something to do with who you are to begin with. How strong. How patient. How content or how angry. So far, Beto seemed pretty free.

Riding home from San Sebastian that day, helmet hanging from the handlebar, feeling the wind catch your hair, you dodged the few traffic cops that cared enough to chase you for driving without a helmet. As you smoked the first cop car, you realized just how similar you really were to Beto Zamora. It was a game you played.

Driving away from the boys after buying eight grams, your hog wants to decide what to think of the rotten petrol you filled up with earlier. It decides. It sputters and you barely keep it running. Then, after a righteous backfire, that bitch wants to fly.

You shotgun some coke and kick into third gear and build speed, up towards where there's nothing but dark, winding road and coffee plants. The only sound in the world, you and the hell you are raising.

Getting back now, it's close to five. Too lazy to open up the big doors, you chain up your Harley outside. Just as you click the padlock closed, a taxi pulls up. There's three girls inside. You don't need a Berlitz course to know that this is a good thing.

They're friends of a dolly you spent a few hours with a while back. She'd come to your bar with a group, and while they were drinking, you left for her place, then brought her back an hour or so later. That was when Mario was still there, before he tried to kill you.

She lived in the row of cottages behind the huge meat processing plant, Cinta Azul. You'd always heard that it was a dangerous place. Poverty brings dangerous to desperate, wherever the poor live. This was such a place. Rooms out in back of the front cottages rented daily, weekly, monthly. Whatever. Very little asked. Just stay alive to pay tomorrow.

Pulling up, you chained your bike to the one tree out in the parking lot—really just dirt and stones. She told you not to worry about the bike.

To get to the rooms, you followed her through a concrete

hallway with dim moonbeams coming through from the roof-less top to light your way. There was a common shower and la-trine on one side off the hallway. You thought how interesting a place like that could be in this dark. Then you thought about your bike. Maybe you would have been worried, except that you couldn't take your eyes off the girl walking in front of you, her ass swishing and swinging.

She whispered that she'd wet her pants. She didn't mean with urine, by the way. She told you they were spotted with fluids she claimed she couldn't stop.

You told her to keep the juice flowing. She shuddered as if a cool breeze had suddenly swept down from the hog farm be-hind the cottages and along the river. You remembered fra-grances. Her perfume, then the hog farm, and finally, the baking smells of alcohol from the still they worked day and night over at the farm. Pigs and drunk Costa Ricans—twenty-four-hour lunacy.

Down here, every Costa Rican you meet tells you, *"Pura vida."* Pure life. As you reach for baby love's naked shoulders once she drops her blouse, you laugh, thinking about the hog farm.

Baby, now *that's pura vida.*

Sure enough, when you pulled her pants down, there was a dull white froth and more juice smeared onto her underwear. You ripped her panties off and her cunt began to squirt like a fountain. For a minute you felt like Superman. Then you dragged your finger against her dark, purple lips and juice was all over your arm—an explosion of desire.

Definitely that was your feeling when you went back there on your own, days later—four in the morning. You gambled your bike for flesh. It's not like you could drive up quietly. Everyone in the whole joint, rooms and cottages, knew you'd just driven up. Gringo loco. Looking for that "good thang."

That's what need can do. Needing dope, a woman—any-thing. Need means taking a chance.

But oh, lookee here. It's her three friends. So you let them in and put the dog out in the back. He's pissed. He'd gotten into one of the ladies' purses and when you saw him running around with a tampon in his mouth like a cigar, you realized he'd steal the show.

You get everyone a drink. Then put on some New York Dolls and sit back to view the scene. Warm soft light, no noise outside, and three semi-to-very hot pros sitting close and show-ing a lot of leg and chest.

There's nothing sexier in the whole world than being with a woman in a closed bar. All right, maybe only to you. But mul-tiply one woman times three and you'd hardly get an argument from too many men.

If the girl you'd slept with out there by the factory was nasty good, her friends this morning remained, as yet, unquan-tified. They were an unknown pleasure. Or maybe?

That's all right. You know that there's nothing they can steal. You serve them beer. That's cheap. Their company suddenly is ludicrous. No one seems to want to see your office, or to check the plumbing out with you in the woman's washroom.

Still, you strut like the little red rooster. It's the Sal Palermo show, all the way live, at the bar of no problems.

Except that they want to smoke some reefer. You got coke—cocaine, that is; forget about Coca-Cola—you got that too. You got every brand name and variety of booze they allow in the country. You figure you're fairly easy to look at. In other words, in such a poor place, you have pretty much everything.

Everything you got here, except reefer. You just sold fifty kilos. Not that the girls would have known that. Now, all you wish for is a joint. Like, "Lord, is that too much to ask for?"

232 / *Blood, Guts, & Whiskey*

Invariably, someone will have to roust a taxi, take them "down, down," and buy some pot. It's light out—after six, when the taxi pulls off. Now there's two dollies. Now you're tired. It's a wash. Fuck it. But, not only that, you'll be up till next winter if you keep falling for this shit. Your eyes hide under raccoon circles of black.

Just as invariably as the one is leaving in the taxi—divide and conquer—the other two have suddenly found so many things to talk about that now they practically ignore you. That's fine. You want them gone. Maybe you will sleep a little if you can.

But every time you write the girls off and return to the study of the tequila bottle you are slowly emptying along with too many beers to count, the girls chat away and you can't help but hear the word *moto* repeatedly.

David Johanson wails "Lonely Tenement" while you start to put one and one together. *Moto.* That's motorcycle in Spanish. And as far as you know, you're the only one present with one.

You start to doubt seriously that they're talking about what a good find you are because you're charming, handsome, and you have this extraordinary motorcycle. They play fake when you look their way. Sometimes, although you'd barely seemed to notice, you catch them whispering. You know a setup. This one is a cartoon of poor subtlety.

When the taxi returns and everyone is reunited, they all decide that what would really be swell is for all of you to go back to their place—the surreal dump—"cottage nightmare row," where who-the-fuck-knows-what can happen to a gringo in that labyrinth at seven A.M.

What a great idea. Why stay here where there's every amenity imaginable, and now, even some pot to smoke?

No, they won't hear of it. Promises start to circulate about blowjobs given by all three. Crazier sex than you've ever had.

Well, sure, they couldn't know about the girl and the snake. You laugh. They all are telling you at once to follow them on your *moto*.

You say, "Right, right, the *moto*. Sure. Why stay here where it's cool and safe and we have booze, coke, places to fuck, when I can drive my Harley over to a sweltering shitbox and risk my life?"

All three girls laugh and nod, yes, of course. Still, they add *moto* enough times that you begin to get the picture. They are very hopeful to see you at the cottages.

You tell them enough "Cynical Hall" wisecracks to let them know there is no chance you are going to stay here alone when you can go hang out with three women in a shithole.

One of the little bombshells with the circus tits is on your phone. *Moto* is heard over and over again. Obviously your bike is part of some grand agenda among quite a few early risers, or late going to bed, gals and pals.

When you hear her on the phone, you go out in front of the bar and unchain your hog. Coming back into the bar, you start to swing the heavy link chain with fast and cutting kung-fu moves.

The girls have already called a taxi. Now it seems as if they are all in a hurry to get out into the heat and go back to their slum.

You don't mind getting rid of them. They want you to drive up there on the bike. Each girl has managed a promise that you will never forget the sex this morning.

First, you ask, "What sex?"

Finally, to get them all out, you let them know you'll be following shortly on the bike after you have taken all the tampons away from the dog, then feed him his three double-sized cans of tuna.

Another taxi shows up and everyone kisses you on the lips

234 / Blood, Guts, & Whiskey

and cheeks and all try for an excuse that might force you to get a better look at the six sets of darkly tanned breasts. A nipple here and there. They want to do you harm.

In this city, even one tough bitch can be every bit as dangerous as a man. In this fucking world, you always keep reminding yourself, you will always be a visitor. Not a tourist, but never exactly ever really one of them. And these bitches here? They suddenly don't seem human. Just flesh and long sharp nails. Harpies to rip you apart. Leave your bones to rot. Not the future Mrs. Palermo here, you say to yourself and laugh.

They leave and you're laughing again. The coke is in your blood now. The river inside of you has turned the corner and gets white-water status. You almost growl. Your blood, it's telling you that you aren't tired at all. It's telling you to go over there and tempt fate. Have some fun.

So you go with your loose chain—the one you've become an expert knocking the shit out of street punks with, spinning it and twisting it and lashing out. Already, it's claimed an eyeball in San José one night when you stumbled too far from the Bar Dominica. You'd been attacked. Dangerous little shits that come at you in packs.

You go visit the ladies. In a taxi.

Pink cottages. All of them in a row, and at the end, a hallway that takes you to the sweatboxes out back. Right about now, the hot sun starts to bake those corrugated roofs. If anyone is trying to sleep, they must be real tired. Or already dead.

The only relief from the heat might be in the cool cement walls of the hallway or in the communal shower.

But this morning, there's a few doors open. Especially—you see with a tinge of respect for the ace consistency of a moron— the door to the dolly you visited. You say out loud with a laugh, "Oh what a coincidence. It's you-know-who. And she wants me to come into her room. Not a fucking chance."

And she's standing there. It's such a poor trap, you think. And still, you hear, *moto. No moto.*

They don't know you've taken a taxi. They want this so bad, they forgot to even listen. When you walked in, their minds started to race. No one thought it strange that they didn't hear the bike.

All they are thinking is that they must now find a way to get you in a room. Obviously, they thought it was a sure thing—that you'd go into the old girl's room. Why shit, you think—after all, you two are practically married now. Why wouldn't you go in there?

That's what the ladies are bugging out trying to answer. Not why they didn't hear you come up.

Now, like out on the highway, driving without a helmet, you want to play cat and mouse for bigger stakes. Maybe this morning, it's your life you'll be gambling with.

Here comes another woman—older, so absolutely a first pick of yours for "Most Insidious. Most Dangerous. The Boss." When you learn that she's the landlord, you smile. Instincts. Working.

This one? She's mean. That's what age has done for her. It's replaced her beauty with meanness and a fragile wisdom of the world. She wants her girls here to toss you on a scrap heap, and she is furious with them for not pulling this off like clockwork. That's when you really laugh. In her face.

You're thinking about Costa Rican clockwork. It's an oxymoron. Everyone is late. Just like you're making yourself late right now—late for your own funeral.

She must be wailing at them, you think. You hear her say *estúpido, tonto* enough times to appreciate that their airtight plan has unraveled. And the boss, she's not going to let her girls forget so easily. Besides, if they hadn't come out to your place, they could have earned her some real money right here on their backs.

You also hear, *moto.* She has obviously just arrived from the entrance, maybe just drove up for the ceremony—the celebration of a gringo locked up like a rat in a cage, locked in a fucking oven-backed tin can.

That would have been the second thing she had expected to see, not you alive and well and swinging enough chain in arcs and wide loops in front of your chest to seriously maim anyone who rushes you.

The last thing she expected to see was you alive and out in that courtyard, swinging your chain and matching evil look for evil look.

But what's really got her going is that the first thing she did expect to see, your Harley, doesn't even seem to be out there.

Like, "Where is this fucking Harley?" Only she doesn't say Harley. Because she thinks, like they all did, that you'd recognize the word *Harley,* but that you might not understand the Spanish word for motorcycle. They may as well have asked you to stamp "Stuck on stupid" all over your ass and forehead.

No, she is starting to rethink this one. In fact, she just fucking leaves.

It's just that you won't let your feet take you all the way into the ole girl's room. You laugh and manage in Spanish that you've been there already. Then, out in the courtyard, you let them circle. There's another room. They pretend there's a lady inside. Only she won't open her door.

This must be plan two, you think. Like, if you're not going into a room with a girl you know, why in the fuck you going to go into a room with someone you don't know? You stay clear of that room, still swinging your chain. None of the girls want to come near you. Plan two has also proved to be a poor one.

You ask them if they figured it would be nice for you to stay in a locked, 112 degree hellhole while they steal your *moto.*

But there is no *moto.*

That's what the dude is asking now.

Oh good, you think. The guns have arrived. And he'll have to be a real quick draw before losing a cheek or an eye to the chain. So you get in close. Keep smiling.

He just showed up. Out of nowhere, so to speak, once the boss left. You're starting to enjoy yourself more and more and decide all at once that this is worth missing a few hours sleep. What also intrigues you is that you aren't even a mile away from your bar. You wonder, *What in the fuck are these people thinking?*

But you already know the answer to that. They aren't.

This guy—you've never seen him in town, so you can expect he doesn't know that you are certified. You will kill this punk if you have to. But all he wants to talk about is the *moto.* The one he came to steal.

No one can tell him fast enough that they need him to help get you into that room. While they're jabbering, you also jabber—you go Chicago, pure street on him, your back constantly against the wall, the chain spinning nunchacku-style in front of you, a blur of steel. He can't come any closer and he can't make a move quick enough if he does have a gun—there's just not enough room in the courtyard.

He also can't stop smiling. It must be the only way to hide his surprise.

Someone, the boss maybe, or these women, have gotten him out of bed to come over for a kill—to roast a duck.

But all he can see is a mad gringo, also smiling and talking Spanglish a mile a minute. All he can really see is a world of hurt coming from an older, and obviously wiser, bird of prey. He gets it. He gets that you get it. Still, you can tell that he can't believe it.

He keeps asking, *"No fucking moto? Verdad?"* It is true?

By this time, you have gotten back some of that rooster

from earlier in the morning at the bar, when you were the barn-yard boss.

And so that's how you leave there, feeling better and better. Laughing. Bare-chested, feeling that beautiful heat from the sun once you're out in the front lot.

Big bad rooster.

He follows at a distance, but he already must have known he'd get his ass kicked, plain and simple. And down below, on the road from Cinta Azul to the Roble, a horn honks and screams can be heard.

Suddenly gunshots from that car. Arms waved out the window, one still with a pistol in its hand. Tattooed arms. Zamora's boys coming back from a morning delivery at the plant.

The kid behind you slows down. He recognizes the Zamoras, and for the first time since he arrived to strong-arm you into one of those empty shacks, he hears your name called.

Maybe leaving the trap, he was figuring, you win some, you lose some. Now, he stops and you wonder just what he's thinking now.

"*Hey Sal! Gringo Loca! Mi Cumpa!*"

They stop and you run down for a ride to your bar. You can't say what the punk behind you is thinking, but after you jump into the car, after you fired a shot at the ground by his feet and he about jumped into that only gnarled tree in the lot, you sure know that he is definitely thinking something.

Even from that distance, you could see that his face had gone completely white.

You hand Oscar, the shift leader, his pistol. It's new. He wanted to get your attention and thought he'd also test out the SIG Sauer nine-millimeter. Everyone has already slapped your back, complimenting you on making the muscular Nicaraguan dance out in that empty lot where your motorcycle was supposed to be.

When you'd jumped into the car, you'd asked Oscar quickly to lend you the gun.

He proudly handed it over to you and clicked off the safety. A bag of coke was already going around in the car and the music stayed loud. Once you ripped that round, Oscar smirked, then asked what you wanted done.

You just said, "Respect."

He nodded, muttered, *"Con respecto,"* and sped towards the lone figure in the empty parking lot in front of the pink cottages.

Bad Move

Dave Zeltserman

The news came on while I was still waiting for my ham and cheese sandwich, and it was when they showed the police sketch that the good citizens sitting around me started offering their opinions on what should be done to the freak when he was caught. A glazed toothless sod a few barstools down yelled out that castration would be too good for the bastard, and some fat tub of lard next to him suggested instead feeding the freak into a wood chipper. More of them threw out their ideas on the matter, and all I could do was sit there and take it, all the while feeling a hot burning around my neck. Of course none of them knew the drawing was supposed to be me. The man in it looked wild-eyed, his greasy black hair well past his shoulders, his beard making him look like the Unabomber's deranged cousin. Four days ago I shaved off my beard and clipped my hair short, then had a barber give me a buzzcut and dye what was left yellow. After that I moved into another rooming house. Still, though, listening to them talking about what a fucking freak I must be was hard, especially with them claiming that I was trying to hurt that baby. They didn't understand any of it. If Dr. Bendleson was around he could explain it to them. But he wasn't, so I just had to listen to them blathering on and on.

Four days ago we were a week into this goddamned heat wave. I tried staying in my room; I knew Dr. Bendleson would've wanted me to, but I couldn't. It was just so damn hot in there, my head feeling like it was going to split apart. I needed air, but as soon as I was outside and saw the way the good citizens were gaping at me, I knew I had made a mistake.

I might've still been okay if that woman hadn't blocked the sidewalk with her baby carriage. As I stood there waiting for her to move her damn carriage, all I could see was red, every vein in my head throbbing like they were going to pop. Finally I asked her if she thought I was standing there for my god-damned health. She gave me a slow look then and pulled the carriage back an inch so I would still have to step into the street if I was going to pass by. That was all it took to send me tumbling into the abyss. The next thing I knew I was yelling at her, telling her that she was no better than any other piece of dog crap littering the street and how if she thought she was better than me *she* was the one fucked in the head. I grabbed her baby carriage and pushed it into traffic.

I was deep into the abyss by this point. The baby carriage made it across okay, but then it bounced off the curb and started to roll back, and that's when she jumped into the street after it. A car swerving to avoid the carriage clipped her, and next thing she was laying in the street clutching her hip and making the most god-awful mewling noises.

A crowd had gathered. I'm a big man, almost as wide as I am tall, and all my hours lifting weights at Bendleson's hospital left me as hard as stone. They should've known better. When one of them grabbed at me, I popped him in the jaw and his mouth exploded into a pink spray. And then I ran.

Since then I stayed holed up in my room. But yesterday I finished the box of crackers that I'd bought, and I needed food and I needed to get out of that stifling hot room. So I went to this bar thinking I could grab a quick sandwich. But as they kept talking about me, I could feel myself slipping closer to the abyss again.

Something touched my arm. Through the haze I saw that a lady had moved onto the barstool next to me, and she had a small delicate hand resting on my arm, her fingernails painted a deep bloodred. A dark brunette with soft red lips. I couldn't look away from those lips. She smiled, clearly amused, and said something about a drink. I should've warned her then about what a bad move she was making, but I couldn't, not with the way she had pulled me from the abyss, and not with the way her hand felt on my arm. I waved the bartender over and had her order what she wanted. After her drink was brought over, she moved close so that her lips brushed against my ear, her breath hot against me. What she whispered to me was both an invitation and obscene. I should've turned her down. I'm not dumb, I knew she wanted something other than what she was offering, but I couldn't help myself. I left with her.

She took me to a hotel. A nice one. When we got to the room she didn't waste any time slipping out of her clothes and standing naked in front of me, her eyes glistening, her body slender and firm and challenging. Then she was on me, her mouth hard against mine. After a while it was like I was with a wild animal the way her body buckled and heaved. And she ended up doing every single dirty thing she whispered in the bar.

It was a long time before she was done. Before we were laying together in a sweaty heap, trying to catch up with our breathing. She was stretched out on top of me and I could feel her chest rising and lowering. Eventually it slowed. Not right away, but eventually.

She got up to use the bathroom. I watched until the bathroom door closed and then searched through her pocketbook.

According to her driver's license she was married and her name was Doris Keegan. I copied down her address. Then I lay back down.

The bathroom door opened. She moved across the room and sat cross-legged on the bed, grinning at me. She was still naked. "Did I wear you out?" she asked.

I shook my head. That just made her grin more. She asked what my name was. I lied and told her Paul. She lied and told me hers was Susan. And then she crawled back on top of me and slowly unwound her body like a cat. She moved herself so her face was inches from mine. And then we were going at it again, more wild this time with her looking as if she were caught up in a hurricane. As she thrashed about on top of me, her eyes rolled inwards, and her body shuddered in orgasm. Next thing I knew she was off of me again and heading towards the bathroom. "You got me all sweaty," she said.

The shower turned on for a few minutes. When she came back into the room, she slipped her clothes back on. "I have to run, Paul," she said. "That was fun. How about I meet you Wednesday at one at the same bar?"

"Maybe. I'm not sure."

She laughed at that. "Let's hope you can squeeze me into your social calendar. Room's paid for so take your time leaving." And then she was out the door and gone.

This whole thing was crazy, her picking me up and taking me back to the hotel like this, but it made sense in a way I couldn't quite explain. I tried to remember the last time I'd been with a girl. So damn long, almost too long to still be real.

I rolled onto my side. I had my eyes shut tight trying to block Doris Keegan out of my mind, but I couldn't. All I could think of, all I could see and smell, was her. I knew this was a mistake, both for her and me. I almost reached for the telephone. I sat frozen, wanting badly to call Bendleson. But if I called him I would have to tell him about my headaches and the baby carriage and all the rest of it. I didn't see how I could. I got dressed and left the hotel.

I didn't sleep at all the next night. Wednesday was two days away and all I could think of was Doris. Images of her raced through my mind. Every time I closed my eyes I'd see her naked, slender body gyrating crazily. It got to the point where I was afraid to close them. By morning my head ached worse than ever.

By midday I couldn't stand it any longer. I soaked a towel in ice water and gave myself a rubdown with it. I looked out the window. The sun was so bright I had to turn my eyes away. I got dressed and headed outside.

I found a pay phone and called information and got Doris's phone number. My heart raced while I dialed the number. A woman answered who turned out to be their housekeeper. I asked if she knew where Doris was. At first she wouldn't tell me, but finally let it out that Doris was probably having lunch at the Plaza. "I'm sure you'll find her somewhere in the hotel," she added under her breath.

I walked the three miles to the Plaza Hotel. It was hot and muggy and by the time I got there my clothes were soaked through. Doris was there in the restaurant, and with her was a good-looking man about my age. The two of them were laughing. I couldn't help noticing the soft curvature of her throat. So soft. The way the light reflected off it. For whatever reason Doris turned her eyes towards me, and then her smile froze as our eyes locked. I turned and headed for the door.

Doris must've run after me. By the time I got to the street she was alongside me, her face flushed. "Paul," she said. "What are you doing here?"

I tried to keep from looking at her. "Nothing."

"You knew I was married, right?" she asked. "That's hubby in there. I hate the bastard."

"You didn't look like you were having a bad time."

"Oh no?" She raised an eyebrow. "I can put on a pretty convincing act when I want to, can't I?"

She was grinning from ear to ear. My throat felt dry. I could barely swallow. "Pretty funny, huh?" I asked. She pushed herself up against me and answered me by pressing her mouth hard against mine. When she pulled away her eyes were sparkling. "I better go back before hubby gets suspicious," she said. "We'll meet later. Tell me where you're staying, tough guy."

I couldn't help myself. I told her. A glimmer showed in her eyes. "I'll meet you at three," she said. "Don't get all upset and jealous if I'm a couple minutes late, okay Paul, darling?"

I bit my lip and nodded.

I watched as she turned back to the Plaza. She wore a form-fitting yellow silk outfit, and I stood staring, almost hypnotized by her slender hips. She turned once, realized the effect she was having, and flashed me a knowing smile before disappearing into the Plaza.

I stood frozen for a couple minutes and then I went back to the Plaza's lobby. A short time later Doris and her companion entered from the restaurant. They didn't see me as they walked to the registration desk. The guy she was with whispered something into Doris's ear and she broke out into a soft easy laugh. The desk clerk handed them a key and they walked across the lobby to the elevator. Before the elevator doors closed they were wrapped up in each other, too wrapped up to bother noticing me or anything else.

It was an hour before they came back down. Both of them had their hair slick wet. They still hadn't noticed me. I waited until they said their good-byes before following the guy.

He turned out to be Connor Fairchild, a lawyer working a couple blocks away. After following him to his office, I headed back to my rooming house.

*   *   *

Doris was an hour late and seemed in a rotten mood. "Nice place you got," she remarked as she looked about my flop-house room. "Why don't we call room service and order up some champagne?"

I stared at her silently. "That's what I love about you, your gift of conversation." She glanced at her watch and then met my stare, a brittle smile straining her lips. "I guess I'm giving you a hard time, huh?"

I didn't say anything. She sat down next to me and put her hand behind my neck, rubbing me gently. "I'm sorry, darling," she said. "I'm a little messed up right now. I hate him so much." She paused, and then added under her breath, "I can't stand him being alive."

"So that's your reason," I said.

She gave me an odd look.

"Why you picked me up at that bar," I explained.

She backed away from the bed, disgust washing over her face. "That's what you think?"

I stared at her, confused. She backed farther away from me. "How could you even suggest something like—oh my God, I know why you seemed so familiar. The drawings in the news-papers! You're him, the guy who tried to kill that baby! You shaved off your beard and cut your hair, but you're that freak!"

She stood staring at me as if I were a pile of crap. A hotness overwhelmed me. I tried arguing with her but she screamed over me, telling me how filthy she felt knowing I had touched her. Then she was asking me over and over again if I get off on hurting babies.

I begged her to stop, but she wouldn't, and the more she kept at it the closer I got to the abyss. Everything turned red, her, everything. There was so much noise coming from her. I felt swallowed up in it. I had to make it stop. And then some-how it did stop and there was a different kind of noise. And my hands squeezing something soft.

The noise finally stopped. And then from out of the abyss I saw his face, his eyes bulging, his tongue thick and blue. I had no idea who he was but I was choking the life out of him. I let go and he fell to the floor. His chest heaved in short violent spasms, and when he turned his head to me I could make out deep purple bruises around his neck. All the strength drained from my legs and I sat down on the floor next to him. "Who are you?" I asked.

He started coughing and it took him a while before telling me, "You know damn well."

I shook my head. "One second a lady is screaming bloody murder at me, the next I'm just about killing you. I have no idea who you are."

He gave me a cold stare. "My wife is Doris Keegan. You've been blackmailing her." He blanched, added, "Forcing her the past six months to have sex with you."

"That's what she told you, huh? She picked me up in a bar two days ago. That was the first I ever saw of her."

Uncertainty dulled his eyes. "She came to me this afternoon and told me all about it and . . ."

Someone was pounding on the door. Before I could get up the door swung open and a cop came in. He had his gun drawn, and as he looked from me to Keegan and saw the bruises along Keegan's neck, a hardness shadowed his face. He pointed his gun at my head and suggested I get on my stomach.

I didn't move. "You better do it, boy," he ordered softly. Out of the corner of my eye I could see Keegan smiling uncomfortably. "What's the problem, officer?" he asked.

"There was a call someone's being murdered here."

"I'm afraid there's been a mistake, officer," Keegan said. He showed the cop his driver's license and explained how he was a vice president at the Commerce Bank. Almost choking on his words, he added, "I assure you there's nothing to worry about here."

The cop had a tough time buying that. "How'd you get those marks on your neck?" he asked the bank vice president.

Keegan said that his tie had gotten caught earlier in a shredder machine. The cop gave him a slow hard look, but lowered his gun from me and reluctantly left the room. Keegan blindly stared at the door as it opened and shut, then dropped his head into his hands. I saw it all then. I knew what Doris had tried to do. I'm sure Keegan did too. But he didn't know how bad a move Doris had made. He didn't know me well enough to know that.

"She got you pretty worked up before sending you here?" I asked.

He nodded, his head still buried in his hands.

I could see her doing it. I could see her working him into the same blind rage she had worked me into, and then sending him up to have his neck broken. I asked him if he understood what happened. Again, he nodded, his head still buried.

"She must've been sure I'd kill you. She timed it so the cop would come up here after you were dead, probably figuring he'd kill me too. If he didn't, if he only arrested me, I'm sure she'd have a good story planned. Both her and her lover, Connor Fairchild. Did you have any idea she wanted you dead?"

He shook his head. His knuckles were a hard white as he pressed both hands together.

If I was capable of it I would've taken the first bus I could back to Bendleson's hospital. But that wasn't something I was capable of. Not a guy like me. I told him what we were going to do next and he sat and nodded, his eyes lifeless. After a while he left.

It was no accident Doris met me in that bar. She must've been out searching for me because she knew all along about me and that baby. She must've been one of the faces in the crowd. And she thought she knew what I was and what she could do with me. She was almost right. Almost. But not quite.

It was four thirty. I tried to think things out. Where was she now? At home, waiting for the cops to deliver the bad news. How long would she wait? As long as it took.

Would she call Fairchild? No, that part was easy. She couldn't risk it. Not if the cops got suspicious and checked her phone calls. Or his.

So I knew where to find her.

Outside it was still hot as hell. The air hazy, dead. I gave a quick glance at the sun and had to turn my head away, my eyes smarting.

The hookers were already out along the street preparing for the five o'clock rush. Each and every one of them looked like Doris. At least at first. After a while I realized they really didn't. Some were older, some fatter, thinner, darker. Some had bleached white hair. Some were probably bald beneath their wigs. But they all seemed like Doris.

I finally found one who did look like Doris. Same dark oval face, soft red lips, curvy slender body. At first she wanted no part of me, but when I explained what I wanted, she took my money. We both took a cab to Connor Fairchild's office build-ing and I waited outside while she did what I paid her to do, which was leave a message for Fairchild that it was urgent that he meet Doris at her home at seven. When she came out she told me it went smoothly, that she gave the message to Fairchild's secretary without him ever seeing her.

I took a cab to Doris Keegan's house. When I knocked on the door and she saw me there her face went blank. I pushed my way past her.

"I killed him for you."

Her eyes were wide and confused. "Your husband," I ex-plained. "The guy I saw you with at the Plaza. I had followed him back to his office on State Street, so I knew where he worked. After you left my room I went back there and waited for him. How come your last name's Keegan and his is Fairchild?"

The confusion drained from her eyes. For a moment she

looked very old—older than any of the street hookers I saw that day. She moved slowly to a chair and sat down.

"I knew you wanted me to kill him. You didn't have to spell it out any more than you did. So I waited until he left his office building. It was easy. No one saw a thing."

"What about the other man?" she asked in a tired, sick voice. "The one in your room?"

"Nothing," I said. "Who was he?"

The phone rang. A clock on the fireplace mantel read six thirty. Right on schedule. Doris picked up the phone and mostly listened, only uttering a few words. After she hung up, she said, "That was my husband. Whatever favor you tried to do me, you blew it."

"Wait a minute! You pointed out Fairchild as your husband and—"

"I lied." She smiled sadly at me. "I guess you're in some trouble now."

I didn't say anything. "You murdered a man," she continued, watching me carefully. "All on your own. And I didn't ask you to!"

"Yeah, right. Sure you didn't." I looked down at my nails and picked at them. "Anyway," I said. "I'm not in any trouble. No one saw me."

"But you are, Paul, darling. You told me. And I know about the baby."

"That's right. But you wouldn't tell anyone about that. Especially not the cops, at least not about Fairchild. They'd know I wouldn't kill him without your help."

She laughed a strangled cat type of laugh. I ignored her and continued, "I guess I should explain something to you. I've spent years in a hospital. Quite a few years."

She laughed again. That same strangled cat sound. "No kidding."

"No kidding. Although it's not really so much a hospital as a private sanatorium. Sometimes I have pretty bad problems and I need to stay there."

I paused, thinking about Bendleson, about how much I wanted to go back. I took a deep breath and told her about Bendleson and his hospital. About what a respected nuthouse he ran and how I always have a room waiting for me thanks to a trust fund my parents had set up. I explained to her how if Bendleson knew about the baby he would insist that at a subconscious level I knew I wasn't putting it at risk. Of course I screwed up in my thinking, not realizing the carriage would bounce off the curb and roll back into harm's way. But he would still insist I would never intentionally harm anyone unless manipulated into it. It was always how he'd explain the things I'd do and the authorities always bought it.

She stared at me with a look of utter exhaustion and asked how much was in my trust fund.

"Quite a bit. But I'm only allowed a small allowance. My pop set it up that way as an incentive to stay with Bendle—"

"All right!"

Her face darkened as she sat thinking, then a flicker of light showed in her eyes and she smiled at me.

"You're right," she said. "I did want you to kill my husband. And I wanted us to be together afterwards."

I nodded. "I knew you did."

"Of course you did." She stood up and started towards me. "A smart guy like you would." She lifted her head, brutally pushing her lips against mine. I could feel all the angles of her small body as it pressed against me. From the corner of my eye I could see her hands curling, her red nails like sharp cat claws.

"You could still do it for me," she said, her mouth inches from mine, her breath so damn hot. "He told me he's coming home at seven fifteen and the bastard's always on time. You could make it look like a robbery."

Of course I knew what was buzzing through her mind. It

was now twenty to seven, which would give her about forty minutes to find a gun. She'd find one. Later, after I'd been shot dead, she'd explain to the cops how her husband had given her the gun for protection.

I could see it all in her eyes.

I nodded and she pushed her lips hard against mine, driving her tongue deep into my mouth almost suffocating me with it, and when she pulled back her eyes sparkled. "After it's over, we'll be together. And we'll be very rich." She pushed herself away. "I better get going. Maybe I'll go shopping and buy myself something black. For mourning." We both laughed at that.

She stopped at the door before leaving. "Don't worry, Paul," she said with the utmost sincerity. "It will all be over soon."

Connor Fairchild rang the doorbell at seven o'clock as scheduled. When I answered the door, he tried turning away but I grabbed him by the collar and swung him into the house. "Find yourself a seat," I ordered as I slammed the front door shut.

He turned slowly towards the living room and then tried to rush me. I blocked his punch and gave him a hard jab above the heart and he just sort of sat down. This time I half dragged him to the living room and threw him onto a loveseat while I took the sofa.

"After Doris and I had our three-hour bed marathon yesterday, she decided to change the plan. Basically same plot, just different players with you and her husband dead. This way it would be lover and jealous husband having it out. I'm supposed to cut your throat. Keegan's going to be here in about fifteen minutes and then I'm supposed to hold him until Doris comes and blows his head off. Doris wanted me to do both of you, but that didn't seem fair. So I let her pick Keegan.

"I had to fight with her to see you today," I added. "I was afraid if she called off lunch you'd get suspicious. But she promised she'd think of me the whole time. . . ."

I leaned back into the sofa and relaxed. Fairchild's face was twisted into a sick grimace. He asked what I was waiting for.

"I haven't decided yet if she's worth killing for," I said.

A key sounded in the front door. Then the door opened and closed. We both waited silently as Keegan's footsteps echoed from the hallway.

When he entered the living room I took him by the elbow and sat him down. He gave a lousy performance of acting surprised, barely muttering a word, but fortunately Fairchild was beyond needing any convincing. Then we all sat and waited. When I heard the faint clicking of Doris's high heels on the stone walkway, I turned to Fairchild. "I've made up my mind," I said. "She's not worth it. Beat it."

Fairchild bolted from his chair. I followed him to the hallway. At that moment Doris walked through the front door. She was holding a gun at chest level. When she saw Fairchild, her mouth dropped open. Fairchild's own mouth twisted into a slight smile. "Surprised to see me, baby?" he asked, his voice sounding as if he were being strangled.

"Of course I am, darling!" I think she meant it. She must've forgotten about her gun because she kept it at chest level as she moved towards him. Fairchild caught her with a backhand across her mouth, then struck her again, sending her sprawling into the living room. She was still holding on to her gun.

She tried screaming at him, screaming what the hell was going on, but Fairchild was blind and deaf to the world. He was on top of her, his hands grabbing her head, his skin dead white around his eyes. His shoulders tensed as he started to jerk her head sideways. She was still holding her gun. Keegan sat impassively watching. I turned and started walking away.

As I reached the door I heard a weird sound. Maybe more like two sounds combined into one. Like a gunshot and a neck cracking.

What did they expect with a guy like me?

Stepping outside was like stepping into another world. The heat had finally broken. I stood for a moment, disoriented, listening to a weird stillness in my head. Then a soft breeze blew from the east and I turned my back to it, letting it push me along. With a guy like me there'd always be other Dorises and Fairchilds. But that would be later. For now I let the breeze send me back towards Bendleson's hospital.

You're Gonna Get Yours

Stephen Allan

Raymond winced every time someone from his old life called him Brick House, and got right pissed when some young punk called him that; almost as pissed off when someone called him "nigga." So, when the little snot ran up to him while he was eating his lunch on the back end of his rusting truck, and said, "Brick House, my nigga," Raymond wasn't pleased.

"The name's Raymond to most people," Raymond said as he took another swig from his beer can, hidden in a brown paper bag. He had held the laborer position for nearly a year and felt comfortable enough with the foreman to drink a beer or two on the work site.

"Nigga, please."

Raymond dropped his beer and snatched the scrawny punk by the neck.

"Some white trash piece of shit called me a nigger once and I spent fifteen years in jail," Raymond said. "That racist prick spent those years in the fucking cemetery. I don't give a shit what color you are, nobody calls me a nigga. Do we understand?"

"Goddamn, man," the punk said. "I just come over to tell you about Jerome."

Raymond let him go.

"What about him?"

"They say he's in the ER."

"What for?"

"That nig . . . I mean that boy got himself beat up real good."

Raymond hadn't seen his son since he got out of Angola four years ago. He tried to make contact, but Jerome was too much into the gang life. Guns, thefts, drugs, and whatever else he and his buddies could find. All of them barely in their twenties.

"What's your name?" Raymond asked the kid.

"EZ."

"Your mama give you that name?"

"Nah, but people been calling me EZ most of my life."

"Well, EZ, you gonna tell me which hospital he's in?"

EZ told Raymond.

"His crew gots to know," EZ said. "You know where they hang?"

Raymond didn't know any of Jerome's friends.

"Can't help you."

Raymond walked away to tell his foreman about his son and ask for the rest of the day off.

The woman behind the ER's triage desk gave Raymond directions to Jerome's bed. He found his son sitting on a stretcher, bandaged around the head with his arm in a sling. There was dried blood on his Saints T-shirt.

"What happened?" Raymond asked.

Jerome looked up from a *Sports Illustrated*, but went back to his magazine without answering.

"You gonna pretend I'm not here?" Raymond said.

"I don't need you here."

Jerome was a skinny kid, not quite twenty. While Raymond was away, his ex worked two jobs and didn't have time for Jerome, and the school system couldn't have cared less.

"Where are your boys?" Raymond asked as he pulled up a plastic chair to the foot of the bed. "I figured they'd be here."

"They're gone."

"What do you mean gone?"

"Dead."

"Shit," Raymond said. "Accident?"

"Yeah, someone accidentally shot 'em all."

"When?"

"Man, what the fuck you care for?" Jerome's eyes seemed wild, but there was fear in them. "Why are you even here? How'd you even know I was here?"

"Some piece of work, called himself EZ," Raymond said.

"Fuck," Jerome said and stood up. The first step caused his face to wince. "Fuck."

"What are you trying to do?"

"Jesus, it hurts."

"Just stay there."

"Can't," Jerome said, his eyelids pressed tight. "Gotta get out of here."

"You ain't gotta do nothing but wait for the doctor," Raymond said. "EZ was going to tell your friends where you are."

"Are you deaf or just dumb? I just told you that they're all gone."

"EZ didn't know that. He was asking about where to find them."

"What'd you tell him?"

"What could I tell him? Nothing."

A nurse opened the privacy curtain. She grabbed Jerome's arm and injected a syringe of liquid into it. "Tetanus," she said, holding the empty syringe for Raymond to see. Jerome asked when he could leave.

"The guy will be right in," the nurse said and left, pulling the curtain closed behind her. Raymond watched her ass as she went.

"At least they got some good looking nurses working here," Raymond said and turned back to his son.

Jerome was grabbing at his throat. He scrambled out of the bed and fell onto the white floor. His lips turned blue and his body began to shake wildly.

"Nurse," Raymond yelled. "I need someone in here."

The curtain slashed open and two women in scrubs crouched down beside Jerome.

"He can't breathe," Raymond said.

The women rushed as they tried to put some metal instrument into Jerome's mouth. One said she couldn't get through. The other hurried to a drawer beside the bed and grabbed a scalpel. She handed it to the one knelt beside Jerome. She took the scalpel to his throat and slit it open. The first woman handed her a piece of tubing, which the second one pushed into the bleeding hole. Instead of air, blood and what looked like vomit spewed out of the other end. The shaking stopped and the blood and bile slowed its flow from the plastic tubing.

"What the hell happened?" the first nurse said.

"The tetanus shot," Raymond said. "The nurse gave him the shot and when I turned around, he was choking."

"Tetanus?" the second nurse said. "He didn't need a tetanus shot. Who gave him the shot?"

"A nurse," Raymond said.

"What was her name?"

Raymond tried to recall a name tag or an ID badge hanging around her neck, but he couldn't remember seeing one.

"A tetanus shot wouldn't do this to someone," the first nurse said.

* * *

The cops came but they didn't care. Raymond was in too much shock to ride them, so he sat and answered every question, staring at his son covered with a white sheet.

After the detectives left, orderlies came for Jerome and wheeled him away from his father. One of the officers had said that an autopsy would need to be performed. A nurse told Raymond that Jerome's body would be released to the caretaker when the pathologist was through.

Raymond left the hospital and headed home. Not wanting to take the bus, Raymond walked close to four miles to his small efficiency. When he reached his place, he didn't bother to turn on the lights. He simply grabbed a cleaned-out jelly jar and a half empty bottle of Wild Turkey and sat down on one of the frayed lawn chairs he used for furniture. The whiskey was gone by the time the moon came out. Raymond stared at a small picture of Jerome that hung on his grimy wall. He was six or seven and wearing a football uniform. Three teeth were missing from his smile. Raymond kept his eyes on the photograph until the heaviness of the drink consumed him and he fell asleep.

The pounding on the door woke him. He stood up from the chair too fast and his head swam from the alcohol. The microwave's clock read three thirty. Raymond didn't own a gun, so he went to his kitchen utility drawer and brought out a chef's knife. He went to the door.

"Who is it?"

"It's EZ, man." His voice was low, a conspiratorial whisper. "Open up."

"I don't know you," Raymond said, looking through the eyehole.

"You know me, we met today, nigga," EZ said. "Sorry, not nigga. I mean, yeah, whatever. But you know me."

"Just because we talked for five minutes, it don't mean we're close."

"Just open up. This is about Jerome."

"Jerome's dead."

"Yeah, I know. People been saying he was juiced."

"What else have people been saying?"

"Let me in and I'll tell you."

Raymond unlocked the door and opened it. "Put your hands up in the air," Raymond said, motioning with the knife in his hand.

EZ did as he was told and Raymond patted him down. He told EZ to turn around and saw the gun hanging out of the back of his black jeans. Raymond took it and slid it into the back of his own pants.

"What's the gun for?"

"I get scared of strangers when I walk home from school. What do you think it's for? This place is mad since the floods, man. It's like cowboys and Indians out there on the streets some days."

Raymond had been in Angola during the hurricanes and flooding. He got out four months later to find his city, or at least his part of the city, virtually destroyed. Almost everyone he knew had moved away.

"All right, come in and sit down," Raymond said and turned on the light.

EZ stood next to the chair Raymond had been sleeping in and pointed down at it.

"Man, don't you got like any real furniture?"

"It's hard for an honest man to have anything nowadays," Raymond said.

EZ sat down in the chair, shifting his weight back and forth. Raymond grabbed his one dining chair from his kitchen table and sat in front of EZ.

"You said you had something to say about Jerome," Raymond said. "What is it?"

"Can I get my gun back?"

"Don't trust you."

EZ pleaded, but Raymond remained firm.

"What is it that you know?" He still felt a little drunk and wished he had splashed some cold water on his face. He even looked over at the faucet when he talked to EZ.

"Okay, first of all, I liked Jerome. He was always nice to me. Helped me with shooting baskets, things like that. I never ran with him and his boys, because the others were complete motherfuckers."

"Stop jabbering and tell me what you know."

"Word is, it was Harold, the guy who runs the gang Jerome was with. I guess Jerome went around about this money they'd taken during some bank robbery during the floods. Everyone suspected these motherfuckers, but no one ever saw the cash. Jerome said the money was real and he was getting big enough to take it himself."

"He came out in the open and told people he was going to rip off these guys?" Raymond asked.

"Like I said, it was what I heard. It looks like Harold is takin' care of things. I think if you hurry, you get him and the money."

"Don't care about the cash."

"Well, you can hunt him down."

"You know where I can find this guy?"

"Yeah, he's been staying with his cousin. Lives in one of them new trailers the government bought. It's in a boarded up lot on Christopher Street."

"What's the cousin's name?"

"Wallace."

"Okay. I'll hit their place today."

"You better take something with you if you plan on knocking on that door. Those motherfuckers be holding a lot of firepower."

Raymond took out EZ's gun.

"This should do," Raymond said.

"That's my gun, registered and everything," EZ said. "Something goes down, and they trace the gun, the cops are coming for me."

Raymond thought about it for a minute, then unloaded the gun's clip and took out the bullets and handed everything back to EZ.

"Go home," Raymond said.

"So, what are you going to take with you?"

Raymond looked at his kitchen counter where he had placed his chef's knife in the sink. Getting caught with a loaded weapon was not good for someone on probation, but cutlery wouldn't be a problem.

"I guess I'll think of something."

"You hear anything, I'll be at the courts down by Christopher," EZ said.

The knife didn't feel like enough; he wished he had a gun. Those guys in the trailer would be packing. It was hard to close the distance to someone when all they needed to do was pull a trigger to stop you. He concealed his weapon by holding the blade along his arm, the sharp edge out. He knocked on the door and heard them scramble inside. There was some mumbling that he couldn't make out, and he was sure he heard a clip click into some kind of firearm. He knocked again.

The door opened a crack and a pug-faced man looked out.

"You got the wrong place," Pug-face said.

"I'm looking for Harold," Raymond said.

Pug-face looked back into the trailer, said something to the others, and then returned to Raymond. "Nigga ain't here."

Raymond let the words slide.

"You know where he's at?"

"No," Pug-face said. "I don't know no Harold. Get out of here, old man."

Pug-face went to close the door, but Raymond put a brick in the way.

"The fuck, man?" Pug-face said.

"Where's Harold?"

"Nigga, I'm gonna shoot you, you don't move that brick." Pug-face lifted his foot to kick the brick out of the way, but Raymond grabbed him by the back of his knee and pulled him down. He then pulled the punk closer to him and placed the point of the knife against the man's stomach. Pug-face tried to break free.

"You squiggle anymore, you're liable to get stabbed, man," Raymond said.

Pug-face called to his friends. The door swung open wide and Raymond saw the barrels of two semiautomatics pointed at his head.

"Stop it with the knife," one of the gunmen said. "I ain't afraid to blast your brains out of your skull."

"I didn't come here for trouble . . ."

"You found it, motherfucker," the same gunman said.

"I'm just looking for Harold."

"There's a shitload of Harolds in this city."

"This one runs with a gang that supposed to live in this trailer."

"Who told you that?"

"Doesn't matter."

"Like hell it don't matter," the gunman said. "I want to know the name of the dead man who told you about this trailer. Was it Marcus?"

"Don't know any Marcus, besides that ain't neither here or there right now," Raymond said.

"What the fuck you talking to this nigga for?" Pug-face said. "Shoot him."

The gunman's pistol had lowered a bit, but he raised it back up. Raymond dropped to the ground and rolled under the trailer, the gunshots echoing through the hot air behind him. The tight fit under the trailer caused Raymond to shimmy on his back. The three guys jumped onto the dirt. Raymond managed to scramble out the other side before they were on their bellies and shooting at him.

"Go around," he heard one of them say. Raymond ran to the end of the trailer and leaned against the side with his blade out. The second gunman sprinted around the corner. Raymond brought his knife around and sunk it into the guy's belly. As he doubled over, Raymond pulled the knife out and brought it down into his back. Raymond felt the steel hit the sides of bones on its way in. The guy let his pistol fall as he dropped to the ground. Raymond grabbed the gun and came up in time to see Pug-face come around the opposite corner with a shotgun. Pug-face let off a few rounds, pumping the weapon with each explosion—but the shots went wide.

The gun in Raymond's hand jerked several times with massive power before Raymond realized that he had squeezed the trigger. It was more reflex than conscious thought. Pug-face's shoulder and chest burst with blood. He slammed down to the dirt on his face. Raymond paused too long at the two bodies in front of him. A gunshot came from underneath the trailer and Raymond felt a sudden scorching heat hit his calf. A few more shots missed him as he ran to the front of the trailer. He found some cover behind a Ford Bronco and held the pistol up. It was out of ammunition. He no longer had his knife and the gun was useless.

He crouched up to see through the vehicle's windows, but they were heavily tinted. He tried the driver's door and found it unlocked. He looked inside for a weapon of some sort, but found none. The keys were in the ignition. Raymond climbed in. From inside the cab he could see his surroundings. He watched the trailer from both sides for the gunman and then spotted some movement underneath. The gunman pulled himself from under the trailer, his gun in ready position. Raymond turned around for anything in the backseat, but as he did, his hip hit the horn. The gunman swung around and started blasting the Bronco's windshield. Raymond ducked under the dash, reached up, and turned the truck on. He put the thing in gear and pressed a hand against the gas pedal. Raymond slammed against the insides of the truck when the vehicle hit the trailer. He heard a scream and looked up over the dashboard. The gunman was pinned between the truck and the trailer, his arms trapped at his sides. Raymond got out of the truck and went over to the gunman.

"I'm gonna kill you," the gunman said, but it came out soft. He was a dying man.

"Tell me about Harold," Raymond said.

". . . kill you," the gunman repeated and then went limp.

The sirens were close and Raymond knew that this was a dead end. He stood up and went back and looked for his knife. It was still in the second gunman's back. He pulled it out and wiped the handle with the bottom of the second gunman's T-shirt. He grabbed Pug-face's shotgun and ran off in the opposite direction of the cop cars speeding towards the scene.

EZ was leaning against the metal fence of the basketball courts watching a three-on-three game. Raymond came up beside him.

"Harold wasn't where you said he'd be," Raymond said.

"If he weren't there, he could be anywhere."

"What do you know about a guy named Marcus?"

"Marcus? Good man."

"He got some kind of beef with Harold and his buddies?"

"Something like that. He used to hang with all of them niggas. Then there was some fight and he took off and joined up with some motherfuckers."

"You know where I could find this guy?"

"Sure," EZ said, and pointed to one of the players on the court. "That one in the green shorts, that's him."

A cruiser with its lights flashing and siren screaming flew by. Raymond ducked.

"Damn, why're you acting all wiggedy?" EZ asked.

"Got into a bit of trouble back at the trailer."

"What kind of trouble?"

"The kind you don't want anyone asking about."

One of the players on the court sunk a shot from twenty feet back. "Game, motherfuckers," the kid said. Marcus grabbed his stuff against the fence on the opposite side from Raymond and EZ.

"Yo, Marcus," EZ said. "Got a man here wants to talk to you."

Marcus stood up with a Gatorade in his hand. He looked at Raymond and downed the drink, but kept his eye on Raymond.

"What's he got to talk about?"

"You know Harold?" Raymond asked.

"Yeah, I know that motherfucker," Marcus said. "But you should try his cousin, if you're looking for him."

"His cousin is dead. Along with the rest of his crew," Raymond said.

"Harold do it?"

"No, I did."

"Well, you'll excuse me if I don't cry," Marcus said.

"When I went there they asked me if you were the one who told me where they were. Why would you be the first person they'd think of?"

"Maybe because things between Harold and me never got solved."

"What things?"

"Why should I tell you?"

"Because Harold killed my son."

"Who's that?"

"Jerome."

"He that scrawny thing used to hang out at the 7-Eleven on Burbank Avenue?" Marcus asked. "He was okay. Sorry."

"What happened between you and that crew?"

Marcus looked at EZ. "You vouch for this guy?"

"Yeah, he's okay. Just looking for the guy who did his son."

Marcus thought for a moment and then nodded his head. "Yeah, okay, I'll tell you." Marcus put his fingers through the chain fence and rested his arms there. "I was part of that crew. We'd do the usual shit that every other crew out there does. Everything was split between all of us, so everyone got the same amount of money, no matter who did what. If you were part of whatever was going down, you still got your share. Now, just before the flood I went up north to my grandma's, so I wasn't around for the mess. I found out that Harold and the boys came across a lot of money during that time, but when I got back to the city, Harold said I wasn't with them no more. I told him I knew about the money, but that little bitch ignored me. That money never surfaced. No one in that crew spent any extra cash, you know, like some crazy amount out of the ordinary. So, maybe there wasn't any."

"If Harold wasn't with his cousin, where would he be?"

"If he ain't there, and he ain't on the streets committing crimes, then that nigga must be flying in the air or something."

"There's got to be somewhere," Raymond said.

"Well," Marcus said, "his grandmother used to live in this house on Asylum Avenue, before she was kicked out by the bank. He used to go out there and take care of her. Do her shopping and shit."

"You remember the address?"

"Can't remember any house numbers, but it was on the corner across from a drugstore. It had a big picture window on the side and on the porch. I think it was yellow back then."

Raymond thanked Marcus and started walking towards Asylum without saying another word to EZ.

The drugstore was abandoned, still boarded up with trash strewn all over its cracked parking lot. A realty sign was nailed to one of the plywood panels. There were still a lot of houses and buildings up for sale on Asylum Avenue, but the house that Marcus described had a new coat of yellow paint.

Raymond walked up the porch steps and knocked on the door. He looked down the side street the house shared, Grant Street, and saw a lot of FOR SALE signs. Something on the ground caught the corner of his eye. He walked over and saw that it was another FOR SALE sign, but this one had a giant SOLD sticker on it. When the lock turned, Raymond's attention went back to the door. It swung open and a medium-sized man in a wife-beater shirt stood there. Raymond had a good six inches on him.

"You Harold?" Raymond asked.

"What you want?"

"I wanna know if you're Harold."

A car horn blared behind Raymond and he switched his footing so he could look at the car without losing sight of the man in the door. It was a small foreign car with a couple of different colors—bodywork done with whatever panels were available. EZ was behind the wheel. He got out of the car.

"That's him, that's Harold," EZ said.

Raymond reached up and took Harold by the throat and pushed him inside.

"Why'd you kill my son?" Raymond said. "Why'd you have to go and kill my son for?"

"I didn't kill nobody," Harold said.

"Bullshit," Raymond said. "You paid some crack whore to poison him."

Raymond took the pistol he stole from the trailer out of his pocket and placed the barrel in Harold's mouth.

Harold sounded like he was trying to say something, but Raymond pressed the gun's metal down on his tongue.

"Wait," EZ said. "Don't shoot him until he tells us where the money is."

"Don't care about the fucking money," Raymond said. "I only care about seeing this motherfucker's brains on that wall."

"Man, that's just stupid," EZ said. "Nigga, where's the fucking money at?"

"That's it," Raymond said. "Say good-bye."

Before he could pull the trigger, he felt the metal end of another gun pressed against his ear.

"We're gonna get that money first," EZ said.

"What the fuck do you think you're doing?" Raymond said.

"You think I was following you around because I cared about Jerome? I barely know that nigga. And yeah, I said nigga, nigga. What are you gonna do about it?"

"Put the gun down."

"Fuck that," EZ said. "Harold, where's the money?"

Harold mumbled something and Raymond took the pistol out of his mouth. "There ain't no money."

"Don't give me that bullshit," EZ said. "Everyone knows you got that money."

"There ain't any money," Harold repeated.

"He's telling you the truth," Raymond said.

"How that fuck do you know?"

"This house we're in, it was just bought. Fresh paint outside and a realtor's sign with a sold sticker on it laying on the lawn."

"Shit, a hundred thousand is a lot, but not enough to buy no fucking house," EZ said.

"You notice these places around here?" Raymond asked.

"Every other one is up for sale. There's still trash and shit all over the neighborhood. The prices of these places aren't what they were. This piece of shit just waited until the house went on sale and used the entire bundle to pay for his grandmother's old place. I bet this place went for real cheap. Ain't that right?"

"Something like that, so what?"

"So, you had my son killed for this house," Raymond said. "Every memory, everything he was, it's all gone so you can have some dumpy house that someone you used to know used to live in. It ain't nothing but plywood and paint, but my boy was a good person. He may have fucked up a time or two, but he could have still gotten away from people like you. He could have left this godforsaken place and become something, instead of a piece of meat on some coroner's cold slab.

"Now, I gotta ask you, was this place worth it? Was this place worth my son's life?"

"Place got memories for me, man," Harold said.

"Well, you only got so much longer to remember them before I kill you," Raymond said.

EZ backed away from Raymond, but kept the pistol pointed at him. "You ain't killing no one until—"

"Until what?" Raymond asked as he moved away from Harold. "That money you keep thinking about is in the hand of some lowlife real estate guy who's picking up percentages off people's devalued property. There's nothing here."

EZ stepped forwards again, but Raymond pulled out his knife and hit EZ's gun arm. EZ dropped the gun and grabbed his forearm. Raymond picked the gun up and pointed it at both EZ and Harold. He looked around the room and saw an electric drill attached to a long extension cord.

"EZ, take that extension cord and tie up Harold."

EZ did as he was told, tying Harold to the staircase.

"That little bitch Jerome was talking shit," Harold said. "He deserved it, saying about how he knew about the money and was going to take it from me. Can't let shit talk like that go ignored."

"You heard him say this?"

"Nah, it came from EZ here. EZ was the one told me."

"He's lying to you," EZ said. "Why would I say something like that?"

Raymond grabbed EZ by the collar and slammed his fist into the little prick's stomach. EZ went to the floor.

"To get Jerome killed," Raymond said. "You knew about me, about my reputation for dealing with people. You knew I'd go looking for Harold, and you served him right up for me. All you had to do was follow me."

"I was going to give you a cut," EZ said. "But I didn't say nothing to this motherfucker about Jerome."

"Bullshit," Harold said.

Raymond tied EZ next to Harold, ignoring EZ's insults. He went outside and unraveled the garden hose, cut the metal end off, and then cut off a piece of hose about six feet long. He took empty paint cans from the porch and took the hose and can to EZ's car. He unscrewed the gas cap, placed one end of the hose into the tank. He put his lips around the other end and sucked up the gas. As soon as it hit his tongue, he placed the end of the hose into the metal can and spit. When the can was full, he pulled the hose out and went back inside.

He dumped the gas all over the living room floor and then went back out for another can. He splashed gas all over the walls in the small dining room and on the staircase. When Raymond stepped into the kitchen, he found the girl who slipped Jerome his deadly shot. She was sprawled on the linoleum, still wearing the nursing scrubs she had on before. Rubber tubing stretched tight over her bicep and a needle hanging out of the crook of her arm. She could have been dead or alive; Raymond didn't care. He splashed gas around her and then spit in her face. She didn't move.

Raymond grabbed an empty Coke bottle from the kitchen counter and stuffed a piece of newspaper into it with just a little bit hanging out at the top. He walked onto the porch and took out his lighter. He lit it, watched the paper burn into the bottle. He then threw it in the middle of the wooden floor. The glass broke and the fire ignited the gas-soaked floor and walls in an instant of intense heat and flame.

Raymond walked away from the screams coming from EZ and Harold and headed across the street to the abandoned drugstore. He sat on the cement bench that was on the side of the building and watched that yellow house burn and burn. Each second he didn't hear a siren was better than the last.

Fool in Search of a Country Song

Andy Turner

No matter what you tried, you could bet your ass mud had your name on it in the parking lot of Hank's Gentleman's Club. It could have been bone dry for a month or more, but Hank's would still have deep, black holes filled to the tip-top with thick-ass mud, willing and waiting to claim your tires or your shoes. My truck landed in one of them holes when I missed Hank's entrance, flying instead over the curb and into the lot.

My foot splashed down in a mud puddle soon as I stepped out of my truck. I still had on my steel-toed work boots, so I didn't give a monkey's ass about getting mud all over them. For a second before going on, I stared at my breath in the air. It was a little after eleven. I could hear the jukebox wailing as soon as I got near the door. Hank fired the DJ a few weeks back for trying to spy on the girls while they were changing. Hank said damn DJs cost too damn much when you got a perfectly good jukebox that makes money instead of damn costing money and trying to sneak a peek at the girls. Damn pervert.

About ten guys were inside, most of them sitting by themselves at tables. Two of the dancers were sitting together at a table, waiting to go on, sucking on Newports and talking about George Clooney's ass.

Ed Looney was sitting at the runway with his dollar bills clinched tight in his hands, eyes intent on the dancer as she was shakin' it every which a way. Ed was always at Hank's, always at the same seat, eyeballing the dancers, always wearing a black shirt and black jeans. I stared at the dancer while she was flopping around. The lights flashed against her shiny body. Red, purple, then pink. She was wearing two pink tassels across her nipples and had on a matching G-string. She was older than the rest. Heavy in the ass and big, fat lips. As I stared up at her lips, she licked them, first the top, then the bottom. I stopped staring.

Hank's was beer only. People turn mean on you when they get liquor in 'em, Hank said. Pain in the ass to get your liquor license back, Hank said. Just make sure the damn stall door is closed before you open the bottle, Hank said.

"Blue?"

"Yep," I told Hank, giving a buck and getting a frosty cold Pabst Blue Ribbon and a mason jar to pour it in.

"What's the story?" he asked, wiping his hands on his shirt that read, "Every time I get my shit together, I step in it."

"Not nothing. Just tickled as shit to be off for the weekend."

"Boy, you got a gravy job, what you complaining about? The shipyard ain't shit. You should try running this place. Horny, drunk bastards."

"You're full of it, Hank."

"Sheeit. Last night I caught some twisted son of a bitch trying to squirt off right there at the runway. Tried to hide the shit with a copy of goddamned *Soldier of Fortune* magazine. Beating off at the damned runway. People wouldn't used to even think about doing something like that. How would you like someone to come down to the shipyard and slap their pecker right where you were working?"

"Well, I ain't as attractive as you, Hank."

"You got that right, smartass."

I sipped on my beer and took in Hank's from my spot at the bar. A "Gentleman's Club." Horseshit. Hank calls it that, but you'd be hard-pressed to find anyone in Hank's who calls himself a gentleman. Sure as shit ain't gonna find anyone out there calling us that.

"Another one?" Hank asked as I downed the rest of my Pabst.

"Sure. Cindy won't be home before three anyway."

It had been that way for six months or more. I worked until five at night, and she left at five and didn't get home until after three in the morning. I was normally either asleep or passed out by the time she got home. I went to Hank's a few nights a week, always on Friday. Cindy and I might see each other for a little while in the morning, but normally I was doing stuff outside and she was inside cleaning or watching damned *Judge Judy*. The rest of the time? Hell, we'd just argue. We'd stopped screwing. I'd touch her and she'd kinda twitch up. Wouldn't even bother to tell me she had a headache. Just say, "Naw, my back's been acting up again." What was she doing to her back?

A young girl, couldn't have been a minute over eighteen, came onstage. She reminded me a little of Cindy when she was that age. Straight brown hair that just nibbled at her ears. Brown eyes the color of MoonPies. I thought about Cindy as I watched her dance. I remembered when shit was better. That's what fools do instead of trying to change anything. When we were in high school, Cindy and I would spend whole afternoons at her parents' house with our tongues down each other's throat. One of those times we jumped in the shower with all of our clothes on, ripping them all off until we were both naked. That was our first time. I was so scared her dad was gonna bust in and shoot off my dick. I didn't know what I was doing. My hair was long then, and the water had caused all my hair to fall down on my face. I remember trying to push it back, trying to keep up with what was going on.

Blake Matthews, a one hundred and ten percent asshole I knew in high school, stumbled in while I was looking at the jukebox, trying to make up my mind as to whether I should play Merle Haggard or Willie Nelson. As "Pour Some Sugar on Me" played, I blew Blake a kiss; he gave me a dirty look. I picked Hag. I was in a Hag mood. I decided to play pool and pretend like the ball was Blake's head. I wrote my name on the board. No quarters on the table.

"Show me them titties," was how Blake introduced himself. Hank eyed him.

The game ended as the one guy sank in the eight ball. He had a smile that told me he was gonna kick my ass good in pool.

"Rack 'em up, Junior," he said, extending his slender hand for me to shake. "My name is Cooper, but you can call me Cooper."

Cooper was a skinny guy with long, greasy red hair that dripped out of a Rusty Wallace racing cap. The whole time he talked he rubbed his chest square in the center. He lit a cigarette and stuck it in his mouth before rubbing more chalk on his hands. Chalk was all over his shirt and pants.

"Don't think I've seen you in here before," I told him, chalking my stick.

"First time. I live in Carolina. Came up here 'cause my friend told me he was gonna hook me up with some action, you know. Shit fell through, so I came here to look at a couple few titties."

He moved around the table, knocking in three low balls without even looking up at me.

"Besides, this ain't far from where I live. My house is right on the border. In fact, I can piss across my ditch into Virginia. Not that I do—necessarily." Another high ball dropped in the corner pocket. And he just kept going.

"Damn. Looks like I'm screwed."

"Don't worry, Cap'n. I'll use Vaseline," he said, knocking in the last, lonesome solid but scratching in the process. He had gone on for so long that the cigarette that hung from his lips was half ash.

I knocked the cue ball off the table and it landed under a chair by the runway. Someone in the back yelled, "Another one dollar in the jukebox." As I picked it up, I noticed a guy wearing a Dale "The Intimidator" Earnhardt jacket and snakeskin cowboys eyeballing me like I'd just banged his grandmother. Dale was a tall bastard with a Tom Selleck mustache growing above his lips, which turned to a smile when he noticed I was looking at him.

"I Think I'll Just Stay Here and Drink" came on the jukebox, so I felt obliged to get another Pabst for me and Cooper after tossing the cue ball back on the table. Cooper thanked me for the beer, took a sip, nodded at the right corner pocket, and knocked in the eight ball.

"Shit."

"Play again?"

"Nah, I think I'm just gonna finish my beer and head home."

"Suit yourself, ace."

Melanie came onstage to dance. She ran her hands through her hair before walking up the steps to the runway. The little she had on was all black.

Merle sang, cutting through my insides like a honky-tonk surgeon.

Blake was getting drunker and more obnoxious. Ed Looney sat beside him, not saying a word, looking up at Melanie. Blake kept jumping up and down in his seat, knocking into Ed and spilling his beer all over him. Nothing. Ed was quiet. John Lee Hooker came on the jukebox. *Boom, boom, boom.* Melanie grabbed hold of the pole, a confident smile sliding off her lips.

She teased a young guy who had leaned in close to the runway, dipping those blond curls on his face, tickling his eyeballs.

"Hey, Melanie. You and me after you get off. What do you think? Sound good, honey?" Blake yelled at her, spilling more beer.

Nothing.

"You hear me?"

Still dancing. "C'mon, baby." *Boom, boom, boom.*

"Don't try to ignore me. I know you hear me. Slut."

It was like something ripped. Ed rose from his seat, giving the meanest look to Blake I had ever seen one man give another.

"I'm trying to look at the titties," was all he said.

"Fuck you, loser. Why don't you just go home, fat fuck."

Hank came over.

"You're gonna have to leave," he told Blake. "Carry your ass down the road."

"I ain't fucking leaving," Blake said, taking a swing at Hank and landing his fist deep in Hank's ribcage.

He caught Hank off guard and Hank ended up flat on his ass. While Blake was looking down at Hank, Ed Looney chopped Blake dead in the neck. That son of a bitch fell to the floor right next to Hank. Blake's rat head bounced once on the floor like a scoop of mashed potatoes with gravy. He tried to talk and couldn't. The back of his head was dripping blood on the floor. Couldn't get his ass off the floor.

"That had to hurt, partner," Cooper offered as he walked by on his way out, scratching his nuts.

Ed sat back down like nothing happened, with a look that resembled satisfaction, but it was Ed, so it also resembled not much at all. Someone tried to help Hank up, but he refused and got up on his own. Hank kicked Blake hard as he could in the stomach with his cowboy boot. Blake let out a pathetic whimper that was something like an acknowledgment that he was a dumbass. Hank grabbed Blake by the seat of his pants and tossed him outside. "Don't bring your ass back in here," he said, before adding, "at least not for a week or two." Hank returned behind the bar and resumed beer slinging like nothing had happened.

Melanie had put on a black slip and was in the corner smoking. I asked her if she was okay, and she said, "That little shit ain't worth worrying about," as she blew out smoke.

"Well, at least you have Ed protecting you."

"Damn straight. You better act right, hun."

"I'll keep that in mind." And tipped my hat towards her like a jackass.

Shaking my head, I walked over to Hank. "One more Pabst for the road, Hank."

"Be careful on your way home, Billy. Cops sure enough will pull your ass over."

"I know, Hank." I put the beer in my coat pocket. "Have a good night."

One of the strippers, Two-Ton Tammy, went out before me and got in someone's passenger seat. She came up with that moniker herself and was known to add "with two top-notch tits." She was a big girl and damn proud of it. Boasting a pair of 40 Gs, killer attitude, and sex appeal to spare, Tammy could make a linebacker blush—and cum in Hank's parking lot for an extra forty bucks. "Holy humdinger, here's a lady with hellacious hooters, gentlemen" was how Little Bobby, the pervert DJ, once introduced her. Rumor had it that Tammy became a stripper soon after her mama drained a Liquid-Plumr cocktail.

Dale was leaning against my truck when I got outside.

"What do you want, Dale?" I asked.

"My name ain't Dale. It's John, and I'm the man who's fucking your wife." He pulled his hand from his back and brought out a .38 special.

He pointed it at me and said, "Here's how it's gonna be. Cindy wants a divorce. You're gonna give it to her. You ain't gonna say shit about shit and I won't beat the living shit out of you or shoot you." He brought the revolver down. "I know you might think this is a bit overly forceful, but I like to get my point across."

"Fuck you," seemed like the appropriate thing to say, so that's what I said.

Dale-John spit, then said, "You ain't fucking nobody. Cindy said you ain't fucked in six months. That's fine with me, because I prefer her pussy clean and to myself. But she said you spent all your time chasing skanks at this run-down titty bar, playing that old, pity me, country shit. Shame, shame."

A man who fucks your wife and points a gun at you can still have a point. But I didn't feel like agreeing with him.

"I'll fucking kill you. I've got guns too." I didn't. "But why don't you put the gun down and fight me like a man, you son of a bitch."

He kept the gun instead and stepped towards me and punched me in the gut. I swung at his head, missed, and then felt like I was going to throw up. As I stumbled backwards, I noticed Cooper coming up slowly behind him and he had a shotgun in his hands. He smiled at me. Buying him that beer had apparently been a smart purchase.

Cooper put the gun to Dale-John's head and said, "Hey, asshole, why don't you cease and desist?"

Dale-John froze and said, "Who the fuck are you? This ain't none of your fuckin' business."

"Well, my name is Cooper, and I'm from North Carolina. Drop the gun on the ground, son." He cocked the shotgun for emphasis.

"Your ass is mine, faggot." But he did what Cooper said.

"Hey, Billy, why don't you grab that gun and we'll call the cops on The Intimidator here. Have I mentioned how much I fuckin' hate Chevy's?"

I picked up the gun and started to walk inside and tell Hank to call the police. But with visions of his hands touching my wife and him smiling like Luke Cocksucker, I turned back around and smacked Dale-John in the mouth as hard as I could with his piece. The blood from his mouth raced him to the ground as he fell to his knees. He spit out a few teeth or parts of teeth and said something, but I wasn't listening.

Cooper stopped grinning for a second. Two-Ton Tammy ran out of Cooper's car and went to help Dale-John.

"I appreciate it. I owe you," I told Cooper.

"Always here to help, man. Shit, thanks for making my Friday night interesting." The smile returned.

Hank came running out the door and I knew I owed it to him to explain what happened. But my mind was swirling and I just got in my truck. I took the gun with me, figuring I would toss it in Lake Mead like real soon. I pictured Cindy and me in the bathtub together long ago, two horny teenagers, smiling and red-faced. I put the key in the ignition and a cassette playing Merle Haggard's "The Emptiest Arms in the World" was turned up too loud. I left it that way.

I took the beer out from my coat and drank it as it foamed over. I reached down to get the bottle of Jim Beam I kept under my seat and put it between my legs, wondering which back road I would pick to throw a pity party. Old Myrtle Road would do. I hit reverse—way too hard—and my back end bucked wildly when my truck hit a mudhole.

She was standing in the wrong spot. I couldn't stop in time. Two-Ton Tammy screamed as Hag howled for the lonely.

Mercy First, First Mercy

David Harrison

People stop taking their meds all the time.

I'm sorry I killed that dog, though.

Just, stuff gets stuck in your head—am I right? Am I right? Aggravation. Insults.

Childhood . . .

Or a plainclothes named Barlow and, behind him, his over-wrought partner, the one who's pacing, rolling his eyes through one-way glass along the dirty wall of an airless interrogation room.

"From the top," Barlow says.

This ain't my first time; I know that's an order.

Still, I ask for another cigarette.

Wrong brand, but if I know another thing, it's that beggars can't choose. I close my eyes, inhale—deep—imagine the nicotine like pretty paint rolled on my inside walls. . . . When I open my eyes, I'm guessing I've smiled, 'cause Barlow wants in on the joke and the partner looks, more than ever, loaded for bear.

"Seriously," Barlow says.

But he's the one smiling now—I'm almost sure of it. Doesn't

make me nervous so much as it makes me mad that I don't know how long the three of us are gonna be stuck together in this sneaker box of a room. "I'm sorry I killed that dog—"

"The top," Barlow interrupts. "That's an order!"

My stomach growls. I'm probably hungry. There're coffees they'd brought me, all gone cold, collecting in Styrofoam cups atop the dented steel table between me and Barlow. I don't drink coffee—won't, either—I told them early on. Again I ask what it takes to get a Canada Dry around here.

Barlow tells me, "Water."

With my hands cuffed behind me, I spit the cigarette butt from my mouth to the floor; I turn, lean, drink from a straw though the water's lukewarm. I'm picturing the nicotine running and streaking, and I don't think my eyes are even closed. . . .

The top? I liked the dog fine. Some kind of retriever. Square head, thick haunches, dark tail taut like a whip. So black he looked blue when the light hit him right.

And I swear he didn't talk.

I tell Barlow and his partner, "Wouldn't stop barking, though—"

Partner peels himself away from the window—in time to slam a big hand down on the table. "From the beginning!"

"I'm right here," I say. Then, to Barlow, "He always shout like that?"

"Take five, Frank."

Partner—name is Frank, I guess—leaves.

Barlow says, "Just you and me."

I want to point to my temple, tap some, correct him. But the cuffs. Fuck it.

"Danny," I say.

"The boy—"

"My brother."

Barlow's bushy eyebrows arch. He thumbs through my file. "Uh-uh."

"Deceased," I tell him. "Long time ago." Mercy is where and whenever you find it.

Barlow only sighs.

"My father was a welder," I continue. "He caught fire once—all up and down his one arm. Wound up limp, all smooth, real ugly—like candle wax left in the sun." Pop liked me and Danny to touch it. . . .

"The boy."

A one-track steel trap this Barlow, lucky devil. So, I try to concentrate—I really do. . . .

The boy? His father spoke Spanish. *La madre* went mute. I heard their works through thin walls when I should've been sleeping. Poor kid, in the treacherous dark with his pitch-black dog . . .

"Boy's name was Antonio," Barlow interrupts.

If he says so; I mostly remembered big ears, skinny legs, bruising all up and down the kid's arms. Clumsy, my ass. Or am I thinking of Danny? Old gets new, again and again. . . .

And again.

Barlow says, "Antonio Diaz . . ."

"I offered him gum once."

". . . age eleven."

I tell Barlow how the kid took a stick, but didn't know to thank me. Up close, his eyes had looked old. "Swiveled his head like he might get caught stealing, you know?"

Barlow knows of what we speak; I can see it in the way he shrugs his shoulders, in the way he taps one foot, in the way he writes left-handed. The scrape of his soft pencil across the notepad sounds like a wagging tail. . . .

"We never had no dog of our own," I say, thinking Barlow ought to know. "My brother stole a turtle once."

"Danny."

"Tyson."

"Tyson?"

Danny's turtle's name was Tyson. Got found, all right; Danny offered to take Tyson back to the pet store, make things right, whatever it took. Pop handed Danny a hammer instead. . . .

"You got kids, Barlow?" I ask.

"You think we got nothin' but time around here?" But he puts down his pencil. Then, he's looking around the entire tiny, shitty room; he's spreading his arms, slowly, and pointing or something—crazy bastard—like he's a television spokesmodel or some goddamn thing.

"I'll show you crazy," I hear myself tell Barlow. But the cuffs; I sit back down.

"Pop handed Danny a hammer."

Like that, Barlow is writing again.

And writing.

I gather I must be talking: Hammers. House pets. Parents. Pulp. I see sweet Danny's eyes, but my rap to Barlow is all about old man Diaz, about how I figured out which Fridays were paydays from the bumps in those nights, from the barley stink of freshly drained forties in the Dumpster, from Saturday bruises still swollen and purple before time turned poor, skinny Antonio yellow. . . .

"Man died much too quick, you ask me. You know the sound it makes when you drop a flat rock onto mud?"

Before Barlow can answer, I'm on to the missus, *tu madre*, the mute. "How dare she?" I ask him. Hurt like a bitch when she dug those nails into my neck. And teeth on her too; left one of my earlobes about on a thread. "All of a sudden she's a fighter?"

Barlow's scribbling like a genuine madman now. It makes me think I'm talking about the kid, about Antonio, *D* for Diaz, for Danny, for damn sure, 'cause just growin' up is murder enough, but it's worse to be waiting and wishing when you know that things don't change, things won't ever change, old is new, new gets old, like father, like son, brother's keeper, losers weepers. . . .

"*D* for done?" I ask.

Barlow nods as he puts his pencil down. He twists in his seat, shoots the same nod out that mirrored glass.

Like that, the partner, Frank, is back. Still ugly, but I'll be damned if he doesn't have my ginger ale.

"Where and whenever." I laugh and lean and sip and slurp. "Danny buried Tyson in the woods behind our house." I found arrowheads out there once; I straight away showed them to Pop. He snatched the lot, made me watch when he put them in hamburger meat, fed the neighbor's collie. . . .

Dogs bleed.

Kids see.

Danny loved that turtle.

I love Danny. . . .

So, meds or no meds, maybe I ought to tell Barlow and Frank how a hammer's only good enough for fathers, for mothers, for goddamn dogs who just wouldn't stop with the barking and barking. And barking . . .

But I've said enough.

"Crazy bastard," Frank mutters as Barlow leads their way out.

At last, giving me my own clear view to the one-way glass. I see Antonio's eyes, grown wide as Danny's did in the final instant, not scared nor brave, not empty though, either, just already dead at eleven years old, long gone before I snap his neck, past lost before I save a soul. . . .

"Mercy, me."

This ain't my first time.

Overclocked

Lawrence Clayton

I got the worst fucking luck.

The downtown local broke onto the subway platform like a rogue wave, and I was nearly pulled under by the riptide. I wrapped an arm around an upright steel column, encrusted in decades of tough, brightly colored institutional paint. Someone had started an archaeological excavation, exposing a multitude of layers, geological strata millimeters deep, and no sign of the naked underlying steel. Like a coward I crouched in the lee, waiting for the surge to pass. About the only thing I had going for me was that I was headed opposite the commuters on their way to work.

Sometimes I believe I live inside a giant pachinko machine, I swear. I couldn't decide if it was way too early in the morning or way too late at night.

I felt shaky. Nauseous. Like a shadow on a cloudy day. Too much coffee, my stomach twisted in knots in protest; and the numbing effect of the alcohol was beginning to morph into a splitting headache. I wanted methamphetamines. I wanted valium. I wanted to eat a mile of pussy. I was still technically on the clock.

On a stainless steel edge, I smoothed a crumpled twenty that had until recently lived a solitary existence in the bottom of my blue jeans. I fed it into the slot, and shockingly, the machine accepted it on the first try.

"Would you like to add money to your MetroCard?" No. I didn't have a MetroCard. I wanted to get one. That was the problem. The solution, however, didn't seem to be revealed on the touch screen. I hit cancel. "How may I help you today?" No sign of my twenty. "Please insert credit card or cash to begin." I looked around. The token booth, encased in inch-thick Plexi, stood empty. "Thank you for riding with MTA."

More Trouble Ahead.

It was going to be a long walk. For a minute I just stood there, looking at the thing. I swear, if a machine could look smug, this one did. I considered digging my ten-inch Crescent wrench out of my tool bag and doing a number on its smug little touch screen, but frankly I didn't have the energy. I sighed, probably too loud and too dramatically, and headed up the urine steps into the morning sun.

Technically I was still on the clock. Technically I should have still been at the bottom of a very deep pit in a very tall building on the walkie-talkie with Joe Blow, trying to dial in load sensors whose manufacture and installation had been botched twenty years ago by a company out of Ohio that no longer existed; but then technically I'm not supposed to drink whiskey at work either and that's never stopped me, now has it? Seven hours of this shit is more than enough for anyone, certainly more than enough for Joe and me, and the rats in my peripheral vision give me the fucking creeps, and who really gives a shit if we cut out a little early? Not me.

Fuck this, man. It was kind of weird to be out and about this early in the morning. The light was strange. I had this strong paranoid feeling that I was being watched, but I chalked it up to caffeine, amphetamine withdrawal, and general paranoia. I checked over my shoulder a couple times nonetheless. Hey, you can't be too careful. An ounce of prevention is worth a pig in a poke, or something like that.

I picked up the mail on the way up to the apartment. Crap, whole lotta crap. Doctors Without Borders wanted more money. Man, you write them one lousy check and they never leave you alone. What else? Another rejection slip. A CD in a cardboard mailer for Nate. He'd been getting a ton of those lately. The Con Ed bill. Christ on a flipping crutch!

"Hey, Nate?" If there is one thing I really, really cannot stand, will do almost anything to avoid, it is conflict. My share of the electric bill, however, even considering our sixty-forty split, currently represented more than the sum of my total liquid assets, and rent was coming due again.

Nate poked his head out of his bedroom. Actually what we call his bedroom is just a sheet of half-inch plywood drywall—screwed into the far end of our railroad studio. It is a bedroom in that it encompasses just enough space for Nate's futon, and in that he sleeps in there. Not that I've ever actually known him to sleep.

"The electric bill just came in. It's for over nine hundred dollars." Our power bill had been creeping up for months now. Nate just looked at me. His eyes seemed wobbly. Or maybe it was just me, just that I hadn't slept in a really, really, really long time. "And I can't afford it."

He blinked, slowly, like a sick and twisted Disney version of an owl. Nate is ridiculously tall, six-four or six-seven or something, and has horrible posture and greasy black hair that he neglects to cut. So why does he always remind me of an owl? Maybe it's the nose. "Don't worry about it," he said. "I'll take care of it."

"All of it?"

"All of it. Give me the bill. I'll write them a check."

Wow, big spender. I handed over the bill. "This came for you too," I said, passing him the cardboard CD packet.

"Cool," Nate said, but he was no longer interested in me. He was already loading the CD into the one computer he owns that actually has a CD drive. A couple dozen fans kicked in as sleeping integrated circuits grouchily blinked the cobwebs out of their collective eyes and shook an electronic leg. A nearly subsonic sixty-cycle hum grated on my eardrums, and the temperature in the apartment edged up a degree or two.

Over the months, our apartment had been engulfed by a crawling infestation: what might appear to an uneducated layman (i.e., me) to be dozens of crappy old PCs, stripped of their cases and peripherals and wired together with red, blue, yellow, and green jumper cables. For a while Nate had been paying me (twenty bucks a pop, cash) to pick them up off the street for him, old computers that people were throwing away. Where he gets the money, I have no idea, because he certainly doesn't have a job and hardly ever leaves the apartment. He is some kind of computer genius—he fixed my pokey old PowerBook up real good, runs faster than brand-new now—but we don't even have our own Internet connection. We steal Internet (via a homemade tin can high-gain antenna that Nate cooked up from some recipe off the Interweb) from the Crazy Lady Coffee Shop across the street that is going to be closed soon because a Starbucks just opened up on our block. Nate is clearly a little crazy, but quite frankly that's the kettle calling the pot black.

It was only ten, but sometimes Daisy can be convinced to open the Good Times a little early; so I took my rejection slip and girded my loins for a nice long wallow. Daisy is a friend, and also happens to be my valium supply, and when she's in a good mood I can drink for free or half price. And I like looking at her tits. I hadn't been properly laid in a really long time, and the tension between my legs achieved some kind of cranky equilibrium with the tension between my ears. I really needed to score some meth and do some writing. And now I had an erection.

Honestly, I never do speed at work. I only use it to help me write. Nights, I'm an elevator mechanic—days, I'm a novelist. Or at least a short story writer. A thus far unpublished short story writer. And I need the valium to mellow out the meth; otherwise I get too jittery.

Daisy was behind the bar, polishing the greasy wood surface with a greasy rag in an earnest display of the futility of the Protestant work ethic. The steel gates were still down, but she let me in and set me up with a can of PBR and a shot that took some of the edge off. I told her the story of the thieving Metro-Card machine, and she shook her head in sympathy, but didn't offer me any free product. So I had to be content to watch her cleavage, which jiggled pleasantly under the cutout collar of a black Iron Maiden T-shirt. Daisy's got a bit of a gut, but frankly I didn't really mind that at all. What she has got is a really cute set of tits that I wouldn't mind having a closer look at, if it weren't for that damn ring on that damn finger of her left hand. I wouldn't mind, not one bit.

Feeling sufficiently insulated, or just fatalistic, I tore open the rejection slip. It was from one of your more pretentious literary journals, a story I had sent in months and months ago, and more or less given up on ever hearing back on.

Is it possible to hallucinate a complete page of text? I think that it probably is; and my head was in the kind of state that I assumed that was exactly what was going on. Holy shit. I killed my PBR and reread the letter that wasn't even a form letter.

My rejection slip wasn't. It was a congratulatory note, an acceptance letter. I read it again. *Foie Gras Journal* was happy to publish my fresh and wryly humorous piece. There was to be no payment of course, not even a complimentary issue, cock-suckers, but still. I realized that I was grinning. Daisy landed another ice-cold can in front of me, and I slapped five dollars down on the bar. She looked surprised.

"I just got published," I explained, unable to wipe the big goofy grin off my face.

"Congratulations," she deadpanned, pocketing the five. "When? Where?"

I scanned the letter for a date. Over a month ago. Slackers. But that meant that the current issue, the only issue that mattered, my issue, should already be out.

"I've got to go," I said, standing up and taking a big cold fizzy swallow of beer. And then on impulse: "Hey, what are you doing later on, after you get off work?"

She looked at me a little funny. "I don't know. Depends."

"Do you want to come over to my house?" I felt hot and realized that I was blushing. I've always sucked at asking girls out. As a matter of fact, I can't remember the last time I actually asked a girl out. Possibly in junior high school. The deepest pit in hell, half the reason I'm so freaking maladjusted. "Like, do you want to come over and hang out?" I sounded like a complete asshole.

"I don't know. . . . If my husband found out . . ."

"What time is your shift over?"

"Nine."

"Do you want to meet me over there?"

"Sure."

I gave her our address and left, feeling like I'd just robbed a bank. Nobody ever told me it was *that* easy!

I was headed up to the St. Mark's bookstore, the best and only place I know of to get obscure pretentious literary journals. On the way over, some yuppie woman gave me the evil eye for flicking my cigarette butt onto the sidewalk, and I gave her such a look that she stopped in mid scold and took a step backwards. I was King of the World.

Made my way to the rack in the back where they sell the

indie rags. It took me a minute to locate it, but there it was, the latest issue of *Foie Gras*—shiny and new. I can't believe they didn't even give me a free copy. Cheap fucks. I ponied up my thirteen bucks (thirteen bucks?!) and hit the street.

As I worked my way south and east, I flipped through the magazine. There I was, right there in the table of contents, my name in somebody else's ten-point black Helvetica. Of course they had mangled the title, but whatever. I paged through the journal (I can't believe the crap they publish) not wanting, I suppose, to appear too eager to get to my own story. (Appear to whom? I have really got to get some sleep.) About midway through, there it was, next to a poem about a boyfriend some chick had had when she had been a counselor at some summer camp. I pulled up to a convenient standpipe and started to read:

> *Dear Douchebags,*
>
> *My hands are shaking with disgust, making it hard to type. Your pathetic excuse for a lame-ass fucking joke of a so-called literary journal fucking blows. It is literally worthless: I wiped my ass with it and got a fucking paper cut. I can't believe you so-called editors are wasting perfectly good air with your pathetic respiration. Why don't you do humanity a favor and donate your fucking worthless organs to charity? I mean there are poor villages in Guatemala that could use your shriveled undersized testicles and livers. Give me a fucking break. . . .*

And so on, for almost four pages. I realized as I read the first sentence that this was not the story I had sent them something like nine months ago: this was the follow-up letter I had sent them after not hearing back from them at all after six months. I'd just banged it out and dumped it in the mail. I'd never even worked up a second draft. Reading it critically now, I wondered if maybe I shouldn't back off a tad on the methamphetamines when writing. "*Goddamn prepubescent troglodytes, writh-ing around like a bunch of epileptic whores in a strobe light fac-tory . . .*" How fucking weird, yet hilarious, yet surreal, yet pathetic that they reject my perfectly good story and then go and publish my bizarre tirade. Oh well, whatever. At least I finally got published.

I nearly got run over on the way back to the apartment. I was crossing the street towards our place, at the crosswalk with the light in my favor no less, when a convoy of three shiny black unmarked SUVs came screaming through the intersec-tion. I was rereading my piece in *Foie Gras* again (it grew on me) and didn't even notice them until they were on top of me. No horns, no sirens, nothing; just strobe lights in their hazards and a blatant disregard for human life. I vigorously gave them the finger as they receded down the street. "Fucking cock-wipes!" I imagined myself screaming at them. "Motherfuckers!" But then I imagined the SUVs stopping and coming back for me. I pic-tured them jammed full of Blackwater ex-green berets, bristling with high-tech weaponry, probably whisking Dick Cheney off to a brunch meeting. I wondered what would have happened if I'd managed to kick one in the fender as it passed. I'd probably get disappeared down to Guantanamo, that's what.

It was hot as hell in the apartment, but the electronics hum had gone down several decibels. Nate was sitting sprawled on the peeling linoleum floor of our kitchen, eating Chinese food out of a Styrofoam container. I don't think I had ever seen Nate eat before. I had always assumed that he stayed so skinny be-cause he spent all his money on cocaine. That and electric bills. But come to think of it, I had never seen Nate do coke either.

"Your friend Michael is here."

Michael McAsshole is most definitely not my friend. He is my drug dealer, and I think he is genuinely psychotic, and sometimes it amuses him to pretend to be my chum.

"Why did you let him in?" Mike is over six feet tall, with an oversized carrot-topped head, and he is an ex-marine (or so he claims). He is radically antisocial. And he sells me my speed.

"He insisted." Honestly, I'm not addicted to meth. But how the fuck else am I supposed to write during the day when I have to work all night? Have you ever stood in ankle-deep muck water at four in the morning, wrestling with half-inch diameter seven-by-nineteen grease-impregnated aircraft cable? Have you ever tried to sit down and write a chapter after doing that for eight hours? Well, okay then.

Michael was sprawled out on our couch, his big ugly boots propped up on the pillow, drinking a beer (my beer, and the very last one I had in the fridge too, I thought), toying with a plastic Ziploc bag with a bunch of pills in it. He gave me a big shit-eating smile when I walked in. I gave him his eighty bucks. He gave me the baggy. That should have been the end of it. But he just lay there, giving me that weirdo twitchy grin.

"You know," he said, "I've been worried about you."

Nate's computer (that is to say the only one of Nate's twenty or forty computers that actually had a cover and a CD drive) beeped and ejected a freshly burned CD.

"Excuse me." Nate slouched into the room and retrieved his CD from the drive tray. There's never anything interesting on Nate's CDs, the ones he gets or the ones he mails out. I've snooped, looking for porn. All there is is big text files, full of numbers. Math geek stuff. Most definitely not my bag. Nate slipped the CD into a dust jacket and slipped the dust jacket into a padded pre-addressed envelope.

"You know," Mike went on, draining the last of his (my) beer from the bottle and idly picking up one of Nate's old CDs from the end table, spinning it on his index finger like a Frisbee, "I think you've got a real problem. I think you've been doing way too many drugs."

Michael does hallucinogens at least three times a week. I think Mike does more drugs than anyone I know.

"I think you should seek out professional help."

I found myself literally leaping at Mike on the couch. Clutching my baggy in one hand, I brought my mouth to within an inch of his big hairy Irish ear.

"*Fuuuuck yoooou!!!*" I screamed.

Time could have stood still, except I could still hear my heart drumming away in my chest. I didn't know what to expect from Mike. I'd never done anything like that before in my life. He's a lot bigger than me.

"Um, excuse me," said Nate. "I've, ah, got to step outside and mail something. . . . Can I get you anything? While I'm out, can I get you something? A pack of cigarettes?" Usually Nate sends me out to mail his packages, and pays me off with a pack of cigarettes or something.

The door closed behind Nate. I didn't know what to do. Mike just lay there on the couch, an old data CD balanced on his finger at a crooked angle, looking at me, twitching. An excruciating minute passed. And another. He looked at me. I looked at him. He opened his mouth to say something.

I never found out what he was about to say, because right about then is when they kicked the door in. It was really loud and it all happened really fast. The door crashed open, and about a dozen guys all in black with Kevlar flak jackets and black riot helmets with clear plastic visors stormed into the apartment, rushing through the kitchen, scattering dirty dishes in front of them like fall leaves on the wind. Before you could say "habeas corpus," they had a black hood over Mike's head, plastic zip-cuffs around his wrists, and were dragging him back out to wherever they had come from.

I just stood there.

A bunch of guys in spacesuits came along later, and started disassembling Nate's computers, putting them into clear plastic bags, and hauling them away. They tried to take my PowerBook, but I objected. "Hey, that's mine," I said, and they left it alone.

Eventually I got myself a tall cold glass of water and took a pill and settled down to do some writing. The guys in space-suits were still coming in and out of the apartment, but they were reasonably quiet, so I ignored them. Nate came back later on, looking frazzled, but he didn't say anything about what was happening, and locked himself in his bedroom for the du-ration.

Daisy came by a little after nine. She had lust in her heart, a ring on her finger, and a bunch of pills in her pocket. Her breasts were just as big and luscious and inviting as I had imag-ined. She had a wicked scar on one of her boobs, a long white burn mark, all the way down to the nipple. It was slag, she ex-plained, from back when she used to do a lot of welding. A bit of molten metal had gotten down her shirt and run down her tit and into her bra. It looked like it had been really painful. But at the same time, I thought it looked really sexy, in an odd way.

Her thighs were strong and pale, and she was very wet and ready for me. She tasted nice, not like peaches or anything, but clean, salty, and tangy. Real.

I remembered that I had to be at work again in three hours; we had to get those load sensors ironed out. But I knew Joe Blow would cover for me.

Care of the Circumcised Penis

Sean Doolittle

My boy was already back in the hospital room, swaddled and peaceful, at breakfast in Sheila's arms, by the time I figured out the nurses had played me like a dime-store paddleball.

Right down that hallway, one of them told me. First double door on the left. Five minutes later: Left? I'm so sorry, hon, I meant right. A different nurse sent me down a completely different hallway. The nurse at the main station finally told me to wait while she checked the room schedule; after several minutes, she apologized and told me the computer seemed to be down.

I cornered Dr. Baldwin when he stopped by to check on Sheila's incision. He listened to my tale and sighed. "I suspect the floor staff may have developed something of a system," he admitted. "We've run into problems in the past."

"With the same nurses?"

"Fathers," he said. At my confusion, he added, "Some find the experience a bit . . . traumatizing."

"I guess I don't understand."

"How to put it." Baldwin angled his head. "You've heard of people who become faint at the sight of blood?"

"Sure," I said.

The doctor nodded slowly. "Think along those lines and you'll be in the ballpark." When I still didn't catch his drift, he held up his pinkie finger meaningfully, then scissored across the first joint with two fingers of his other hand. I felt a quick shiver between my legs.

"Oh," I said.

"It's a simple procedure," Baldwin assured me. "But let us say that some men underestimate the visual impact." He shrugged. "And of course there's the screaming."

"Jesus, Doc." The phantom shiver in my nethers had already given way to something deeper—a kind of creeping, clammy unease I couldn't quite name. "The baby really screams?"

"I'm still talking about the fathers." Baldwin scribbled something on Sheila's chart and slipped it in the sleeve outside her door. "A colleague of mine once had to fend off a distressed Papa Bear with his surgical stool. True story."

Later, in the quiet of the afternoon, while Sheila slept, I ran a quick diaper patrol. The boy was clean and dry, and I suppose I knew that before I pulled the tape. I peered carefully beneath his dressing, a small square of blood-dotted gauze, and there it was: a raw little nub, glistening with ointment, a shocking jot of scarlet against the white. I felt the shiver again.

"Sorry, partner," I said.

He blinked at me. A sweet velvet ache wrapped me up and I leaned in close, grazed his soft cheek with the back of my finger. He smelled like a loaf of fresh-baked bread. At my touch, he turned his head reflexively, working his little mouth, rooting for a nipple.

"Dinnertime," Sheila murmured behind me, her voice warm

and drowsy. The bed hummed as she thumbed the control button, raising herself upright.

"Hey there." I smiled over my shoulder. "Good nap?"

"Eh." Her IV tubes rattled against the pole by the bed as she
seesawed her hand in front of her. Her eyes were puffy; her hair
hung lank and ashy around her face. She looked exhausted, as
unmade as the cot in the corner where I'd slept the night. I
thought I'd never seen her prettier.

"Soup's on," I told the boy, wrapping him up in the blanket
the way the nurse had showed me, lifting him out of the bassinet.

"He looks like a little bean." Sheila smiled with her whole
weary face, stretching out her arms. "Come here, little bean."

I handed him over, then sat down carefully on the edge of
the bed. Already I could feel the cooling spot where I'd carried
him against my chest. I helped arrange the pillow so Sheila could
get him situated. She winced as he latched on, then sighed.

"How's your pain?" I said.

She smiled and settled back. "He makes it go away." She
tilted down her chin, watched him going to town in his little
knit hospital cap, light blue with penguins on it. After a minute,
she looked up at me, hid her mouth with the back of her hand,
and whispered, "How's Junior Johnson?"

"Still attached," I told her. "As far as I can tell."

"Don't even joke," she said, stroking his cheek. "Poor little
bean."

"I'm still kind of pissed they wouldn't let me in to watch," I
said.

She made a face. "Why? It sounds awful."

I took in the sight of my son at his mother's breast. The
curve of his cheek, rising and falling. His tiny nose mashed into
her soft flesh. His big eyes scrunched up tight. My heart felt
full. Because I'm right here, partner, I thought. Today. Always.

"So sweet," she said, and touched my hand, though I was almost sure I hadn't answered aloud.

* * *

There were flowers everywhere, most of them from people I didn't know. Balloons floated around the ceiling like cartoon jellyfish, and tissue paper bloomed from the trash. My cousin Marie brought a stuffed panda bear the size of a husky eighth-grader. Sheila laughed and clapped her hands when she saw it.

"I feel like it's watching me," I told Marie on the side.

"Good," she said. When I looked at the thing, hulking in the corner with its droopy eyes and stitched-on smile, Marie tiptoed over and kissed my cheek. "Congrats, fave cuz."

A few of the girls from Sheila's work stopped by on their lunch hour to coo and pass the boy around. Sheila's parents came and went. They didn't like me very much, but I could tell they were making an effort. That could have been wishful thinking on my part. I gave them credit anyway.

My old man stopped by for a few minutes, reeking of Winstons. He didn't hold the boy, but he kissed Sheila's forehead. She called him Pop, and patted his grizzled neck with her hand, and I'm pretty sure I saw relief in her eyes as we left the room.

"Little bugger didn't want to come out," the old man said on our way to the elevator. "Did he?"

"I guess not," I said. It had been a tough go for both of them, nearly twenty hours of hard labor that ended in an emergency cesarean. The boy had been blue when they pulled him out, and he didn't cry for almost half a minute. Meanwhile, in the midst of all the slicing and dicing, one of the docs had accidentally torn a hole in Sheila's bladder. She'd be peeing through a tube for the next week or so.

My old man laughed the way he did. Like gears grinding. "Can't say I blame him. When the hell you going to give that boy a name?"

I told him we were working on it.

"First grandson, and I don't even know what the hell to call the little shit."

"We've got it narrowed down."

"Already, huh?"

"Take it easy," I told him. "You'll be the first to know."

He screwed up a special smirk just for me.

"All right. Third or fourth to know. Definitely in the top ten."

"Don't be an asshole."

"Get the button," I said. "You're closer."

We waited for the elevator in silence. I hadn't seen my old man in a year or more; we'd agreed to get some breakfast in the cafeteria, his treat. I knew I'd be paying for breakfast. While we stood there, I wondered what my mother would have thought of all this. I wondered if the old man wondered. Then the bell chimed, and the doors slid open.

We exchanged places with a guy stepping out. He was about my height, better dressed, trailing a faint swirl of cologne. Blond hair combed back, damp from the rain outside. As soon as I recognized his face, my blood went hot.

He'd already recognized me. He met my eyes squarely, then looked away as the doors closed between us.

I stood inside the elevator, pulse thudding in my temples, feeling my old man's gaze. He leaned against the rail, bit off a hangnail. Said, "Friend of yours?"

"No." I stared at the console for a beat too long before jabbing the button to open the door.

The elevator carried us down.

The ride was slow torture. I didn't realize my fists were clenched until I felt my fingernails biting my palms. When we reached the main level, the old man stepped out. I stayed put.

"Pop," I said. "Rain check, okay?"

He looked at me a moment, then shrugged his shoulders. The doors slid closed again.

* * *

"Don't worry," the guy said. By the time I made it back up-stairs, he'd already closed our room door behind him. If the sight of me coming intimidated him, he didn't seem to notice. "I'm leaving."

"So soon?" I said.

"I'll be back," he said. "You can just be ready for that."

The guy had a name. Nathan Greenleaf. Once upon a time, he'd been Sheila's boss at work. "Call me Nate," he'd said, the first time we'd met. I called him Fuckface.

"Look, give it up," I said. "You had your shot. She picked the other guy. It's a sad story."

He shook his head slowly, like I was too dumb to see the point.

"Fair warning," I told him. "If I see you again, you'll wish I hadn't."

A few of the nurses were starting to pay attention now. I glanced at the desk and saw one of them with her hand on the phone, a tense look in her eyes.

"Fair warning," he said. Cool and calm. "You'll see me again, Dan. With an attorney of my own, if that's what it takes. I want a blood test. And I'll get one."

The way he talked—as if we were on some kind of first-name basis with each other just because he said so—I could feel the warning signals, familiar as a gang of bad old friends. The sudden calm in my belly. The hum in my blood. The tingle in my fingertips. The shimmery film of red all around.

I took a deep breath. Thought of Sheila. Of all the promises I'd made. I thought of my boy. My boy.

"How many times do you need to hear it?" I forced a chuckle, tried my best to speak to him the same way he'd just looked at me: like a small, sad soul. "I mean, dude. Seriously. How many different ways does she need to explain the math?"

"For a bookkeeper, her math's a little shaky," he said. "Or maybe yours is."

My knuckles began to itch. "My math is fine."

"We'll see." He straightened, smoothed his jacket.

I think that if he hadn't smiled, I might have been able to hold it together. If not for that last, brief, tight, smug, little shit-eating, Fuckface grin, I think the deep crazy itch in my fists might have gone away on its own. Instead it became unbearable, and I knew I'd scratch it. I thought of all my promises, but my left arm had already tensed in my sleeve.

I heard myself say, "Blood test, huh?"

As if from nowhere, a hand fell lightly on my wrist. A leathery, strangely soothing grip. Easy does it.

I hadn't sensed anyone approaching. But I knew the hand without looking. By the time I smelled Winstons, my fuse had fizzled, and the red film had lifted.

"So," my old man said. He looked between the two of us, smiling brightly. "Where you figure they keep the morphine in this joint?"

Sheila had been crying. Seeing me, she wiped her eyes quickly and dummied up, put on a quick smile so forced and false that it broke my heart to see it on her face.

Her mother stood by the bed, holding the baby, swaying gently on her feet like the old pro I knew her to be, having rocked as babies Sheila, her three older sisters, and a younger brother who'd caught a bad break in Afghanistan. As I walked in, her father seemed to consider my presence a moment. Then he returned his gaze to the rain-streaked window.

Before stepping back into the room, I'd taken a walk around the floor to clear my head. For at least twenty minutes, I'd stood on the far side of the ward, looking through the glass at all the other new babies. I'd watched a few other new dads doing the same. I'd wondered if they'd really be able to tell which kid was theirs without the Crayola-colored name tags on the bassinets.

Sheila and her folks thought I'd missed the show. I got it. Fuckface had only been here a few minutes, and as far as they knew, I'd been downstairs having breakfast with my old man at the time. I didn't see any point in shattering the illusion.

"What about Brandon?" I said.

Sheila sniffed, paused, turned a bewildered eye my way. Her mother stopped swaying the baby. Glanced towards her husband.

Sheila's father looked at me again. This time his eyes had hardened. Quietly, he said, "What about him?"

"For the man here," I said. I walked to Sheila's mother. Touched her shoulder with one hand, my sleeping boy's cheek with the other.

My boy.

I had never asked Sheila everybody's big question. Long before this moment, I'd decided that I never would.

"He needs a good name," I said. "A good name. What do you think, sweet?"

For a moment, Sheila looked at me like I'd climbed down out of the ceiling tiles. Brandon hadn't been anywhere among the ten piles of names we'd discussed, though speaking it now, I wasn't sure why. It had been her kid brother's name. Why not?

Her eyes began to glisten. I didn't need to ask everybody's question because I could see the answer caught in her tears: I don't know. But her smile came back, and this time it was real. That was enough for me.

She said, "Mom?"

Sheila's mother rocked her grandson and said nothing. When I glanced up, I found her looking at me with a tenderness so sudden that it must have surprised her as much as it surprised me.

Sheila said, "Daddy?"

Her father looked at the floor.

Silence.

We waited.

At last he cleared his throat. A touch hoarsely, he said, "It's a good name."

"You ask me," my old man said, "you shouldn't had that boy mutilated in the first place."

"Nobody asked you, Pop."

"I mean it just ain't called for."

I sighed, looked out my window at the passing streetlamps, hazy yellow blobs in the cold November drizzle. "It's a simple procedure."

"Uh-huh."

"They do it for hygiene."

"Hygiene. Cuttin' off what God gave you is what it is. Poor devil."

"Anyway," I said, just wanting the conversation to be over. "A boy grows up, he ought to look like his dad. Down there at least."

My old man steered with his wrist on the wheel, Winston crooked in the first knuckles of his other hand, trailing smoke out the gap in the window. He chuckled softly, a loose phlegmy rattle in his chest.

"What?" I said.

"Damned if I didn't tell your mother the same thing about you boys," he said. "Guess she saw it different."

I had nothing for that. So I let it go. Hell. I hadn't brought it up in the first place.

The old man slowed the car, then turned off the main drag, onto a service road. The Buick's slick tires crunched over a scatter of gravel and broken glass. Streetlamps grew scarce. Darkness pulled in around us.

"Pop?" I said.

"Mm."

"You planning on telling me what the hell we're doing all the way out here?"

Rain check on breakfast, he'd said forty minutes ago, talking to me on his cell phone from the hospital parking lot. He'd cruised back around after visiting hours in a dented old Buick I'd never seen before. Said he figured we could get a burger and a few beers. Maybe watch the game.

I'd said that sounded fine. Instead, he'd driven us here: a trash-blasted warehouse complex out by the airport. Not many sports bars around.

"Quick stop," he said, turning off the service road onto a narrow strip of buckled asphalt. "Take a jiff."

We rolled through an open gate on a high chain security fence. The old man pointed the Buick towards a corrugated steel building at the back of a weedy, chuck-holed lot. Oily rainwater fanned away from the tires as he cut across. A pair of rust-streaked bay doors grew close and bright in the headlight beams.

"Pop," I said.

He pulled around to the side entrance, out of view of the main road. Behind the building, beyond the high fence, lay a dark empty sprawl. Somewhere in the distance, the lights of the airfield twinkled through a sheer screen of mist.

I didn't like the feeling I was getting. Just as I opened my mouth to say so, a descending jetliner roared over us, momentarily erasing all other sound. I could feel the thrum of the big plane's turbines down in my guts. I saw its great winged shadow cover us, spread over the land, slide away.

When it was quiet enough to be heard, I said, "Tell me what's going on."

"Hell, I felt bad." The old man clapped me on the knee and killed the motor. "I never did think to bring a present."

* * *

They'd duct taped him to a metal folding chair in the middle of the warehouse floor. Wrists, ankles, thighs, chest. A single shop light glowed hot overhead, throwing long shadows. My stomach did a slow, sick roll.

"Damn," my brother Dave said when we came in. "I was startin' to wonder." He grinned broadly and hopped off a crate, pulling a pair of white buds from his ears. He shoved the earbuds into the pocket of his leather jacket, along with his iPod, came over and gave me a bear hug. He smelled like whiskey. Whiskey and Winstons. Maybe a little pot underneath.

"Congrats, little bro. Sorry I ain't been by to see the ankle biter yet." He patted my cheek. "But we brought ya somethin'."

I looked over his shoulder at Sheila's old boss, shirt ripped, blond hair a mess, eyes wide and wild above the stretch of silver tape pressed over his mouth. Call me Nate. Seeing him in the chair, centered in that puddle of hot yellow light, I felt a strange feathery sensation. Like something I'd wanted slipping away.

"Dave," I said. Kept my voice level. Glanced at the old man. "You shouldn't have."

"We overdid it," the old man said. "But what the hell. It's for family."

A weight in my hand. I looked down at the gun Dave had pressed against my palm. Medium frame, short barrel. Blued finish. It would be clean, I knew. My fingers had fallen into position without being told.

"Let's jump," Dave said. "I'm about fuckin' starved."

Six feet away, Greenleaf began to wheeze through his nose. We all looked. At the sight of the gun in my hand, he cried in his throat. He writhed and bucked against the duct tape holding him fast. If he wasn't careful, I thought, he'd tip the chair over, and then where the hell would he be?

I thought of my promises. The ones I'd made to Sheila. The ones I'd made to myself.

"It's for family," the old man said again, as if I hadn't heard him say it the first time.

Sheila's parents didn't like me very much.

They don't know you, Sheila always said. And she was right.

They had no idea.

But standing in the cold empty warehouse, the heat from the overhead shop light warming my skin, I thought that I saw a better road out of here. I thought that maybe, in Greenleaf's swimming eyes, I'd glimpsed a possible version of the future. The version I wanted.

Because the guy was scared. The kind of deep scared you don't forget when it's over. The kind of scared you don't ever want to be again. The guy was scared, and I had six credits to go at the technical college. A job fixing computers for Sheila's father, if I wanted it.

So I said, "You didn't know what you were dealing with. Do you see that now?"

Three hard nods. Eyes red, tears streaming. Silver tape slick with snot and sweat.

I raised the gun, pressed the muzzle to his forehead. Wanting him to feel it. Wanting there to be a round spot he could look at in the mirror later.

"And now you know," I said. "Don't you?"

More nodding. Skin beneath the gun barrel oily and pale as warm cheese.

I thumbed the hammer back a notch. The single click echoed sharply in the empty space around us. Greenleaf made a keening, huffing sound in his throat, squeezed his eyes closed. Tried to lean away.

I applied more pressure until his face turned up to the ceiling, washed in the stream of bright light from above. When I thumbed the hammer back the rest of the way, a musty reek rose up between us. I looked down. Saw the sodden fabric of his khakis matted darkly against his thighs.

"Now you know," I told him.

And I knew we were done. There would be no lawyers. No blood tests. No worries. My boy.

I de-cocked the gun. Handed it back to Dave.

My brother looked me over. I could read the question clearly in his eyes: You sure? When I nodded, he shrugged. Scrubbed my head with his knuckles, the way I always hated when we were kids.

A plane came in low over the warehouse, filling the space, drowning us in rolling waves of noise. I turned to find the old man. As I did, I saw Dave straighten his arm. I saw the gun buck, but amidst the roar of jet engines I couldn't hear the bang. I saw the side of Greenleaf's head open up and cough out a dark wet wad. I saw him jerk, then go slack in the chair.

The in-riding jetliner pulled a blanket of new silence behind it.

The sharp smell of gunfire drifted faintly in the air.

I stood there.

"Shit, Gandhi," Dave said. "I knew you were gonna be all charitable, I wouldn't have let the prick see my face." He snapped open a cell phone, punched a number. Said, "Yeah. The place on Giles. Bring a sponge." He closed the phone, tossed the gun in the dead guy's piss-soaked lap, looked at the old man, looked at me. Said, "Who's up for hot wings?"

Apply Vaseline gauze to penis for two to three days. This is what the checklist of care instructions from the hospital says. Clean the penis with clear, clean water (no soap, no pre-moistened wipes) until healed.

What the instructions don't happen to mention is that a newborn infant poops nothing but thick black sludge for the same two or three days, and sometimes it gets all over everything. Meconium, they call it. It's like roof tar. Just as black and sticky as sin.

Not so easy to clean up with clear, clean water, checklist or no checklist, that much I can tell you. But I figured out that if you take some of the Vaseline you're supposed to use, and you kind of smear it all around the trouble spots, the black stuff doesn't stick quite so much, and pretty soon, the kid clears the last of it out of his system. Fresh start for everybody.

"This is so weird," Sheila says. She's on the couch with her bare feet on the footstool, Brandon propped up in her lap. "What do you think could have happened?"

I sit beside her, making funny faces at the boy. They told us in class that a newborn can't see much farther than a foot or so, but I make the faces anyway. I let him grip my pinkies with his tiny fingers. I wonder if he'll turn out to be blond.

It won't mean a thing to me if he does. Blond, brown. Tall, short. Straight, gay. Whatever he is, whatever he isn't.

"Probably nothing," I tell her. "Maybe he just left town or something."

"In the middle of the week? Without telling anybody?" She frowns. "On his way to meet somebody?"

I shrugged. "I guess it's a little weird."

It's been three days since the news first reported the disappearance of local business attorney Nathan Greenleaf. Apparently, Greenleaf keyed out of his condo's parking garage at 9:04 P.M. on the night of the twelfth. He'd been traveling to meet a companion for drinks at a nearby bar and grill. He hadn't arrived, and nobody's seen him since.

The cops left our place a half hour ago. It was true I'd had words with Greenleaf earlier that day. It was true that he and

Sheila had a dating history. It was true that he'd sought a paternity test.

It was also true that a Hooters waitress named Mandi had confirmed my presence at one of her tables between the hours of eight P.M. and midnight on the same night. According to Mandi, whom I've never laid eyes on, she'd had her hands full with me, my brother Dave, the old man, and half a dozen of our friends. None of whom I've ever, to my knowledge, actually met.

"Hooters," Sheila says. She gives me a look. Shakes her head slowly.

"I'm totally innocent," I tell her. "It's where the old man wanted to go."

"I'm sure it was brutal for you." In a singsong voice, she tells the boy, "Your daddy and your grandaddy are terrible. Just terrible." She smiles big, lifts his chubby arms high. "Yes, they are."

The baby gurgles, squirms a little, and loads his diaper loudly, right there in her lap. We look at each other and laugh our heads off. It's the cutest damned thing.

About the Authors

Stephen Allan has a Master of Fine Arts degree in Creative Writing, not that anyone has been impressed by that. He has written over twenty short stories and flash fiction pieces, which have appeared in various magazines, Web sites, and anthologies. Steve lives in Maine with his beautiful wife and two adorable children.

Jedidiah Ayres lives in St. Louis.

Eddie Bunker, Mr. Blue in real life and in Quentin Tarantino's film *Reservoir Dogs*, was the author of *No Beast So Fierce, Little Boy Blue, Dog Eat Dog, The Animal Factory, Stark*, and his autobiography, *Mr. Blue*. He was co-screenwriter of the Oscar-nominated movie, *Runaway Train*, and appeared in over thirty feature films, including *Straight Time* with Dustin Hoffman, the film of his book *No Beast So Fierce*. Edward Bunker died in 2005 and subsequently another novella was found along with some short stories, of which "Death of a Rat" is one.

Lawrence Clayton lives in New York City where he (grudgingly) works for a living. He really is not a misanthrope, although he seems to have fooled a large number of people. He holds a BFA in Minding His Own Business, and gets along better with ironworkers than any of the other construction trades. More of his writing can be found in Porta-Johns across the eastern seaboard, and at www.grimandchronic.blogspot.com.

Hilary Davidson's debut novel, *The Damage Done,* will be published in October 2010 by Tor/Forge. Her first story for

Thuglit, "Anniversary," was featured in the anthology *A Prisoner of Memory and 24 of the Year's Finest Crime and Mystery Stories.* Her crime fiction has also appeared in *Beat to a Pulp*, *Crime-Spree*, *Spinetingler*, and *The Rose & Thorn*. In her non-thug life she's a New York–based travel writer who's authored eighteen guidebooks for Frommer's, including several about her hometown of Toronto. She remains certain that she is the only writer in the world who has published work in both *Thuglit* and *Martha Stewart Weddings*. Visit her online at www.hilarydavidson.com.

Sean Doolittle is the award-winning author of five crime and suspense novels, including *Safer*, his latest. Doolittle's books have been translated into several languages; his short stories have been anthologized in *The Best American Mystery Stories*, *The Year's Best Horror Stories*, and elsewhere. He lives in western Iowa with his family and is working on a new novel.

Glenn Gray is a physician specializing in radiology. His stories have appeared in *Plots with Guns*, *Pulp Pusher*, *Beat to a Pulp*, *Powder Burn*, *Word Riot*, *Underground Voices*, *Bewildering Stories*, several issues of the print pulp zine *Out of the Gutter*, and others. He's at work on a medical thriller.

Pearce Hansen is a fifty-ish melancholy Dane, born on the eastern shores of San Francisco Bay and currently living in Northern California anonymity with his wife.

Jordan Harper is a staff writer for *The Mentalist* and was a member of the 2009 Warner Bros. Writers' Workshop. He was born and educated in Missouri. He's worked as a rock critic, a scalper, and a professional TV watcher. His fiction has appeared in *Thuglit*, *Out of the Gutter*, and *Demolition* and the anthology *Hardcore Hardboiled*. His short story "Johnny Cash Is Dead" was shortlisted for a Derringer Award and selected by the Million Writers Award as a notable short story. "Like Riding a Moped" was selected by the Million Writers Award as a notable story and appeared in the anthology *Sex, Thugs, and Rock & Roll*. He is adapting the story into a screenplay. "Red Hair and Black Leather" was shortlisted for the 2008 *Best American Mysteries*. His reviews and articles have appeared in the *Village Voice* and among other papers. Read his work at www.jordanharper.com

David Harrison went to Princeton, hated Wall Street, and drove a truck. He lives and writes northwest of Boston, teaching Literature and Life Skills at the Lowell Middlesex Academy Charter School.

John Kenyon is an Iowa newspaper editor who has published short stories with *Thuglit, Demolition*, and other online outlets. He also writes the blog Things I'd Rather Be Doing (www.tirbd.com) where he covers books, music, and pop culture.

Dana King's short fiction has appeared in *Thuglit, Crooked, New Mystery Reader*, and *Powder Burn Flash*. *New Mystery Reader* has also published over one hundred of his crime fiction reviews and several author interviews. He lives near Washington D.C., and pays the bills working as a consultant at an undisclosed location. It's not one of those "he'd tell you, but then he'd have to kill you" deals. He's just not going to tell you.

Edgar-finalist **Craig McDonald** is an award-winning fiction writer, journalist, and editor. His debut novel, *Head Games*, was selected as a 2008 Edgar nominee for Best First Novel by an American Author. It was also a finalist for Anthony and

Gumshoe awards. *Toros & Torsos,* McDonald's second novel, appeared in autumn 2008 and made several "year's best" lists. The third novel in the Hector Lassiter series, *Print the Legend,* is available from Minotaur Books. His nonfiction books include *Art in the Blood* and *Rogue Males: Conversations & Confrontations About the Writing Life.* His short fiction has appeared in several anthologies. His Web site is www.craigmcdonaldbooks.com.

Brian Murphy's face makes it impossible to talk out the side of. When all he possesses in the entire world is elegance, Brian Murphy still considers himself a rich man. He is a formula writer. The formula? It's a diabolical mix of authenticity and perspective—true stories tweaked. The formula? It's called living first, writing later. It's called, writing "on the real." Currently, he is completing his novel *Cool School* with the representation and ultimate guidance of legendary literary agent, Nat Sobel. Sobel discovered Brian, after reading some of his work at *Thuglit.* Were it not for Big Daddy Thug at *Thuglit,* years back, Brian would still be sending out queries. Brian Murphy's e-mail is iggypopcb3@yahoo.com.

Stuart Neville has been a musician, a composer, a teacher, a salesman, a film extra, a baker, and a hand double for a well-known Irish comedian, but is currently a partner in a successful multimedia design business in the wilds of Northern Ireland. His debut novel is published in the USA by Soho Crime as *The Ghosts of Belfast,* and by Harvill Secker in the UK as *The Twelve.*

Derek Nikitas is the author of *The Long Division* and *Pyres,* both from St. Martin's Minotaur. *Pyres* was nominated for an Edgar Award for Best First Novel. His fiction has appeared in *Thuglit, Plots with Guns, Ellery Queen Mystery Magazine, Ontario Review, Killer Year: Stories to Die For, The New Dead,* and elsewhere. He teaches in the creative writing MFA program at Eastern Kentucky University.

Colin O'Sullivan is an Irish writer living in Japan. He is the author of two books: *Anhedonia* (short stories) and *Majo* (a novella for teenagers) both published by the now defunct Rain Publishing in Canada. He is currently looking for a new publisher. His fiction and poetry regularly appear on the web and in print. He lives in Aomori with his wife and two children.

Michael Penncavage's story "The Cost of Doing Business" originally appeared in *Thuglit* Issue 24 and won a 2008 Derringer Award for best mystery. He has been an associate editor for *Space and Time* magazine, as well as the editor of the horror/suspense anthology *Tales from a Darker State*. One of his stories has recently been filmed as a short movie. Fiction of his can be found in approximately sixty magazines and anthologies from three different countries including *Alfred Hitchcock's Mystery Magazine* in the USA, *Here and Now* in England, and *Crime Factory* in Australia. Organizational affiliations include the Mystery Writers of America, the Horror Writers of America, and the Garden State Horror Writers.

Tom Piccirilli is the author of twenty novels including *Shadow Season, The Cold Spot, The Coldest Mile, The Midnight Road,* and *A Choir of Ill Children*. He's won the International Thriller Writers Award and the Bram Stoker Award and has been nominated for the Edgar Award, the Macavity Award, the World Fantasy Award, and Le Grand Prix de L'Imaginaire. Learn more at his official Web site www.tompiccirilli.com.

Justin Porter was born and raised in New York City. He still lives there. His stories have been featured in *Thuglit, Pulp*

Pusher, Plots with Guns, Big Pulp, and others. His articles have been featured in *The New York Times.* He can be reached at six.gun.chimp@gmail.com. Drop him a line.

A native of New Jersey, **Kieran Shea**'s fiction has spread across the Internet's crime zine ghetto like a glorious case of the shingles. Recently the disease has mutated into print with his work appearing in *Ellery Queen Mystery Magazine.* He lives outside of Annapolis, Maryland, where he bitterly kicks the tires on the status quo and drinks far too much coffee. His Web site is www.kieranjamesshea.blogspot.com.

Andy Turner lives in Milwaukee, where he works as a freelance writer and editor, serves as an English lecturer at a local university, and hosts his own radio show on which he plays (frequently spastic) music exclusively from independent labels. He is a former newspaper reporter and has written for numerous music publications, including *No Depression, Pop Culture Press, Harp,* and *Country Standard Time. Thuglit* published his first venture into crime fiction.

Scott Wolven is the author of *Controlled Burn* (Scribner). Wolven's stories have appeared seven years in a row in *The Best American Mystery Stories* (Houghton Mifflin). The title story from *Controlled Burn* has been selected to appear in *The Best American Noir Stories of the Century* (Houghton Mifflin). Wolven's novels *False Hope* and *King Zero* are forthcoming from Harcourt. He is finishing another collection of short stories, *Whipsaw.* Wolven lives in upstate New York.

Dave Zeltserman's short crime fiction has been published in venues such as *Alfred Hitchcock's Mystery Magazine* and *Ellery Queen Mystery Magazine.* His third novel, *Small Crimes,* was named by NPR as one of the top five mystery and crime novels of 2008, and by the *Washington Post* as one of the best novels of 2008. Dave has six more novels to be published, including *Pariah*. His thriller *28 Minutes* has been optioned by Impact Pictures and Constantin Film.

Raise Your Glasses . . .

As you may or may not know from the previous anthos, culling down a year's worth of the best crime fiction the world has to offer can be a nightmare. A headache. A want-to-claw-out-my-eyes-and-scream kind of responsibility. Doing the Web site is hard enough. Doing these books—well, you get the point. So even though we couldn't fit the following writers into this year's anthology, they all deserve a lifted glass and a heartfelt thanks for being part of the few, the proud . . . the thugworthy.

Carl Moore—Tom Sheehan—David Moss—Anonymous 9—Joe Clifford—Steven Wellington—Jonas Knutsson—Brian Haycock—John Schulian—Ellen Neuborne—Richard Farnsworth—Crit Minster—Patrick J. Lambe—Barry Baldwin—Robert Palmer—Adrian Ludens—Ben Nadler—Michael Colangelo—Randy Chandler—Leslie Budewitz—Nolan Knight—Keith Gilman—Kim Cushman—Hugh Lessig—Stephen Beckwith—Mark Joseph Kiewlak—L. V. Rautenbaumgrabner—Tony Black—Matthew Stern—Robert Aquino Dollesin—Allan C. Kimball—Steve Newman—J. A. Tyler—Raise your glass. . . .

Further thanks go to Michaela Hamilton over at Kensington Books for putting up with our shit. Hell, would you? Exactly. Raise your glass. . . .

Raise your glass up as high as you can for:

JOHN (Johnny Kneecaps) MOORE.

I'm such a douche that I forgot to thank him in last year's anthology. Without John, there would never have been a *Thuglit*. He is an editor supreme and a Web dude like no other. Without John's technicals and knowledge, we'd be banging rocks and throwing our own feces like the filthy sub-humans we are. That's why he gets the bigger font—to make up for last year.

For Sam Drake Robinson (Little Daddy Thug)—you're not here yet, but by the time this comes out, you will be. Weird . . .

And finally, for Allison. My Lady Detroit and the reason it's all here. Don't raise your glasses. Just get out of the goddamn room already. Can't a couple get some privacy? Pervert . . .